A DREAM OF
DRAGONS

A DREAM OF DRAGONS

LAURETTA L. KEHOE
AND
MICHAEL R. KEHOE

TATE PUBLISHING
AND ENTERPRISES, LLC

Published by Tate Publishing & Enterprises, LLC
127 E. Trade Center Terrace | Mustang, Oklahoma 73064 USA
1.888.361.9473 | www.tatepublishing.com

Tate Publishing is committed to excellence in the publishing industry. The company reflects the philosophy established by the founders, based on Psalm 68:11,
"The Lord gave the word and great was the company of those who published it."

Book design copyright © 2016 by Tate Publishing, LLC. All rights reserved.
Cover design by Dante Rey Redido
Interior design by Gram Telen

Published in the United States of America

ISBN: 978-1-68301-520-8
Fiction / Christian / Fantasy
16.04.21

To Kat, Cathy, Mike, James and Robert, our greatest creations.

Greater love has no one than this, than to lay down one's life
for his friends.

—John 15:13 (NKJV)

They say it takes a village to raise a child. It also takes almost a village to write a book. In this case it involves our beta readers; our beautiful daughter, Kat Dienethal, RN and Amy Solbach who provided medical advice in addition to story changes; Deborah Riley who prevented a cotton candy ending; our niece Christina Spaulding who in adddition to editing, with her husband, Travis, helped us throw Michael out of a plane; Kelli Petsche; Shannon MacDavid; Maxime Laboy who not only beta-read once but twice when she served as our proofreaders along with Cheryl Hoffman; Angela Raysa and Tina Goddard who provided psychological advice; and final copy proofing by Connie Wright, Gabrielle Higgins and Kim Huyler Defibaugh Also, this book wouldn't have been possible without the assistance of our author friends, established in their own right but who took the time to read the manuscript and provide their time-honored advice and edits; Chris Stevenson, author of *Wolfen Strain* and *The Girl They Sold to the Moon*; M.A.R. Unger, author of the *Matti James Mystery* Series; Sean Brink, author of *The Space Between* Series; Chris R. Powell, author of *The Path that Shines: A Story of Life, Love and Loss*; and Laura Vosika, author of *The Bluebells of Scotland* Trilogy.

1

Just Another Day

June 15
Monday

Henry Williford awoke and lay motionless, enjoying the comfort of his queen-sized bed in his one-story home in Venice, Florida. Today was just another day in the life of the freelance commercial artist.

The fog in his head began to dissipate as his senses slowly came online one by one. He could hear the gentle humming of the air conditioner down the hall and the ticking of the clock on his dresser. His own breathing and heartbeat were in sync with the house. He exhaled, relaxing every muscle of his six-foot-two-inch frame, and became one with the mattress. His eyes were still off-line while his mind accessed the day's tasks that awaited him in his studio. When he stretched out a kink in his back, all hell broke loose. Six cats and three dogs stretched out on his bed all ambushed their beloved master at once. The dogs slobbered him with love and affection while the cats articulated their demands for breakfast.

Like a rock star hounded by a throng of adoring fans, Henry and his entourage made their way to the kitchen for their morning feeding. Morning chores checked off, he slipped into his jogging clothes for an early morning run on Venice Beach, just the thing to get his heart pumping and his creative juices flowing.

The Florida air felt muggy as Henry hopped into his black 1999 Chevrolet Camaro, shoving his runner's backpack onto the passenger's seat. There wasn't much traffic on Venice Avenue, the near empty street divided by rows of tall palm trees on a grassy median leading him to the ocean.

When Henry arrived, he parked his car several spaces from the boardwalk and got out to stretch before his run then walked to the raised wooden bridge spanning tall wild grass to the sand beyond. He checked to see if his sports wristband was indeed in sync with his cell phone so he could track his progress. Earbuds in place, he selected a playlist of Elvis Presley's greatest hits, took a deep breath of fresh ocean air, and then began his morning jog on the wet sand along the shoreline. Henry had been an early riser his entire life and enjoyed the solitude of having the beach all to himself while the nine-to-fivers were just crawling out of bed.

After a few moments, and the second verse of "Hound Dog" ended, Henry noticed something on the beach not one hundred yards in front of him. It was the wrong color to be a manatee and didn't look like any piece of driftwood he had ever seen. His curiosity was piqued, so he picked up his pace. In mere moments, he came up upon this mysterious anomaly and stopped dead in his tracks.

He was shocked to find a young woman lying on the shoreline, naked and alone. It looked as if she had just crawled out of the ocean. She was still wet and shivering, lying on the dark sand, the waves washing over her feet. She appeared to be in her early twenties with well-developed legs and arms and long golden hair. She was lying on her left side with her head down, knees bent, and arms around her chest in the fetal position. The girl was conscious with eyes wide open. A quick glance assured Henry that there were no visible injuries.

Henry scanned the horizon, but there was not a single boat in sight. If she had fallen overboard, it was very unlikely she would have been able to swim that many miles to shore. There were no footprints in the wet sand on either side of her. Henry was reasonably certain she didn't walk here on her own and wasn't carried here by anyone. There was no evidence of anyone else in the area. It was as if he had walked into a scene of a bad movie.

He turned off "The King" and removed his ear buds. Then he knelt down in front of her and placed one hand on her shoulder while lifting her chin with the other, turning her face towards him.

When he looked into her eyes, he fell into the ocean of her blue gaze, forever shifting his world around him. He tried to speak but couldn't find his voice, spellbound by the beauty of this tragic vision. Henry painted for a living, capturing the beauty of many a female model in every medium from charcoal to oil, even bedded a few, but never had he witnessed beauty quite like hers. Immediately, something began to stir inside him, causing his heart and mind to trade places. Henry was lost in another place and time, like having an out-of-body experience inside his own head.

Henry's mouth felt like cotton; and his voice, when he found it, was strained. "Heh…hello. Miss, are you okay?" Her sapphire eyes blinked, her only reply a frown of confusion. Henry raised his voice. "MY NAME IS HENRY. ARE YOU OKAY?" A look of panic leaped onto the young woman's face as her eyes darted back and forth in fear.

Henry tightened his lips in a scowl and cursed himself. "Oh great! I frightened her," he muttered to the empty beach. "Like she wasn't scared enough already. Stupid!" Henry softened his voice and smiled, hoping to put her at ease. He asked again, "Are you all right?" She responded by shaking harder, her wide eyes looking for an escape. It was obvious that she didn't understand a word he was saying.

Henry sighed and ran his hand through his red hair. "What to do, what to do!" He expelled a long breath and turned again to peruse the empty beach. The answer fairies didn't appear with any revelations on what to do when you find a strange naked girl on the beach. It was obvious that he was just going to have to figure this one out on his own. He pulled out his phone and began to dial 911, but then he hesitated.

"Well, I can't just leave you here like this," he said, putting his phone back in his pocket. *What the hell am I doing?* "At least let's get you covered up." He removed a poncho from his runner's pack and carefully offered it to her. She stared back at him, more confused and frightened as ever. It was alarmingly clear she had no idea whatsoever of what was going on.

Henry set the poncho on the sand and offered his hand in an effort to help her sit up. She stared back as if it were some foreign object until she reached out her own hand, examining it with the same bewilderment, wiggling her fingers, and opening and closing her hand. Henry shook his head in astonishment and disbelief. It's one thing to not know who or where you are, but to not know *what* you are just took this encounter to an entirely new level. Henry needed a moment to regain his composure. *What the hell was going on here?*

Undaunted, he took the initiative, taking her hand into his only to find himself swept away, sucked into a vortex of emotions. Her features had softened a bit as she looked back into his. His heart was pounding as he helped her up to a seated position and retrieved the poncho. He still had a naked girl on the shore and was anxious to get her covered before some passerby showed up and started asking questions or, worse, making accusations. Cell phones had become both a blessing and a curse. The last thing he needed was to end up on YouTube.

He rolled the poncho up, holding the opening wide to place it over her head. She recoiled for a moment; but eventually, after patient repeated attempts and gentle spoken reassurances, Henry somehow managed to gain a grain of trust. She allowed him to push the opening over her head and then over her shoulders. Henry breathed a sigh of relief when her trembling seemed to abate a bit under the security of the garment.

Henry, the rescuer of needy causes, swooped in again to save the day, even if it meant facing possible kidnapping or human trafficking charges for his troubles.

"Henry," he said, pointing to his chest. "My name is Henry. I'm going to help you." He reached out to touch her shoulder and was relieved when she didn't cry out or cringe. "Let me help you get up." With his free hand, he held hers and moved the other from her shoulder to her upper arm, gently pulling her to her feet. She wobbled a bit then found her balance.

"I've got you," he said. The girl did not move; she just stared back at him. Henry stood there a moment, pursed his lips to make a smacking sound, and sighed. He put one arm behind her legs and the other behind her back and lifted her up. Although still visibly afraid, she did not cry out.

She was lighter than he had anticipated. In addition to his morning runs, Henry worked out regularly at home and at the gym. A single guy living in Florida had to keep up with the six-pack competition on the beach. Even with his weightlifting, he didn't expect her to be as weightless as she was. The exhilaration of the moment must have caused his adrenaline to kick in, he reasoned. He also sensed she was more relaxed and calm in his arms.

Pondering more questions than answers, Henry realized he was back at his car already. He put her in the passenger seat, continuing to talk to her in a reassuring voice and trying to keep her calm, like he would to a wounded animal. "I'm not sure what happened to you, but I will do everything I can to help you. First let's get you home." A puzzled look was his only reply.

He took a blanket he kept in the car and wrapped it around her. Henry took his place behind the wheel and noticed her jump as he started the engine. Panic filled her face when the vehicle began to move. Her head snapped back and forth in wide-eyed amazement as he entered the roadway. "It's okay," he assured her. "Everything's going to be okay."

He continued to talk to her the entire drive home to keep her focused on his voice rather than the sounds of the car's V-8 engine and the *whoosh* of cars passing them from the other direction. He kept his speed five miles under the limit for the drive home, not wanting to risk belting her into the seat and causing her more alarm.

"I know you're scared," he continued. "Once we get you inside and warm, you'll feel better. I'll do whatever I can to help you. Only a few more blocks and we'll be there." While he talked to her, he glanced back at her whenever he could to ensure that she was listening to him. She sat in the seat with her knees up to her chest and clung to the blanket, but the sound of his voice held her in its warm embrace, keeping her eyes focused on him rather than the Florida landscape as it passed by.

Henry ran several scenarios through his mind as to how he could help this young woman while he cruised along. "I need to get Heidi involved," he told her as part of his continuing diatribe. Heidi was his younger sister. Heidi Haley Williford-Mason. "She'll know what to do." Henry hoped. "You'll like her. She's always been there when I needed help."

The car pulled into the driveway of his orange stucco home that backed onto a small lake where the alligators silently lay waiting for their next meal. It was his parents' home before they died, and now it was his. "We're here," he announced, turning off the ignition. "I'm going to call Heidi, and then I'll come around and get you out." Still no response, but her trembling subsided and she didn't seem as frightened, curled up as she was. Henry sat in the driver's seat and pulled out his cell phone to call Heidi. The girl stared at the phone, and her eyes widened.

"Heidi," he began when she answered. "I need your help. Can you get over here now?"

"Well, hello to you too. Wait, why? What the heck did you do now?" Heidi demanded.

"Nothing! I swear! I just need your help. Come over, and I'll tell you why."

"Give me half an hour." Heidi sighed. "Let me get the kids up and ready." Henry had lost track of just how many times Heidi had to pull his bacon out of the fire over the years. This was no different.

"Okay," Henry told his peculiar guest. "Help is on the way." He got out of the car, ran around to the passenger side, and opened the door. He took her hand, prompting her to get out of the car. "It's okay," he said gently. "Come on out." The girl slowly got out of the vehicle, bumping her head along the way, then stood still, unsure what to do next, her eyes glued to Henry.

Henry nodded. "All right. Let's get you inside." He picked her up and carried her into the house while she clutched the blanket around her. "I wish you could understand what I'm saying. It would make things so much easier."

He took her to the sofa and set her down. She pulled her legs up with her feet on the sofa and her knees up to her chin, clinging to the blanket. Immediately, the cats and dogs rushed over to her and began sniffing her feet. The cats jumped onto the sofa, rubbing their faces against her legs, while the dogs licked her, wagging their tails with enthusiastic acceptance. Even Mack, a blind orange tabby, could sense her presence and was drawn to her. And Flack, a red dachshund with paralyzed back legs, struggled in his doggie cart, rolling himself over to join the furry welcome party. Henry had never seen his pets so drawn to any other newcomer, especially this fast, but this mysterious guest seemed to be a magnet for animal affection. For the first time, she appeared to respond, her eyes softening and her hand reaching out to pet each of them.

"Strange," Henry observed. "Never saw them react like that to anyone else."

Henry seized the opportunity to dash into the kitchen, sensing he was leaving her in good hands, or paws as it were, while she was distracted. He rifled around in his refrigerator to see what he could offer her to eat or drink, hastily grabbing a bottle of lemon-flavored water and a box of wheat crackers from the counter. He returned to find the scene much the same as he had left it. Setting the crackers on the coffee table, he opened the bottle and offered it to her, only to pull it back when she did not take it from him. She did not seem to understand what the bottle was. She was staring at it with the same bewildered look she had on the beach when she looked at her hand, as if for the first time.

"Okaaay." Henry closed his eyes then opened them.

"Let's try something else." He took a drink from the bottle then handed it back to her. "Drink."

She cautiously took the bottle from his hand, looked at it, and held it back to her mouth, spilling the water down her front and onto the blanket. She jumped a little as the cold water ran down her neck to her chest (as did Baby, the small calico cat who happened to be rubbing her face against her at that moment), but then she took the bottle again and put it to her mouth, swallowing the cool liquid. She did not know what to do with the bottle after she drank, so Henry took it from her hands and set it on the table.

Finally, Henry thought to himself, *we're making progress*. Next, he took a cracker from the box and offered it to her. As before, she did not respond, so he ate one first then handed one to her. She stared at the cracker for a few seconds then took it, bringing it to her mouth while Henry chomped his teeth to show her what to do. She chomped her teeth back in response and put the edge of the cracker in her mouth, nibbling at it like a mouse. A moment later, she gobbled the remaining cracker and opened her mouth, indicating she wanted more. Henry gave her both the crackers and the water.

Eventually she had eaten half a box of crackers and managed to drink the entire bottle of water. Henry sat back and really looked at this strange young woman, her soft cheekbones, a pixie nose, those piercing blue almond-shaped eyes, and a wide mouth. All framed by that golden mane of hers.

"What do we do now?" he asked the universe who refused to provide him any direction. "Damn you, Answer Fairies!"

There was a sharp knock at the door a heartbeat before Heidi and the kids burst into the house without waiting for Henry to answer, a diaper bag on one arm and a purse on the other. Two-year-old Natalie, called Nattie, was also in her arms, clutching her favorite "bankee" in one hand while sucking the life out of the thumb of her other. Five-year-old Nathan was in tow, glued to her side. "What's the matter now?" She closed the door behind her before anyone could escape.

"This," Henry said, standing by the girl with his hand out to her. "I found her on the beach this morning naked and scared. She doesn't seem to understand anything I say, and I just don't know what to do with her."

Heidi's jaw dropped in both surprise and disbelief. "What the hell did you get yourself into this time, big brother? Honestly, it's a miracle you survived on your own before I came along! Did you at least call the police?" Heidi put her purse, diaper bag, and Nattie on the floor.

"No," Henry admitted. "I don't want her to get lost in the system if I can help it. Besides there's something weird about her. It's like she's totally helpless." Henry wasn't ready to admit to himself, let alone his sister, that he felt connected to the girl in some inexplicable way. "Can you help me with her? You're a girl."

"Wow, figured that one out all by yourself, did ya?" Heidi quipped. "What gave me away? Popping out two kids or my boobs?"

Heidi walked over to where the girl was sitting. "Okay. First we need to make sure that she's not injured in any way, and if she is, get her the appropriate medical attention if we need to, system or no system. Then, we need to get her something to wear. Do you have some shorts and a shirt we can use for now? I can run by SuperMart later and pick up a few things for her. Then we need to figure out what to do after that. Are you going to keep her here?"

"Yeah, I guess. I'm not sure what else to do."

Heidi watched Nattie join Nathan, who was already playing with the animals. Not having any pets of their own, the kids always looked forward to going to Uncle Henry's house to have fun with them. "That should keep them occupied while I handle your latest crisis."

She sat by the girl and introduced herself. "Hi, I'm Heidi. I'm going to see if you're hurt, okay?" No response. Before she had the kids, Heidi was a nurse and was accustomed to working with difficult patients. She had a gentle bedside manner and a way of putting people at ease. This young woman was no exception.

The girl did not flinch when Heidi removed the blanket and poncho before making a quick physical examination. "Doesn't appear to be any sign of trauma, pulse and breathing are fine," Heidi said, relieved, as she looked at the girl's eyes. "That's good."

Henry returned with a white T-shirt with a large Tampa Bay Buccaneers logo on the front and a pair of shorts that tied at the waist. Heidi nodded in approval as she took possession of them and then turned her attention back to girl on the couch.

"Okay, sweetie, here are some clothes for you to wear. The bathroom is just down the hall." She pointed to the second bathroom between hers and Henry's old bedrooms.

The girl just blinked in bewilderment, looking back and forth between the clothes and Heidi's smiling face. Heidi tugged on the shoulder of her own shirt. "Shirt? Clothes? Dressed?" She rolled her eyes and then glared at her brother. "Oh, for heaven's sake, Henry! Leave it to you to discover the world's only barbarian Barbie! What are ya gonna drag home next, Betty Bigfoot?"

She took the girl's hand, helping her to stand. "Come on, honey." She smiled, lowering her voice. "Let's get you decent." Heidi wrapped the blanket around her, supporting her while she took small slow steps. She allowed Heidi to guide her. It was almost like she didn't know how to walk. As they crossed the threshold of the bathroom, Heidi barked a command to Henry to watch the kids.

What the hell did I get myself into indeed? Henry then realized his niece was sampling tuna-flavored Friskies from the bag she pulled from the cupboard and spilled on the floor. He quickly grabbed the bag and started to pick up the loose pieces.

Over Nattie's screams at the loss of her treats, Henry heard his sister speaking in that caring mother voice she often used with her own children on the other side of the bathroom door. He couldn't make out what she was saying, but he could tell she was in full mother hen mode and was going on and on about something.

In addition to being seven years younger, his sister was a foot shorter than he was, standing only five feet two inches. She had short brown hair and big brown eyes and still carried a few extra baby pounds after having Nattie. She made up for her lack of height with attitude and tenacity.

After what felt like an eternity, the bathroom door finally opened, and the two girls emerged. Henry felt relieved that this mysterious Jane Doe finally had some clothes on. Heidi led the girl back to her previous spot on the sofa. Then she turned on her heels, grabbed Henry by the arm, and dragged him a few feet away, forcing him to sit down in a dining room chair.

"Do you have any idea what just happened in there?" Heidi asked.

"Of course I don't," Henry replied in his defense. "I was out here the whole time."

"I was being rhetorical, you idiot!" Heidi scolded. "She just urinated on the bathroom floor!"

"What?" Henry's brow furrowed with confusion, his mouth open in a sneer.

"You heard me. There is something seriously wrong here. She's as helpless as a newborn baby. As soon as we got in there, she stopped, started shaking, and the floodgates opened up. I immediately sat her down on the toilet to finish. Dude, you really need to learn how to put the seat down by the way!"

"It's my house."

"Whatever, the point is I had to teach her how to go to the bathroom. It was like she had never even seen a toilet before, let alone used one."

"You should have seen her in the car. She was the same way. After we got home, I had to teach her how to eat and drink."

"Exactly my point. If I hadn't checked her pupils myself, I would think she was on drugs or something. I don't think she's mentally challenged either because she apparently can learn things really fast. After I showed her how and where to take care of her bodily functions—I'll spare you the gory details—she just kept flushing the toilet over and over with a proud look on her face."

"Wow, um, thank you for that," Henry stammered. "I've only potty trained dogs before. I don't know what I'd do without you, sis."

"Well, this isn't some stray dog you picked up on the side of the road. You can't just post her picture on Facebook and hope somebody claims her. You really should reconsider calling the authorities."

"I know you're right. You always are."

"But you're not gonna listen because you never do." She bent down and picked up Nattie, who had moved on to snacking on the dogs' kibble in the large metal bowl on the kitchen floor.

Heidi just stood there for a moment, shaking her head, thankful the child hadn't grown a tail.

"Who is she? Where the hell did she come from? Why is she so helpless? These are all questions that need to be answered, big brother." She scooped up her purse and diaper bag, Nattie struggling in her arms.

Henry pressed his lips together and shook his head. "You're right, of course, and I want to know as badly as you do. It's just that I've never met anyone like her before." He hugged his sister. "Thanks for coming by on a moment's notice. I'll think of something. Love ya, sis."

"I love you too," Heidi said with one hand on the door and the other around Nattie, who was covered in crumbs. "I'll be back with some more suitable clothes and undergarments. You need to think about what you're going to do, Henry, if you're not going to call the police. Say good-bye, kids."

Nattie smiled, enjoying a postmeal thumb, and little Nate just waved a tiny hand good-bye. With that, Heidi turned around, Nathan at her side, and left, shutting the front door behind her.

"Bye, kids," Henry called.

Henry turned his attention back to his odd guest, only to discover she was missing. He found her in the bathroom using her newly discovered toilet-flushing talent. "I guess you can stay with me for a little while at least." His guest only responded with another flush. Just another day.

2

Learning to Speak

Henry led his guest out of the bathroom and back into the living room. She sat back on the sofa and then began making sounds with her mouth directed at the animals. She started with just single sounds but then seemed to mimic the meows and barks of his pets with surprising accuracy.

Watching her "talk" to the animals gave Henry an idea. He sat down in front of her on the trunk he used as a coffee table, pointed to himself, and said with a breathy *h* and strong emphasis on each syllable, "Henry. My name is Henry. HEN-REE."

The girl looked at him only a moment before she opened her mouth. She seemed to be forcing the air out of her lungs, as if she was breathing hard on glass. She put her head forward and pushed to get the sound out and was rewarded with "Heh...heh... Henreee."

He smiled and nodded as she said his name. "That's right! My name is Henry! But what do I call you? I guess you can't tell me your name, so let me think about what name is best for you."

He thought a bit and then offered his solution. "Let's try something that's easy to say. How about 'Anne'?" He pointed to his chest and affirmed, "My name is Henry," then pointed to her and spoke in a clear raised voice, "Your name is Anne."

The girl rocked forward again, as if the action would push the sounds of out her mouth, forcing the air out as she did with his name. "Amm." Her face brightened; and for the first time, he saw her smile with a wide face-splitting smile, showing bright, perfect teeth.

"Close," Henry encouraged. "Let's try again. ANNE," he repeated, keeping his mouth open and his tongue pressed against its roof so she could see how to say the letter *n* as well as hear it.

"ANNNNE."

"Yes, yes, very good!" Henry praised her efforts. "That's a good start!"

He got up from the table and, holding her hands in his, helped her to her feet. "I wonder how she would react to…" Not finishing his thought out loud, he led her to the full-length mirror in the hallway. Standing next to her in front of it, they both gazed into this mysterious new wonder as Anne scrutinized her reflection. She was astonished to see two Henrys and kept looking back between the real Henry and his doppelgänger. Henry couldn't help but think what an attractive couple they made when suddenly Anne jumped when she realized Henry's partner in the mirror was her. Henry smiled, amused while she watched her image move whenever she did. Henry waved his hand to show her how it all worked.

While watching Anne fascinated by her own appearance, the artist in him couldn't help but notice subtle changes in the portrait of his own reflection, the slight wrinkles in the corners of his emerald green eyes and thin worry lines starting to dig across his forehead. At age thirty-two, the last few years had been rough ones, and it was starting to show.

"It's okay. It's just our reflection, see? I wanted you to see what you look like." Pointing at his reflection, he confirmed, "I'm Henry." Then pointing at her reflection, he said, "And you're Anne."

"Anne!" she repeated, covering her mouth at seeing her reflection speak.

Henry kicked his head back and roared with laughter.

Anne started laughing too, touching her reflection with one hand and her real face with the other. Turning her attention to Henry, she reached over and grabbed his face.

"Otay…doze are my wips," Henry explained, speaking between her slender fingers. Anne's finger tips explored his thin lips, caressed his square unshaven jaw, and tickled his high cheekbones. Henry explained what everything was as she moved from feature to feature. "And that's my nose," he said as she ran her index finger down the bridge of his straight nose, stopping at the tip. Anne touched each corresponding feature on her own face, which was now beaming, finally grasping the concept.

For the first time since stumbling upon Anne on the beach, Henry felt relieved and encouraged. "It's going to be okay, Anne. We're going to figure this out together, one step at a time. You're probably still hungry, and I should get you something better to eat than crackers. C'mon, let's go to the kitchen." She followed him to the kitchen, and Henry sat her down at the table while he pulled out several items from the fridge.

Anne was playing with Groucho, the Turkish Van with a black "mustache" under his nose, like his namesake. She was having a kitty conversation with the feline, answering his meows with varied versions of her own.

Henry returned with a plate of assorted indulgences and placed them on the table and then sat down beside her. He gave her some apples, strawberries, and, especially to her delight, chocolate. "I thought you might like that." He smiled. Her reply was to grab another piece of candy. "Whoa, slow down there, sweetheart," Henry cautioned, pulling the plate closer to him. "You don't want to give yourself a tummy ache."

Anne pouted in disapproval and turned away, folding her arms across her chest. Then something caught her attention on the floor. It was a bowl of hard food Henry kept out for the cats. Mistaking it for more chocolate, she reached down and grabbed a handful, stuffing it into her mouth before Henry could stop her.

"NO, WAIT!" he shouted, but it was too late. Anne gagged, trying to spit out the mistaken morsels stuck to her tongue. Henry had to suppress the urge to laugh and quickly guided her to the kitchen sink. He grabbed a paper towel and, facing Anne, instructed her. "Stick out your tongue, like this." He demonstrated.

Anne complied with an urgency brought on by the nasty taste in her mouth. He wiped off what he could and then turned on the cold water.

"Here, rinse out your mouth. Watch me!" Henry bent over the sink, cupped his hands under the running water, slurped some up, brought his hands to his mouth, and then spit. No further demonstration was needed. Anne elbowed him out of the way and followed his example. Henry put one arm around her shoulders, wiping her face dry with a towel.

"I'm sorry. Sometimes I forget how new all of this is to you, for whatever unknown reason. How about another piece of chocolate to get rid of the bad taste?" He gave her one last piece, thinking to himself that some lessons are best learned by experience, even if it is unpleasant.

Undaunted, Henry was determined to get through to her. They moved from room to room so he could teach her the names of different objects. She learned what a cat and a dog were and each of their names. Book, sofa, lamp, etc.—it was amazing how she picked up on everything.

Henry felt a bit like Annie Sullivan with his own Helen Keller, going around the room grabbing or touching items so he could teach her what they were called. They named everything in the living room and then moved to the dining room to learn the names of the dining room table, chairs, buffet table, and china cabinet.

They were in the kitchen taking out everything in the drawer of kitchen utensils when Heidi walked through the door, with Nathan and Nattie trailing behind. She had a couple of SuperMart bags in her hand. "I got her some clothes, underwear, and…" She stopped. Henry and Anne were picking up individual pieces of kitchen utensils spread out on the counter. "What are you two up to?"

"You won't believe it!" Henry put down a rolling pin on the counter and turned to Heidi. "She's incredibly smart! She's picking up on stuff like it's nothing! We've spent the last hour and a half learning the names of everything! It's amazing how fast she's catching on!"

"Really!" Heidi said, putting down the bags on the kitchen table. "That is amazing!"

"Guess what else? She has a name," Henry said, not waiting for a reply. "I call her Anne."

"Anne?"

"Yeah, I thought that would be easier to say. I didn't know what else to call her. I don't think Mom would've minded." Anne was their mother's name.

"And she understands that's her name?"

"Yep! Not only that, she knows my name too. Let me reintroduce you to your new estranged sister. Ahem, Anne," Henry said with his hand on Heidi's back. "This is—"

"Heidi!" Anne said, smiling. Both siblings' jaws dropped.

"That's right," Heidi replied in disbelief. "But how?"

Anne pointed as she spoke. "Heidi, Henry, Anne."

"She must've remembered your name from before." Henry beamed like a proud parent. "I told you she was a quick study." Turning to his niece and nephew, he said, "And these two monsters are Nathan and Nattie." Henry grabbed each one in a big hug as he said their name.

Nathan ran right up to Anne, saying, "My name is Nathan! Say my name!" Nattie just hid behind her uncle's legs, peeking out and smiling at Anne from behind her pacifier, not quite as brave as her big brother.

Anne smiled at him and said in a clear voice, "Nathan."

"Remarkable!" Heidi said. "Have you thought about what to do with her tonight?"

"I'll clear out the spare bedroom," Henry replied, putting the utensils back in the drawer. "I'm just using the futon as a bookshelf anyway. Those books can go on the floor." Henry and Heidi both loved to read, a joy they inherited from their mother, and both homes were filled with bookshelves spilling over with loose books. "I guess we'll just see how tonight goes before I decide anything further."

"Well," Heidi said, looking at her watch. "I need to get these kids fed. You wanna watch them while I do a fast-food run? Afterward,

I can show her what I bought and see if it all fits. It will be nice to see her wearing some proper clothes."

"Sure, you know what I want. Double cheeseburger with no pickles and large fries. Get something for Anne too and get her a chocolate shake. She likes chocolate."

"Okay, not even going to ask. Just hold down the fort, and I'll get lunch."

Heidi left, and Henry watched Nathan take over teaching Anne, taking her into Henry's studio, where he showed her the box of toys Henry kept for those days when he took a turn watching the kids.

Anne picked up Nathan's *Big Book of Animals*, and the two of them sat there for a while. Anne pointed to an animal while Nathan provided its name. Anne tried to repeat each name, having difficulty with a few but seeming to enjoy the time with Nathan. Henry crossed his arms in front of him and smiled as they played with names.

Half an hour later, Heidi returned with the food. "Nathan, Nattie," she called. "Come and eat. I got chicken nuggets." Nathan took Anne's hand and led her to the table to join him in his favorite fare. Henry pulled out a chair and helped Anne to sit while Heidi put a cheeseburger, small fries, and a chocolate shake in front of her. Henry picked up his own double cheeseburger and took a bite, showing Anne what to do with the food.

Anne poked at the cheeseburger as if it were alive and then picked it up with both hands and brought it to her mouth. She took a small bite, smiled, and then began to eat the cheeseburger with renewed relish in the taste. She then turned her attention to the chocolate shake and stared at it for a while. After a moment spent watching Henry drink his Coke, she took the straw into her mouth and...nothing happened. She backed away and looked pleadingly at Henry.

"Oh yeah, I forgot how new all of this is to you. You just learned how to drink from a bottle a couple of hours ago. Wait, I know." Henry removed the straws and lids from both of their beverages and handed the milkshake back to Anne. Holding his own cup up to his lips, he said, "Drink," and proceeded to demonstrate to Anne how to drink from a cup.

"Drink," Anne repeated and mimicked his movements. She pulled her cup away and pronounced "chocolate" from beneath a big, frothy foam mustache. Everyone at the table burst out with laughter at the sight.

"Yes, that's right. It's called a chocolate shake." Henry chuckled. Anne continued enjoying her meal, oblivious to what was so funny and, just like little Nattie, she was wearing almost as much as she was consuming.

In between taking a few bites of her salad, Heidi asked, "Have you given any more thought as to what you're going to do with her? Are you going to be able to get your work done with her here? I mean, look at her. She's going to need a lot of attention."

"I don't know, haven't really thought that far," he said between handfuls of fries dripping with ketchup. "I can put all the extra stuff in the guest room in my studio, and she can sleep in there until I figure out who she is and where she came from or what I'm going to do for the long term. I'll also check for any missing person reports and see if anyone matches her description. I don't want to call the police unless I have to."

Henry took a drink from his Coke and sighed. "I have a few days before my next piece is due. I can afford that time to sort this out." Henry was in the middle of a set of illustrations for a nursing student manual and only had a few more to complete.

"Okay," Heidi said then shrugged. "Let me know if there is anything I can do to help. We can take it one day at a time."

When everyone was finished with their lunch, Heidi cleaned up both Nattie and Anne and then cleared the table of the trash. "Well"—she dusted off her hands—"let me see if she can fit into these clothes." She took Anne's hand and nodded to her. Anne stood up from her chair and followed Heidi as she grabbed the SuperMart bags and headed to the guest room. "Kids, mind your uncle."

In the guest room, Heidi took some of the stacks of books off the futon and put them against the wall. She put the bags on the futon and selected a lilac-colored cotton blouse. "Let's start with this," she said.

Anne just tugged at her T-shirt, saying "Heidi," not sure what to do.

"Oh, let me help you." Heidi nodded and put her hands up. Anne mimicked her and put her hands up as well. Heidi reached out and took the bottom of Anne's T-shirt, pulling it up and over her head. She then took the lilac blouse and put Anne's arm into one sleeve, then the other. Heidi buttoned up the shirt for her, stood back, and nodded her approval.

Then Heidi said, "Let's get those shorts off," pointing at Henry's old and ragged running shorts. Anne pulled them down. Heidi helped her step out of them, leaving them in a puddle of clothing on the floor. She took a pair of underwear out of the package from the SuperMart bag and held them out, ready to help Anne step into them. But Anne took the underwear from Heidi and, after staring at it a moment or two, put her feet into the leg holes and pulled up the garment. Heidi gave her a pair of purple stretchy shorts, and Anne repeated the process, pulling the shorts up around her waist.

Heidi patted the futon. "Sit down. Let's do something about that hair." Anne sat beside her while Heidi took out a brush and comb and brushed out Anne's long blonde hair until the golden mane shimmered.

Pulling the comb through the golden threads of Anne's hair, Heidi also found herself drawn to this strange girl, wanting to care for her as if she were her own child, or sister perhaps. She understood why her brother could not leave this enchanting girl on the sands alone. Heidi brushed the shimmering strands, pulling her hand over them and smoothing out the tresses while Anne sat still on the bed beside her.

Finally, Heidi put the brush down, admiring the bright shine of Anne's locks of spun gold. "Okay," she said, standing up. "That's more like it. Let's join the others and see what disaster awaits." Heidi held out her hand, helped Anne up off the futon, and led her back into the living room and to Henry.

"Wow!" Henry stood up from the floor where he and Nathan were playing with Legos while keeping Nattie from eating them. "She really is pretty, isn't she?" he said, stunned.

"That she is." Heidi smiled, staring at her brother's guest. "Okay," Heidi grabbed her purse, diaper bag, and Nattie. "I think you've got things under control here. Come on, Nathan."

"Bye, Uncle Henry! Bye, Anne!" Nathan shouted.

"Call me if you need me," Heidi said, walking out the door and closing it behind her.

Henry took a deep breath and turned to Anne. "Now what can we do?"

Anne. She had a name. It was "Anne." And the one who found her was "Henry." The fear she felt when Henry first found her began to fade to be replaced by excitement, especially when she learned to say the words. She knew Henry and Heidi and Nathan and Nattie and Sam and Charlie and Groucho and Baby and Mack and Flack and Bond and Elphaba and Loki...so many new names!

Anne went to the pile of toys on the floor in the studio and brought *The Big Book of Animals* to Henry.

"Okay," Henry said with a smile. "Let's see what else I can teach you."

After they finished Nathan's books, she pointed to other books on the shelf. Henry pulled out a few illustrated books and showed Anne his world. For several hours, they looked at books on what she learned were travel, architecture, history, famous paintings, Hollywood icons, and even comic books. Her thirst for knowledge was as insatiable as her enthusiasm.

A book of fantasy art really caught her attention. She was mesmerized by every image in the book, page after page of beautiful women, some with wings and pointed ears, while others were scantily clad in armor holding swords or glowing spears. She learned these were fairies, elves, and warrior princesses. Some pages depicted strange animals like unicorns and griffins and strange creatures Henry called trolls, ogres, and goblins. She wanted to say each word for every picture she saw in the books. There were so many words! She sat next to Henry flipping through the pages while Henry provided the name of each picture she pointed to.

One drawing, which took up two pages, made Anne freeze and stare while the page shook in her trembling hand.

"That scary guy is a dragon, and that's fire coming out of his mouth," Henry informed her.

Anne couldn't reply or speak. She just stared at the book, touching the picture as if it was a living being. Her chest began to hurt, and her eyes filled with tears that spilled onto the page. Of all the wondrous things they had explored together that night, it was a picture of a dragon that touched something deep inside her, creating an intense yearning for what she did not know, or even why.

"What's the matter, Anne? Why are you crying?" Henry touched her cheek to turn her face to him and wiped away the tears rolling down her face. Henry took the book and shut it, putting it on the table. "None of the things in this book are real. They're just pretend, make-believe." Henry smiled at her. "You've been through a lot, and it's getting late. You must be tired. Come on, let's get you to bed."

She reached out and picked up the book, holding it as if she could not let it go. "Okay." Henry let her keep the large volume. "You can keep it, but you do need to get some rest. It's been a long day."

He led her to the guestroom and pulled out the futon to become a bed. Grabbing some linens and a blanket from the closet, he guided Anne to the bed and helped her to lie down, covering her with the blankets. She kept the book, holding on with both hands. The bed was soft beneath her, the mattress and the blankets enveloping her in a warm cocoon.

"Get some sleep, Anne. Things will look better tomorrow." Henry turned off the light and closed the door, leaving her alone in the dark.

Anne lay clutching onto the book of fantasy creatures like Nattie clutched her blanket. Salty tears ran down her eyes into her hair and onto the soft pillow underneath her. She could not understand what was happening, only that she could not stop crying.

She didn't know anything really, except that she was with Henry and that she was not alone. She liked learning the words and making the sounds. It made her feel good inside, like when she made the sound Henry called "laughing."

That was until she saw the dragon. What was it about the strange picture that made her feel this way? She did not know what dragons were, only that they made her hurt inside. She could not even tell Henry why; she didn't know herself.

Eventually, her sobbing ceased as the need for sleep took over, pushing her into a deep slumber.

3

I am flying! I inhale a deep breath of sweet morning air while I glide effortlessly along on the strong, swift current. Closing my eyes for a moment allows me to enjoy the cool wind against my face while I soar over majestic crystal mountains. Their sparkling summits of breathtaking colors stretch way beyond the distant horizon, reaching up into a silver sky glistening under a brilliant white sun. Far beneath me is an ocean of emerald green that laps at the side of the mountains and crests white wherever the water slams against the lower outcroppings.

Sharing the sky with me is an enormous dragon with powerful, great white wings. He is the largest of all the dragons except for The Two. His massive wingspan is as wide as he is long. He flexes his strong pectoral muscles to propel him high up into the clouds, his wings beating the air down. I struggle to keep up, following him to the highest peak, which has a flattened top. I see the numerous multilevel structures made of bricks hewn from the crystal mountain. Looking down, I see countless shelves extending out from the mountain that shine in different colors. Each shelf leads to an opening that serves as each individual dragon's lair. The higher the dwelling, the higher one's status is in our world.

I watch several other dragons fly on and off their shelves at different heights on the mountain. Their bodies are long and slim, with shorter front legs than hind, four toes and sharp talons, and a tail that ends in three flowing fins the same color as their wings. Their faces are elongated, with ears that sweep up to sharp points and turn in the direction of even the slightest sound. Their mouths are the length of their heads, with two thin slits for nostrils at the end of their snouts.

All of us have smooth golden skin that glimmers in the sunlight, while the membrane covering our wings varies in color and brightness. There are dragons with wings of dark gray, lighter gray, silver, dark blue, light blue, yellow, red, purple, and white. My own wings shimmer with an iridescent glow reflecting all the colors of the other dragons.

Suddenly, there is a deafening crack of thunder, and I look up in disbelief to see the sky torn open with a sickening black flash. Out of the wound, several large ebony dragons come gushing through the severed jugular of the heavens. An icy chill runs down my spine at the sight of these monstrous invaders adorned with huge black wings spanning twice the length of their bodies. The mountain trembles when they touch down, standing upright on two long legs with large feet with elongated razor sharp claws that slice the pristine crystal beneath them like flesh.

My heart leaps into my throat, and I watch in horror as they spew fire from their great mouths, scorching the crystal mountain and its frightened inhabitants. Their nostrils are raised and large, emitting smoke from the deadly inferno within. Their evil eyes blaze as red as the flames they expel, mercilessly burning the golden dragons attempting to flee. My heart hammers in my chest, and I scream out in terror, helplessly witnessing this hellish genocidal inferno incinerate my kind.

4

Return to the Beach

Startled, Henry sprang up in his bed. Something was seriously wrong. He could hear Anne screaming and the dogs howling; all hell was breaking loose. He was out of bed and down the hall in a heartbeat, bursting into the guest room and almost ripping the door off its hinges in the process. He was shocked to find Anne screaming with her eyes closed and arms flailing as if fighting off imaginary foes on top of her. "Anne," he shouted, trying to grab her hands. "It's all right! It's only a bad dream! I'm here! Calm down! I'm here!"

Anne continued to fight him for several minutes, even after she opened her eyes, until she realized where she was. He could feel her body shaking from the horror of her nightmare. She frantically gasped to catch her breath.

"It was just a bad dream, Anne," Henry whispered. "Everything's all right!" He could see she was covered in sweat and the sheets were soaked. When she recognized him, she threw her arms around him and sobbed into his chest. Her body still trembled, and she clung to him with everything inside her. Several of the animals came in and jumped up on the bed to offer their comfort and support.

"It's okay," Henry repeated. Putting his hands on her shoulders, he held her at arm's length so he could look into her eyes. "It was just a bad dream." He wiped away her tears. He knew she did not understand all of what he was saying, but she seemed to respond to the soothing tone of his voice. Combined with his gentle demeanor and the purr of a concerned kitten, she stopped shaking. She reached out to pet each animal that had rushed to her aid.

"Tell you what," Henry offered. "I'll stay here with you until you fall asleep again." He sat on the floor next to the futon, surrounded by his furry supporters, and held Anne's hand. He caressed her forehead while she settled back into the mattress. Eventually, Henry heard her breathing slow as she fell back asleep. He stayed with her a little while longer, gazing at her beauty while she drifted off. His hand brushed across her cheek while he bent down and kissed her forehead. Silent as a cat, he crept out of the room, turning off the light along the way.

Anne did not dream again the remainder of the night, and all was peaceful. Henry lay on his back with one arm tucked behind his head, staring at the ceiling and vigilantly listening to every sound. The Answer Fairies never did make an appearance that day, but thankfully, the Sandman was on duty. Eventually, Henry slipped into a restless slumber.

June 16
Tuesday

As with every morning, Henry's four-legged alarms went off before his electronic one had the chance to perform its assigned task. "Why do I even bother setting it?" As soon as he got to his feet, the tail-wagging choir broke out into their morning chorus. Before heading to the kitchen, Henry went to check on Anne. He was relieved and surprised to see her sitting on the futon, calm and awake.

"Well, good morning, sunshine! I hope you're feeling better." Anne replied with a smile. Despite her ordeal, she appeared to be no worse for wear from her nightmare mere hours before. "Let me get these guys fed. Then I'll make us something to eat." He helped her up and led her to the kitchen where he fed the animals and then poured out two bowls of cereal with milk, which he put on the dining room table. He pulled out a chair. "Let's sit down and eat."

Anne followed his lead, picking up the spoon and taking small bites. After spilling several flakes on the floor, which were immediately lapped up by dogs, she finished the entire bowl. Henry was reminded of Nattie. She usually ended up wearing more than she consumed. Henry finished his bowl then wiped Anne's chin with a napkin before clearing away the dishes.

"I will put the DISHES in the SINK in the KITCHEN while you wait on the SOFA, okay?" Henry put emphasis on key words he hoped Anne remembered from yesterday's teachings while pointing toward the sofa.

Anne went back to the living room and sat on the sofa, followed by the animals. He noticed that she remembered each of their names when she called them to her like a game. Henry washed the bowls and poured himself a cup of steaming gourmet coffee. Standing in the doorway, he inhaled its aroma before slurping down the first sip. He stood there for a while watching her interact with his pets. He marveled at how different this girl was. He had never met anyone like her!

He finished his coffee and went to where Anne was sitting. "Let's try to find out a little more about where you came from," he suggested. "But first let's get you into some fresh clothes." He took her by the hand and let her back to the guestroom.

After rummaging through the clothes Heidi had purchased the day before, he selected a pair of blue shorts, a white T-shirt with the face of a cat on it, and a pair of underwear. He laid them out on the futon for her to see. "Here, put these on," he instructed, tugging at the shirt she had on. He hoped she would be able to undress herself and was surprised when she nodded and pulled her shirt off right in front of him. "I really need to have Heidi get you a bra," he said, more to himself than to her as his eyes returned to their sockets. Picking up the new clothes and pointing at her, he said, "Put these on, okay?" Without waiting for a response, he shoved the clothes into her hands and then dashed out of the room to give her some privacy.

Back in his own room, Henry shut the door, spun around, and leaned his back up against it, exhaling as if he had dodged some imaginary bullet. He had come to accept the yet-to-be-explained psychic connection he felt toward Anne, but he wasn't quite ready for this physical attraction he was feeling. How could he help it? She's like a living Malibu Barbie with breast implants on steroids. *Yeah, it would just be my luck to bed this beauty only to discover she's the daughter of some powerful drug cartel kingpin, with amnesia.* Henry laughed at the absurdity of the thought. It was a welcomed distraction.

With his pulse and manhood back down to normal, Henry undressed and headed to the bathroom to take a shower. The master bath had a large garden tub and a separate shower enclosed by glass. He opened the door and reached inside to turn the water on and waited a moment for it to heat up. Once inside, he allowed the cascading water to roll down his body and wash away his concerns. When he reached for the bottle of shampoo on the shower caddy, he froze! Anne was standing in the bathroom watching him! He cracked open the shower door, grabbed the towel from the rack, and wrapped it around his exposed body.

"What are you doing here?" he exclaimed, stepping out of the shower, the water still running. It wasn't like he'd never showered with a girl before, but this was not one of those times.

Anne ignored his query and stood there fascinated by the running water. She kept looking back and forth between the shower and her dripping host as if trying to solve a puzzle. A moment later, she stripped off her clothes and marched into the shower. She didn't seem to have any reservations on disrobing in front of Henry or seeing him nude. He realized that to her, this was just another new experience, just like every previous moment had been ever since they first met. She squealed when the warm water came in contact with her skin. She stood under the cascading torrent, enjoying the sensation of it caressing her body.

Henry stood there dumbfounded, trying to stay calm and objective while this erotic scene played out in front of him. Here was the most beautiful girl he had ever seen standing naked in his shower, her flawless figure glistening in the flowing water. The whole experience felt like some surreal wet daydream.

Henry jumped when Anne reached through the open door and grabbed his arm, snapping him out of his trance and pulling him inside to join her. Along the way, Henry removed his towel and tossed it onto the edge of the tub before closing the door behind him.

"Okay, that was unexpected!" Henry exclaimed. "Now what?" He panicked while Anne ran her fingers through the streaming water rolling off his chest. Henry cleared his throat, took a deep breath, and closed his eyes so he could think without being distracted.

All right, he thought to himself. *She's as oblivious to my nudity as she was of her own when I first found her naked on the beach.* Then he realized she was just as innocent and unaware as his niece and nephew were whenever they bathed together. *Get a grip on yourself, man! You can get through this. Just teach her how to wash herself.*

Henry opened his eyes and locked his gaze with hers. *Just keep your eyes fixed on hers, and you'll be fine.* He sighed, grabbed a bar of soap, held it up in front of her face, and said, "SOAP. This is SOAP. We use it to WASH ourselves. WASH," he instructed, taking her arm with his free hand, making circular movements with soap while her arm lathered up. "Then we RINSE." He moved her arm directly under the stream of running water, making the foam disappear. Anne was amazed at this new wonder she was experiencing. Henry could see in her eyes that she understood. He placed the bar of soap in her hand. "Your turn."

"Soap," Anne stated, holding it up. "Wash." She grabbed Henry's arm, intending to scrub away. But she stopped when she saw the tattoo that covered his right shoulder and arm. It was beautifully illustrated, one of Henry's own designs he once saw in a dream, of a golden dragon with its head covering his shoulder and the body entwining down his arm. The wings wrapped around his pronounced muscles with its tail reaching down his forearm. Anne caressed his arm, tracing the lines with her fingertips.

"Dragon?" she whispered, hypnotized by the design.

"Yes, it's a dragon," he responded. "It's a tattoo, a picture like in your book."

"Tattoo," she repeated, continuing her exploration with her fingers. "Dragon."

The touch of her caress sent waves of desire through Henry's body. She slowly traced the lines along his arm up to the dragon's face on his shoulder, lightly drawing her hand over the open mouth of the beast.

Henry closed his eyes, consumed by the passion that was building inside him. His breathing was shallow and fast, his body surrendering to her touch.

"No!" Henry recoiled, finding that he could breathe again.

Startled, Anne looked back at him, confused.

"No, no, wash yourself," Henry instructed while making circular motions on his chest.

Anne thought for a moment before a look of understanding lit up her face.

Good, Henry praised himself, *I think she gets it.*

"Yourself," Anne chimed, reaching over and washing Henry's chest.

Henry stayed her hand by placing his over hers. He realized he was at a crossroad of what could happen next and what should happen next. The low road led him down the path of taking advantage of her naiveté and giving in to his primal urges. The high road demanded he show restraint and respect and not taint this moment by stealing Anne's innocence. For Henry, the decision was an easy one. He had become a man of honor and didn't want to take advantage of someone for whom he was developing deep feelings.

His hormones, however, were kicked into overdrive, and there was no denying that cold hard fact—*hard* being the operative word. Anne was looking at him in a way she never had before. Suddenly, the moment had changed, and they were both sharing it.

Anne reached down, taking hold of Henry's manhood. Henry could tell from her expression and demeanor that she was moving beyond her insatiable curiosity to arousal. Something was stirring inside both of them that he didn't need to explain. The language of the heart speaks for itself.

Henry gently held her hand and said, "MAN. Henry is a man." Then removing her hand, he placed it between her legs. "Anne is a WOMAN." Anne closed her eyes and began to explore her own body. He knew her mind and body were connecting in an exhilarating, life-changing way. She ran her hands over her breast, her hips, her…"Okay! That's just about enough of that," Henry admonished with a smile. "We're here to wash, remember?"

Thankfully, the hot water was beginning to run out, and the shower was getting colder. *Not a moment too soon*, Henry thought, relieved. "Okay, Anne, let's try 'monkey see, monkey do.' Here is a bar of soap for you and one for me. Do as I do." Henry started rubbing the soap all over his body, and holding her wrist, he moved her hand to encourage the same. She mimicked his every movement. He used Nattie's baby shampoo when it was time to wash their hair so it wouldn't sting her eyes. Every time she looked at Henry's groin, she would proclaim "Man," and Henry would turn away. Watching her rub the soap on every part of her body, the white foam covering her, made him very uncomfortable.

When they were rinsed, Henry turned off the water and retrieved two towels from the bar, wrapping one around himself to conceal "Man" and holding the other out for her.

She stepped out of the shower and into the oversized towel and wrapped it around herself, rubbing it down her body to absorb the water.

Henry picked up her clothes. "Put these back on."

To Henry's surprise, she dropped the towel on the floor right there in the bathroom and took the clothes, putting them on without any difficulty. The awkward silence was deafening while the two of them got dressed for the day.

After they were dressed, Anne marched right up to Henry, grabbed his groin, tilting her head. He nearly jumped right out of the clothes he had just put on. He wrestled with the fact that modesty had not only flown out the window but it had gotten sucked into the jet engine of a passing airliner and was totally annihilated. He sighed, realizing what her questioning look meant and took a deep breath. How was he going to explain the difference between men and women to someone who had no understanding of human anatomy or even the English language?

He led her to the sofa and sat her down and then sat beside her. "I am a man." He pointed to himself. "You are a woman." He pointed to her. "Our bodies are different."

"Man." Anne touched his chest. "Woman." She touched her own.

"Yes, a man has…different parts…than a woman."

"Why?"

"Why? Wait, what?" Henry stammered.

Where the hell did that come from? Oh crap, she must've picked it up from Nattie. She's going through that annoying "why" stage right now. "How the hell do I explain this…I mean it…no, no, not *it* it. I mean us!" He really hadn't thought about having a sex education talk with a grown woman and wasn't prepared for it. "Men and women are different so that together they can make babies. No wait!" He waved his hand. "You don't know what a baby is, let alone where they come from. That won't help." He interlocked his fingers behind his head and looked at the ceiling, begging for an answer.

He put his arms down and exhaled. "Hey, remember when I promised we would to try and figure out where you came from?" Anne nodded. "Come with me to the beach first. We can talk about this later." She did not respond but stood up when he stood and took her hand. Henry sighed again, hoping this diversion would work for the time being.

With the awkward conversation about the birds and the bees tucked away for the moment, he led her to the car. "Let's start at the beginning, where I found you." He opened the door, and she got in. Anne seemed unfazed when Henry fastened her seatbelt. "This is to keep you safe," he said with a smile. He then took his place behind the wheel and fired up the engine, and they began their trip back to Venice Beach. Anne was much more comfortable in the car on this trip and didn't seem frightened at all. Just the opposite—she seemed to be enjoying the Florida landscape as it passed by, asking about what she saw. Henry tried to tell her, but there were too many questions, too fast to keep up with her.

Henry parked the car closer to the wooden boardwalk, ran around to open the passenger door, and unfastened the seatbelt for Anne. She got out without any difficulty, and he led her across the wooden walkway over the tall waving grass to the bright sands beyond.

When they reached the edge of the beach, Anne stopped, that same panicked look on her face when Henry first found her. She stood there paralyzed, looking at the sand and the water beyond. An unseen and silent evil had crept up and seized her. She did not move, afraid to put her foot in the sand. Henry could tell something terrible must have happened to her that was connected to this beach in some way. He had hoped returning to the beach might jog her memory. He hadn't stopped to consider it may cause her to relive some horrific trauma.

Oh boy! I sure hope this wasn't a bad idea. Maybe I can distract her and give her something else to think about. "It's okay," Henry assured her. "It's just SAND." He stepped onto the sand, pulling her with him. He knelt down and picked up a handful of sand, spilling it from his hands. "Sand," he repeated.

Anne snapped out of her trance and was back in the moment. She knelt down in the sand beside him and scooped some up in her hand, letting it trickle from her fingers. "Sand," she responded. The sand sparkled when she held it up. Henry saw her relax, as if the fear was trickling out of her like the sand that trickled through her fingers.

"Water!" Anne pointed out to sea.

"That's right, water. We called this large body of water the OCEAN, and all of this sand is called the BEACH. Do you remember anything?"

She stood up and walked barefoot across the sand to what she now knew to be the "ocean." Henry followed, still in his flip-flops. Anne knelt down on the wet sand and let the sparkling liquid wash over her fingers, only to rush away to come back again. He saw by the lightening of her face that the horror of the previous night, triggered by her return to the beach, slowly began to slip away with each ripple of the water that retreated from the sand. She became mesmerized with the movement of the water, her breath in tune with the waves washing in and out, the swishing sound a balm to both of their spirits.

Henry knelt beside her. "Can you remember anything?" She did not answer. "Maybe it's too early yet." He took his flip-flops off and sat with her in the wet sand, watching the waves play with the sand, splashing over their feet. A few determined shark teeth hunters walked around them with their sieves on the end of sticks, drudging the sand to find the millions-year-old black shark teeth and maybe an interesting shell or two. More visitors started to arrive at the beach, laying out their blankets and setting up beach chairs to enjoy the Florida sun.

They sat for about an hour. Henry finally stood up, saying, "Let's give it more time," and he helped Anne to her feet. "We can come back another day. Maybe you'll be able to tell me then." He retrieved his footwear, and together, they walked barefoot back to the car over the sand that had begun to heat up with the rising sun.

On the way home, Henry asked Anne one more time if returning to the beach sparked any memories at all. "Do you remember anything at all?"

She thought for a moment and then shook her head. "No pictures," she said. Henry nodded. He sensed she was able to comprehend more than her limited vocabulary allowed her to communicate. At least he hoped that was the case. Or maybe it was just wishful thinking on his part.

"We can give it a few more days then go back and see if you remember anything. In the meantime, let's drive for a while. You had to get to that beach from somewhere. Maybe some other building or landmark will help your recollection. Besides, it's a beautiful day. It would be a shame to waste it all indoors. How about some music?" Henry turned on the car's radio.

Anne reacted to the music. Her body started to sway, and her head nodded with the beat of this new sound she was experiencing. She turned to Henry. "What?" she asked.

Henry raised an eyebrow, not sure what she meant at first. Then he realized it was the songs on the radio. "Music," he replied. "What you hear is music."

"Music?"

She tilted her head, not understanding.

Henry exhaled a long breath. "When someone talks, you hear different tones. Sometimes the voice is higher"—he changed his voice to reflect the word—"or lower," again changing the tone of his voice.

"Higher?" Anne mimicked him, speaking in a high voice. "Lower." She dropped her voice to a bass note.

"Yeah, like that." Henry nodded. "Music is the same thing, different tones or notes played on instruments. The voice you hear is the person singing. I guess you could say it's a special way of talking. There are many different types of music," he explained. "Too many to really learn about, but I can show you a few."

Anne nodded with that face-splitting grin, eager to learn something new. Henry smiled, pleased to see that she did not seem to be suffering from the night terrors. It made him feel good when he saw that smile. He would do anything to keep it there.

Henry tapped a button on his steering wheel and gave a command. "Elvis Presley, 'Love Me Tender.'" It was a simple song, and Elvis's voice was slow and mellow. Anne listened to the song, rocking to the slow beat of the melody, her eyes closed.

When the music ended, Henry explained, "That is what they call a love song or a ballad. Would you like to hear more?"

She nodded, sitting up in her seat and waiting for the next new experience.

"Okay," he said, choosing another song. "Let's ramp it up a bit. We call this one 'rock and roll.'" Hitting the control on the wheel again, he spoke his command when prompted. "Elvis, 'Jailhouse Rock.'" Anne bounced with the fast beat of the song, lifting her hands and arms and moving her feet up and down in time to the song. Henry found himself rocking to the song as well, tapping his left foot.

"Did you like that? The guy singing is Elvis Presley, and those were two of his songs." The look on her face told him all he needed to know. Her eyes were bright and her smile wide, and she waived her hands in front of her, eager to experience more.

"Elvis Presley!" she shouted. He laughed.

"Yep, that was Elvis. Okay." He smiled as they pulled up into his driveway.

When they got back into the house, Henry let the dogs out into the backyard and picked up his phone to call Heidi. She answered on the fourth ring. "Nattie!" she yelled as she picked up the phone. "Put that down! Hello?"

"Hi, Heidi. It's Henry. You got some time today?"

"Henry who?" she answered.

"Come on! You know who it is!"

"Then why tell me, doofus!"

Henry grimaced, swearing under his breath. "Do you have time today?" He didn't mind most of Heidi's satiric wit, but he didn't have the patience today.

"Yes, what do you need?"

"Well, I need to get Anne to talk a little more so that I can find out what happened to her. She seemed to learn quickly from Nathan's stuff. I thought maybe I could borrow some of the kids' books for her."

"Sure," Heidi agreed. "I'll bring over some of Nathan's books. Think that will help?"

"Can't hurt. What else can I do? I need to know what happened."

"Okay. Do you want me to bring some lunch?"

"Sounds like a plan. I could really go for some tacos. See you in a few." He put the phone down and came and sat by Anne on the sofa. "Now what do you want to do?"

She pointed to some books on one of the shelves. Henry chose one of his art instruction books of models posing, and they worked on learning the words for actions rather than names of things. This model was sitting, this one was standing, yet another was lying on a bed. At times he got up and physically acted out a movement, such as walking, waving, and eating. By the time Heidi arrived with lunch, Anne knew several verbs. When Heidi handed Anne her first taco, she announced, "Anne eat" to which Heidi and both kids giggled.

"That you do." Heidi laughed. "You go, girl." After lunch, Henry cleaned the table while Heidi cleaned up Nattie. Anne had learned yet another new word, "spicy," after sampling the hot sauce. Heidi handed Henry a bag containing many of Nathan's books, 1-2-3 picture books, ABCs, and First Time Books—first time at the zoo, the grocery store, along with many others. "Have fun, you guys," she said as she packed up the kids and left.

Anne spent the rest of the afternoon learning how to read books from prereader and very early readers up to a five-year-old level. Anne's ability to learn new things was amazing. She absorbed book after book until they exhausted all the books that Heidi had provided. By six o'clock that evening, Anne knew the alphabet and was able to read simple words.

It was around that same time when Henry got a call from his editor, Elliott Schoenfeld, reminding him that his latest illustration for the student nursing textbook was coming due. Henry assured him that it would get done, which got him thinking about what he would do with Anne when he had to work. He could reach out to Heidi like he did for everything else. *I'll deal with it tomorrow.* Exhausted from the long day, Henry just made a couple of sandwiches for their dinner and then turned on the television for a break from the books.

Anne's eyes grew large as the screen came to life. She was overwhelmed with the new experiences the television presented. She went up to the screen and tried to interact with the people and images as they flashed by. She tried speaking to the people on screen that were talking. She kept repeating the new greeting Henry had just taught her, "Hello, I'm Anne," to no avail. One time, she tried to reach out to grab a taco that was on a commercial. She kept scratching and clawing at the screen, trying to touch what she thought was real. Henry could see that she was getting frustrated and joined her in front of the television. He had to admit he found the scene a bit humorous and adorable at the same time. He held her hand before she could do any damage to the TV or herself.

"It's not real," he assured her. "They're pictures that move, see." Henry tapped on the screen. "They're not really here."

She stared at the television with a scowl on her face, watching the people and objects zip by in an ever-changing series of pictures and sounds. She sat on her haunches for several minutes, staring at the screen before she realized what Henry meant.

"Come sit on the sofa." Henry helped her up. "We'll be more comfortable." The two of them retired to the sofa and cuddled close together. Anne sat watching the images of little people moving on a fifty-four-inch flat screen with intense concentration, listening to how they spoke and to the music in the background. Henry hoped she wasn't on sensory overload with so many different images and sounds to process, but she seemed like she didn't want to miss any part of it.

He found a program about the lions on the Serengeti plains. Anne watched the large animals and got excited whenever she recognized one and shouted out each animal's name to Henry. "Lion…leopard…zebra," she squealed, at times even mimicking their roars. Henry kept it on the Animal Channel. He didn't want to frighten her with explosions, gunfire, or zombies. Not to mention how hard it would be to try and explain those phenomena. Watching a wildebeest getting torn apart for dinner was upsetting enough. Anne buried her face in his chest until he sounded the all clear. They spent the rest of the evening viewing programs about difficult cats with behavior issues and a documentary of a dog show.

Around midnight, he realized she had fallen asleep on his shoulder and that he was nodding off himself. He picked Anne up in his arms and carried her to the guest room. She didn't wake at all when he laid her on the futon and tucked her in. He sat there for a few moments admiring her and reflected on the day. It was amazing just how much progress she had made learning to communicate in this strange new world. At least that's what it was from her perspective; Henry was convinced of that. How or why didn't seem as important anymore. All that mattered now was him being there for her. He kissed her cheek before whispering, "Sweet dreams." Then he headed off to bed.

5

I am back at the majestic crystal mountains, and I marvel at their beauty, sparkling and shining like the gems within them. The crystals grow and form into flower-like shapes in colors of blue, red, yellow, green, white, and, on occasion, the precious rare purple. All the rare purple crystals are reserved for Aesmay, The One, the greatest, most powerful, and wisest of all the dragons. He lives on the very top of the mountain in a purple palace trimmed in gold. The sacred teachings say it is the same gold the first of the golden dragons were made from before the Creator breathed life into them.

We harvest the crystals that grow in the mountains, using the power of our minds to cut the crystals out, carving out a lair in the mountain's side, and then using that material to build shelves for landing and takeoff in front. The higher one's position is in the golden dragon order, the higher one's lair is on the mountain.

Most lairs are shared by a dragon and his mate. I share my lair with Kenta, my guardian, protector, and closest friend. My lair is constructed of crystals hewn from the highest and oldest of all the mountains: Draeche Engael. It is located right below the purple palace where Aesmay watches over all of us. We have lined our lair with white crystals that reflect our beautiful wings.

Suddenly, my serene moment is shattered! A flaming ball of fire slams into the shelf outside our dwelling. The crystal sounds like it is crying when nearly all the ledge outside our home shatters and falls into countless pieces. Many of the golden dragons attempt to flee into their structures, but they cannot escape the scorching missiles raining down on them from the black dragons above. Kenta wraps his enormous wings around me to protect me. I see his beautiful wings hit by the fire, and he screams in anguish when they begin to burn. He leaps off the jagged remains of our platform and dives down to the water far below with the black dragons in pursuit. I feel the intense heat searing around me, burning my fellow dragons in their attempts to flee. I sense inside me the cry of each of my brothers and sisters who are consumed by the white-hot flames. My heart explodes at the senseless slaughter of my kind. Several of the black dragons swoop down upon me, slamming me onto the ledge and slicing me with their razor-sharp claws. I try to claw my way off the platform, but they hold me down. Darkness descends over me, and I fall away into nothing, screeching.

6

Learning to Draw

Henry's heart was pounding when, once again, he found himself rushing to Anne's room and responding to the sound of her screams. *She must have had another nightmare,* he realized with growing concern. *This is two nights in a row now!* Upon entering her room, he found her much like he did the night before except this time, mixed in with the cries and screams, she was shouting "No! No!" and something about "Kenta!" *What's a kenta? She must be babbling. She is just learning to speak after all.*

Sitting on the bed beside her, Henry placed his hands on her trembling shoulders, called her name, and gently shook her in attempt to free her from whatever nocturnal hell she was in. "Wake up, Anne! Wake up! It's okay, sweetheart! I'm here. Everything is going to be okay!"

Anne continued thrashing for a few more moments before she settled down. She struggled to open her eyes, her face moist with tears and sweat. Her golden locks hung in wet strings down her back. Her teeth chattered until her body stopped trembling. She panted for a breath, the fear beginning to loosen its grip on her heart.

"It's okay, honey. It was just a nightmare. The pictures were not real. Just like the television. They can't hurt you." Henry helped her sit up in bed. "I'm here now. It's okay." Anne looked around the room, holding on to him until she was fully aware of where she was. By this time, the bed was crowded with furry well-wishers that tried to lick her face in an effort to show their support.

Anne finally stopped shaking at the calming ministrations of the pets and Henry's soothing voice. All she could say was "Henry" and hold on to him with the desperation of one who had just faced her darkest fears. Her tears fell on Henry's shoulder, and her arms clung to him with all their strength. Henry just held her tight, wishing he could do more to take away her dread. But he didn't even know the source of her torment. How could he possibly hope to eliminate it? For the moment he just held on to her, allowing the warmth of his body and the sound of his voice to wrap around her like a comforting blanket. His heart ached for her, questioning again what could have possibly happened to this poor girl to cause her to have such vivid nightmares.

"I'm here," Henry said. "I'm not going anywhere. I'm right here." Relieved, he felt her relax in his arms and settled her back onto the bed. "Go to sleep, Anne. I'll stay here with you." He attempted to sit on the floor next to the futon, but Anne would not let go. She was like a frightened child who insisted on sleeping in her parent's bed. They lay down together, and she held on tightly to Henry, only relaxing her grip when she finally drifted off. Henry vowed to remained vigilant the remainder of the night, determined to be there for her if the terror that haunted her dared to return. He almost made it until dawn before he nodded off.

June 17
Wednesday

"I don't know what to do," Henry told Heidi over his cell phone. "She must've really gone through something terrible to give her such horrific nightmares."

"How is she now?" Heidi queried.

"She's fine. She's sitting on the floor with the kittens at the moment. I have got to get some work done today. I'm way behind on my deadline. But I'm afraid to leave her alone. She's so helpless and curious at the same time. I don't want her to get into something she's not supposed too. I'm worried she might get hurt, but I can't watch her every second."

"If you like, I can pick her up and bring her over here to my house for a while. The kids love her, and she's great company for them. Besides, I'd like to get to know her better myself. She and Nathan can go over some more of his books together."

"If you don't mind, I'd appreciate that," Henry agreed. "What time can you be here?"

"Let me get the kids fed and dressed, and I'll come right over. See you at nine thirty or so?"

"Perfect! That will give us just enough time to have a quick bite and clean ourselves up for the day. Thanks, sis. See you soon."

Henry popped two sausage-and-egg breakfast sandwiches into the microwave, punched in the appropriate cooking time, then pressed start. While Jimmy Dean's buns heated up, he quickly poured a couple of glasses of fresh Florida orange juice. Anne was silent while they ate, but she appeared to be okay after last night's ordeal.

With every tummy in the house full, Henry led Anne to his bathroom after stopping at her bedroom to grab some clean clothes. He taught her how to brush her teeth with the same "monkey see, monkey do" method, and she caught on immediately. He then turned on the water in her shower and set it to the right temperature. He demonstrated how to turn the water on and off before fully explaining to her exactly what to do. "When you are all done washing yourself"—Henry pointed to the shower holding up the soap and shampoo—"turn off the water like I showed you." Henry touched the faucet handle. "Dry off with the towel and get dressed." Henry held up the appropriate item at the proper moment. "Okay?"

"Okay!" Anne replied, smiling as she started to undress. Henry just sighed and shook his head. *I'm never gonna win this battle, am I?*

"I'm going to be right outside, so if you need anything, just say my name and I will be right here." He turned to leave.

"Henry wash?" Anne asked with a sad, confused look.

Henry stopped in his tracks. "Heidi is coming over to take you to her house today," he said. "I will wash after you leave with her. I've got to get some work done."

"Henry wash," Anne pleaded.

"You'll like it. She has a really big house with a pool. You can play with Nattie and Nathan..." Henry stopped midsentence because Anne was now pouting and looking at him with those big blue eyes of hers. Combined with the fact that she was completely naked again, Henry had to admit, she had a compelling argument. "Oh, what the hell! Why fight it?" Henry resigned, not too disappointed in his decision. "But no touching Man, okay?" Anne just smiled and nodded in reply. Then she tore his shirt off.

Dressed and ready for the day, Henry wanted to invite Anne to his studio to share his art with her while waiting for Heidi to arrive. Once Anne was gone, he could focus on his work without any distractions. Besides, it would be a nice opportunity for Anne to experience some new surroundings and interact more with her new extended family. "Come with me," he offered. "I want to show you something very special." Anne followed him down the hall to the large corner room.

She gasped when they entered his studio and saw his latest illustration of how to suction a tracheostomy tube on the electronic drawing tablet. The sight of seeing a detailed illustration of a person lying on his back with his throat cut open while a pair of disembodied hands were inserting a menacing foreign object into the void could be unsettling to anybody. Especially when drawn by someone as talented as Henry. He knew she had no idea of exactly what it was she was looking at, but he could tell it upset her just the same.

Henry smiled. "Not very pretty, huh? I agree. Look over here on the wall." Henry made a sweeping motion toward the wall on their right. It was covered in countless doodles, sketches, and drawings, all in various stages of completion. Just about anything one would imagine to find in an artist's studio hung there on display—everything from nudes to portraits, from ocean scenes to landscapes, from family pets to wildlife, from technical drawings to architecture. There were even some sketches of cars and superheroes, some real and others straight out of Henry's vivid imagination. Some people tuck facts and ideas in the back of their mind to reference later. Henry's inspirations either ended up on his wall or in a sketchbook or, on rare occasions, on napkins, on scratch paper, and even on the back of receipts.

Henry had converted Heidi's old bedroom into his art studio because it offered the best natural light and it was the second largest of the three. His drawing table was next to an old wooden desk where he kept his laptop for easy access to the Internet, which he frequently used for reference material or to post photos of his work to sell. The desk also provided him extra working space along with convenient storage for his art supplies when needed, except for the very bottom left-hand drawer. Something nasty had spilled in there so long ago; even Henry forgot what it was. The drawer and its fate were both sealed that fateful day, never to be opened again. Next to the desk was a small square black table that held his color printer. A revolving office chair, stained with droplets of paint and smears of every art media, sat between the desk and art table so that he could swivel back and forth as needed.

In a special corner of the studio sat Henry's first art desk that he kept for when Heidi came by with the kids. Like the chair, it too bore the battle scars of countless hours of use from his many years of training as a child. Uncle Henry kept it stocked with washable paint, markers, and crayons. Two of grandpa's old dress shirts that served as makeshift smocks, worn during their lessons with him, hung on the wall nearby. It was sad they never got to meet their grandpa, but Henry liked to feel that this was a nice way to help his dad's memory and legacy live on.

Henry credited his father for being his greatest influence in fueling his passion for the craft. His father studied, and eventually taught, at both the American Academy of Art and the Art Institute of Chicago before moving to Florida when Henry was still in grade school. He recognized Henry's natural talent early on and taught him to draw and paint while other kids were learning to ride a bike. Fortunate indeed is the man who can pursue his passions in life and make a living at it. Henry was that man.

Henry sat Anne in the chair facing the window, where he posed most of his models, to take advantage of the morning's light. After tilting her head into the perfect position, he swept her hair back from her face. Then he held both palms up, touching the tips of his thumbs together to frame her face. "Perfect," he said. "Hold real still for me, okay?" Anne nodded. "No, no, you don't need to answer me, just don't move. I promised you something special, and I have been dying to do this from the moment I first saw you."

Anne smiled.

"Even better, Anne. Keep smiling for me." Henry smiled back and hastily picked up his sketch pad and charcoal pencil. He still preferred working with paper, pencil, and ink over electronic media, although he did use the digital drawing tablet when necessary. He loved the feel of putting ink to paper and watching his inspiration flow from the pen onto the page. The exhilarating sensation made him feel more connected to his work. It was intimate and natural when he could touch the texture of the paper and smell the charcoal. For Henry, it was impossible to bring a blank page or canvass to life unless he engaged all his senses. He almost always had music playing or the sounds of ocean waves rushing against the shore, anything to help create the proper mood or atmosphere to reflect his work.

Henry's hand swiftly danced and darted all over the page. His eyes repeatedly flashed back and forth from her face to his sketchbook. Henry was totally in the zone while his creation took the form of his subject. After a few last broad finishing swoops of his pencil, he dated and signed the piece then turned it for Anne to see.

"Well, what do ya think? Do you like it? It's you, Anne!" Henry beamed.

Anne's mouth was open, and her eyes were wide, sparkling with wonder. She stood up and moved in for a closer look. Henry tore the page from the book and handed it to her. "Here, this is for you. I'll do a full-color portrait of you at some later date, but you can have this for now. It's a drawing that shows how pretty you are."

Anne gave Henry a hug then looked back at her likeness. "Anne, picture, pretty, thank you."

"You're welcome," Henry replied. "I'm glad you like it."

Henry watched her gaze at the flawless rendering of her likeness. She scrutinized every line, curve, and shadow, fascinated by each minute detail. He, in turn, gazed at the real thing, equally awed.

"Heidi and the kids should be along any minute now to pick you up. I'm going to get started on my work. You can watch me if you want or look at some more books if you would like." Anne nodded in reply, her attention still mesmerized by her image.

Henry turned his attention back to the close-up, detailed drawing of the tracheostomy tube that was nearly completed. Anne watched him intensely for a long while as he worked. A few moments later, she retrieved the sketch pad and pencil Henry had used earlier. Unlike earlier encounters where it was clear Anne was oblivious to her strange new environment and everything in it, the pad and pencil didn't appear unnatural to Anne at all. Quite the opposite. In fact, she began to draw, mimicking Henry as he worked. In mere moments, she had the basic overall design of the tube immortalized on the page and was beginning to recreate the technical details, only stopping to grab another pencil from the desk when one either broke or wore down.

Henry paused for a moment to see how Anne was faring. He had gotten that uncomfortable feeling that adults get when there are children loose in the house and things are just too quiet. Looking over his shoulder, he saw Anne slaving away in his sketchbook. Amused by the sight, he asked, "Well, what is it that you are working on so diligently? May I have a look?" Anne's concentration broke as Henry grabbed the corner of the pad, turning it to inspect her work.

This time, it was Henry who was taken back and fascinated. He couldn't believe his own eyes. He held her drawing up to his, comparing the two side by side in total disbelief. "H-how did you do this?" Henry stuttered. "This is incredible! Impossible, but incredible just the same!" Somehow, not only was Anne able to exactly recreate Henry's work but she did so in a smaller scale. *Hell, there aren't even any eraser marks!*

"A surgeon would give anything to have hands as steady as yours," Henry said. Anne threw him a puzzled look.

"Never mind. I'll explain later."

"Do you like it?" Anne parroted Henry's earlier question with a smile.

"Ah, yeah. I like it, Anne. I like it a lot."

"Picture pretty?" she pressed, longing for his approval.

"No, it's not pretty. It's good. You're pretty. This is good, great, amazing even." Henry could see the light in her face start to fade. "Yes, it's very pretty, Anne. You did great, and I like it a lot. Thank you."

"You're welcome!" Anne replied, overflowing with joy.

Henry just stood there, shaking his head. The front door burst open, and Heidi and her brood came pouring in, sparking the dogs into action and putting the cats on alert.

"We're here," Heidi called.

"In the studio," Henry yelled. Heidi and the kids came into the studio, Nathan rushing in and heading straight to the little hand-me-down art desk while Nattie struggled to get out Heidi's arms to join him.

As Anne joined the children, Henry took Heidi aside and shared Anne's sketch with her. "Take a look at this," Henry said. "Pretty impressive work, wouldn't you say?"

Heidi raised an eyebrow, her eyes widening in disbelief. "Wow!" she commented. "Impressive is not the word for it. How the heck did you teach her to do this so fast?"

"That's just it. I didn't teach her anything. She just picked up the sketchbook and pencil and started drawing. I mean really drawing, and drawing well!" Henry shook his head. "Damndest thing I've ever seen! She's a natural! Even the most gifted artist would still need years of training and practice before even hoping to achieve this level of expertise."

"Well," Heidi said. "Where do we go from here? Do you still want me to take her with us?"

Henry thought about it for a moment and realized that having Anne drawing beside him was not such a bad thing. More like a golden opportunity to help unravel the ever growing list of mysteries surrounding this unique creature. "On second thought, no. If that's okay? I'd like to explore and expand on this new phenomenon with Anne. My interest is more than piqued. I truly am sorry I made you come all the way out here," Henry begged forgiveness.

"That's okay. I was planning on heading out this way anyway to get some shopping done. I thought it might be a fun experience for Anne to tag along," Heidi replied, letting him off the hook.

"Well, at least let me buy you guys lunch and get some ice cream afterwards. I'll even throw in some quarters for the kids to ride those mechanical rides they enjoy so much." Henry removed a pair of twenty-dollar bills from his wallet and handed them to his sister. His niece and nephew drew close as he rummaged through the change in his pockets.

"Deal! If it will make you feel better." Heidi's focus shifted back into mother hen mode to rein in the kids. "Okay, kids, time to go. Say good-bye to Uncle Henry and Aunt Anne." After the hugs and kisses, Heidi grabbed Nathan's hand and scooped Nattie back up. "Come on, Nathan, let's go to SuperMart. I need to get Nattie new flip-flops."

"Flop-flops!" Nattie corrected her.

"Yes, flop-flops. What was I thinking?" Heidi agreed. "Call me if you need anything," she yelled as she left the house.

"Thanks, sis!" Henry shouted back.

"Okay, Anne." Henry stretched his arms above his head, cracking his knuckles and arching his back in an effort to relax his muscles. "Let's get to work and see what you can do." He was dying to explore the depth of her ability or discover if this was a onetime fluke. He turned their attention back to the illustration of the nursing procedure while Anne continued to flawlessly copy him. They worked side by side, Henry at his drawing tablet, Anne with the sketchbook in her lap.

At about one o'clock in the afternoon, Henry had completed his illustration and sent it off to Elliott. By this time, Anne had completed her drawing, which perfectly replicated Henry's piece. Henry sat next to her and took the sketchbook out of her hand. "I don't know about you, but I'm hungry. Let's have some lunch, shall we?" Anne nodded enthusiastically in approval.

In the small kitchen with blue flowered curtains his mother had hung years ago, Henry made a couple of ham sandwiches on wheat bread with a glass of milk for each of them. He looked out to the backyard to make sure the animals were safe and behaving themselves, especially keeping an eye on Flack, who was in his doggy wheelchair struggling to keep up with his brothers.

In addition to his passion for art and all things beautiful, Henry had a compassionate heart for all things with four legs. He loved all of his animals, but Mack and Flack inspired him. Mack thrived and played just like any other cat, chasing balls with little bells inside them. At least he was spared the torment of the ever-elusive red dot, Henry often joked. And Flack could keep up with the rest of the pack in his two-wheeled doggie cart that squeaked whenever he turned a corner too fast. His back legs had been crushed by a careless driver, and Henry had saved him from being euthanized. Henry's empathic soul made everyone feel relaxed and trusting around him, especially children and animals.

He had built a series of structures with shelves in the backyard at varying heights where the cats were perched while watching the birds fly by and the dogs played with each other and the rubber tire hanging from a bar going across the yard connecting two of the cat shelves.

When they were finished with lunch, Henry and Anne headed back to the studio. "If you're going to do something, do it right. Let's learn how to draw!" Henry selected a fresh sketch pad from his stock and a box of artist's pencils containing over 150 colors. "Here you go, Anne. These are for you, and this will be your very own sketchbook. This way, we can keep all of your work in one place and track your progress."

Henry began the lesson with graphite pencils, showing her the difference in the firmness of each. He demonstrated that the softer lead pencils produced a rich darker shade while the harder pencils gave a lighter gray hue. They practiced just coloring blocks with each grade of pencil. Anne was fascinated, wanting to experience every shade of graphite from the lighter shades to the rich dark blacks. Henry noticed that when she was intensely working on the drawing, she pursed her lips in deep concentration. When she had filled up an entire sheet making different-shaded blocks, she looked up at Henry with excitement in her eyes.

"More," she demanded.

"Now that you know how to use a black pencil, let's experiment with colors!" Henry directed her attention to the vast array of colored pencils in the set. Anne's eyes perused the ocean of colors stretched out before her in an effort to soak in all the subtle hues. One by one, Henry selected a pencil, handed it to Anne, and then instructed her to repeat its name. She grabbed the next pencil in the spectrum and made different-colored blocks from each one. Henry demonstrated how to make new colors by layering one on top of another. After the individual blocks were filled in, Anne would proclaim the name of the new color, holding up the sketchbook for Henry's approval.

Henry's phone rang. The Taylor Swift "Fearless" ringtone alerted Henry that his sister was calling. "Hi, Heidi. What's up?"

"I'm planning to take the kids to the beach tomorrow. I thought you and Anne might like to come with. Are you done with your drawing?"

"As a matter of fact, I just sent it off. The next one is not due for a couple of days so I got some time. I think going to the beach for the day is a great idea. Count us in."

"Okay. Let's go to Caspersen. It's less touristy, so it's usually not too crowded. Besides, Nathan wants to look for more shark teeth. I'll pack a picnic lunch. Meet me there say around nine o'clock?"

"Sounds like a plan. Do you want me to bring anything?"

"Yes, you can bring your cooler, and pick up the ice and drinks so I don't have to lug mine along. Other than that, I've got it covered. Hmm, speaking of covered, I just realized, we're gonna need a suit for Anne! You can't keep parading her around in those shorts and T-shirts I bought her earlier."

"Yeah, you're right. I didn't think about that. Do you have one she could wear?"

Heidi let out a long sigh. "Henry, how can you be such a clever and talented artist and not be able to see size and perspective in the everyday world? Even before popping out two kids, I could only dream of a having a body like hers. No, I do not have a suit she can wear," Heidi replied sarcastically. "Bring Anne to the Sun Lover's Boutique on West Venice Avenue. They open at eight thirty. Do you know where it is?"

"Of course I do. I hang out there all the time," quipped Henry, taking his turn.

"Ha, ha! Okay, I probably deserved that one. I'll get her all fixed up with a suit and proper undergarments. I don't think any of us expected this to be such a long-term arrangement. While I'm busy with her, you and the kids can pick up the ice and drinks at the Farm store. Be sure and get some juice and water this time, not just soda, or the kids will be hyped up on sugar and you'll be the one chasing them up and down the beach."

"Will do. See you tomorrow." Henry ended the call and smiled at Anne. "We're going to the beach tomorrow with Heidi and the kids. Won't that be fun?"

"Beach!" Anne beamed.

"Okay," Henry said, laughing. "Tomorrow, fun at the beach. For now, let's see what else you can learn today." They spent the afternoon together, with Henry teaching her to draw objects using proper perspective and variations of shading. Anne followed behind while Henry gathered different objects from all over the house and set them on the desk side by side. At first, he would draw the item of choice and Anne would copy him, duplicating both the sketch and his technique. She caught on fast and was quickly drawing on her own, guided only by Henry's instructions. Soon she had several pages full of different shapes drawn in three dimensions with the proper shadowing under them.

Henry noticed that the cats had covertly begun a silent, Navy Seal–style invasion of his art studio, inserting themselves between him and his work or rubbing themselves against his legs, meowing demands. *Wow, dinner time already!* "Okay, Anne. I think that's enough for today. I'm going to go feed all these guys and order us some pizza. In the meantime, do you think you can remember where all this stuff goes?"

"Pizza?" Anne queried.

"Yeah, pizza. Dinner…Food…You haven't tasted yet, at least not as far as I know. I think you'll like it. If you don't like it, then I'll know you're from another planet," Henry joked.

"Huh?"

"Never mind, I'm just kidding. Please just put back what you can, and I'll be back to help you in a minute or two."

"Okay, I will." Anne scooped up an armful of inanimate artist models before dashing off to return them to their original resting places. Henry was momentarily stunned by her first-person reference. *She really is catching on,* he thought.

A short while later, Anne jumped at the sound of the doorbell, having never heard it before. Heidi had her own key for those rare moments when Henry actually remembered to lock the front door. "It's just the doorbell, Anne. Everything's fine. The pizza is here!" Henry said with a salivating smile. He had ordered a sausage pizza with extra cheese from Hungry Hal's Pizzeria because they were the fastest in town. "For the best pizza in a hurry, call Hungry Hal's," their jingle promised. When it came to pizza, Henry was always in a hurry.

With the driver paid and tipped, Henry returned carrying Italy's greatest culinary gift to mankind. The aroma filled the room and their senses as he pulled back the lid. *If reincarnation is real, I'm coming back as a ninja turtle. Cowabunga!*

Anne's eyes were as big as the pie in front of her as Henry plated each of them a slice. "Okay, Anne. This is very hot, so we've got to be careful. Hold your slice with both hands, one on the crust at the back with the other supporting the front. Then just start with a small bite like this." Henry demonstrated the maneuver for her, savoring the delicious morsel. *Pizza is to guys what chocolate is to women.* "Here, let me help you. Try a bite of mine."

Anne took a generous bite of the proffered piece and was surprised when the cheese stretched like a suspension bridge, refusing to relinquish its hold of the slice. Henry burst out laughing when her eyes widened in alarm, and she waved her hands signaling her need for help. He was reminded of those Chinese finger-torture novelties where one gets both index fingers hopelessly trapped in either end.

"Only you could go from being an art protégée to damsel in distress in under five seconds," he teased. "You're okay. It's just cheese, and you just have to pinch it off like this." Henry pinched off the cheese between his fingers at Anne's lips and returned it to the top of the slice. Anne savored the mouthful she had bitten off, now that she had been saved from her perilous plight. In no time at all, they finished off the entire pie, washing it down with diet cola. As Henry had predicted, she liked pizza, and he mentally added it to the ever-growing list of Anne's favorites he kept in his head. The jury was still out on whether she was from another planet or not.

After dinner, they sat down to watch television. Anne was more comfortable watching the screen now that she knew the things she saw were not real. She paid close attention to the way the actors talked, moved, and interacted with each other, sometimes repeating random words. Her language skills were quickly improving, both in vocabulary and comprehension. Henry enjoyed her sitting next to him on the sofa. There was something about this strange girl that touched the dark places in his soul with little pinpricks of light.

They watched a movie about pirates and their ships, with tall masts, billowing sails, and hoisted Jolly Roger flags. Henry explained to Anne about pirates and how people lived many years ago. When she saw the main characters fighting with swords, she looked at him and said, "What?"

"Sword fighting," he said. "The things in their hands are called swords, and it is a way for people to fight."

"Fight?"

"Yeah, um combat, attack. The pirates try to take other people's things by force, and the people fight back to stop them."

"Show me!" she demanded.

"You want to learn to fight with swords?" Henry raised his eyebrows. "Now?"

"Show me!"

Henry smiled, paused the movie, and got up to search for something to fence with. He had a few yardsticks in the garage from when he had work done on the home after his father died and brought them into the living room.

"Here is your sword, my lady." He presented one to her. "Now stand like this and hold out your 'sword.'" He stood in the en garde position—one foot in front pointing forward with his back foot perpendicular to it, his knees slightly bent, and his yardstick raised in front of him. She did the same, holding her yardstick in front of her.

"When you fight, you have eight positions for your blade." He showed her each position. "Then you attack, either thrust or parry." He demonstrated each move.

"Thrust," Anne said, mimicking the move.

"And parry," Henry replied, parrying her attempt at an attack. He turned the movie back on, and they pretended to be pirates as they "fought" across the living room, precariously climbing on top of the sofa and even the pony wall separating the living room from the dining room, trying to keep up with the characters on the screen, at least in basic moves because they really couldn't jump in spinning wheels or climb ropes. But they tried their best. When the movie fight ended, Henry put his 'sword' down, both of them breathing heavy, and said, "That's enough. Let's watch the rest of the movie now."

Anne gave Henry back the yardstick, her face bright with a smile and the exertion of learning a new skill, and then sat back on the sofa while the movie continued. As she did with everything they watched, she asked Henry to explain what was happening throughout the movie.

At some point, he looked down to see that Anne had fallen asleep. Television seemed to be a good relaxing tool for her, it appeared. He laid her down on the couch and covered her with a blanket that he fetched from the guest room and then went to take care of the nightly animal chores. He turned off the television and living room light, leaving her to sleep on the sofa, hoping that this night would be a quiet one and that the demons of her dreams would leave her alone.

7

I am flying again over the green sparkling waters, my golden companion at my side. I am free as we rise up higher into the white sky. We quickly descend down close enough to the water so I can drag my clawed toes, drawing lines in my path. Silver fish jump out of the water as I cross, and I try to catch them.

I dive into the water, feeling the cool liquid wash over my skin and descend deeper into the emerald oceans where the green goes from a light crystal color to a dark, rich verdant tone. The mountains under the surface of the water reflect the darker shades of green blending into a deeper blue. The silver fish stay with me as I descend, soon to be joined by the larger dragonfish, ancestors of our kind, blue fish with long snouts and streaming tails like ribbons, with clawed fins they use to catch the smaller silver fish.

We slow down and settle on the black sand at the bottom of the ocean. I can breathe the water as easily as I can the air and welcome the soft bed of sand. I fall into a restful nap on the sands, my companion next to me. We are happy and peaceful, curled together under the cool covering of the ocean.

I could stay here forever. However, Kenta signals that it is time to depart. Following his lead, we kick off the ocean bottom and, moments later, break though the surface of the water. Together, we head straight to the shelf outside our dwelling, touching down effortlessly as we have countless times before. I enter first while Kenta takes a moment to stand and stretch his wings and back before following me.

I see the first fireball slam into the ledge outside, and Kenta wraps his powerful wings around me in a brave attempt to protect me. I can hear his heart beating before lifting my head from his chest to look into his eyes. His loving smile is soon replaced with anguish, and his eyes tear in the agony of the fire that engulfs him. I choke on the intense heat as I scream.

8

Caspersen Beach

"Anne, wake up! I'm here!" Henry held her close in his arms while she struggled to wake from another nightmare. This was the third night in a row that Anne woke up screaming. He felt useless and could only hold her when she cried in the black of the night. Henry welcomed the opportunity to assume the mantle of her protector, but how does one protect someone from a dream? Henry was frustrated because he couldn't defend her in her sleep.

"What happened?" he asked, holding her tight and rocking her back and forth until she was fully awake. When she was aware of where she was, she looked around the room, searching for the words to describe the nightmare. Her eyes landed on the book about fantasy creatures she and Henry had looked at previously. She grabbed it, flipping through the pages in a frenzy until she found the picture of the dragon.

She pointed to one of the illustrations. "Dragons," she managed to say while the tears streamed down her cheeks. "Dragons…fire!"

"It was only a dream, honey," he said. "There are no dragons. They're not real." *Fire? Was that a clue to what happened to her? Had she been in a fire recently and was reliving the trauma in her dreams?* He would have to check the local news for any reports of fires in the area. *But what was up with the dragons? Perhaps she had a childhood fear of dragons, and maybe the pictures in the book upset her? Yet she wanted to keep the book.* These thoughts raced through Henry's mind as he got his first clue to the content of the nightmares she was having.

"Maybe we won't look at that book anymore," he suggested. "Come on. You can sleep in my room. Let's see if we can keep the dragons away tonight." He picked up the blankets and spread them on the floor of his room near his bed. He encouraged her to lie down on the blankets and covered her with the quilt. He lay next to her on the ground, his arm around her side until eventually the images of fire and dragons faded and Anne was able to fall into a quiet sleep. Henry did not sleep for a long time, plagued by Anne's description of the nightmare, trying to figure out what it all meant.

June 18
Thursday

The next morning when the animals woke them up, Henry struggled to keep his eyes open, finding he had fallen asleep on the floor. He had just gone back to sleep. He used the bathroom and then stumbled to the kitchen to feed the hungry hoards. When everyone was chomping loudly on their various dishes, he went back to his room. Anne was already sitting up on the floor when he returned.

Henry waited for her to use the bathroom and then turned on the shower for her. He gave her a fluffy blue towel and said, "I will be here if you need me." Then he stepped out, leaving the door open just in case she needed help and flopping on the bed to grab just a few more minutes of sleep. He was relieved that she was able to take care of her own hygiene, shower, and dress without any help. When she was ready, Henry took care of his own needs while Anne played with the animals. Anne did not come into the shower this time, so Henry was able to relax and enjoy a leisurely shower.

They ate a quick breakfast of bagels and cream cheese and Henry's beloved coffee, which Anne really seemed to enjoy as well. Then they departed to meet Heidi and the kids on Venice Avenue. Henry headed out on Tamiami Trail to Route 41 and then to Venice Avenue.

They got to the Sun Lover's Boutique at around nine thirty to find that Heidi was already waiting for them with a stand-back-kids-give-me-room-I'm-about-to-kill-your-uncle look on her face, the kids running on the sidewalk in front of the shop.

"Nice of you to show up," she snarled.

"Sorry," Henry apologized. "Another rough night."

"You couldn't call?"

Yeah, and get yelled at twice!

"It's real easy. You push one stupid button and say 'Call Heidi.' The phone does the rest."

"I was in a hurry to get here. Again, I'm sorry," Henry lamented, reaching for his wallet.

Heidi frowned and shook her head. Henry had barely gotten his credit card halfway out of its slot when Heidi yanked it out of his hand. "Thank you! You take the kids, and I'll take Anne shopping."

Henry put his hands out in supplication. "What do you want me to do with them?"

"Go get drinks and ice! After that, I don't care! You're in charge!" Heidi grabbed Anne's arm and marched her towards the store.

"Shopping?" Anne asked, ever curious.

"Yes, but not just any shopping. Today we're shopping for clothes. Trust me, you're gonna love it!"

Henry was left standing on the sidewalk with his niece and nephew. Both of them looked up at him in eager anticipation while he contemplated his next move. Henry took his job as uncle very seriously and strived to be a good role model.

"Okay, kids." He took their hands. "Who wants ice cream for breakfast?"

Heidi and Anne entered the small boutique where a wall of different bathing suits hung.

"Let's see what size you are first," Heidi said. She found a saleswoman who came running up with a measuring tape.

"Such a lovely girl!" the older woman with a name tag that said "Doris" exclaimed. "What is your name, dear?"

"I am Anne."

"Anne, how sweet. Now stand here dear." She motioned to a platform in front of some mirrors at the back of the store. Anne did as instructed. "Hold out your arms, dearie," Doris crooned. Anne put her arms out to her side. Doris took the tape measurer and put it around Anne's bust, then her waist, and finally her hips.

"Be still," Doris admonished. The measuring tickled, and Anne couldn't help giggling. Heidi giggled right along with her, the two of them acting like schoolgirls. Doris, ever the ultimate professional, continued with her work, noting the tall girl's measurements, despite her furrowed brows.

"Now, what can we help you find today?" Doris asked, putting away the tape.

"My friend needs a bathing suit, and oh yeah, a couple of bras," Heidi said.

Doris smiled and nodded. "What kind of suit would you like? Over here"—she indicated the left wall—"are our one-piece suits, and over here"—she pointed to the opposite wall—"are our bikinis. Anne is a perfect size 6, and we have plenty to choose from. If you choose a bikini, I would recommend a 34D for the top. Please take your time, and I will gather up some of our brassieres for her as well." Doris trotted off to retrieve the garments, and Heidi and Anne began to rifle through the one-piece suits.

"What is brassiere?" Anne asked.

"It's something that we women wear to hold up our breasts." Heidi pointed to her own ample top, made even more ample from breastfeeding both kids.

"Breasts?" Anne put her hands on her unhindered breasts and cradled the fullness of her bosom. She stood in front of the mirror, obviously fascinated by her appearance. "Breasts," she pronounced.

Heidi smiled at Anne's innocence. "Maybe a bikini *would* look good on you. Come on." She dragged her over to the bikinis.

"Bikini," Anne repeated. "What is bikini?"

"It's a swimsuit that has two pieces, one for your breasts and one for your bottom." Heidi pointed to Anne's rear.

Anne then put her hands on her backside and caressed the curvature of her bottom half. "Bottom."

Heidi smiled and shook her head. "You are unique. I'll give you that."

Heidi started to pull several bikinis off the rack to show them to Anne. "There are several different kinds and colors. Anything strike your fancy?"

"Ooooh," Anne cried when Heidi held up a bright pink bikini with aqua highlights.

"Nice choice!" Heidi took Anne's hand and pulled her to the dressing room. "Try these on," she instructed.

Heidi told Anne to take her clothes off. Anne did, and the two girls stood for a moment, taking in the beauty that was Anne. "Henry sure does have good taste." Heidi smiled. Standing behind Anne, Heidi reached around with the top and put the cups over Anne's breasts. "Hold this," she said, tying the back and neck.

"Let's try the bottom." Heidi handed Anne the piece. Anne put the bottom on, turned, and posed in front of the mirror. Heidi nodded and smiled. "Henry is one lucky dude," she said.

Anne returned the smile. "Henry is one lucky dude," she repeated.

Heidi laughed. "I think we got a winner! We'll take this one." The hot pink complimented her light skin, and the cut of the suit highlighted all her curves.

"You'll need a cover-up too." Heidi pulled her out of the fitting room. "Doris, we're going to take this one. She'll wear it today to the beach. I'll need a cover-up for her too."

"Very good," Doris said. "Here are some of our finest brassieres in her size." She held out six bras in various colors and styles.

"Anne, pick which ones you like, as many as you want."

"Pretty," Anne said, choosing several lace bras in pink and white and blue and red satin as well.

Heidi walked Anne over to the cover-ups and picked out an aqua sheer garment.

"Excellent choice," Doris said. "And I have the perfect sandals and hat to go with that." Doris retrieved a pair of aqua sandals and a large woven floppy aqua hat, putting the hat on Anne's head. Anne took off Henry's old oversized flip-flops that she was wearing and put her feet into the sandals.

"Now look in the mirror, dear." Doris turned her to a large mirror in the center of the store.

Heidi and Anne gazed at the woman looking at them in the mirror. The figure reflected back was a breathtaking beauty in pink and aqua, her long golden hair flowing from under the hat.

"They're gonna have to change the name to heartbreak beach after you show up wearing that," Heidi said, beaming. Both girls looked at each other and giggled.

While Heidi paid for the clothes, Anne picked up her old clothes and flip-flops.

"You can put those in the bag." Heidi handed her the bag with the bras. When the transaction was complete, she took Anne's arm. "Now let's go find that lunkhead brother of mine," Heidi said, heading for the exit.

Henry was sitting on a bench outside the shop with the kids, cleaning up the ice cream that Nattie had smeared all over herself. When the girls approached, Henry slowly looked up. "'Bout time you two showed up. Is my card maxed ou—" He froze, dropping the napkin on the sidewalk, oblivious to Nattie hitting him, demanding that he clean her face. His mouth dropped open and his eyes grew wide when he saw Anne standing there in her new bikini and sheer cover-up.

"Aahhh, ummm, Anne," he managed to say, "you're beautiful!"

"Henry is one lucky dude." Anne smiled back. Heidi and Anne both laughed, then Anne added, "Anne like shopping." That made them laugh even more.

Of course you do. It's part of the female DNA. Glad I got my credit lines increased. Heidi corralled the kids back into her car, and they all headed to the beach.

Heidi picked Caspersen Beach because it was known for the abundance of exotic shells and prehistoric shark teeth lurking in the shallow water beneath the sand. Henry parked his car and pulled out the large cooler filled with their drinks. They walked over the wooden boardwalk spanning over the tall wild grass surrounded by palm and mangrove trees to the beach beyond. A light wind was blowing in over the water, bringing with it the tang of the sea. Several people were in or near the water, either swimming close to the shore or bent over with little metal sieves in their search for a fossilized treasure. Henry explained to Anne that the sieves shifted through the sand so that the searcher could find the shark teeth blackened over millions of years resting in the ocean. There was a hypnotizing whoosh of the waves on the shore, mixed with calls of seagulls overhead and the din of the beachgoers enjoying the Florida coast. Washed-up seaweed lined the uncultivated sand nearer to the water. The beach was narrower than Venice Beach, left in its natural condition, and did not have the benefit of lifeguards.

Heidi spread a blanket on the sand and let the kids go to the shoreline. She sat down while the children walked up and down the beach with their strainers looking for shark teeth. Henry put down the cooler with the drinks he had purchased, sugar-free as instructed, then he and Anne sat on the blanket next to Heidi. The kids ran over excited to show them the colorful shells they had found in the few minutes they were there. Nattie didn't have any shark teeth, but she displayed the twigs and pieces of broken shells she had picked up. Nathan showed them the three black shark teeth he was lucky enough to find.

"Uncle Henry! Uncle Henry! Look what I got!" Nathan beamed. "I got shark teeth!"

"I got snells!" Nattie yelled, dumping her treasures on the blanket.

"Yes, I see your pretty snells. Good job." Henry examined Nattie's broken shell pieces as if they were priceless gems. Nathan pushed his strainer in front of Henry.

"Look at my shark teeth!"

"Wow, those are really cool, Nathan. Hey, do you think the Tooth Fairy visits the sharks every time they lose a tooth?" Henry teased.

"Noooo, sharks don't have pillows to leave quarters under, and the Tooth Fairy can't swim," Nathan said with authority.

"How could you possibly know that the Tooth Fairy can't swim?"

"Because her wings would get all wet, and she couldn't fly anymore!"

Damn, the kid has a point. Who's teasing whom here?

"Besides, sharks don't use quarters!" Nathan added confidently.

"She could bring them a fish."

"I don't think so, Uncle Henry."

"You're probably right, Nate. After all, you are the smartest five-year-old in the world," Henry replied.

Having obtained approval from Henry, the kids then turned their attention to Anne, who also examined the treasures and said "pretty" to each of them. Satisfied that their finds were appreciated, the children ran back to the water's edge to keep looking. Anne got up from the blanket and followed them, bending down in the ankle-deep water to pull out handfuls of sand to see if she found anything of interest.

"She had another nightmare last night," Henry informed Heidi. "Every night. I'm not sure what to do. This time though, she was able to tell me what she dreamt about. Dragons and fire."

"Dragons and fire? Do you think she maybe was involved in a fire herself recently?" Heidi asked.

"That was my guess too. I told her maybe we shouldn't be looking at the pictures of dragons in the *Fantasy Creatures* book, but she doesn't want to give it back. She seems to *need* it. That's the only way I can describe it." He watched Anne head deeper into the water, the kids having given up their hunt and turning their attention to chasing each other with handfuls of seaweed.

"Where is she going?" he said and got up to follow her.

"She's going deeper into the water, Henry," Heidi answered. "Do you think she'll be okay?"

"I better go with her. She didn't even know how to walk when I first found her. I doubt very much that she knows how to swim." His eyes were fixed on Anne the whole time, and he was already on his feet heading towards her. Anne was chest-high in the water. He ran in to catch up with her, fighting through the waves that tried to take him back. Since there were no lifeguards on Caspersen Beach, he just wanted to make sure she would be okay.

Suddenly, Anne disappeared under the water. Henry called her name and dove in after her, finding it difficult to see in the murky water at first. When he finally caught sight of her, she sank down to the bottom of the ocean and opened her mouth, letting the salt water rush in. Her eyes popped opened wide in disbelief, and her hands flew up to her throat. Henry immediately grabbed her and pulled her up to the surface, grasping her in a tight grip across her abdomen, forcing the water out of her mouth and lungs.

"What are you doing!" he shouted, pulling her back to the shore. She coughed up more water, gasping for breath with tears in her eyes while Heidi ran over to offer any help.

"Why did you do that?" Henry held her as other beachgoers gathered around, asking if she was okay. Heidi gathered up the kids while she assured the onlookers everything was under control. The few nosey tourists who gathered there soon disbursed when they realized there would be no ambulance or TV news cameras.

"Sweetheart, why did you do that?" Henry repeated in a soft concerned tone.

Anne finally stopped coughing and said in between gasps of air. "No breathe in water!" she managed through her tears. "No breathe in water!"

"No, honey, you can't breathe in water." Henry cupped her face. "Why would you think you could?" She didn't answer, her tears washing over his hand. "Please don't ever try anything like that again, okay?"

Anne stared at the water as if she had just lost her best friend. She didn't want to move, but Henry insisted they return to the blanket. Heidi was calming the kids who were also crying because they were scared something had happened to Aunt Anne. Heidi assured them with hugs and cookies. When they saw Anne back on the blanket and apparently okay, they went back to their game of seaweed tag.

"No breathe in water," Anne repeated, shaking her head.

Heidi opened another bottle of water for Anne to drink to ensure she flushed out any salt water she may have consumed. "Drink this, honey. It will help flush out the salt water." She looked at Henry. "Good thing you followed her in."

"I don't know what she was thinking." Henry pressed his lips together, shaking his head. "Why would she think she could breathe under water?"

"Maybe it's more a matter of her not knowing she couldn't. The good thing is you were there to get her out. She'll be okay. It's probably best if you stay with her for a while."

"I'm not going anywhere," Henry said. "I'm not leaving her side."

By this time, the kids had grown tired of pelting each other with seaweed and came back to the blanket. Nathan sat by Anne and offered his advice. "You hold your breath when you go into the water. Like this," he said, taking a deep breath and holding it, his little cheeks blowing up like balloons. After a few seconds, he let out a long exhale and started panting until he caught his breath. "You try it."

Anne smiled, took a deep breath, and held it for about thirty seconds before she let it out. "That's a long time," Nathan observed. "Can you hold it a whole minute?"

"There will be no more breath-holding," Heidi announced, opening up the picnic basket and handing out sandwiches and little bags of chips. "Now it's time to eat." They ate their lunch in the warm Florida sun and watched the seagulls walk in the waves before taking off into the air above them. When the kids were finished with their food, Nattie lay down and was soon asleep. Nathan grabbed Anne's hand.

"Help me find more teeth please," he begged. Anne nodded and got up to join him at the water's edge, but she did not go in farther than her knees. Henry went with them and stood on the sand, watching her like a hawk and pondering the earlier events while fulfilling his vow to watch over her. What was it about this unusual girl? Why would she think she could breathe in water? Henry disagreed with his sister on this one. She didn't see what he saw. She tried to breathe water and was shocked at the outcome. He continued to maintain watch as she and Nathan walked down the beach in their search, always keeping a close distance to the pair.

After they had collected a dozen shark teeth in Nathan's basket and several small shells, they came back to the blanket. Heidi took the treasures and put them in a plastic bag to wash later when they got home. "I think we've been here long enough," she said, packing up the basket and Nattie. "Time to go."

Henry shook the sand and crumbs out before folding the blanket, and then they headed back to the parking lot. The kids took advantage of one last opportunity to splash one other when they stopped at the outdoor showers to wash the sand off their feet.

"Why don't you both come over on Saturday?" Heidi asked. "James is home, and we can barbeque. He really wants to meet Anne."

"Okay," Henry said, holding the door for Anne to get into his car. "What time?"

"Come around lunchtime. We can swim in the pool where it's a little more controlled." After everyone said their good-byes,

Heidi loaded the kids into the car and headed to her house in downtown Venice.

Both Henry and Anne were quiet on the drive home, each lost in their own thoughts. Henry contemplated the events of the day, wondering if they were connected to her nightmares in some way. Anne stared out the window but was oblivious to the Florida landscape as it flew by. Henry would have loved to know what she was thinking about. Why did she think she could breathe under water? She seemed disappointed she couldn't do something she insisted she had done before. But how could she without proper equipment? It was impossible.

When they got home, Henry led Anne to the sofa and sat beside her. "Anne," he began. "Why did you think you could breathe underwater?"

Anne hesitated, trying to find the words to express herself. "I see"—she pointed to her head—"breathing in water. In dreams."

"Well, maybe in your dream you can breathe underwater, but in the real world you need special equipment to help you breathe." Anne looked confused, so Henry picked up a scuba diving magazine in the pile of mail and showed her a picture of a diver under the water.

"No," she insisted. "I breathe in water long…no…help."

"Anne, honey, that's impossible. No one can breathe underwater without some kind of gear. You can't see it, but we live and breathe the air around us. Remember when Nathan taught you how to hold your breath? The two of you were breathing air. Both of us are breathing it right now. You see this thing on the diver's back? It's called an air tank, and it has air inside it for him to breathe through this tube in his mouth. He takes the air with him so he can breathe underwater. Without it, he would have the same problem you did."

Anne looked down at the wooden floor of the living room. "I no breathe in water." Her eyes looked sad, but she did not cry.

"I can't…The correct way to say it is I can't breathe in water. Just like I can't bear to see you sad." Henry flashed her a reassuring smile then stood up. "I have an idea. Let's draw with colored pencils some more." She returned the smile, and together, they went into the studio to amuse themselves with Henry's colored pencils. The diversion helped to lift Anne's spirit, and she found joy in blending different pencils to make new colors. Henry hoped that she had forgotten her sorrows by throwing herself into the drawing.

That night, Henry had Anne sleep in his room again so that if the nightmares returned, he would be right there to help her, remembering his vow to never leave her side.

9

I am lying next to the largest of all of the dragons, my father. His wings are enormous and iridescent like mine. I am safe near him and curl up comfortably near his hind legs. I shut my eyes while he tells me again the story of our kind.

He tells me that in the beginning, the Great Creator made the Firstborn, including the Two—my father and the Other, his brother. The Two were given dominion over our realm to teach them of the Creator and to live in peace with one another.

The Two assumed the form of the golden dragons, their iridescent wings rippling with the echo of all the dragon colors. Over thousands of years, the dragons grew to be in a form and mind like the Two, but none would be equal.

The Other chose many mates from the golden dragons with whom he had many offspring. But my father does not take a mate from the dragons. He longed for one that would be equal to him, one he could love, so he surrendered his own heart to create me. I am the one he loves.

The Other comes before him while he is telling the story and demands that I be given to him as his mate. My father reminds the Other that he has many mates. Because I am forbidden to mate, he cannot command me to be the Other's. The Other becomes angry and threatens that he is worthy of me, that he will have me.

The black dragons come with fire! I see the Other come, but he does not look the same anymore. He is different! His skin is black and hard, no longer smooth like mine. His nostrils are large and round, spewing smoke from inside. His angry red eyes are focused on me while the other black dragons spit fire at our kind, burning them as they flee. The Other approaches me, and I feel the fire of his breath.

10

Trip to Jungle Gardens

This time when Anne woke up screaming in the night, fighting the demons of her dreams, Henry was right there at her side. It was upsetting to witness the horror of her night terrors right from the beginning. Each night that Anne had to endure this torment tore at his heart, leaving him feeling helpless to stop it. He was determined that he would find the cause and a way to chase the demons away.

June 19
Friday

The morning came with sunlight shining through the bedroom windows, illuminating the couple curled up on floor. Henry had intended to sleep on the floor while Anne took his bed, but after her nightmare, she held on to Henry for solace and would not let him go. Henry didn't want her to, ever. While Henry rolled over to divert the sun from his eyes, his thoughts shifted from the previous night's ordeal to breakfast. He had a large number of mouths to feed. Anne, however, leapt to her feet as if the terrors of the night never happened. Acting as if she read his thoughts, she dashed off towards the kitchen, daring him to catch her. She beat him, leaving Henry behind her. Even little Flack in his wheelchair left him in his dust. "Et tu, Flack," Henry accused.

When he entered the kitchen, Henry was surprised to see Anne dishing out the pets' food. Henry could tell by her wrinkled nose and sour expression that she didn't much care for the pungent order. "Smells just as bad going in as it does coming out, doesn't it?" Henry joked before something very odd caught his attention. All the animals were sitting quietly, waiting to be fed, tails wagging and tongues drooling of course, but otherwise very behaved. *What the hell? Isn't that the damnedest thing I've ever seen?* With their bowls full and in hand, Anne turned around and placed them on the floor two at a time, calling each pet by name. One by one, they came when summoned and started chomping away. *No, I stand corrected. THAT'S the damnedest thing I've ever seen. Coming from a guy who found a naked woman on the beach who didn't know how to talk or where to pee but could draw as well as Da Vinci, that's saying something.*

Not wanting to interrupt what had to be a filming of a new *Twilight Zone* episode, Henry maneuvered his way around the smaller animals and headed for the coffee pot. It didn't really matter what he ate in the morning; as long as the mystical brown liquid was there to fortify him, he could face anything. Before he could reach his destination, Anne intercepted him, stopping him in his tracks.

"No, I make coffee," she said, then she measured the coffee into the filter and poured the water into the coffee machine.

As the water dripped through the grounds to the waiting pot below, Henry couldn't help but think maybe it was his turn to wake up screaming. *I have to be dreaming. It's the only logical explanation, or perhaps she really is reading my thoughts. Easy, Henry, just go along. You can check the closet for seed pods later.*

"You do!" Henry smiled. "Well, that's terrific. Thank you!" When the dripping stopped, she took a cup from the cupboard and poured the coffee into it before handing it to him. "Thanks again," he said. Then he inhaled, hoping the aroma might help clear his head. Holding the steaming cup to his lips, he slurped the first few sips, blowing cooling breaths across the surface. About halfway through the first of what would be many cups, he looked up at Anne. "I have an idea for today."

"Idea?"

"Something I want to do," he explained. "I am going to ask Heidi to take you to see some animals while I talk to someone at the Venice Police Department to see if I can find any answers about what happened to you."

"Zoo?" Anne cocked her head, remembering the pictures in Nathan's books.

"Something like that. It's a place you can go and see some of the animals you're learning about. You can even feed some of them. You seem to have a knack for that." *I swear if I hear they all line up for her one by one, I'm having Heidi admit me.*

Anne nodded, squealing. "Zoo…Animals…Feed!"

"I'll take that as a yes," Henry said, smiling. He picked up his phone, which he had left on the table. Hoping it was charged enough to work since he forgot to plug it in, he dialed Heidi's number.

"Hello, big brother," Heidi answered.

"Hello, little sister!" Henry returned. "Can I ask you a favor?"

"Like you do every day, or is this a *special* favor?"

Henry smirked. "I don't ask you every day."

"Just about."

"Okay, fine. Here's today's *faveur de jour* if you will! Happy?"

"Actually, yeah, I am."

Henry sighed. He could almost feel the smugness in her tone and see the look on her face in his mind. "Hey, in all seriousness, can you take Anne somewhere where she can see some animals? I'm going to stop by the police department and talk to someone about her. I really need to find out what happened."

"It's about time," Heidi scolded him. "I suppose. But you really do owe me, you know. Not for this, because the kids would love having Anne go with them, but just because I am really the greatest sister in the world!"

"You just better hope I don't find any seed pods in my closet," Henry replied, only half-joking.

"What?"

"Nothing. Just thanks, and I'll bring her around as soon as we're dressed."

"Okey dokey," Heidi replied. "We'll go to Jungle Gardens." She hung up.

Henry got up from the chair and went to where Anne stood with a carton of eggs she had taken out of the refrigerator. "Let me help you with that," he said, getting out a bowl, a pan, and a spatula. "Time you learned to cook." They had fun cracking and scrambling the eggs, making quite a mess.

Anne wanted to wash the dishes, having observed Henry do them these past few days, so he let her. Well, to be honest, he was grateful that she wanted to because he never enjoyed doing dishes. And he was glad she was learning her way around a kitchen.

When Anne finished cleaning up the kitchen, she came into the bathroom where Henry was shaving. He wanted to be more presentable when he talked to the detective he had arranged to meet: Detective Ed Ortega. Anne stood by Henry and reached out to touch the shaving cream covering his face. She rubbed her fingertips together to explore the texture and then applied it to her face in an effort to imitate him.

"No, Anne," Henry said. He took a towel and wiped the cream off her face. "You don't need to shave. This is one of those differences between men and women."

"I do not shave?"

"Well," Henry said, picking up the razor, "not your face anyway. Go ahead and get in the shower. I'll take mine after you."

Anne stood for a few minutes, watching him as he dragged the razor down his cheeks, up his neck, and under his nose. When he was done, he rinsed his face and patted it with a towel. Anne reached up to touch his clean-shaven cheeks, fascinated by the change in his appearance.

Henry let her explore, then he touched her hand as she caressed him. "Get in the shower, Anne," he said with a smile. "We have a lot to do today."

She did slowly, her eyes on him as she stepped into the shower. Henry closed the door for her. "I'll be right outside if you need me." He left the bathroom.

When she was finished showering and came out with a towel around her, Henry took his turn while Anne got dressed in shorts, a pink T-shirt, and her floppy hat. Once dry, Henry put on a pair of khaki shorts, a light blue polo shirt, and loafers.

Heidi heard Henry pull up at around ten o'clock. The kids were already chomping at the bit to get to the park, and they ran around them when they entered the front door, chanting, "Jungle Gardens!"

Heidi was packing up Nattie's diaper bag when he entered the house. "How long do you need?"

"Can you give me about three hours?" he replied.

"Sure! I think we can keep busy for that long, probably longer. Tell you what. I'll call you when we're ready to head home, and you can meet us here."

"Sounds like a plan!" Henry kissed Anne on the cheek. "Have fun, Anne. I'll see you in a little while."

"Thank you," she said. Henry left, and Heidi finished packing up the diaper bag. "Let's go!"

"She's a pretty girl," Detective Ed Ortega remarked, looking at Anne's picture on Henry's cell phone. Detective Ortega was an older man in his late fifties, with graying hair that was mostly gone. He preferred wearing black Ray-Ban glasses instead of contacts, which made the seasoned officer look even more intelligent. He carried a few extra pounds, but it was obvious from his muscular build that he preferred the health club over the doughnut shop.

Ortega sat at his desk at the Venice Police Department surrounded by a computer monitor and keyboard. Several stacks of case files were piled so high that Henry couldn't see the photos in the frames peeking over the top. Assorted desk necessities and a badly chipped coffee mug with a shield and the word "Sergeant" completed the scene. Henry could only assume the cup held some sentimental value, which would explain why it had never been replaced with one depicting his current rank.

The two had met when Henry entered the Navy and Ortega was the ensign overseeing his unit's weapons training. Ed was nearing retirement, and the pair had only worked together for about a year before Ed left the Navy and joined the police department of their hometown of Venice. Years later, Henry looked him up when he returned home; and they stayed in touch, especially when Henry needed help with a speeding ticket or the identity of the occasional naked woman washed up on the shore.

"And you say you found her about a week ago on Venice Beach?"

"Yes, Monday, June 15 to be exact. I went to the beach to take a run and found her lying near the water in a fetal position, naked and terrified."

"And you didn't think to call 911?" the detective probed, raising one eyebrow.

"No," Henry admitted. Ortega shook his head, scowling at his old friend.

"Was there any sign of trauma or injury?" Detective Ortega jotted something on a notepad.

"None that I could see. Other than being terrified, she appeared unharmed."

"It would've been better if you had called the police, Henry. We could've gotten her proper medical attention, had psychological and physical examinations done, and gotten her finger prints. We could have done more to find out who she is a lot sooner."

"Yeah, I know you're right, Ed. But for some reason I felt compelled to help this girl. That's why I'm so worried about these nightmares. It's obvious she's reliving some traumatic ordeal that ended up with her all alone and naked on that beach."

"And you say she is having these nightmares every night, but the only thing she can tell you is that there was a fire involved?"

"The only things she told me so far are that she was breathing underwater, not quite sure what to make of that, and that she always sees fire. How the fire is involved is still a mystery, but my best guess is that she may have been in a fire at some point or lost someone close to her in one. But other than the nightmares, she remembers nothing about who she is or how she got there. Nothing at all!"

"How tall is she?"

"She's about five ten, a little shorter than me. I'm six feet two inches. I guess she weighs about 130 pounds. Long blonde hair and bright sapphire eyes."

Detective Ortega lifted one corner of his mouth in a smirk. "I haven't heard of anything that would fit with your description, but I'll do some digging. And you said she doesn't remember anything?"

"Nothing at all." Henry shook his head. "It's almost like she was just born. She didn't know how to walk, talk, use the bathroom, or even eat! It's amazing though how quickly she's learned how to do all these things. I've never met anyone like her!"

Detective Ortega closed his notebook. "Can you e-mail me that picture? E-mail address is on the card." Henry nodded, typing in the detective's email on his phone from the business card Ortega handed him. "I'll do some digging and get back to you if I find anything. I'll check with the Sarasota Sheriff's Department and Florida State Police as well. If there are any records of her, we'll find them."

"Thanks." Henry stood up and extended his hand. "I really appreciate it."

"No problem." Detective Ortega stood and walked Henry to the front doors of the police station. "Thanks for bringing this to my attention. Let me know if she remembers anything at all. The smallest detail could unlock the biggest clue."

"I promise I will."

"Oh, and Henry, try not to get too attached to this girl. I don't have to be a detective to see that you're sweet on her. If something pops in missing persons, I'm gonna have to step in in an official capacity. Do you understand?"

"Yes, I understand. And you're right. I know."

Henry nodded and left, hoping he did the right thing.

His next step when he got home was to log on to the Florida Crime Information Center Web site and put in the information about Anne to see if there was a match. Finding nothing, he then pulled up the local newspaper Web sites and researched recent articles about fires, especially at sea or anything about a missing woman, but nothing seemed to fit with either Anne or the area where he found her. Frustrated, he sat back and frowned. Hopefully, Detective Ortega would have better luck.

While Henry was busy playing junior detective, Heidi and the gang were having the time of their lives at the Sarasota Jungle Gardens. It was obvious to anyone, Heidi observed, that Anne was thrilled to see the animals in the flesh instead of pictures in a book. They moved from habitat to habitat. Nathan and Anne had a contest to see who could say the name of the animal first. Then Nathan would speak the sound the animal made or what he thought they would make. But they were both stumped when they came upon Putter the Prairie Dog. Nathan, Anne, and Nattie squeaked like a spider monkey or squawked like a macaw as loudly as they could, laughing with delight if they got a response. Heidi just chuckled. She was used to this with Nathan and Nattie.

They wandered down the sidewalks of the park, surrounded by large willow trees and green ferns bordering ponds where flamingos stood on their long thin legs; and beautiful peacocks walked uncaged, their train of feathers spread in colorful delight. They bought some feed from the machines at the flamingo habitat, and Heidi recorded them on her cell phone, taking turns feeding the large pink birds. Nattie went first and showed remarkable courage, extending her tiny hand to a towering male. Heidi told her to think of him like he was Big Bird from Sesame Street with a sunburn. Her turn ended when she started eating the pellets herself. Big brother Nathan was a bit more timid and uneasy. Not to be shown up by his little sister, he stood stiff as a statue when it was his turn. Heidi remembered a past visit when he was Nattie's age and an overzealous flamingo nipped his tiny fingers, proving the old adage, "once bitten, twice shy" to be true. "Keep your hand flat, and don't curl your fingers," Heidi told him. She was very proud of him facing his fear like a brave little soldier.

Anne, of course, drew the largest crowd of animals since she was an adult and could hold a much larger amount of food and partially because, well, she was Anne. Like everything and everyone she encountered, Heidi noted that Anne completely immersed herself in the moment. She had a way of squeezing every drop out of a new experience and soaking it all up like a sponge. She giggled and smiled when their tongues tickled the palm of her hand. They only stopped because they ran out of quarters to buy more feed. They had almost left the flamingo habitat when two of the birds began following them for a short while.

They enjoyed a picnic lunch before attending the bird show. From her reaction, Heidi guessed it was Anne's first peanut butter and jelly sandwich. The bird presentation showcased assorted species of exotic birds, including parrots, macaws, cockatoos, and others. All had been trained to perform tricks on tiny bird roller skates, ride little bird bicycles, and play bird basketball. Heidi watched this charming girl laughing like her children, tucking the sight away in her heart. Anne was as delighted as the kids, fascinated by the little feathered thespians and their antics.

They were all a little afraid of the crocodiles and alligators at the reptile habitat, except the fake croc that everyone loved to sit on for pictures. All of them felt intimidated by their size and long rows of sharp teeth. Nathan was the only one in the group that enjoyed seeing the snakes. Even Anne wasn't very impressed. Snakes just don't have that warm fuzzy vibe most animals do. Nathan alone started hissing in an attempt to make snake sounds in front of the tanks. Heidi was relieved when he didn't get any response from the slithering creatures.

At the mammal habitat, they had fun saying the word "lemur." Anne kept saying "lemur" and "flamingo" because she said they were really fun names to say. They strolled through the gardens on brick paths surrounded by a variety of trees, including fruit, palm, bamboo, pine, and even a bunya-bunya tree skirted by dense ferns. The kaleidoscope of nature blossomed everywhere, from the vibrant exotic birds and multicolored butterflies in the butterfly garden to the many species of flowers blooming around the walkways and trees.

Anne lingered in the gardens gazing up at the trees that canopied the walkway. She touched every tree, fern, and flower, feeling the texture of the plant and leaning down to take in its scent. Heidi could see it in her eyes as she drank in the rich colors of the environment and the wildlife. Anne was frozen in awe at the beauty of creation until Heidi gently took her arm, guiding her through the rest of the park.

On the way out, they stopped at the gift shop; and Heidi bought them all stuffed flamingos, even Anne. The fun continued on the drive home from Sarasota on Route 75, with Anne and the kids looking for any animals. Every time someone saw a herd of cows grazing in the pastures bordering the highway, the car erupted in a chorus of moos. Heidi watched Anne and the kids play their cow-game and smiled, amazed at this strange girl her brother met. Heidi hoped that having Anne in his life would finally bring Henry out of the refuge he had retreated to after the death of his fiancée, Heather, several years ago.

When her SUV was near to Heidi's house, she turned on the Bluetooth and called Henry. "We're almost home," she said, pulling into the street where they lived.

"I'll be there in a bit. Did you guys have a good time?" Henry asked.

"We had a wonderful time. Not sure who enjoyed it more— Anne or the kids!"

"Happy to hear it. I'll see you soon."

Back home, Heidi ushered the kids inside, flamingos in tow, while Anne gathered up the diaper bag and bags of souvenirs left in the backseat. She brought all the bags into the house while Heidi put together some dinner for them, heating up frozen chicken nuggets and slicing up an apple. By the time she had the food on the table and the kids seated, Nattie in her high chair, Henry had pulled up.

Henry walked into the front door. "Uncle Henry! Uncle Henry!" Nathan said, coming up to his uncle. "We saw alligators!"

"And lemurs," Anne added. "Leeemuuurrrrs!" This set Nattie off on a chorus of "leeeemuuuuurrrsss" while she played with her nuggets, pretending they were lemurs climbing on trees of apple slices.

"Sounds like you all had a lot of fun." Henry smiled then picked up Nathan.

"Did you find out anything?" Heidi asked.

Henry shook his head. "Not yet. Eddie is going to contact other state agencies and check missing persons, but so far, zip." He hoisted Nathan up in the air, almost hitting his head on the ceiling fan, making Heidi cry out. "Careful!"

"Sorry, he's getting so tall," Henry replied, in his defense.

"Yes, he is, and you chopping his head off will put an end to that real quick, won't it?"

"Sorry, Nate. Before you know it, you'll be picking me up," Henry said. Nate smiled and ran back towards the kitchen before all the chicken nuggets were gone

"Do you want some dinner?" Heidi offered. "It's only frozen chicken nuggets, but I can fix you something else if you want."

"No, that's okay. I'm sure Anne's had enough fun for one day. I promise I will bring her back on Saturday," he assured the pouting kids. Anne picked up her stuffed flamingo, kissed the children and Heidi, and went over to stand with Henry by the front door. "Thanks again, Heidi," Henry said, hugging the kids and his sister.

On the drive home, he was quiet, lost in thought about Anne.

"We will find." Anne put her hand on his arm.

He reached over with his left hand, his right on the steering wheel, and covered hers. "I know," he said with a smile. "I just want to help you find the right answers to make the demons go away."

"What are demons?"

"Demons are nasty things that hurt people. They're not like us, with a body, but they are more like a…" Henry tried to find an image that would convey what he wanted to. "Like the bad things in your nightmares. Sometimes people just refer to things that make them sad as 'demons,' which is what I think is more accurate. I don't think there really are these evil spirits waiting to do us harm. It's all just stories parents tell little kids to scare them into behaving. There is no God and no Satan."

"What is God and Satan?"

Henry sighed. "Allegedly, God is this great being in the sky that supposedly made the earth and everything on it. Satan was one of his angels who got mad at God and wanted to do what he wanted to instead of what God wanted him to do. So God made him leave the place in the sky, what we call Heaven. And before you ask, angels are the good spirits that God created to protect us, or so they say. You'll see pictures of them dressed in white robes with giant wings on their backs."

"They are not real? Like tele…vision?"

"Yep. I think it's all just stuff someone made up to make us all feel guilty so they can keep us in line. In my experience, none of it is real. I used to believe in God and the whole religious scene. My family used to go to church every Sunday."

"What is church?"

"It's a place where people go to be with God. I stopped going years ago." Henry didn't say anything more after that. He was lost in the memory of a day when he was ten years old. After a visiting pastor delivered an inspiring sermon about the love of Christ, young Henry felt compelled to go forward to receive Jesus into his heart while the organ played "Just as I Am." He loved Sunday school and couldn't get enough of the words of Jesus he learned while there, wanting so much to live a life worthy of God.

But memories of those other days when he was in a church also came flooding back—memories of standing in front of his mom's casket; memories of friends killed in combat in Iraq during his tour as an individual augmentee and the empty words of the chaplains; memories of staring into a hole dug into the ground at the coffin lowered into it and the sound of dirt hitting the top of the vault, hiding his fiancée Heather away from him forever. He stood by the grave long after everyone left in his service dress blue Navy uniform, watching the workers fill in the grave and feeling abandoned and betrayed. That was the day his faith finally died. Finally, there were memories of his father's funeral with young Heidi at his side, now his responsibility.

He couldn't understand how a "loving God" could allow these things to happen to someone who loved God as much as he did. What Father doesn't protect his children? How much more could God take away from him? Tormented day and night, he begged for the answer to one simple question: "Why?" Henry's hands tightened on the steering wheel while he shoved his memories back into the corners of his mind. *Damn it! It's been ten years! Doesn't it ever get any easier?*

He glanced at the speedometer and realized he was cruising way over the speed limit and eased back on the gas. *Get a grip, Henry. Focus on the now, on Anne. Don't let your anger at God get you both killed.*

"I'm sorry, Anne. Not a good subject to talk about." He looked over at her and forced a smile.

She put her hand on his leg, and that warm slender hand acted as a balm, helping him to relax and put his grief away.

Maybe someday he would tell Anne about the night he landed in the hospital with a fractured skull and with no idea how it happened. He only remembered waking up and staring into Heidi's distraught eyes. At that moment, he vowed to his sister that he'd change. Henry kept that vow, stopped partying, and obtained a degree in graphic design.

Maybe someday, he would tell Anne about who he was and why he retreated into his own world filled with his animals. But not today. Having Anne beside him somehow made life easier. Besides, she had enough to worry about without being dragged into Henry's private hell.

Anne didn't say anything after Henry stopped talking because he seemed to be getting upset by the conversation. She wanted to reach out to him to take away the pain she saw on his face and to see his wonderful dimples when he smiled. She felt his pain as if it were her own. She didn't even know what to say, so she just put her hand on his leg to let him know without words that she understood.

She did not comprehend what he was talking about with angels and demons, but in her heart, Anne somehow knew that whatever these beings were called, they were real, as real as she and Henry were. She didn't know what they were or how she knew, but she did. What she didn't understand yet was whether she should be afraid of that or relieved.

11

I am the most beautiful of all the dragons, and they all adore me. But one dragon loves me even more. He has great and powerful white wings, and other than the Two, he is the largest and mightiest of our kind. I fly across the white sky with him, watching the powerful pectoral muscles of his wings thunder as they push down the air in his path. I feel joy rise in my heart as we rise in the sky. We climb high into the air, as if we will touch the white sun above us. We fly all day and never tire, stopping only to admire the beauty of our home.

But the Other wants me and so he watches us—watches me. I see the evil in his eyes as he follows me wherever I go, and I am afraid.

12

At James and Heidi's House

June 20
Saturday

Heidi and her husband, James Mason, lived in a two-story tan stucco home with five bedrooms and a three-car garage. James was Henry's best friend in high school before James attended law school and Henry enlisted in the Navy. James had a successful probate and business law practice in Sarasota.

It was one of those romances where a best friend's baby sister went from pigtails and a pain in the neck to all grown up and beautiful. They got married when Heidi was in her second year of nursing school at the University of Florida. After she graduated as a registered nurse, she obtained a position at Venice Regional Medical Center. She became pregnant with Nate soon thereafter. When Nattie came along, James and Heidi made the decision that while the children were young, Heidi would be a full-time mommy and resume her nursing career after the kids were both in school full time.

When Anne and Henry arrived, Heidi opened the double oak front doors with decorative glass panels. The doors were mounted between two large picture windows. Beneath the windows stood manicured bushes lined with small flowers. Two large palm trees and a mature century plant adorned the lawn.

"Hi, Anne," Heidi said. "I would like you to meet my husband, James. James, this is—"

"The beautiful and mysterious Anne I've heard so much about!" James interrupted. "It's a pleasure to meet you," he continued, extending his right hand toward her. James was just a few inches shorter than Henry, standing at six feet, with a hawk nose, bright blue eyes, a businessman's haircut of his brown locks, and a well-trimmed goatee surrounding his thin, downturned mouth.

"Hello!" Anne exclaimed, stepping past his hand and throwing her arms around him in a giant hug. "I'm Anne."

James stood there speechless with a shocked but pleasant look on his face.

Henry laughed.

"Um…Anne," Heidi started to say before Anne turned and locked her in her embrace.

"Hi, Heidi!"

"Hello, Anne." *We're going to have to have a little talk about appropriate physical contact.* Heidi pried herself loose. "Come on, I'll show you the house."

James put his arm around Henry's shoulder, and the two of them disappeared inside the house and headed toward the backyard, probably in search of a cold one. Heidi took Anne on a tour of their home, starting in the white marble foyer to the raised living room with white carpet and antique Chippendale furniture. Over the sofa was a large oil painting of the family that Henry painted, with Heidi seated on the chair holding ten-month-old Nattie in her arms, James behind her with his hands on her shoulders, and Nathan sitting on the floor at her feet. The painting was framed on either side by photographs of the family, James and Heidi's wedding, the children's baby pictures, and a picture of Henry and Heidi with their parents.

Anne stared at the painting, tracing the raised edges of the brush strokes with her fingers.

"You like it? Henry did that."

"I like it!" Anne affirmed.

Next, they went through the formal dining room with a mahogany colonial set that sat eight. On the wall between the two rooms was another large oil painting of children playing on the beach. Heidi bought that at an estate sale.

Heidi walked Anne through the kitchen with marble counter tops and an island counter in the middle surrounded by glass and mahogany cabinets. Different plates of food were already set out on the island waiting for the afternoon festivities. Off the other side of the kitchen was the den, decorated like an old ship with dark paneling, nets, a ship's wheel on the left wall, a home theater with movie-style seats in front on the long wall opposite the entry, and a large stuffed marlin mounted on the right wall over bookshelves.

"James caught that fish two years ago," Heidi said, pointing to the marlin. "It put up quite a fight."

"Caught it?" Anne asked, confused. "Why would you want to catch it?"

Heidi gave her a strange look. "Perhaps Henry can tell you all about fishing. It's a sport guys like to do. The boys go often. Come on, let's go upstairs. I'll show you the bedrooms."

James used the downstairs bedroom as his home office, and the remaining four were upstairs. In the master bedroom was a king-size bed with tall bedposts, a fireplace, and French doors opening onto a balcony overlooking the back yard. The bathroom had a Jacuzzi tub big enough for two and a custom-designed shower with four shower heads.

Nathan and Nattie each had their own bedroom with a bathroom shared between them. Nathan's was themed with superheroes, and Nattie's was princess bedding and paintings of ballerinas on the wall. The last bedroom was a guest room.

They concluded the tour at the backyard, where the men were seated on lounge chairs next to a large pool with a rock waterfall on one side, an attached spa on the other, and a water slide for the children. Three steps led into the shallow end on the side near the spa, with the pool going to a depth of ten feet at its deepest end. A full outdoor kitchen and a patio set completed the area. The fenced-in yard had a swing set near the tall pine trees with a sandbox next to it. The kids were outside riding three wheelers around the patio. Screaming Anne's name, they jumped off their bikes when they saw her.

"Anne, come play with me," Nathan ordered.

"No! Play with ME!" Nattie shouted

"Let's go!" Nathan demanded. "I want you to play with me. Do you want to see my room?"

"No, Nate. She wants to see my room with the princesses, not Ireman," Nattie insisted.

"It's IRONMAN, not Ireman," Nate corrected her. The debate continued as the two of them dragged Anne back into the house.

Heidi joined the men chatting by the pool.

"Do we have any idea yet as to who she is or where she came from?" James asked, handing Heidi a beer from a cooler between him and Henry. The coals in the barbeque were already glowing. Soon they would be ready to grill James's famous teriyaki steaks marinating in the refrigerator. He had a special sauce he called his "secret weapon" that gave it just the right flavor.

"No," Henry said. "I did talk to Eddie who's checking into it, but so far there are no matches to her description. And I've checked missing persons on the FCIC, but nothing that would fit her."

"What are you going to do for the long term?" James took a sip of his beer.

"I'm going to let her stay with me. She's not just homeless. She's helpless. Ask Heidi. When I found her, she was as helpless as a newborn."

"That's my point. It has to be a lot of work for you. Why bother with the burden? Just turn her over to the authorities."

"I don't think Henry wants to do that," Heidi said, sipping her own drink. "You know him."

"Yeah, I know, the knight in shining armor for lost causes."

Henry smirked. "Yeah, I guess I am. I never met a stray animal or blonde I didn't like." He tried to do his best Groucho Marx impression, complete with an invisible cigar.

James laughed, choking on his beer.

"I don't see a problem as long as Henry can get his work done," Heidi continued. "Anne seems to enjoy the art as well."

"Legally, he's taking a big risk. What if something happens to her while she's under his care? Didn't she almost drown the other day?"

"Yes, but that's because she didn't know she couldn't breathe underwater," Henry said.

"Why would anyone think they could breathe underwater?" James asked.

"That's my point," Henry answered. "No one else is going to watch over her like I am. Turn her over to homeless shelter and she won't last a day. She's too vulnerable."

"I see your point. Just be careful," James said as a caution.

"Besides, she understands more and more every day," Henry said. "I'm hoping soon she might be able to tell me what happened to her. At first, I thought she might've been caught in a fire. Then there's something about being in the water. My guess was that she was on a boat that caught fire and fell off? But there's not a mark on her, no sign of physical trauma. Just emotional."

James shook his head. "Weird that no one seems to have reported her missing. You'd think someone would know her."

Heidi turned to go into the house when she heard Nattie scream bloody murder at Nathan. "There are a lot of people who are alone in this world who don't have anyone to report them missing." She went to break up the kerfuffle. She found them upstairs in Nattie's room. Anne was trying to keep them apart and was holding on to Nattie. Nathan had taken Nattie's doll out of her hands and was using it as a hammer to bang his turtle fighters' evil nemesis into submission.

"Gimme back my dolly! Gimme!" Nattie screamed.

"No!" Nathan yelled back. "Dolly is killing the bad guy! Bam, bam!"

"Nathan Alan Mason, you give your sister back her doll this instant!" Heidi yelled. Nathan looked sheepishly at her and handed the doll back to his sister. "Are you okay, Anne?"

"I am okay." She laughed. "Nattie has dolly now."

"Go on outside with Henry," Heidi said. "I'll get the kids ready to go in the pool. We'll be right out."

Henry stood when Anne came out the patio door to join them by the pool.

"Hi, Anne," James said. "Are you enjoying the house?"

"Pretty house," Anne replied. She sat by Henry and took the can of lemon soda he offered her.

"Well, guess I better get the steaks started." James put his beer down and went to the kitchen to retrieve the night's main course.

"Are you okay?" Henry asked Anne. "I know the kids can be a handful sometimes."

She nodded. "Yes. I laugh with Nathan and Nattie." She put the can down and looked at Henry. "Anne go in water please? No breathe."

"Okay, we can go into the water, but you have to promise me you'll stay close and listen to everything I tell you."

"I will," Anne promised.

"I will teach you how to swim and breathe air. We'll stay in the shallow end until I feel it's safe for you to go deeper."

"Shallow, deeper?" Anne questioned.

Henry thought for a moment. "If there is very little water, like up to your knees"—Henry held his right hand at his knee parallel to the ground—"then you are in shallow water. If the water is over your head"—Henry stretched his arm high above him—"then you are in deep water. Do you understand?"

"Yes. Shallow, deep." She mimicked his movements.

"Very good," Henry said. "Are you ready to go into the water?"

"Yes, I am."

They had come prepared to swim as both of them already had their swimsuits on. Henry just had to pull off his T-shirt, remove his sunglasses, and kick off his flip-flops. Anne was wearing a cover-up that looked like an oversized baggie blouse. Henry chuckled when James almost dropped the plate of meat at the sight of her unveiling when he walked back into the yard and then looked around to see if Heidi saw his reaction. Henry knew James loved his wife and would never cheat on her, but Anne's beauty caught him off guard. She was stunning, and she was with Henry.

Henry went first, using the steps leading into the pool's shallow end before Nathan could jump in and splash them. Anne was next, and the two of them walked to the middle of the pool where it was waist-deep. The kids came out of the house and followed. Nathan performed a perfect cannon ball splashing them with the cool water. Heidi was right behind them with Nattie in tow, looking adorable in her princess water wings.

"Nathan, front and center," Henry barked. Nathan torpedoed across the pool, stopping right in front of the two of them. "Yes, Uncle Henry?"

"Remember those swimming lessons I paid for last summer at the park district so someday I can teach you to scuba dive with me?"

"Yeah."

"Would you like to show Anne how to swim for me?"

"SURE!"

"Great, here's what I want you to do. Swim back and forth from side to side right in front of us. Go real slow so Anne can see how you swim. Then you can show us how fast you are, okay?"

"Okay. WATCH ME, ANNE!" Nathan plunged forward and swam freestyle. Henry was impressed with the young boy's form. Either he was a natural, like his uncle, or had been practicing on his own. Whatever the reason, this little guy could swim, and Henry knew he would jump at the chance to show off for Anne.

Anne watched Nathan pass back and forth while Henry described what he was doing.

"Do you see how he has his head in the water and is looking straight down? That keeps his spine in line and prevents his hips from sinking." Henry gently touched each part on Anne's body as he named them. "You don't want to swim with your head up looking at what's in front of you. Also, see how he rotates—moves—from side to side, one arm stretched in front of him while he brings the other one up. That keeps his shoulder from getting hurt and lets him take a breath of air. You don't want to swim flat. Keep your legs straight and don't bend at the knees. When you breathe, remember to breathe early and keep your arms straight and fingertips pointed down so you don't pull crooked. Do you understand?"

"I understand."

"Are you ready to give it a try?"

"Yes!" Anne replied, diving into the water.

"Wait," Henry said, alarmed. "I wasn't finished."

Anne skimmed across the surface of the water at a fast pace. She thrashed her legs and churned her arms like a windmill. Always the quick study, Anne was making progress and holding her own, but she expended way too much energy, and Henry knew she would tire out soon. He marveled at how well she was doing for her first attempt and couldn't help but notice her muscularity and power, the artist in him drawn to her anatomy. The water glistened on her skin, accentuating her form.

Henry tapped Anne's shoulder when she made another pass. "Anne, Anne! Stop for a minute." Anne stood up and with both hands brushed her wet hair back away from her face.

"Anne swim, I swim," she said, smiling and dripping.

"Yes, Anne swim. I mean, you swim…uh, swam. Now you got me doing it! Yes, you did. You swam well, but we still need to work on it. Here, watch me." Henry grabbed the edge of the pool with both hands and stretched out in a prone position, floating on the surface. "Watch my legs." Henry kicked his legs while bracing himself with both arms. "See, you don't have to kick so hard. Now you try it."

Anne joined him on the ledge and kicked her legs to match Henry's movement. "That's it. You've got it. Keep kicking but much slower. I want to try something." Anne obeyed Henry's instructions, and he stood up and placed both arms under her torso. "Okay, let go of the edge but keep kicking. I'm going to hold you in one place."

Anne released her grip, and Henry guided her to the pool in four feet of water. "Okay, now I'm going to let go, and I want you to slowly swim to the end of the pool and back to me." Henry dropped his arms and watched Anne paddle off. She turned around when she reached the end of the pool and headed back towards Henry. About two-thirds of the way back, she took a deep breath and submerged below the water. Henry gasped and for a moment felt a wave of panic. Then he relaxed when he could see her streaming toward him underwater. She emerged right in front of him, stood and said, "I no breathe."

"Damn!" Henry said, impressed.

The moment was broken when a well-aimed beach ball slammed into the back of Henry's head with a loud ping.

"Dinner is ready," Heidi announced. "Be sure and wash up." Nathan doubled over with laughter after witnessing the attack. Nattie continued playing with her princess ponies, oblivious to what had just happened.

They all enjoyed a feast of steaks, chicken, hotdogs, corn on the cob, potato salad, and a garden salad. After dinner, Heidi brought out ice cream and made sundaes for everyone. Anne added several items to her ever-growing list of new foods she liked.

13

On Being a Woman

While everyone sat around the patio talking and eating, Anne jumped up, feeling something uncomfortable in her bikini bottom. She ran into the bathroom near the pool to look. When she pulled her bikini down, it was red with blood that trickled down her legs. She was horrified at the sight. What was wrong with her? She had no idea why she was bleeding! Bloody images from her nightmares of dragons being ripped apart flashed in her head. The fear that she had managed to push down since Henry found her fought its way to the surface of her resolve. She stood in the bathroom looking down at the blood on her legs, her hands up in the air in front of her, and screamed Henry's name.

She heard Henry banging on the door. "Anne! What's the matter?"

"I am bleeding!" she cried. Heidi's voice came closer to the door. "Let me in, Anne. I can help!" Anne opened the door, dripping blood onto Heidi's bathroom floor, her bikini still pulled down around her knees. Heidi stepped inside, closing the door behind her.

"She's started her period," Heidi called to the men on the other side of the door. "I got this."

"All yours, honey," James answered.

Henry knocked on the door. "Can I help with anything?"

"Yeah, keep an eye on the kids. I got this."

Heidi helped Anne take off her suit, told her to sit on the toilet, and then left the bathroom, returning with fresh clothes. She brought sanitary pads with her and put one on the underwear she included with the clothes. "Wipe the blood off your legs then put this on," she instructed. Anne did as she was told, and Heidi was relieved to see her relax a little. Heidi put the lid of the toilet down and told Anne to take a seat. She leaned against the sink and put her hands on Anne's knees.

"Haven't you had your period before?"

Anne did not seem to comprehend what Heidi was talking about. She looked at Heidi with a confused look and then shook her head. "What is 'period'?"

"You have what all us women have had to go through since the beginning of time. You should have started years ago. I don't understand why you don't remember having one. Anyway, there is nothing wrong with you. This will happen every month. It's a natural thing, and there's nothing to be afraid of. When it starts, you can put a pad in your underwear like these." She grabbed a few from the package she brought with her. "Change them often, depending on how much blood there is. When you are more comfortable, I will show you another way to protect your clothes." Anne took the small plastic-wrapped packages from Heidi's hands and stared at them as if she'd never seen them.

"Women have, not men?" Anne asked. "Men shave, not women?"

"Well, we do shave but not our faces. But yes, this is something only women get. Go ahead and get dressed." Heidi took one of the small towels off the rack. "I'll take care of your suit and the bathroom. Then we'll talk more about it." Heidi started to clean up the blood that had leaked on the floor. Anne pulled the second towel off the bar after she saw Heidi cleaning the floor and knelt down to help her. "Thanks," Heidi said, but inside, she couldn't get over how scared Anne was of something she should have been used to at her apparent age. Heidi then wondered, how old was Anne anyway? They didn't even know her correct age, only that she appeared to be in her early twenties, maybe the same age as Heidi, which was twenty five. There was no way of knowing for sure. But she was certainly old enough to have been a woman for several years now.

After they cleaned up the bathroom and Anne was dressed, Heidi took her by the hand and led her into the den. She took one of her nursing books off the bookshelf and opened it up to an anatomical picture of a woman. Heidi described how each part worked, including menstruation. While she pointed out the female anatomy, Anne pointed to the backyard and said, "Henry is different!"

"Yes." Heidi couldn't help smiling. "Men are different than women." She turned the page to the illustration of a man's anatomy.

Anne pointed to the evident male parts. "Man!" she exclaimed.

"I guess you've seen that, huh," Heidi said, chuckling. "Yes, that is called a penis, and the things underneath are testicles. Men and women have different parts that they join together to make babies."

Anne cocked her head. Heidi nodded then put the book down and explained the birds and the bees to Anne, including detailed descriptions of intercourse and childbirth. When she was done, she asked Anne, "Do you understand?"

"Man and woman are different but make babies? Like Nathan and Nattie?"

"Yep, like Nathan and Nattie. All of us were babies at one time. We all have a mother, the woman, and a father, the man."

"Do I have mother and father?" Anne asked, her eyes glistening with the threat of tears.

"Yes, you do," Heidi said, taking Anne's hands in hers. "We just have to find them. And we will. Henry's doing everything he can. Do you have any more questions?"

Anne looked at the floor and shook her head.

"Let's go join the rest of the family," Heidi said, standing up.

"Everything copacetic?" James asked upon their return. Henry went over to Anne.

"Are you okay?" He put his arm around her shoulders.

"I am okay," Anne said, smiling. "Heidi told me about man and woman." She pointed to Henry's groin and said, "You have a penis!"

Henry blushed and nodded. "Yes."

James laughed until Anne pointed to him and said, "You have a penis!" James stopped laughing at Henry, his face taking on a nice red hue as well.

Henry put his hand on Anne's elbow, guiding her to a lounge chair to sit down. "Thanks, Heidi." He looked at his sister. "Wasn't ready to get into that with her yet but"—he shrugged and sat in his own chair—"glad I dodged that bullet."

"You just dodged the opening salvo, buddie boy. You've got mood swings, cramps, and the joy of shopping in the feminine hygiene aisle to look forward to." Heidi sat in her chair and stretched her arms above her head, crossing her legs. "Glad to be of assistance," she said with a gloating smile.

Henry glared at his sister, knowing she was enjoying every minute of his discomfort.

They sat in the lounge chairs on the patio while the coals turned into ash and the pool lights turned on, glowing a light blue under the water. They talked until the sun went down and it was time for the kids to go to bed. Henry decided it was time for them to leave as well. Kisses and hugs made the rounds, the kids heading to their bedrooms and Henry and Anne to home.

When they got home, Anne picked up a picture of Henry, Heidi, and their parents.

"Mother and father?" she asked.

"Yes," Henry replied, coming over and taking the picture from her hands, staring at it. "This is my mom and dad before they died."

"I do not know mother and father," she said, a faraway look in her eyes. "Tell me."

Henry smiled. "Sit down. I'll get the photo album and show you." He took a blue photo album off the bookshelf and sat down beside her on the sofa. "That's my mom and dad." He pointed to a picture of the couple dressed in wedding attire. The man wore a light blue tuxedo with a white ruffled shirt and a dark blue bowtie. He had brown hair and blue eyes with a sharp nose and high cheekbones, like Henry.

The woman was smaller, only up to the shoulders of her husband, with red hair, her veil pulled back over a diamond tiara on top of her head, a low-cut dress revealing ample breasts highlighted by a pearl necklace above them. She had green eyes and a small mouth with full lips. There were several more pictures of the couple in different poses—at a party holding up glasses of beer, at the beach, at a birthday party for Henry's mother. Anne spent a long time looking at each one, photos of newlyweds joining their lives together and growing as a couple—through two children, her illness, up until her death of breast cancer when Henry was eighteen.

After his mom died, he left home and joined the Navy. His father was so overcome by grief at the loss of his wife that within a couple of years, he had a major heart attack. Unfortunately, while recuperating in the hospital, he also had a major stroke that left him an invalid. Heidi was sent to live with James's family until Henry came home, which is where their romance started, even though James was much older than she was.

When Henry was discharged, he assumed the role of parent, taking care of his father until he passed away a year later. Heidi was only fifteen when their father died, so Henry became Heidi's legal guardian at the age of twenty-two. Now looking back at the pictures, the pain of his parents' deaths came back to haunt him.

Then Henry took out another album. "This is me when I was a baby." He pointed to a picture of a little redheaded baby in the typical hospital first photo, his little fists raised before him like a prizefighter. They went through the years of Henry's life as if watching a movie. She saw pictures of him in grade school, the birth of a little sister, playing Little League baseball, obtaining belts in Taekwondo, through high school, his stint in the Navy, and even his life with Heather.

"Who is she?" Anne asked when they got to photos of Henry and Heather, a part of his life that he had thought he had safely tucked away.

"She was going to be my fiancée," Henry replied. "She died several years ago."

"Fiancée?" Anne repeated.

"I was going to marry her, like the pictures of my parents." He put the book of his life down and picked up the album of his parents, turning to the wedding photographs once again. "I loved her and wanted to spend the rest of my life with her."

"Love," Anne repeated. "What is love?"

"A question for another day." He sighed, putting the books and his grief away. After Heather's death, Henry was devastated and retreated into his own world, swearing off love. Oh, he dated once in a while, but it never went farther than a one- or two-night fling. He didn't want to face another heartbreak. He wasn't ready for love again or to talk about emotions that he had, to date, kept bottled up inside, locked away.

That night, Henry lay awake while memories of his parents and Heather pressed heavily on his heart, bringing up the pain of their separation and death.

While Henry struggled with his memories, Anne struggled to reach the recesses of her mind to try to bring up any image of a family or even the ghost of a feeling for a connection. She had to have a mother and father, right? Heidi told her she did. Why couldn't she remember them? Did they look like the people in Henry's books? How could she not know her own father and mother? Were there pictures of her as a child like Henry? Did she play games like Nattie and Nathan? She squeezed her eyes, trying to find something to hold on to, only to find a void like the darkness of the room. When she finally fell asleep, the void filled not with family but with the fiery death of her nightmares.

14

I rejoice as another pair of dragons join in a union. Dragons choose mates from among one another, and once chosen, the union is binding for life. But others may join in the union. The dragons wrap their necks around each other as they join together before all the others. I long for a mate, but the One tells me I am forbidden. I am happy with his rule.

The Other follows me when I go inside the crystal halls at the bottom of the mountain where the dragons gather to meet. He comes to me and demands that I must choose to join with him. I tell him I cannot. I am forbidden to mate. Although the Other has many mates, he tells me that none are like me, that he wants me. He presses me against the crystal walls, his large body hot against mine, and, with a deep growl, threatens me that I will suffer for my choice. I am afraid of his words and leave him and the hall. I escape to the outside, hoping he does not follow.

15

Shopping

This time after Anne's nightly episode, Henry brought her to sleep with him in his bed instead of lying on the floor with her. "No point in standing on formality anymore," he told Anne. "We end up together every night anyway. We might as well be comfortable. Besides, maybe if you're with me, you'll feel more secure and you won't have a nightmare at all."

Anne nodded, laying her head against his chest. Henry held her tight until he heard the soft, steady sound of her breathing when she finally fell back asleep. The sensation of her soft body pressed up against him made it difficult for him to sleep. He so wanted to caress her and give in to his building passion for her, but he would not let his own desire overrule his concern for her. His heart was taking him to a place he had closed off long ago after losing Heather.

Looking down at Anne's golden hair, he couldn't help but think of Heather, of her passion about her work and her intense joy in life, so much like this woman lying next to him. Henry, James, and Heather were best friends in high school. While Henry enlisted in the Navy, Heather and James went to college to study prelaw. She too had long blonde hair and laughed at everything, even Henry's bad jokes. He had a very odd sense of humor. Heather kept him sane when he was dealing with his mother's illness and eventual death.

He listened to the sound of Anne's steady breathing and relaxed, allowing himself to remember that day when he was on leave after a twelve-month deployment in Iraq where he caught a bullet to his right thigh. He drove down to Orlando from the naval air station in

Pensacola, Florida where he remained stateside, stationed there as an airplane mechanic. Henry had arranged to have two of his MP buddies, whom he knew were visiting family nearby, to interrupt their date and pretend to arrest him. During the pat down, they would discover a heart-shaped diamond ring that he intended to propose to her with while in handcuffs. Odd sense of humor indeed. He only had six more months of his enlistment to go and wanted to settle down with Heather, making love and making babies.

Somewhere just south of Tallahassee, while he stopped at a gas station, he got a call from James telling him that Heather had been hit by a drunk driver while driving to Orlando to meet him and died instantly. Henry's heart was as crushed as Heather's car, and his capacity for love died with her. He didn't even have time to grieve because soon after, he had to take a hardship discharge to care for his father after his stroke.

Henry buried his pain deep inside him, shying away from any relationship that would make him feel vulnerable. But there was something special about this lost girl that stirred something inside him from the very first moment they met on the beach, emotions he had never felt before and a connection to her that he could not explain. At that moment, while holding her secure in his arms and whispering comforting words in her ear, his heart opened up that hidden place and his feelings for her came flooding in. He didn't know it yet, but Henry was falling in love.

June 21
Sunday

Henry was opening and closing the kitchen cabinets in a desperate search for coffee for his morning fix. With both his search and his cup coming up empty, he decided it was time to go to the grocery store.

Henry hustled Anne into the car and headed straight to the nearest Starbucks drive-through. He ordered a ham-and-cheddar breakfast sandwich and a tall Pike Blend for himself and whole grain oatmeal and orange juice for Anne. He could feel order slowly returning to the universe with every steamy sip, while Anne stabbed at her oatmeal with a plastic spoon. *Wow, I think I might have actually found something she doesn't like to eat.* By the time he finished his coffee, Henry was pulling into the SuperMart parking lot. He thought this would be a good opportunity to buy some more clothes for Anne and, of course, necessary items for her female issues.

Anne stepped out of the car into the parking lot and stood in awe at the hustle of shoppers coming and going into the very large building with big yellow letters on the side that spelled "SUPERMART." Henry took her elbow and guided her towards the entrance, her head turning from side to side, trying to see all the action happening around her.

Upon reaching the door, a startled Anne jumped back when the automatic door magically opened. Henry burst out laughing. Anne watched the door open and close as shoppers came and went. He pointed out the sensor above the door and tried his best to explain to Anne how it worked. Anne kept her eyes glued to the device and craned her neck to watch the device when they passed underneath into the store.

Finally inside, they started at the produce section. Anne stood at the first bin, her gaze taking in the colorful piles of the different varieties of fruit and vegetables. She picked up an apple first, said "Apple," then took a bite of it before Henry could stop her. Then she went to the oranges and picked one up, saying, "Orange!" Henry held her hand down when she brought the orange up to her mouth to take a bite.

"No, Anne," he said. "We can't eat that until we get home. We have to pay for it first. It's not ours until we pay for it. Just like when we bought your swimsuit and went to the beach. Food at the store is no different. We can't just eat it just because it's food and sitting out here."

Anne released her grip on the orange and let it fall back into the bin. Then she extended her other hand to return the apple to the stack.

"No," Henry said, "you took a bite out of it, so we have to pay for it now. Finish that one, and we'll put the core into the bag and pay for it when we check out. Good thing they're on sale per apple and not per pound." Anne smiled and crunched away while Henry bagged a few more apples. He could see the excitement on her face, seeing all the different sizes, shapes, and colors of all the various fruits and vegetables.

She continued to each bin and picked up an item and showed it to Henry, either telling him the name or asking what it was. Henry bought one of several different types of fruits and vegetables to take home for her to try.

They finally left the produce section and headed to the meat department. She picked up a package of beef and asked him the name.

"This is the meat department, and that, my dear, is beef. Hamburger to be specific. Over here are some ribs, and this is steak like you ate last night. It comes from a cow. All of this is meat of one kind or another. They also have chicken, pork, and fish right next to us," Henry explained, pointing.

She looked at the package and said, "MOO!" Several people turned around and stared at her, smiling. When it didn't answer, she frowned. "Does not look like cow."

"Well," he began, "the cow isn't alive. They cut the cow up into smaller pieces so we can eat them."

She cocked her head to the side. "Why?"

"Because we can't eat the whole cow," he said, smiling.

She lifted one corner of her mouth in a smirk and then picked up a package of chicken. "What is this?"

"That is chicken."

"CLUCK!" she yelled. It didn't answer either. The other store patrons who watched her laughed. "It not look like chicken." She shook her head. "Chicken nuggets?" Henry nodded. She picked up a package of pork but didn't "oink" at it, understanding that even though this was an animal that she knew, it wouldn't make the right sounds anymore. Henry was very grateful for that.

Anne walked over to take a closer look at the piles of fish lying on a bed of ice inside a glass case.

"Dragons eat," she told him, pointing to the fish.

"No, that is not dragon's meat. It's a fish that swims in water, like you saw on TV and at Jungle Gardens."

"No…dragons…eat…fish," she insisted in long, drawn-out words to get her point across.

"Anne, I told you there are no such things as dragons. They are only make-believe, not real. They don't eat fish or anything else, except the occasional knight in shining armor in the movies."

"NO, DRAGONS EAT FISH!" Anne insisted, her eyes moist and lips pressed tightly together.

Henry was taken back by both her tone and the look on her face. He could see in her eyes that she truly believed—no, somehow in her heart, knew—that dragons ate fish.

"Okay, okay, calm down! My mistake." Henry held both hands in front of him and motioned as if he were patting the air. "I'm sorry. I didn't mean to upset you. If there are dragons in wherever it is you come from and they like sushi, who am I to argue?"

"NOT SOOSHE FISH!"

Great, her first period. Our first argument. This is just great.

"Sooshe, eh, sushi *is* fish, sweetheart. I believe you, okay? No reason to get so riled up. Would you like to eat fish too?" He hoped to change the subject from dragons.

"Have to buy first," Anne reminded.

"That's right, have to buy first. Thank you. Would you like me to buy you some fish and we can take it home and eat it later?" Henry had the butcher wrap up a couple of pieces of halibut, first having him chop off their heads after weighing them. He hated eating or preparing anything that was looking back at him.

Noticing Anne's mood hadn't improved, he said, "Let's go look at some clothes," hoping to distract her. "We'll come back to the food." Anne followed Henry towards the women's department. Letting Anne push the cart seemed to brighten her disposition.

Shopping in the women's section wasn't any easier. Anne's shopping gene kicked into high gear, and she was drawn to the racks of clothes like the proverbial moth to a flame. She darted from rack to rack, snatching up several different items, asking Henry what each one was called. She seemed a little puzzled when several of his answers were the same. "Expensive!" Henry finally told her to stop and picked out a few things in her size, according to Heidi's instructions, and told her to try them on. He didn't stop to think that she wouldn't know where to go to try them on and quickly stopped her before she put the clothes on right there in the middle of the store.

"Anne," he said in a low voice, taking the shirt off her head, trying not to laugh or run out of the store. He wasn't sure what he would do. "You can try them on in a fitting room."

"Fitting room?" she looked around. "With Heidi!" She remembered the swimsuit store.

Henry took her to the middle of the clothes section, where the ladies attending the fitting rooms just smiled, having watched the whole episode. "Go in here, take off your shirt, and try this one on. Then come out and let me see how it fits."

Anne did as she was told, and after about an hour of looking at different items and trying each and every piece on, they settled on a couple of sundresses, more bikinis, three pairs of shorts, two pairs of jeans, and six shirts in varied styles. Henry put them all in the cart. "I think we need to get you some shoes too," he said.

"Shoes?"

He pointed to the aqua sandals she had on that Heidi had bought her. "Like those."

"Flop-flops!" She called them the name Nattie had given them.

"Yes, flop-flops." They went to the shoe section and picked out tennis shoes, white sandals, and a pair of beige flats. Henry figured that these would pretty much go with all the clothes they bought, not seeing the need to have a pair to match every outfit.

It took them four hours to get through the store because she wanted to know the names of every single item they picked up. Several times he had to pull her along and drag her away from that moment's fixation. At one point, Henry told her not to ask about every item or they would be there all day. She sulked a little, but she soon cheered up when the cart began to fill with brightly colored items. Henry continued letting her push the cart, hoping it would keep her mind off the impromptu "I spy with my little eye" game they were playing.

With the clothes all picked out and the few remaining food items selected, one task remained—taking care of Anne's monthly needs. Henry sighed and took the list from his pocket his sister had prepared the night before. Anne was strangely quiet as Henry tried to shop casually and not draw attention to himself. Clearly out of his element, Henry struggled to make sense of a never-ending barrage of feminine products. Super Absorbent this, Ultra-Thin that, Super Long with Wings…*Wings? What in the hell are the wings for?* Deodorant, overnight, maxi, douching, yeast infection, vaginal discharge. He never knew it was so tough to be a woman. *I swear I'll never bitch about jock itch again. This is seriously messed up.*

Henry was about to give up and head to sporting goods, buy Anne some fishing waders, and just hose her down in the morning when a store clerk stocking a nearby shelf took pity on him. "Can I help you, sir?" the young girl asked politely.

"Oh heavens! Yes, please!" Henry looked at her name tag. "Yes, please, Darla, if you don't mind?" Henry handed her his list. "This is what I need and lots of it because I want to stock up…I mean *she*— she wants to stock up." Darla looked at Anne. Anne smiled back, looking Darla straight in the eyes and pointed to Henry, stating, "He has a penis." Anne obviously remembered her conversation with Heidi from the night before when she was first introduced to the surrounding products and their purpose.

Darla didn't know what to say. She slowly uttered, "Yeah, okay."

Henry's mind was back in sporting goods. This time his thoughts were of loading the largest pistol they had and ending his misery.

"I'm sorry. You must forgive my friend. She's not from around here, and she's, well, she's special."

"Oh, I see. Okay, no problem," Darla replied awkwardly. "Let's get you taken care of."

Henry hated using the word "special" because he knew Darla would take it exactly the way Darla took it and not call security. Anne, of course, really was special, but in a way only Henry understood, and he didn't want to take the time to try and explain. Because Darla stocked the shelves, she knew exactly where everything on the list was and soon had their cart packed with enough products for an entire sorority. Henry thanked Darla over and over and made Anne push the cart out of that aisle.

Finally, they had all they had come for and headed for the registers. As Henry emptied the cart onto the belt at the checkout line, Anne pointed to each newly discovered prize and announced its name loud and clear to the checker. The poor guy did his best not to laugh when Anne said "Super Maxi with Wings," and he had a hard time keeping his eyes on his work and not on Anne.

Henry started to push the cart out of the store, but Anne hip-checked him out of the way and ran with the cart to the car with the excitement of a child with a new toy. Henry regretted buying her those tennis shoes and was barely able to stop her before she hit the car. Anne watched impatiently while Henry loaded everything into the back, and they drove off.

Back home, Henry unloaded the groceries, and Anne dashed inside with her new clothes. While Henry put the food away, Anne was in the kitchen, taking stock of her haul and showing everything off to the animals gathered around her. "This is a blouse, this is a tank top, and this is an expensive." Henry just shook his head and smiled, marveling again at this special girl while he continued to put the groceries away, especially, thank God, the coffee!

All the food was put away, and the "Super Maxi with Wings" products were piled high on the counter. *We'll find a place for all that later*, Henry thought to himself. He felt embarrassed just looking at them. Henry realized he had to make room for all of Anne's things.

They had a late lunch, which they made into dinner, and spent much of the evening cleaning out the closet in the master bedroom to make room for all of Anne's new clothes. Henry emptied out several drawers in a long oak dresser that had an attached mirror topped by a curved wooden shelf. A second taller oak dresser was on the wall opposite his bed. He piled all the clothes from the closet and the dresser in a stack on a red easy chair in the corner of his room. Henry showed Anne how to fold her clothes, and she put some of them into the dresser. She examined each piece, feeling the fabric and holding it up to admire it before putting the piece away either in a drawer or on a hanger. Henry finally put away the stack of clothes on the red chair, finding he actually had enough room for all his clothes between the closet and the taller dresser. He just needed to put them all away neatly.

When they had finished making room for Anne's things, including the feminine products, which Henry had tucked away deep inside a bathroom cabinet, Henry went to the kitchen and scooped out a generous portion of ice cream into two bowls to make sundaes. After smothering both bowls with lots of chocolate syrup and whipped cream, he was about to clean up the mess when Loki the cat leapt onto the counter and began the task for him. He left the Norse cat of mischief the hell alone and opted instead to join Anne on the sofa to watch a superhero movie, content to feel her lean against him.

Anne loved *Superman*, starring Christopher Reeve, and Henry never grew tired of watching it either. So far, there wasn't a movie they watched together that Anne didn't like, but they had yet to watch anything from the horror genre. Henry was afraid it would be like pouring gasoline on a fire for the girl who had nightmares each and every night. Instead, he preferred to quietly observe while Anne watched the film, engrossed with the fascination of a child, truly believing that a man could really fly or pick up a yacht with one hand.

Her ability to so easily believe in the impossible was refreshing on one hand and unsettling on the other. To accept this strange, new world Henry was slowly introducing her to on blind faith alone reminded him of how gullible he used to be when he was younger.

As a child, there was a time when Henry believed in the impossible and had a very strong faith as well. This was before the harsh realities of life tore his world apart and his heart turned against God. Now, however, with the joy and happiness Anne had brought into his life, little tugs of hope began to pull at his heart, threatening to make him confront those long-suppressed aspirations of a child who once looked at the world as an exciting and never-ending adventure.

Her simple trust in things like believing that a man could really be from another world reminded Henry of the comfort and security he felt as a child, and part of him was longing for that peace again. His heart was at the brink of opening him up to the possibility of falling again into the arms of a faceless God, knowing He would be there to hold him. Henry was fighting a battle inside between the light he basked in as a child who once believed and the darkness that consumed the man who refused to. Maybe this moment with Anne, combined with looking at the old photographs with her, was freeing the child Henry had locked away deep inside. But the man refused to surrender.

When the movie was over, Henry took care of the necessary needs of their paralyzed dog and scooped the four litter boxes. He put the bag of soiled litter into the large garbage and then wrapped it up to take it outside. While he was walking back toward the house, the light illuminating the backyard was blocked for just a nanosecond, causing Henry to stop, turn around, and scan the yard. But the moment was so quick that he dismissed it as a result of the battle going on inside him.

16

I watch the little dragons learn to fly for the very first time from my shelf high up on the mountain. Soon after the golden dragons mate, the female lays her eggs at the bottom of the ocean. The eggs are watched by all the dragons until they hatch and the dragonets are brought up to the crystal mountains, where they are kept under the warm bodies of the larger dragons.

The little ones are learning to live above the water, and while they chase each other, they flap their wings and briefly rise off the ground in an effort to fly. Their wings are not yet fully developed, and they come crashing back to the ground. But that does not stop their games, each one of them insistent to be the first one to stay in the air. When they tire, the adult dragons take them back to their shelves to eat the silver fish they had collected for them and then rest. Some of the little ones have just hatched and are trying to walk, bravely venturing out from their warm refuge under the wings of the large dragons.

Suddenly the sky bursts open with a loud thunderous crack, and the terrified little dragons cry out, scrambling to hide under their parents! The enemy cuts through the sky, blotting out the white sun like a black cloud of evil spreading across the sky. They spit fire from their large mouths, consuming everything in their path. The little ones cry and cling to their mothers and fathers and then succumb to the intense flames engulfing them.

The black dragons form into a group like a flock of birds and fly straight down, plunging headfirst into the sea. One by one, they take turns scooping up all the eggs from the shelter of the bottom of the ocean and bringing them to the surface. There, they slam them into the side of the crystal mountain and crush them with their large feet! The remaining golden dragons cry out in their attempts to rescue the fragile eggs, only to be scorched by the mouths of the monsters crushing their babies. The blood of the little ones pools around their little bodies in the broken shells while the black dragons search for any hidden ones. I try to reach them, but I cannot help them.

17

Watercolors

Henry felt Anne shudder in his protective embrace and moved closer to her, spooning around her while she fought off the dragons in her nightmare. The nightmares were now a part of their nightly routine. He was thankful that his presence combined with the fact that Anne now knew what a nightmare was allowed her to actually sleep most nights, although she was still restless. He wondered if they would ever stop, and he resolved to seek professional help in the light of the morning.

June 22
Monday

When the morning came and the nightly fires burned out, Henry decided that today was a good day to pull out his watercolor supplies to teach Anne how to paint in a new medium. To start with, he built a still life set of an apple, an orange, and a banana. He also put on a CD collection of classical pieces, part of his efforts to introduce her to different types of music.

He tacked the heavy paper down on the board for Anne and taped down a sheet directly on his table for himself. He filled two large jars with water then squeezed small amounts of different color paints on the egg carton water color pallet.

They started by drawing the objects, which Anne already knew how to do. Once the drawing was complete, he took a spray bottle and filled it with water.

"Spray your sheet with the water, like this," he demonstrated, spraying water on the thick paper until the page was soaked. She did the same with her sheet.

"Now choose your colors. Remember what we learned about with the color pencils regarding making different colors?" She nodded. "When you want to make a new color with paints, you take a dab of one and mix it with the other on the pallet." He mixed up an orange shade then brushed it over the wet page to make a soft splash of color on the pencil sketch. Henry added a little bit of burnt sienna to the shadow with just a dab of purple to reflect the color of the cloth on which the fruit was placed.

Anne watched for a little while then sprayed her own sheet with water. She mixed up her own orange and let the paper absorb the color. Then she laid down red for the apple with a bit more red in the shadow under the orange than Henry did. She watched as Henry left some spots uncolored so that he could create highlights and then put the color to her own painting. Every once in a while, Henry would stop and spray the paper when it dried out so they could keep the consistency of the paint uniform and flowing. They added the purple in the cloth then a light blue backdrop.

When the paintings were finished, Henry sat back and smiled at Anne. She had paint all over her, but she was smiling with an open mouth that threatened to split her face. "More!" she finally said.

Henry took the paintings off the wooden boards and got out more sheets. This time, he took a white cup and plate and put them on a green kitchen towel. He wanted to give her different shapes so that she could see how these items were shaded with the colors. They cleaned their brushes and drew the objects on the paper. Henry watched Anne learn the basics of watercolors, thinking to himself, *She's found her medium.* She seemed to enjoy it so much that they completed two more paintings. They spread the wet paper all over the room, making sure the door to the studio was shut to keep from getting paw prints on the paintings.

Then Anne started to draw something that wasn't set up. She drew what started out as a serpentine-like creature but soon emerged as a dragon with wide wings in the sky above a mountain. He sat up, his heart jumping, when he realized she may be recreating what she saw in her dreams. She sprayed the page after she had drawn the creatures then dipped her brush in yellow and then in a little brown, trying to create a golden color to apply to the creature.

Henry stood behind her and watched as the picture began to emerge of a dragon flying in the sky over mountains that reflected many colors. The dragon had small thin upper arms and longer rear legs, both with four toes ending in sharp claws. The face of the dragon was elongated but smooth, unlike traditional visages of dragons, on a stretched thin neck. The eyes were white with no pupils; and the nostrils were more like slits at the end of the lengthened snout, almost like a cat's nostrils. The wings were twice the size of the dragon's body with small bony supports covered by a membrane yet to be painted.

She sprayed the page with more water to get the maximum wetness on the paper over the wings then took a thin brush with barely any paint on it and made small lines of color in the membrane of the wings that were quickly absorbed into the water. She did this with several different colors, making the wings look like the rainbow of oil on water. She left the sun in the sky unpainted, the white of the paper as its color.

When she had finished the drawing, she stared at it, transfixed by the image. She held the smaller brush in her hand until Henry reached down, gently took it from her, and put it in the jar of water.

He put his hands on her shoulder then ran them down the top of her arm and back up to her neck. "Is this your dream?"

"Yes," she said, coming out of her almost trance-like state. "This is the good part before the fire."

Henry wasn't sure where to go with this. He didn't want to push her to talk about the fires, but he was encouraged that she was able to put something from her dreams into a visible representation. "It's a beautiful picture, Anne. Very pretty."

She reached up and touched his arm. "Like the dragon tattoo."

"Yes," he said, smiling. "Like my tattoo."

Anne turned around in her seat and picked up her brush. "I do more!"

"Hold your horses there, ma'am," he said, chuckling. "We need to take a break and get some food inside you. We've been painting for five hours now!" They went to the kitchen where Henry, with the help of Anne, who decided she wanted to learn to prepare food, made turkey sandwiches with avocado on multigrain bread. Chips, bottled water, and some of the fruit Henry had used for the still life completed their lunch.

"Tell me about the dragon tattoo," she asked him while they were eating.

He took a drink from his water. "I saw it in a dream when my mom died and somehow it made dealing with her loss a little easier. For some reason, the image gave me peace. I decided to make it permanent after that."

"I like the dragon on your arm," she replied.

Henry looked down at the tattoo on his bare arm as if seeing it for the first time. Then he shrugged and took a bite of his sandwich.

Heidi's name flashed on the caller ID when Henry's phone rang. His mouth was full, so he answered it, chewing in Heidi's ear for a few seconds before he got out a muffled "Hullo."

"Are you eating?" Heidi demanded.

"Yeth." Henry swallowed. "Yes. What's up?"

"You're a pig. You know that, right?"

Henry gave a loud belch in reply.

"Oh, gross! Can you watch the kids tonight without teaching them any of your bad habits? James and I want to go to a movie."

"Yes and no promises." Henry looked at the clock. "What time?"

"Can I bring them around six? I'll bring some movies Nattie wants to watch and pick up burgers for everyone."

"Make it pizza, and you've got a babysitter," Henry countered, pressing his advantage.

"What is it with you and pizza?"

"The only thing I like better than pizza is pizza that somebody else is paying for. It's especially tasty when that somebody is you."

"Fine. I'll get your stupid pizza."

"Don't forget the extra cheese," Henry reminded.

"Don't you forget to cut it up into small pieces so Nattie can eat it. The last time you fed her pizza, she ended up wearing more of it than she ate."

"Actually I think the dogs got most of it," Henry corrected.

"Whatever!" Heidi replied, exasperated. "The point is she has to eat. That's why I was going to get burgers with fries. At least she has a fighting chance."

"I'll make sure she eats. Will this be overnight?"

"If you don't mind."

"Oh, what do you two lovebirds have in mind?" Henry teased. "Late-night skinny-dipping in the pool? Kinky sex in front of a raging fire in the fireplace? Naughty role-playing in the bedroom involving costumes and restraints?"

"You need serious help, big brother. You know that, don't you?" Heidi interrupted. "And since you asked, the answer to your question is all of the above."

"WHAT!"

"None of your damn business is what! Besides, how do you think Nate and Nattie got here in the first place? I didn't buy them off eBay. Is six o'clock okay or not?"

"Yeah, that's fine. We'll see you in a little while, and don't forget the pizza." He ended the call and looked at Anne. "Heidi is bringing the kids over for us to watch. They're going to stay overnight. Won't that be fun?"

Anne smiled and nodded. He knew she loved being with the kids. They decided that there wasn't time for any more painting and spent their time until the kids came cleaning up the guest room and setting up the playpen that would serve as Nattie's crib. The kids had spent the night in the guest room before and seemed to do okay. Henry left the door open so he could hear if there were any problems. He wasn't too concerned about dividing his attention between Anne and the kids because of Charlie, his Golden Rottie. Charlie and Nathan had bonded the very first moment they met, and Charlie always slept curled up on the floor near Nathan during overnight stays and naps, protecting him like the good dog that he was. Henry pitied anyone who tried to get near either of the kids without Henry's okay. Must be the Rottweiler in him taking over the Golden Retriever, like Hyde did to Jekyll.

At six o'clock, Heidi and James knocked on the door and came in. James had Nattie in his arms with the diaper bag on his shoulder. Heidi had a small suitcase and two pizzas from Hungry Hals. Nathan trailed behind her. Heidi brought overnight diapers just to be prepared for any eventuality during the night or if her brother was asleep at the switch, the latter being the more likely scenario. "We're here!" she announced.

Henry and Anne came out of the guest room and greeted them with hugs and kisses. "What movie are you going to see?" Henry inquired.

"That new vampire movie," James said, putting Nattie down. "You know where the vamps come out in the daytime."

"Sounds like fun." Henry smirked. "What time will you pick the kids up tomorrow?"

"Ten o'clock?" Heidi suggested.

"Okay." Henry took the pies from Heidi, inhaling their aroma, and then turned just in time to see Nathan run to the studio door that was shut. "Wait, Nathan!" Henry shoved the pizzas into a startled Anne's hands then dashed over to distract Nathan from opening the door and letting the animals in to tromp all over the paintings.

Henry came back to the conversation with Nathan in tow to see Heidi hand several DVDs to Anne. "Here are a couple of movies for Nattie. She may not sit through the entire movie, but it will distract her for a little while."

"Okay," Henry said. "Have fun, guys. We'll be fine."

Heidi and James kissed the kids and left. "Nattie's movies," Anne said, handing the movies to Henry. "What is this one?" She pointed to the picture of a princess sleeping on a bed.

"*Sleeping Beauty*," Henry replied, putting the films near the television. "Do you want to see that one?"

"Yes." She smiled.

"Everyone, come eat while it's still hot," Henry called, getting plates and drinks from the kitchen. The kids ran to the dining room, followed by Anne, who placed the boxes on the table. Henry returned and put Nattie in a high chair he had on hand for her when she came over. Henry made good on his promise to cut up Nattie's food. After dinner, they went to the living room to watch the movie.

While Henry was putting the movie in the Blu-ray player, he unwittingly passed gas. Just as he had belched at his sister, he made no attempt at discretion and just let 'er rip, making an all-too-familiar sound.

Nathan looked up from his turtle figures. "What was that?" he demanded.

"Oh that? That's a duck that's been hiding in here somewhere. We can't find him."

Nathan stood with his little hands on his hips and a scowl on his face and retorted, "Ducks don't fart!"

Henry couldn't help but laugh as he fessed up. "You got me, Nathan. That wasn't a duck."

Anne smiled and said, "Quack! Ducks say 'quack'!"

"Yeah, and they don't stink either. Eeeeewww! Uncle Henry, gross!"

No promises, he reminded himself, just in case this got back to Heidi.

Nattie decided to join in and ran around the sofa, saying, "Quack! Quack! Quack!" Henry chased her around the living room flapping his arms like wings. "I'm gonna get the duck! I finally found the farting duck." Nattie giggled and squealed every time her uncle got close to catching her. Nathan decided he wanted to be a duck too, and eventually, all four of them ended up running around the room, quacking like ducks.

Soon they got tired of playing ducks, and Henry started the movie. From the moment it started, Anne was enthralled. She swayed to the music when the prince and princess danced together in the forest. She laughed at the fairies and almost cried when the princess fell under the sleeping spell. Henry just watched her instead of the movie, his eyes twinkling with the overwhelming feelings for her that were consuming his heart.

When the great black dragon reared up to fight the prince though, Anne started to have difficulty breathing and tried to hide in Henry's arms. He felt her heart pounding in her chest while he held her against him when the fear started to take over. Henry recognized what was happening and stopped the film, reassuring her that it was only a picture and not real. He explained that it was a drawing, like her paintings, and could not hurt her. He promised her that the dragon would be defeated in the end.

She took a deep breath and watched the rest of the movie, Henry's arm securely around her, until the prince slayed the dragon. He knew her fear lifted when the prince found his way to the princess to give her love's first kiss. When they danced at the end of the movie, her dress changing colors, she asked Henry what they were doing.

"Dancing," he explained.

"Show me."

Nattie had fallen asleep halfway through the movie on the sofa, and Nathan got bored and went to play with his turtle fighters. So Henry stood up, helped her to her feet, and then pushed the trunk out of the way. He put his arm around her back and took her hand.

"Put your hand on my shoulder," he instructed, "and follow what I do." He put his left foot forward. "You step back." Anne stepped back with her right foot. Then he stepped forward and to the right with his right foot. She followed, stepping back with her left. He slid his left foot to his right. Anne followed to the left. Finally, he slid his left foot back, followed by the right. She followed in a corresponding step.

"That's it, basically, but you do it to a beat. Like this. One, two, three," he counted, moving his feet. She moved with him, her steps the opposite from his, just like they walked through it. The movie was rolling through the credits, so they followed the beat of the music until the movie ended.

"That is dancing."

"I like dancing," she said, both of them sitting back on the sofa.

"Why did the prince give up his…chair?" she asked. Henry took the movie out of the Blu-ray player.

"Throne," Henry corrected.

"Throne. Why did prince give up throne for the princess?"

"Princess, that's right." He sat beside her on the sofa. "He did it because he loved her and wanted her more than he wanted the throne. He didn't know she was a princess until the end of the movie. But he ended up with both the princess and the throne in the end. All fairy tales have a happy ending."

"Did he not want…throne?"

"Yes," Henry replied. "He did. But he was willing to sacrifice it all to be with the woman he loved."

"What is 'sacrifice'?"

"Sacrifice," he explained, "is being willing to give up something you want for someone else. That is true love."

"What is love?"

Henry shook his head. He hoped she had forgotten about her question. "That is the big secret, my dear. What is love? Some people think it's the way you feel about someone else. Some people think it's what you do for someone else, or even what you really want. Some people believe love is sacrifice. There are many aspects to love. It depends on a lot of things." He shrugged. "It's difficult to give one answer to that."

"How do you know love?"

"Most people spend their entire lives looking for that answer. I don't know. I guess you know love when you find it. That really doesn't answer the question, but I think that's something every person has to answer for himself."

"Do you know love?" she asked.

Henry thought for a moment. "I did. Once." He was lost in memories that were chipping away at the barrier he had put up around his heart. He came back to the real world with Anne and took a deep breath. "With Heather. She was killed in an accident several years ago." He stood up and put the disc away in Nattie's bag. "Let's put Nattie to bed and see what Nathan's up to." He didn't want to open the door any more than it had started to open. He knew it would release the demons of Heather's death to haunt him during the night. It was enough to deal with Anne's nightmares.

That night was no exception, even with the children in the house. Anne did not scream but started thrashing and fighting with the sheets as if with the dragon in the movie, whimpering and breathing heavy, until Henry woke her up. He held on to Anne while she cried, thanking the stars above that the kids didn't wake up.

Henry lay awake for a long time after, staring up at the black ceiling while holding on to Anne. He didn't like what was happening to him since he found her. He'd done just fine for several years now, holding back his feelings after suffering through three deaths in only a few years. Three deaths, three stabs to his heart. But now, while he held Anne as she fought the demons in her dreams, he found he was fighting his own while awake.

First, the demons in his mind started with memories of the long hours spent in the hospital at his mother's bedside up until the time she passed. Henry hated hospitals—the way they smelled, the drab green paint on the walls, the doctors and nurses so overworked and understaffed. She wasn't a lost cause; she was his mother, damn it! Why couldn't they do something to help her?

He loved his mother and wanted to be there for her. He was, even though it tore at his heart to see her suffer day to day. You can only bring so many flowers, and you soon run out of things to talk about. So he just sat by her bedside, holding her hand and letting her know he was still there. He could vividly remember the exact moment when she slipped away. Even though he was blinded by tears and crushed by sorrow, he felt the slightest tinge of relief at knowing she was finally free of the pain, free of the waiting, free of the burden that she felt she was. Real love is a gift to be cherished every moment of every day, and it is never a burden; and to Henry, neither was she.

After joining the Navy following the death of his mother, he had hoped to move on with his life and put the pain behind him, but he couldn't. He missed his mother every day and replayed the hospital visits in his mind to see if there was more he could have done. He wondered every day if she was watching him from Heaven—back when he used to believe in such nonsense. Was she was proud of him or worried about him when he was in combat?

After reliving his mother's passing, the demons tormented him with the memory of the phone call informing him of Heather's death. Heather was like an answer to prayer——someone positive, loving, life-changing. She had always been an anchor from the time they were little kids. When he finally realized how much he loved her, he allowed himself to care again, to feel again, to dream again, and to love again.

Then while he stopped at a gas station for fuel on his way to Orlando, his cell phone rang and his world—his entire life—was turned upside down. He would never know what her answer would have been to his proposal. Unlike his mother, he didn't even get the chance to say good-bye. He not only lost the love of his life, his soulmate, best friend, and lover; he had lost his future—their future. It was ripped away in a heartbeat by some stupid drunk driver. The future of two people and who knows how many children they might have had together. Just gone.

As the tears started to form in his eyes, he clenched his lips together, determined he would not cry or let out the pain. He knew if he did, he couldn't put it back and it would overwhelm him. Right now, he needed to be there for Anne. He didn't need the distraction of his own nightmares to haunt them in the night.

Eventually the demons in his mind tired of haunting him and he finally drifted into sleep, unaware that something still lurked in the shadows around him in the darkened room.

18

I lie on my bed on the highest level of the crystal structure, made from bricks hewn out of the crystals in the mountain underneath the city. Kenta and I listen to the others of our kind who come before us with their concerns. We do not speak with audible sounds but with thoughts and images conveyed to each other.

We hear the concerns regarding our work of cultivating the crystal and building the crystal mountains and shelter spaces from our brethren. He rubs his head against mine ensuring us both that we act as one in our decisions. His massive wings cover me while we hold court under the watchful eye of the One. I am content to be with him with the heat of the white sun above us. We cannot mate, but he is close to my heart.

I try to follow Kenta when he flees into the water, his wings flaming and burning away the white membrane, but I cannot follow him. The black dragons hold me, and I cannot move. Kenta rushes down, but the water does not extinguish the fire that blankets him. It shines like a flower under the water as he goes deeper, but the fire does not go out. I reach out as if I can save him by my desire, but I cannot.

19

Venice Avenue

June 23
Tuesday

In the morning, James and Heidi picked up the kids shortly after breakfast. Uncle Henry had made their favorite pancakes and sausage and was getting pretty good at making them look like Mickey Mouse. Well, Mickey for Nathan and Minnie for Nattie. He used strawberry jelly to paint a bow on hers. He was grateful that they had slept through the night and through Anne's nightmares.

With the children gone, his sister and brother-in-law "satisfied" from the night before, Henry had Anne join him in his studio to continue their work. Henry focused on his illustrations and set Anne up with the watercolors she displayed so much talent with the day before.

Anne was creating a series of watercolors portraying the beautiful golden dragons in their daily life on the crystal mountains—swimming in green waters, lying on various structures, or soaring through the air. She told him that this was what she saw in her dreams. He marveled at her imagination and how masterfully her pieces were completed.

They worked up until lunch then decided they needed a break. Henry thought it would be nice to take Anne to Venice Avenue to visit the unique shops in the downtown section of Venice.

They drove down Venice Avenue, where the little shops painted in pastel colors, with weathered arches and glass windows, invited tourists and locals alike. Henry parked in an open space on the north side of the street; and together, they wandered into the unique shops, spending a lot of time in the Treasures of the Sea shop where Anne picked up several small shells to add to those she and Nathan found at Caspersen and a few larger ones as well that were intricate in design and colors. She wanted to know what each shell was called and made sure to inspect every one of the dozens of bins in the shop. Henry especially enjoyed watching her when she asked the clerk about the names of practically each and every shell. The poor girl was trying to keep up with Anne, who was so excited about her prizes that even with her limited vocabulary, she chattered like a roomful of monkeys. Henry was surprised she was able to breathe through all her questions. It was also nice that someone else was answering her never-ending queries for a change instead of him, although he did feel her pain and sympathized.

When they finally left the Treasures of the Sea shop, they stopped for lunch at a unique little restaurant specializing in fifty different varieties of oversized stuffed baked potatoes. Henry asked Anne about her pictures while eating his potato smothered in broccoli and melted cheddar cheese. Anne was enjoying a ham and Swiss, almost as big as her head, and she was doing a good job devouring it.

"So you see these dragons in your dreams? What is it about them that causes your nightmares? The dragons look beautiful."

"It is not golden dragons. It is black ones, like the princess movie. I do not paint them."

"Why do the black dragons upset you so much?"

"They come…kill…with fire." She stopped eating her potato, the spoon just resting in her hand.

Henry took her other hand to comfort her. "It's okay, Anne. Take your time. Tell me. What do you see?"

"I see dragons burn in fire…I hear little ones crying! I feel them…They are dying!" Her eyes began to fill with tears, and her hands were shaking.

"Who's dying?"

"The others, the golden dragons! All dying! I feel the fire!"

"Anne," Henry asked. "Do you think someone you loved died in a fire but maybe you escaped?"

She hesitated, trying to find the strength and words to answer. "I…I do not know. I feel fire in my dream, but not here." She pointed to her head, and Henry could see the frustration in her expression.

Henry wondered why her dreams were about dragons and exactly what happened to her that caused her to manifest these dragons? He didn't want to push her and upset her anymore, so he stood up and said, "Let's go check out some more shops. Maybe we can find some different shells, okay?" Anne just flashed a weak smile and stood up. Neither of them were able to finish their lunch, having lost their appetites, so they left Double Stuffed Spud Hut to continue on their hunt for unique oddities along Venice Avenue. Henry hoped to restore their good mood along the way.

The rest of the afternoon passed by pleasantly enough. Anne's mood indeed improved with every shop they visited. Henry never grew tired of the innocent wonder and amazement she felt toward everything and everyone around her. She wasn't as chatty and hardly asked any questions at all; instead, she just observed and watched, soaking everything in. For a while, they just sat on the edge of a fountain and people-watched skateboarders, surfers, countless girls in bikinis, people on bikes, dogs, and children.

When Henry's arms couldn't hold even one more bag and Anne's feet couldn't take one more step, Henry felt it was a good time to go home. Shortly after leaving his parking space, he realized just how tired and hungry he was from walking and shopping all afternoon. He decided it would be nice to treat Anne for dinner at his favorite steak house nearby.

Henry drove up to a building he told her was a place where they would eat, and then he helped her out of the car. Anne was confused as to why Henry let a man drive off with his car. Once inside, she was overwhelmed with the delicious aromas. Combined with the sight of the flames as they flared when the meat was turned and the sizzling sound of a fresh piece of beef hitting the grill, her mouth was already salivating.

She was about to sit at an empty table when Henry stopped her and told her they would have to wait until the lady he called a hostess seated them. Henry said, "Party of two, please," to a very nicely dressed woman standing behind a tall little table. She greeted them and led them to a table not far from the pit, where Anne watched men dressed all in white, wearing very tall hats, pile on slabs of meat in varying sizes. Once seated, she marveled at all the elegant silverware, dishes, and glasses laid out on a beautiful white cloth.

Throughout the entire meal, Anne was amazed at the number of people that came and served her food. She said thank you to everyone—from the hostess to the people who brought out their dishes, to the people who took away their dishes, to the young boy that kept their water glasses full, to the very nice man that stopped by to say hello and asked if everything was satisfactory with their meal, to the tall gentleman with a towel draped over his arm who kept asking Henry if he wanted more wine. She hugged the woman in the ladies room who handed her a towel because she was so excited. It was such a treat, except when Henry limited her to only one glass of wine. He said he didn't know her tolerance and didn't want to find out tonight. As it turned out, she really liked the wine, and it somehow made her feel even happier.

After dinner, Henry gave the piece of paper back to the man who took his car, and he went running off and brought it back. He then dashed around the car and held the door open for Anne, who continued to be astonished at how helpful everyone was.

On the ride home, Henry didn't bring up the dreams again. Maybe he would tomorrow, but he thought they'd made some progress tonight, so he'd let it go. It had been a pleasant evening, and poor

Anne would probably suffer through another nightmare before the night was over, so there was no point in sending her to bed already worked up.

Back home, Anne went through all the bags from the Venice Avenue shops, mentally cataloging all her new treasures, while Henry distributed the bag of steak bones he got from the restaurant to some very happy dogs. Not wanting the cats to feel left out, he gave them all a generous helping of treats. "Sorry, guys, restaurants only have doggie bags, not kitten bags," he said in jest. Then the two of them retired to the sofa to watch a little TV and to digest and relax a bit until bedtime. They both enjoyed just being with each other and letting the worries of the night wait for a little while.

Hours later, Anne's nightmares did indeed return, and Henry held her tight until she stopped shaking. It was their nightly routine now, not unlike brushing their teeth or letting the dogs out. It was almost as if her nightly torments were a part of her. Henry was able to tell when the nightmares started by her movements and tried to be proactive, holding her tight before she started screaming. Although she didn't scream out as often, there was nothing he could do to stop the nightmares from coming.

Later that night after Anne finally went back to sleep, Henry thought he might be dreaming when he saw a shadow darken the bedroom window, temporarily blocking the moonlight from shining into the room. He blinked, and the shadow vanished. He could have sworn something, or someone, was there and then gone. It was hours later before he drifted off into a very uneasy sleep.

20

Saphan, the Other, had chosen numerous mates who have born many offspring before succumbing to the evil he now embraced. Some of his sons follow him, in blind loyalty to their father, in part, but mainly because they share his lust for power and blood. The rest of his children are cared for by their mothers, and most of them play with the other young dragons in the cool green waters. I am the only child of the One, taken straight from his heart. I am unique among our kind.

The Other's shadow casts an inky silhouette of death as he descends from the sky, leading his army of black dragons to slaughter all in their path. He is different now, changed, no longer beautiful and graceful as he once was. Now his outward appearance mimics the cold black heart that beats beneath his massive chest. He is colossal in height and width and much larger than any dragon ever known. His red eyes burn with the fire of hatred against all whom he once loved. The mountain crumbles at his roar, sending shards of crystal rocks crashing down to crush the golden dragons' dwellings below, killing all inside. His sons, like all that follow him, are as black as night, but none equal in size or cruelty. All of them spew fire from their mouths from behind razor teeth. The Other takes great pleasure in burning his former mates and laughs as he rips open the bellies of his inferior offspring, spilling their entrails on the ground before setting them ablaze. His mates cry out to him to stop the fire and spare the children, but his laughter drowns out their screams. With a sickening smile, he turns and takes to the skies, leaving them to suffer a slow and agonizing death. Not one shred of compassion or pity remains in this soulless beast as he continues to hunt and destroy all of the golden dragons.

21

The Black Dragon

June 24
Wednesday

Everything felt better in the morning's bright light while they ate a light breakfast of bagels, cream cheese, and coffee. When finished, Henry and Anne went straight to the studio and got to work. Henry headed to his latest illustration of how to properly insert a midline catheter, while Anne took her place at the new table and chair Henry had set up for her. She started to take out her watercolors because she enjoyed that medium more than any other. Henry noticed that there was something about the flow of colors in the water that had a soothing effect on her. She told him that she also felt more connected to each piece, as if her creativity were flowing through her directly onto the paper. That bond was not quite as strong with a pencil.

Today, however, she forewent the watercolors, took out the jar of pencils, and started to sketch out a figure. Henry looked up from his work, noticing how heavily Anne was breathing and the ferocity with which she was drawing. The form of this object was beginning to emerge dragon-like in appearance, although much larger than any of the golden dragons she had previously painted or sketched. This creature had long feet with sharp claws and large pointed ears with hard ridged edges. She switched to a 9B pencil to scratch in the tone of the object, which was black, as black as she could make it. For the eyes, she choose a blood-red colored pencil, making them look so evil that when she completed them, Henry saw her visibly shudder. For its large snarling mouth, she selected a lighter pencil, a 7H, and shaded in long teeth with the lighter gray hue. Its wings were massive and covered with a gray membrane from the same pencil she used on the teeth. Anne used varying shades of red, orange, and yellow to create the flames of the fire exploding from its maw.

Her hand was a blur, scratching back and forth, up and down on the page, tearing through the paper onto the sheet beneath. Tears formed in her eyes, and her breathing now came in deep rasps, but she pushed through to complete the drawing, pressing hard with the pencils as if to punish the paper. Henry had never seen her like this before, and even though he was deeply concerned, he felt it best to let her be while she worked through this.

When she finished, she sat back panting and shaking, wiping away the tears with the back of her hands. Henry let her take her time to gain her composure, and when she was ready, she went up to him and thrust the drawing into his hands. "Fire," she said through clenched teeth. "What I see."

Henry raised his eyebrows, taking in the drawing. He took a deep breath. "Fire," he repeated. "Wow! That is one mean looking son of a...Ahem, no wonder you're having nightmares! This bad boy would keep Stephen King up at night. Damn!" He put the drawing back on the table and asked her, "You still have no idea what these images mean or where they came from?"

Anne shook her head. "I do not know. I see them always when I have the bad dream."

Henry sat back in his chair and sighed. He picked up the drawing again and studied it, with his thumb supporting his chin and index finger stretched across his lips, thinking, pondering, hoping for the damn answer fairies to finally show up. "Well, if we can ever figure that out, we may finally know what happened to you." He looked back at Anne and could tell his frustration was stressing her out even more, and that certainly wasn't helping her disposition any. He placed the drawing facedown on the table and put his hand on her shoulder. "Let's work on something different now. How is your painting of the little dragons coming?"

Anne put the sketchbook away and turned to her board, where an unfinished picture of several tiny golden dragons was tacked down. The little dragons were swimming on the surface of the green water and appeared to be chasing each other in circles while the silver fish jumped over their backs. Anne pulled the watercolors back out, sprayed the paper to refresh the water on the page, and squeezed her colors onto the small "egg" tray. Henry critiqued her painting and made a few minor suggestions, but overall, he had very high praise for her work. He then turned his attention back to his catheter illustration, which he needed to complete today to make his deadline. He was filled with renewed hope knowing that Anne had a breakthrough today, bridging the gap between her unconscious and conscious mind. He knew that something opened up that might help him find the answers to who Anne really was and what happened to her, leaving her so traumatized that she had no memories at all of her life before he found her.

They worked straight through into the late afternoon, stopping only once for a quick lunch. Anne finished the illustration of the little dragons, and Henry completed and forwarded his illustration, confident Elliott would be pleased with his work. With the work done, Henry suggested they go out for an early dinner and maybe see a movie. He wondered if Anne had ever been to a movie theater.

They ate a light dinner at a small bar and grill close to the Metroplex, leaving room for popcorn and candy. Soon after, they arrived at the theater, and Henry bought tickets for the latest animated feature about a princess and her sister in a frozen land with talking snowmen, hoping that the escape from reality would help Anne recover from reliving her black dragon nightmare. Once inside the lobby, Anne's sweet innocence kicked in as she stared and pointed at all the different movie posters and displays with wide-eyed wonder. Of all the moments they had shared together, Henry cherished these the most. He loved the purity of these moments when she was totally open, unguarded, and relaxed. Most of all, it was times like these that he felt she trusted him completely.

After securing the biggest tub of popcorn Anne had ever seen along with, of course, some chocolate, they settled into their seats and let the cares of the day slip away with every frame that flashed by. True to form, Anne immersed herself into the story that unfolded, crying and laughing with the characters as if the scenes before her were her own life.

Seeing how much Anne was enjoying the movie, Henry resolved to take her to Orlando sometime to meet some real, live princesses. He realized that by making that commitment, he was taking a bold step toward leaving part of his past behind. Heather's memory haunted him to this day, and to take Anne to the place he was going to propose to his former fiancée would take great courage on his part, an act of love. Henry had never met anyone like Anne, and to be honest, he really didn't want to meet anyone different. The connection he felt that first moment on the beach was growing stronger with every beat of his heart.

Damn it! Can't we ever get a break? Henry screamed inside his head when Anne shrieked and thrashed from what must have been her worst nightmare yet. Henry held her in his arms and repeatedly kissed her tear-streaked face in between the words that leapt from his heart like a wild animal caged and finally free. "Anne, sweetheart, everything will be all right." Each kiss more passionate than the last. "I'm here, Anne. I will always be here." His tears mingled with hers. Anne began kissing him back, pressing close against him. Finally, their mouths met, and Henry's mind exploded with the same sensation when he first saw her, only stronger.

Henry surrendered to the moment and allowed his body to follow his heart. They began to caress and explore each other, Henry taking his time to allow his experience to guide Anne, her body becoming fully alive for the first time. Part of Henry felt unworthy of such a beautiful woman, winning her innocence and her heart, but somehow he knew it was meant to be; they were meant to be. He could sense Anne was close to crossing the threshold into womanhood, secretly hoping he could extinguish the fires in her dreams and ignite the fires in her heart. Henry was pleased that Anne was totally immersed in this new sensation, her body yielding to the inevitable. The two of them collapsed into each other's arms.

He gently rubbed up and down her arms and then moved his hand to her stomach and up to her breasts. He wanted to go slowly to give her time to understand what was happening and to protest if she wanted, but she moved in rhythm to the ministrations of his hand, which found its way down to her legs, caressing her thighs.

"Anne," he breathed, his hand warm on her leg. "Are you okay? Do you want me to stop?"

"No," she said. "Do not stop."

He didn't.

"Henry," she whispered while he freed them both of their garments. "Is this love?" Finally free to explore all of him, she touched him, feeling the effect her fingers caused, learning with her hands what her eyes had seen. They both took their time discovering each other through touch, taste, and scent.

"Yes…it's one way…of saying love," he said between kisses to her neck then down to her breasts.

He had a momentary panic attack when he realized just how quickly their relationship was moving, but like a man about to jump off a cliff in a hurricane, he was unable to stop it. His lips followed where his hands had gone, and other parts found their way in the darkness. She made a sound when the barrier was broken, then found the movement of the two of them together to be a different kind of fire, one that did not leave her crying but chased the fires and the tears of the previous nights away.

After, they lay silently together, still locked in their embrace for a long while and enjoying the momentary reprieve from the demons that haunted them. Henry felt a weight had been lifted off his shoulders, freeing him from a lingering doubt he didn't even know was there. His thoughts turned to Heather, and instead of guilt, he felt a great peace about his love for her. He hadn't replaced his love for her with another; he simply allowed himself to move on. His love for her would always be there as a memory tucked away in a special place in his heart.

He gently kissed Anne on the top of her head, which was lying on his chest, thinking of the enormity of the step their relationship just took. Softly, he whispered the words, "I love you."

Henry dived headfirst off the cliff into the churning waters below.

Somewhere around three o'clock, Henry was woken by the dogs barking, sounding the alarm. He threw off the covers, pulled his shorts on, and grabbed the Browning 1911 .45 caliber pistol and flashlight he kept in his nightstand drawer. He pulled the slide back on the gun with a loud snap, chambering a round, and told Anne to stay put. He rushed to the kitchen where all the dogs were gathered, scratching at the back door. Henry joined them, patting Charlie and Sam on the head, and then threw open the back door. To his surprise, neither dog ran out. After sniffing the evening air, they began to whine and cower. *What the hell has gotten into them?* Taking one step out of the door, he closed it behind him and examined the lock and door jam. He did not see any evidence of an attempt to jimmy the lock or pry the door open.

Assuming any intruder would have been scared off by the dogs, he decided to walk slowly around the entire house, pistol in his right hand, flashlight in his left. All the windows were intact, and there were no footprints in the soft earth beneath them. He moved his search to the back fence and scanned the pond behind the yard. Everything was eerily quiet and still, as if nature itself was holding its breath waiting for something to happen. Finding nothing, he headed back to the house. As he opened the back door, he thought he saw a shadow move out of the corner of his eye and spun around, pointing his gun. But there was no one there. Just as he shut the door behind him, he could swear he heard what sounded like the flapping of giant wings taking flight.

22

I sit at the feet of the One as the Other comes before Him, demanding that I be given to him as his mate. The One replies that I am forbidden to mate. The Other becomes angry and swears he will not obey the One anymore. The sons of the Other shout out in agreement. No one has ever challenged the One before! We live in peace and honor each other and the One. We do not know of the hatred the Other speaks of.

The Other contends that he should be ruler and leaps at the One. The One lashes back, and they fly into the air, biting and raking at each other with their long, sharp claws. The other dragons watch as control of our world is decided—some in horror, some in glee. The battle rages above, the blood of both dropping on me like rain from the wounds each inflicts on the other.

The One finally throws the Other to the earth and crashes down on him, taking the Other's neck in his teeth, ready to crush it. But the One loves his brother and cannot kill him. He tells the Other he must leave and take his sons with him or he will kill them all. The Other is badly wounded and slinks away in defeat to the black mountains with his sons behind him. I fly to the One to lick his wounds, his golden blood flowing from many places.

23

Let's Write a Book

June 25
Thursday

Henry was enjoying his new life with Anne, or should he say his renewed life with Anne. The two of them spent their days together painting, swimming, or exploring and learning new things. Anne's insatiable thirst for knowledge combined with her childlike enthusiasm for learning was as infectious as it was inspirational. As intelligent as Henry was, he didn't know everything, so together they made each day count by learning or experiencing something new.

Their nights together were an entirely different matter. The time they spent in each other's arms was indescribable. The love they expressed through their passion for each other was inexhaustible and boundless. Everything would have been perfect if not for those damn dragon dreams that terrorized his beloved each and every night. He was determined to find the meaning of these winged manifestations, and he was convinced that the key to that mystery was to uncover their root cause. There had to be something in Anne's past that triggered these demons haunting her dreams. He visited several online sites on psychology and dream interpretation to try to find some answers. His efforts bore little fruit.

There was one positive ray of sunshine that came out of her dreams: Anne's paintings of the golden dragons. She had created quite the body of work, and numerous paintings were piling up, each more detailed and beautiful than the last. Henry noticed each painting had something different to say. Anne's subconscious mind was reaching out through her art. Henry hoped that if he could help Anne focus on the positive and try to get her to talk about what she had brought to life through her art, it might give them some insight to what was really troubling her.

"Anne," Henry called to get her attention, "why don't we write our own storybook?"

"Write?" Anne replied, intrigued.

"Yeah, like those story books of Nathan's we read when you were first learning about, well, everything I guess, the ones with all the drawings and illustrations, remember? We could use your paintings and tell our own story. Wouldn't that be fun?"

Anne squealed and threw her arms around Henry's neck and squeezed. In between repeated kisses to his face, Henry said, "I'll take that as a yes." Prying himself loose, he retrieved his laptop and had Anne spread many of her paintings out on the floor in front of the wall that was already covered with them. Anne leaned against his side with her head on his shoulder, watching the words magically appear along the screen as Henry typed.

"Okay," Henry began. "Let's see if we can spice up the standard introduction just a tad.

> Once upon a time, in a realm far away, lived a peaceful race of golden dragons who resided on a crystal mountain.

Their eyes perused the vast selection of paintings on display before them. Anne pointed to one painting showing the dragons lying on the various heights of shelves on the crystal structure on top of the mountain. In her excitement, she took a quick shallow breath, leapt to her feet, and scurried over to snatch it down off the wall. Holding it up, Henry nodded his approval and motioned for her to bring it over. He typed the description on his laptop to later add to that painting.

Anne picked up another one where the dragons were flying in the white sky.

> They flew high and soared over mountains of crystal, across a sky where a white sun shone bright.

Anne picked up one of the smaller dragons playing in the water.

They swam in the green ocean, where they dove to catch silver fish.

"Dragons eat fish not soo-she" flashed across Henry's memory. He smiled.

Next, she chose the painting with the two dragons, one with iridescent wings on the top shelf of the crystal structure. Henry got his wish. Anne was guiding the story, and he was eagerly following her bread crumbs, hoping they would lead them to some answers.

They were ruled by a good king.

"Wait, what do we name him?"

"The king?"

"Well, yes. But now that I think about it, are we just calling the dragons 'dragons'?"

"*Thraekenya*. That is what they are called. They are the Thraekenya."

"That's pretty," Henry said. "Now what will we call our king?"

"Aesmay."

"Where did you get that name from?"

Anne shrugged. "I do not know. I just know it."

"Okay."

The Thraekenya were ruled by the good King Aesmay.

"That's a good start anyway. Are we going to include the black dragons at some point?"

"Yes," Anne said hesitantly. "They are the story."

"Okay, what do we want to call the black dragons?"

"They are *Tannen*. One time, they were like Thraekenya, but they did not want to stay under Aesmay, the good king."

"You have quite an imagination, Anne," Henry commented. "How do you come up with those names?"

"I feel they are right names," she answered. "I hear them in my head but do not know them."

Good! I think we're actually making progress.

"So the black dragons are the Tannen." Henry resumed typing. "Before we get to the attack, we have to build up the story. How about let's make up a leader of the Tannen. That might help with the 'history' of our dragon world."

"Saphan. He is Saphan, brother to Aesmay."

"So, Saphan and Aesmay were brothers?"

"Yes."

"Okay, so we can use a Cain and Abel approach."

"Cain and Abel?"

"Yes. Cain and Abel were brothers, but Cain killed his brother, Abel, when God found his sacrifice more pleasing. It's in a book called the Holy Bible," Henry voiced in what had to be the worst Charlton Heston impression in all recorded history.

"Why did Cain kill Abel?" Anne looked at him, frowning.

"Well, Cain was jealous of his brother and got angry. A lot of the stories in the Bible are about people doing stupid things. Tell me more about Saphan and Aesmay, so I can see if I can tie them to Cain and Abel." Henry stopped typing, more interested in where the story was going.

"Aesmay was king. Saphan was his brother but did not like Aesmay to be king. He and others got angry and tried to take the mountain."

"Okay, that's good. Do we want to make Saphan change into a black dragon, or should he start out that way?"

"He was a golden one once. Then he turned into a black dragon and killed Aesmay. His body changed."

"Changed? How did it change?" Henry was intrigued with where this story would go. "So he physically changed and then killed his brother? This is more like Cain and Abel than I thought." Henry's heart was racing. Had Anne witnessed a murder, her own father, perhaps?

"He was more like my drawings and paintings. His skin was hard with scales, and his wings were dark. He had fire breath now and was bigger, stronger. His eyes were red, not white like Aesmay's."

"You know what changed about him, but do you know *how* he got like that?"

"No. Aesmay sent him away, and he was changed when he came back."

"Anything else?"

"He could not talk with his mind anymore and had to talk like we do. And he could not make things move with his thoughts but had to use his hands."

"So the golden dragons are telepathic and telekinetic."

"What is tele...kine...tic?"

"Being able to move objects with your mind. So once the black dragons left, they lost their abilities. But why did they change shape?"

"Their body was...twisted...Is that the right word? They changed."

"Okay." Henry typed up what they had just talked about. "We need to think about where we go from there. So Saphan grew angry because he was not king, and Aesmay sent him away. And the golden dragons lived their lives until what?"

"Saphan came back with the others out of the sky with the fire. Then he killed Aesmay and..." She stopped.

"Is this too hard for you? Is this the nightmare?" Henry touched her leg where she was sitting next to him.

"It is hard, but I will tell you."

Henry stopped typing. This was the basis of her nightmares, and he wanted to pay close attention to every detail she told him, hoping to find out the reasons why these images haunted her.

She took a couple of deep breaths to give her the courage to continue. "I am called Aeya in my dreams, the daughter of Aesmay."

"Wait, you're his daughter?" This might be the breakthrough he'd been looking for. She just revealed her father and uncle. If they really existed at all, that is.

"Yes, Saphan hated Aesmay because he would not let Saphan have Aeya."

"Well, this is a children's book, so we might want to leave that part out. So there was a woman—female—involved, very interesting. What happens next?"

"I see the sky open, and Saphan and the others come back. They have fire breath, and I see the others burn. I feel them, all of them, even the little ones, burn and die! Everything about them is different, their teeth, their claws, their size, all bigger, sharper, so the golden dragons are..."

"Powerless, helpless," Henry suggested.

"Yes, powerless. They cannot stop the black dragons. They cannot run from them, and many are ripped apart before being burned. The little ones are stomped on or even swallowed in one bite. Then there is the darkness, and I scream."

"We can stop if you want," Henry took her hand.

"No." She shook her head. "I will try." She took a few deep breaths.

"The sky opens, and the black dragons come down with fire in the..." She went to the drawing of the black dragon and pointed to fire coming from its mouth. "Fire comes from their mouths. I am with another dragon called Kenta, like you and I are together, but he does not make love to Aeya. No one is allowed to. Kenta protects and watches over me. He tries to shield me from their fire breath, and I hear his cries when I watch him burn. They burn all the golden dragons until none are left but me. I see their bodies become black from the flame and hear their screams."

"Wow," Henry exclaimed.

"In my dream, Saphan comes for me. He tells me he will take me. When the golden dragons are all gone, I am covered with darkness. That is when I wake. There is nothing after that."

"Wow, wow, wow!" Henry was stunned. "I am so sorry, honey. I never imagined it was that bad."

Anne had never relived her dreams while awake. In fact, it was quite the opposite. He knew that she always tried to slam the door in her mind shut and lock it up tight, desperately hoping it would never open again. But every night, something compelled her back across the threshold, plunging her into the world of the golden dragons and, eventually, into the nightmares. She could not hold back the tears and buried her head into Henry's chest and sobbed.

Henry held her tight and softly kissed the top of her head. Despite the moment, he couldn't help but smell the fragrance of her hair. His thoughts mingled with her scent, and together, they swirled in his head. Only time would tell if Anne facing her fears and unburdening her heart like this would help or make things worse. Either way, it was good that he had a better understanding of what she was going through.

Time to switch gears and get the day back on a more positive note.

He gently pushed her back at arm's length, kissing her forehead along the way, and brushed away a tear from her cheek. Smiling, he said, "That's enough for today, don't you think? Let's do something a little more lighthearted. You get to choose. Anything you would you like to do?"

"Beach!" she shouted.

"Beach it is. Come on, let's pack a lunch and grab our suits."

Soon they were packed up and headed to North Jetty Park in Nokomis to watch the boats come in through the channel. True to form, Anne was excited to see all the different kinds of boats, some big, some small, sailing through the rock-lined channel into the harbor beyond. The seagulls would take flight every time a horn blew or a bell rang, adding to the spectacle. Later, Henry took her down to the harbor where they met a nice older couple named Ron and Betty White, who were willing to take them out on their small sailboat for a small fee.

The sun was out, and with the wind in their sails, they were miles out on the ocean in no time, the shore a dark line along the horizon. Anne was beaming the entire time, looking as beautiful as ever with the wind blowing back her golden tresses along with her cover-up. Mr. White turned a brilliant shade of red when Mrs. White caught him staring.

Henry tried to teach Anne the difference between port and starboard, and for once, she had a hard time learning something new. Henry told her the trick to remember is port and left have the same number of letters in each. Not having any formal teaching in reading and writing other than with Henry, at least not any that she remembered, that information didn't help her much. To her, right was right and left was left; those were hard enough to remember. Stars were in the sky, not on boards.

After a while, Ron stopped the boat and lowered the sails so Anne and Henry could go for a swim. Together they dove off the *right* side of the boat and swam in the deep ocean while Mr. and Mrs. White watched from the deck smiling, remembering when they were that young.

Henry took Anne out a little farther into the water, swimming out several meters from the boat and enjoying the freedom that swimming in the open water gave him. When they got to a certain point, they raced each other back to the boat. Somehow, Anne always won those races; and if the truth were known, it was because Henry enjoyed the view from second place. Besides, it made his girl happy, and it was the gentlemanly thing to do.

After they boarded, Mrs. White handed each of them a towel and offered them a soft drink while Mr. White hoisted the sails and headed back to shore. Anne told the Whites about a pod of dolphins she saw swimming off in the distance. The joy she found in the little things made Henry smile, and he breathed a silent breath of relief that his attempt to raise her spirits was working out so well. She had an unquenchable love of life that infected everyone around her. Even the Whites couldn't stop from smiling.

The gentle rocking of the boat as it neared the shore helped them both to relax and allowed the cares of the day to drift away with the tide. The sun made its daily descent, leaving behind a sky filled only with clouds of ever-changing colors and seagulls calling out their farewells to the day. All they cared about was scanning the heavens and taking it all in. Happily, there was not a dragon in sight.

Back in their berth in the harbor, there were hugs all around as Henry and Anne said good-bye to their new friends. Henry thanked them when they got off the boat but only after they promised to come see the Whites again and their little sailboat. It was already dark by the time they left the park, stopping to pick up sandwiches to eat when they got home.

But when they finally went to sleep, the dragon fires returned. Henry held Anne tightly in his arms as she shook, and when she awoke and turned to him, a different kind of fire consumed them.

24

There is peace on the mountain since the Other is banished. But the One is sad. I know he misses his brother and did not want to force him to leave our mountain. I try to snuggle against him to let him know that I am here.

The sky explodes! The Other returns! He is no longer a defeated golden dragon but fills the sky with his massive wings and large nostrils that smoke. The Other lands in front of the One and roars his defiance while the other black dragons attack and burn our kind. The Other has a long sharp crystal in his claws, and I scream when he takes the crystal and plunges it into the One's body. The One falls to the ground, the Other stabbing him over and over! Hard claws grab me, digging their sharpness into my skin, holding me, cutting me! I reach out to my creator and watch him bleed golden blood that flows down to wash over my feet. With his remaining strength, he exhales his last breath toward me. I want to fly to him, but I am thrown to the ground and covered in darkness.

25

Dr. Rayback

June 26
Friday

The next day, Henry dropped Anne off at Heidi's house while he went to talk to his psychologist friend, Dr. Angela Rayback. Henry and Angela were friends in college when he went back to finish his senior year. Angela was in her second year. During the first semester of a shared English literature class, Angela's mother passed away. Henry helped Angela at her weakest time, and they spent many evenings studying together, and a little more. They understood their shared grief and found consolation in each other. It was a mutual arrangement, no strings, no commitments, friends-with-benefits type of thing. Henry hadn't seen Angela since he graduated.

Angela's assistant showed him to her office where Angela greeted him with a hug.

"Hello, Henry," she said. "So nice to see you again! You're looking good." Angela was in her early thirties with shoulder-length brown hair and blue eyes. "Can I get you something to drink?"

"Water would be fine," Henry said as he walked into her office. Angela's office was done in a nautical décor with dark paneled wood on the walls. Nautical lanterns served as the light fixtures, and the furniture was rich brown leather pieces. Angela's antique desk was made of oak, with panels set in the side surrounded by raised frames.

All around the office were items from the sea; shells, some large, like the pink conch shell on the end table, to baskets filled with smaller, intricately designed shells. Over the couch was a framed copy of Ivan Aivazovsky's *The Ninth Wave*. Henry loved that painting, feeling like one of the survivors holding on to the raft in the fury of the sea while the hope of a new day rises above the turmoil, like a sail of a ship heading in to the wind. Behind her desk, Angela had a model of a three-masted barque ship, exquisitely made with minute details, including complete rigging and separate sails.

Angela came back and handed Henry a bottle of water and then sat behind her desk. "Now tell me about Anne."

"Well, I found her almost a month ago on Venice Beach. She was naked and scared and couldn't talk to me or understand anything I was saying to her. It was really kind of freaky. She didn't seem to know how to do anything, almost like she was a newborn baby. She didn't even know how to control her bladder!"

"Really?" Angela exclaimed.

"But," he continued, "the most amazing thing about her is her ability to pick things up quickly. She learns at an astounding rate! We only have to show her something once, and she could do it. She's learned to talk, to take care of herself, even to swim. And then there is her art. I've never seen anything like it! She just watched me for a little while, and then she picked up a pencil and drew as if she had years of training! She really is the most amazing person I've ever known!"

"Tell me about the nightmares, Henry. You seemed very concerned about that. You said they happen every night?"

"Every single night."

"And she remembers them?"

"That's the strange thing, the thing that brought me to you today. She can remember every detail about the dreams, including the names of the dragons, but she has no memory whatsoever of her life before I found her. Nothing! I don't understand how that can be."

"Well," Angela began, "severe trauma can cause memory loss, but I've never heard of a case this severe where there is no memory at all. There is a possibility she suffered a physical injury, which may have caused some type of amnesia. I suggest you get her checked out by a physician to be sure."

"I think that's a good idea," Henry agreed. "I'll call Dr. Jackson and set something up." He continued. "Fire is a recurring theme in her dreams. I think she may have been in a fire at some point. And there is something about breathing underwater. My best guess is that she may have been on a boat that caught fire and was thrown into the sea. But what do the dragons in her dream represent?"

"Being in a fire can certainly qualify as a traumatic event, which can cause posttraumatic amnesia. If there was any brain injury, it could cause neurological amnesia. This could be a type of retrograde amnesia, although I would think it would have had to be a severe injury or a large tumor or swelling to cause the extent of loss we are talking about. Any of those disorders have other symptoms, often severe and very obvious. If she's not experiencing any pain, slurred speech, or loss of equilibrium, it's a safe bet we can rule that out.

"Another rare type of amnesia is called dissociative amnesia, and it stems from emotional shock or trauma, such as being the victim of a violent crime. With this disorder, a person may lose personal memories and autobiographical information, but usually only briefly." She put her hands up in surrender. "We can't even attempt a diagnosis until she has been examined by a medical doctor.

"As to why she dreams about dragons, there could be many reasons. Jung believed that dreams of dragons represented the danger of the newly acquired consciousness being swallowed up again by the instinctive psyche, the unconscious. It could be that subconsciously, her past life is fighting against her life as she perceives it now, trying to reestablish itself. Who she was before you found her could be much different than who she is now, for example.

"Freud has a slightly different outlook, believing the dragon symbolized 'the Great Mother' and that fighting the dragon could mean she is trying to break away from her upbringing. There may have been things in her past so horrific that she is trying to escape them. Perhaps an abusive parent, but again, the extent of her memory loss, to regress to the point of a newborn, is puzzling.

"There's yet another theory that dreams of being attacked by a dragon may be one's own basal impulses or overcoming an unconscious need for destructive behavior that she may have engaged in before the memory loss.

"These are all popular theories about why people dream about dragons, but it is difficult to know without spending time with her to try to draw out some of those memories. The point though is that these dreams are representations of something in her past and shouldn't be taken literally. And we certainly don't want to overanalyze them. You stated that Anne has a very vivid imagination. That may be why her mind creates such fantastic and detailed dreams to deal with whatever trauma underlies them. But I think it's clear there's something in her past trying to make its way out, whether it be from a very traumatic event or medically based.

"I would encourage you to have her continue with the story and her pictures. Having her tell the story to you along with creating the paintings is a way to get those repressed memories out in a constructive way. I agree. Her situation is quite unique. I'm going to do some further research on the subject of dragons, and once you have her checked out by a medical doctor, we can get a clearer picture of the cause of both the memory loss and the dreams."

Henry stood up. "Thanks, Angela. I owe you one."

She came around the desk and hugged him. "Nonsense, I still owe you from saving my ass in English lit! Who knows where'd I be if it weren't for you!"

Henry kissed her cheek. "I'll call you once we know what Dr. Jackson says," he said, shutting her door.

On the way home, Henry called Dr. John Jackson's office and was able to make an appointment for Anne for that Thursday.

When he pulled up to Heidi's house, he went around to the back where he heard the sound of children laughing and violent splashing. Heidi, Anne, and the kids were all in the pool, having a wonderful time throwing water at each other.

"Uncle Henry!" Nathan called.

"Hi, Henry," Heidi said. "Come on in!"

"Hi, kids! Not today, sis. Anne, please get ready. We need to go."

"Awwww," Nathan whined. "Can't she stay and play some more?"

Heidi herded the kids out of the pool, carrying Nattie on the way. "No, kids. Daddy's going to be home soon. Henry, are you coming over for the Fourth of July? We'll barbeque and then go watch the fireworks at the Venice Pier."

Henry picked up a blue-and-white-striped towel from the lounge chair and wrapped it around a dripping Anne. "Sure, what time do you want us to be here?" Anne took the towel and went inside to change. Heidi put Nattie down, and she followed.

"How about ten o'clock?"

"Sounds like a plan!"

Anne soon came out with dry clothes on, and they kissed all the faces and left.

In the car, Anne asked Henry about his visit to his friend.

"What did Angela say?"

"She said we should continue with our story and your art. She's very interested in meeting you, but she wants you to see a doctor to make sure there isn't anything physically wrong."

"What is a doctor?"

"Someone who heals you when you're sick or injured. He's just going to look at your body to make sure everything is okay."

"Okay," she answered.

For the remainder of the car ride home and all throughout dinner, Henry was silent and deep in thought. Between the baring of Anne's soul and Angela's insights on amnesia, he had a lot to sort out in his mind. He only wanted what was best for her, but exactly what that was remained an enigma. One fear was that by exposing her to "the system," she would get locked up for observation and have to undergo numerous invasive tests, both psychological and physical. What if she did have some horrible past? Would dredging it up help? Or would it force her to face whatever hell she escaped? He doubted very much that she could have perpetrated any sort of crime or evil act and therefore be wanted by the law, or worse. She was so sweet, loving, and innocent. There was absolutely no way amnesia would change her entire personality too, was there?

Then there were those damned dragons added to the mix, leaving only about a bazillion different scenarios and possibilities as to why they came calling every friggin' night. Each possibility was more perplexing than the last. What was it exactly that Angela said? "Don't overanalyze them." *Yeah, right. That's like telling someone not to think of the color pink.*

Henry's mind was on a roll. *Let me think. There was Freud and his mommy issues. Nothing new there. With Freud, breathing was a mommy issue.* Zo let me zee here, breathing in or ze inhaling iz like da penis going into da voman und exhaling, or breathing owt is like da voman giving birth, ya. *Yeah, no I don't think so. No help there.*

That Jung fella said it was all about her "consciousness being swallowed." Sorry, Jung, that's a little too hard for me to swallow. But hey, maybe the old Anne was trying to move back into her old hangout. It's a nice place to be, let me tell ya. Maybe Mr. Jung is right after all. But then why all the other dragons? And the killing of the babies, not to mention Kenta and the brothers that were her uncle and father. Hey, I just realized no mention of a mommy. In your face, Freud. Ha! No, I don't think her consciousness being on the menu in her dreams is the answer.

Next, there was the "overcoming and unconscious need for destructive behavior" crap. *I love ya, Angela, but the only destructive behavior she's capable of is all the hearts she breaks when she walks into a room hanging on my arm. There is no way in hell I am ever going to believe that my Anne would harm anyone. Heck, pets and wildlife alike fall in love with her just for showing up. If a black heart beats beneath those perfect breasts, the animals would sense it and run from her, not to her. Not to mention the deep connection I felt from the moment I laid eyes on her.* There was no malevolence in that moment—the exact opposite in fact. Even Aeya, her dream counterpart, was an innocent victim and felt nothing but compassion and love for her people. *No, there is another answer, I'm sure. And one day soon, I'll find it.*

As the day and his roll came to an end, Henry could only hope the new path he had chosen for them was the right one. Good intentions do not guarantee good results, but he had to find a way to end these nightmares for her. They were the only dark cloud in an otherwise perfect sky. While he and Anne settled in for the evening, he could only wonder how long it would be before Saphan would rear his ugly head inside of Anne's. *Well, you better watch out buddy. There's a new dragon slayer in town, and you're top on my list.*

26

I am being carried by two black dragons flying over the crystal mountains. I see the fires raging below me, burning the bodies of my creator and my kind. As we pass over the green ocean, the sky grows dark, and the waters turn black. Eventually, even the sun is swallowed by the darkness. We arrive at the black mountains spewing fire from their peaks, the inferno rising up from the center of the mountain.

When we get to the highest of the black mountains, I am thrown to the rocky pinnacle, my escorts landing around me. I have never been in the dark, and I am afraid of what will happen. My body hurts with fear, and I cannot breathe either air or water. I am consumed with dread as the Other lands and comes near me, his red eyes blazing and his mouth open, revealing his teeth dripping with the blood of the One. I try to crawl away from him, but I am held by the others. He laughs as he approaches me.

27

Breathing Underwater

June 27
Saturday

Henry decided he would show Anne how she really could breathe underwater by taking her scuba diving. He was already certified to dive from his days in the Navy, but he needed to get her certified as well, so he signed her up for classes with a local dive shop.

The class was one day with a dive after with experienced instructors. Like everything else she started, she took to the class like a natural, swimming across the pool like an Olympic swimmer and feeling very comfortable with the equipment. Her instructor, a gentleman from Australia named Matt, commented that she picked up diving so quickly he would sign her certification and arrange for her to dive that afternoon—as long as he went with them, of course. Like everyone who met her, Matt fell under her spell. Her zest for experiencing all life had to offer was infectious. Everything was new and exciting to her, and her enthusiasm gave Henry a fresh outlook on life too.

Matt arranged for Henry and Anne to go out on one of their charter boats, a thirty-foot open dive boat with a crew of six. Several other diving students and instructors joined them on the trip. They went about two miles out from the shore to an area where people frequently dive for the Megalodon shark teeth. Matt fitted Anne with a single tank over her back, BCD (buoyancy control device), blue fins, and a mask and helped her put the regulator in her mouth. Henry was able to suit himself up without any assistance, only requiring Matt to perform a safety check of his equipment.

Matt told her to wait and asked Henry to go first to show her how to jump into the water, one foot first, stepping off the boat while holding on to his mask.

She followed with a splash, and Henry gave her the "descend" thumb down hand signal he had taught her, inviting her to join him. Matt came right after and would stay behind her while together they explored the deep. They swam down twenty five feet to the sands on the ocean floor and started shifting through the sand looking for the larger shark teeth. Henry could see the wide-eyed wonder on Anne's face through her mask. He loved diving because it gave him the opportunity to visit another world, a beautiful and exotic world where the inhabitants of one could not survive in the other. That fact prompted a deep respect for this environment and creatures that lived there. They were uninvited guests after all, and he could only wonder if fish were as fascinated with him as he was with them.

Henry guided Anne along the ocean's bottom to explore all the brightly colored coral and plant life. He was thankful she had a regulator lodged in her mouth because he couldn't even come close to naming a fraction of the sea life laid out before them. Anne was probably ready to burst at any moment from the pressure of all the questions he knew were bubbling up inside her. Anne kept her promise Henry made her swear before submerging, not to touch anything without Henry's or Matt's okay first. If she saw anything she wanted to pick up, like a shell or a tooth, she had to point first and wait for the diver's hand signal of either okay or danger. In the ocean, the prettier something was often meant the deadlier or more poisonous it was. One also had to beware of who was lurking under the surface of the sand or had taken up residence in a nook or cranny among the rocks and coral. Sea snakes and eels loved small dark holes, and deadly rock fish lay on the ocean floor, invisible to the untrained eye or unsuspecting passerby.

Anne tried to follow several schools of fish swirling around her, watching in wonder as the brightly colored fish swam by, the schools switching direction when they came nearer. Henry pointed out an octopus he spotted, and she nodded, watching the animal as it pulsed its way across the ocean floor. Matt found a large prehistoric Megalodon shark tooth and brought it to her. Her eyes gleamed with excitement behind the mask as she held it in her hands. The size of this large tooth that filled both of Anne's hands was yet another reminder that they were visitors in an alien world.

After so many nights of horrible dreams, Henry hoped Anne felt like she was in a real dream now, living in the peaceful scenes she painted where she settled on the bottom of the green ocean to sleep. At one point, she signaled she was going down, so the men followed her to the sand. She knelt on the ocean bottom while the sea life swam above her, and she would reach out to try to touch the fish. She sat there for a long time. Henry wondered if she was reliving her dreams, believing they could actually be real, or at least the peaceful parts until the nightmares cut their way into the night.

At one point, Matt checked their gauges and flashed Henry the low air signal. Henry turned to Anne and signaled it was the end of the dive. Anne signaled back okay. The three divers headed back up to the boat. Matt got on first, then helped Anne up, then Henry. When she took the regulator out of her mouth, she could not contain her joy, hugging both Henry and Matt, tears forming in her eyes, her Megalodon tooth held tightly in her hands as if it were a precious jewel.

"I can breathe underwater!" she cried, tears in her eyes, her mouth wide and smiling. "I can breathe underwater! There are so many fish, so many colors! Tell me names of the fishes," she demanded. "What was the yellow one?"

"Tang," Matt replied.

"What was the long silver one?"

"Tarpon."

"What was the orange one?" This went on for a while because she remembered every fish she saw. Then she started asking about the names of the coral: staghorn, elkhorn, lettuce, brain. She asked questions all the way back to the harbor. Matt and Henry tried to answer as many as they could, but she just had too many. Henry was right; she was ready to pop from all the questions.

When they got off the boat, Anne was still smiling, her teeth gleaming in the sun, her eyes bright. Henry thought her face would split; her smile was so big. Henry thanked Matt, and Anne kissed him on the cheek. Henry didn't mind. It was worth it for Anne to have such an amazing day.

Henry couldn't wait to show her his next surprise. Now that Anne had experienced how to breathe underwater, it was about time she learned how to fly!

28

The Other orders the black dragons to bind me with metal chains that hurt. My heart is already broken because my creator and Kenta, my guardian, are gone! How much more can he hurt me? Fear grips my heart, and I cannot breathe in anticipation of what will happen next.

With heavy chains on all my legs, the Other tells his sons to hold me down. He takes the black crystal sword and starts to cut into my beautiful wings! I scream because the pain is so great that it blinds me! I cannot move or get away; sharp claws dig into my body while the heavy chains hold me to the floor of the mountain. The Other saws through my pectoral muscles and bone then wrenches my wings off with his claws, my golden blood flowing onto the ground like a flood. I am sick from the pain and soon unable to make any sounds, my throat raw from crying. There is no reason to hold me down anymore. I do not have the strength to rise.

29

Flying

June 28
Sunday

Henry woke up as excited as a schoolboy on the first day of summer vacation. Today was the day he would reveal his second surprise for Anne and take her to fly in the sky. They were going skydiving! Anne often talked about the joy of soaring through the sky, flying over the crystal mountains in her dreams. They were the happy moments before the black dragons came to spread death and terror upon her nocturnal counterpart and her people. He wanted to recreate that happiness as best he could to offset whatever horrors she may have endured. Maybe, just maybe, with enough positive and happy real life experiences, the bad memories would begin to fade, and new dreams would take their place.

Henry remained mysterious throughout their morning rituals and undercooked breakfast in his rush to get them out the door. Anne had a puzzled look on her face as she watched him. Henry knew she was frustrated, but he wasn't going to tell her where they were going.

"We're going to do something really special today," he said as they got in the car.

"Diving?" she asked, a bright smile on her face.

"Well, sort of in a way, but it's not what you're thinking," he teased.

"Tell me," she begged.

"Nope."

"TELL ME!" she said in a deep voice through clenched teeth, mocking anger and slugging him in the shoulder.

"Hey, behave yourself, young lady. Don't make me turn this car around."

Anne settled into her seat with silent anticipation.

"You'll see when we get there." He pulled the car out of the driveway and headed out toward their secret destination. They drove to the Sarasota Bradenton International Airport where the skydiving school was. When they pulled up to the main entrance and parked, Henry turned to Anne and said, "You are going to fly today."

Anne sat stunned with her mouth wide open for almost a full minute. "Fly?" she could barely speak. "Really, I'm going to fly?" Her face reflected her total disbelief and wonder.

"Yes, fly. Like in your dreams, Anne." Henry put his arm around her. "You are really going to fly!"

As she stepped out of the car, Anne was shaking with anticipation of something she could only dream of was about to actually happen. She followed Henry into the building and stared at the pictures of past patrons on their jumps, the wind blowing their hair straight up, huge smiles on their faces. They had to sit through a brief instruction session and watch a video before heading to the plane with their tandem instructors. Henry and Anne had been given jumpsuits to wear along with a harness, helmet, altimeter, and goggles. A harness was also worn by the instructors who would attach themselves to a partner for the jump.

Anne's partner was an instructor named Travis. He introduced himself, telling them about his history as a retired US Air Force officer, having served on their Wings of Blue skydiving team. He said he loved jumping so much he continued his passion for it after leaving the Air Force and had over a thousand jumps to his credit. He stood about five feet ten inches with salt-and-pepper hair, brown eyes, and had a slender muscular build. After going over the safety instructions one last time, they joined their group and headed for the plane.

Anne smelled something in the air and asked Henry what it was. He told her it was the smell of jet fuel. They climbed the stairs and entered the plane through a wide opening with no door then took their place sitting side by side on two benches that ran parallel along opposite sides of the plane. The jumpers sat next to their instructors in pairs. The chatter amongst the group was a mixture of both excitement and dread.

Anne felt her tummy flop and her ears pop as the plane climbed into the air. She pointed out the window, prompting Henry to look at the Florida coast as they climbed higher into the blue sky. She asked him in a raised voice why the fields, houses, and roads below them looked so tiny. He explained that it was a matter of perspective, like when she drew something far off in the distance. Immediately, she understood.

When the plane leveled off at twelve thousand feet, all the instructors fastened themselves to their students' harnesses, tethering them to each other. The pair closest to the door made their way to the opening and knelt at the edge. Giving each other the thumbs-up, together they leaned forward and disappeared from Anne's view. Then Henry and his instructor jumped. Two by two, they each took their turn jumping; while everyone else scooted up, advancing towards the doorway. While most everyone else was scooting, poor Travis was being dragged by Anne, who nearly pushed the others out of the plane so it could be her turn.

Finally, the moment arrived, and Anne knelt at the threshold of her dream. There she was, gazing into the wide open sky with the wind blowing in her face, inviting her to take her rightful place among the clouds. Travis's fist appeared in front of her face with his thumb up, indicating it was time. Anne didn't waste time signaling back but plunged forward into the open sky with a squeal of delight.

She was flying! She assumed the stable position she had been taught while on the ground, with her arms out at her side and elbows bent at a ninety-degree angle, her hips down, her legs bent slightly, and her knees apart. She closed her eyes for a minute, and she could swear she felt the muscles in her back and chest flexing as if she had wings. Then she opened her eyes, and it felt like she was in one of her dreams, flying into the white sun with her golden companion at her side, the wind in her face. Her heart soared as she did, the smile on her face as wide as the world below her. The wind whipped around her, making her clothes billow out as the ground below slowly drew nearer. She was really flying! Her heart beat wildly, her joy at the experience exploding inside her. She could almost feel the powerful wings on her back as if they were really there, and she stretched her arms wide, letting the air lift her into a state of euphoria while she plummeted towards the earth below. Suddenly, the jerk of the parachute opening behind her instructor snapped her out of the moment.

She transitioned from soaring to floating on the air, and the sensation was amazing. This was beyond her wildest dreams! She was drifting like a cloud. Slowly wafting towards the ground, she looked down at her feet dangling in the open air and playfully kicked them a bit. Then she looked up at the parachute spread wide overhead and watched it ripple as the air passed through it. Travis asked her if she would like to drive for a while, and he pointed her attention to the handles on the sides of the rigging. By grasping one in each hand and pulling down, she could turn to the left or the right. Now this was flying! Anne was really in control, and she was able to soar in whichever direction she chose as if flapping her wings.

The ground was rapidly approaching, and her flight was about to end. Travis instructed her to hold her feet up so his would be the first to touch the ground. Anne could see Henry waiting for her at the edge of the landing sight. He had retrieved his phone before she landed and was holding it in front of him with both hands, smiling. She waved at him a heartbeat before landing and would have run immediately over to him, if not for the hundred and seventy pounds of instructor on her back. Travis detached his harness from hers. He asked her if she enjoyed her first skydive. She was jumping with joy and nearly snapped his neck when she hugged him, saying, "Thank you!"

Henry joined them. "Well? What did you think?!" Anne jumped into his arms, wrapping her legs around his waist and squeezed his neck.

"I WAS FLYING!" she replied, screaming in his ear.

"Yes, you were. I saw. I'm so proud of you."

"I WAS FLYING!" she repeated.

She gave Henry a big kiss and climbed down, only to start bouncing up and down again with joy.

"How did she do?" Henry turned to Travis.

"Oh, she did great, most enthusiastic student I've ever had." He nodded in Anne's direction. "It was also the first time a student dragged me out of the plane too. I've had eager students before, but I never had one that made me feel like I was the one just along for the ride. She's a natural. You should think about signing her up for certification."

"Perhaps some other time. Thank you for taking such good care of her." Henry shook Travis's hand and gave him a nice tip.

"My pleasure. Drop in anytime."

"Yes, thank you, Travis. I WAS FLYING!" Anne added.

"Yes, I know, and you did great. Good-bye, and I really do hope to see you again. If you ever come back, please ask for me."

"We will," Henry promised.

"I WAS FLYING," Anne reminded him one last time.

The jump lasted seven minutes, but for Anne, it was a lifetime of ultimate joy that brought tears to her eyes along with a very large dose of adrenaline. On the way through the gift shop to pick up her photos, she repeated to everyone she saw that she was flying! Henry just smiled, telling everyone it was her first time before realizing how unnecessary it was. Then, when they gave her pictures from the jump, she showed them to everyone who was waiting for their own jump and anyone else who came within five feet of her, exclaiming to each, "I was flying!"

"How are you feeling?" Henry asked her on the way home when she finally stopped talking about the experience.

She turned to him, the smile still wide on her face. "I cannot find words to say! I was flying! I could feel the wings on my back like they were really there! I did not think such a thing could happen. I want to go again!"

"We will," he said, smiling. "That's a promise."

"Thank you," she whispered, barely able to get the words out. "Thank you!"

"You are welcome, my lady."

When they got home, Anne took the pictures and showed each one of the animals, telling them about her flight. They simply sniffed the pictures and went back to whatever mischief they were into. Henry had to recharge his cell phone; Anne had watched the video over and over on the car ride home.

Henry wasn't done yet. "I have another surprise for you. Go look under the bed. There's a big box under there. Bring it out here and open it up."

Anne dashed off as instructed and nearly stepped on half a dozen paws in her rush to get back. In her hands was a large cream-colored box with a big red bow wrapped around it.

"Take a look inside," Henry prompted.

Anne ripped off the bow with one hand and the lid with the other, sending them to opposite corners of the room. She shredded through the tissue paper to reveal a beautiful pastel blue gown with rhinestone accents and matching shoes.

Bibbity bobbity boo, Henry thought to himself. Anne's eyes popped out of her head, followed by the all-too-familiar squeal of delight he had grown so fond of hearing. *More like Bibbity bobbity broke*, he joked to himself. He really didn't mind at all; her love was worth all the gold on earth, Elvis once sang. He would give everything he had if it would end her nightmares, he vowed.

"That's only part of the surprise. Go put that on. We have another special place to go to."

She didn't ask where but ran into the bedroom to change. This time, everything with four legs and a tail gave her a wide berth. Henry slipped into a pair of slacks and a button-down shirt. He emerged from the bathroom moments before Anne reappeared from the bedroom. Webster has yet to come up with a word that could adequately describe the vision that stood before him. *Stunning, beautiful, radiant*—nope, not even close. *Breathtaking* would have to do for the moment. She beamed with joy and happiness and spun around for Henry to see. Henry clicked his heals together, bowed, and extended his hand. Anne took his arm and he escorted her to the car.

"Where are we going?"

"You'll see. It's another surprise."

"Will I fly again? Will I breathe underwater?"

"In that dress? Seriously?"

"Will I see animals? Will I see flowers?" She kept peppering him with questions to which he responded on each, "You'll see."

Finally, they arrived at their destination, the Arthur Murray Dance Studio. "You're going to dance like a princess," Henry said when they walked into the door.

Anne ran into the studio, her smile wide and arms out as she did a pirouette. "Dance!"

They were greeted by their instructor, a tall slender Hispanic man with caramel skin and bright eyes named Sidney. Sidney showed them how to walk first, learning to move in sync with each other. Anne had a little trouble following Henry's lead, and they took turns stepping on each other's feet at first, laughing each time they did, but then they found their groove. Sidney took turns replacing one or the other to make sure they were feeling their way with each other in the movements and direction.

Then Sidney told Anne to put her hand on Henry's arm, and Henry to put his arm on her back near her shoulder blade. He instructed them to hold their arms out together while he restarted the music. Henry stepped forward with his left foot, and Anne stepped back with her right. They stepped to Anne's left then back with Henry's right foot then back again in a smooth box step. Soon the music found its way into their souls, drawing them together as if they were one. Nothing and no one else mattered.

They found their rhythm with the tempo of the music and with each other. Henry gazed into Anne's blue eyes, falling again into that dream state he felt when he first laid eyes on her. Never in his life had he imagined he would meet so wonderful a creature, let alone be loved by one. She was everything to him now. The dance steps became second nature to him, his girl in his arms.

She was a princess in her movie! Anne clung to Henry with everything inside her, feeling his strong arm surrounding her and guiding her across the floor. Sidney kept telling her to look up and to the left, like a princess, but all she could do was look into Henry's eyes. She was drawn into them, wanting to climb into his very soul, to join with him as their bodies did. His hand folded on her back like it was an extension of her, and their joined hands melded into one. She felt like she was floating among the clouds again and dancing on air. She was the princess in a blue dress dancing with her tall handsome prince. No fairytale could come close to theirs, no love as fierce and deep.

She did not want to stop. But soon, the clock struck midnight, or one hour in their case. Their time was up, so they thanked Sidney and left the studio, holding hands and staring into each other's eyes while they tried to find the way out. Sidney smiled and guided them to the door.

Anne was still full of energy, wanting more. Henry decided he would take her to a nightclub so that she could experience the fast life that clubs offered. It was loud, packed, and wild, but she loved it, writhing with the other partiers on the dance floor. They took a break to get some food, and then she was back on the dance floor, screaming with the rest of the patrons and causing Henry's ear to buzz.

Around one o'clock in the morning, Henry had had enough. "Let's go home," he yelled in her ear.

"Okay," she replied, yelling back. They made their way through the packed club and out into the cool night air, where the only sounds were the traffic on Tamiami Trail and the crickets in the bushes. Henry stood for a moment, just enjoying the peace and breathing in the night air to clear his head. But when they headed for their car, he noticed two men in dark clothes and sunglasses lurking by his vehicle. There was a third man behind the wheel of a black SUV that was parked in front of his car with the engine running, blocking it in.

"Hey! What the hell?" he shouted as loud as his sore throat could shout. When they spotted them, the two men began to advance in their direction while the SUV kept pace. Faced with the option of fight or flight, Henry would choose fight every time, but he had Anne's safety to worry about. He thrust his right arm in front of Anne to halt her progress, then he turned his head slightly to speak to her, keeping his eyes fixed on the menacing trio. "Anne, sweetheart, go back inside and ask the big guy at the door to call 911 and then stay by his side." Before Henry could finish his instructions, a group of young partygoers came bursting out of the exit, laughing and carrying on. No longer alone, the mysterious pair jumped inside the SUV and sped off, leaving behind the smell of burnt rubber and a plethora of unanswered questions.

"What the hell was that all about?" Henry asked himself aloud, walking to the car. He turned to Anne. "Are you okay? Did those guys frighten you?"

"I am okay, but what did those men want?"

"I wish I knew. Let's not hang around here and find out, in case they circle back."

Henry held the door for Anne, who climbed into the passenger seat, closing it behind her. On his walk around to the driver's side, he scanned the parking lot and surrounding area for anything or anyone suspicious. There was no way of knowing if there were any more of those creeps, and he wasn't about to be caught off guard. Behind the wheel again, Henry immediately fired up the engine, slammed the gear shift into drive, and stomped on the gas pedal. He swerved a little while putting on his seatbelt, nearly clipping one of the partygoers bent over puking up her spleen. *Hell of a way to pay someone back who, inadvertently, may have saved your life.* He kept a close eye on the rearview mirror on the ride home, disturbed by what had happened at the club. Combined with the weird shadows in his room at night and the dogs' odd behavior barking at imaginary intruders, something didn't feel right.

30

The Other takes my beautiful wings and throws them to his sons. The black dragons fight each other to be the first to tear into and devour my wings. I can only mourn as I watch my wings torn apart and consumed. The Other stands up on his hind legs and roars as his sons feast, the force of his roar shaking the ground beneath me. My golden blood runs into the iridescent membrane, washing out all the beautiful colors reflected in my wings. My back bleeds from the deep wounds, to wash the ground with the tears falling from my eyes. I am forced to watch as my flesh is torn into pieces and consumed by the gloating dragons, afraid of what more the Other will do to me.

31

Dr. Jackson

June 29
Monday

On Monday, they went to see Dr. John Jackson, an older Southern gentleman who had taken care of Henry's parents before they died. He knew that Dr. Jackson would help them without insurance or an ID card for Anne.

They were shown in to the exam room by Dr. Jackson's nurse, Katie, who greeted them with a smile. "Good morning, Henry! Nice to see you again. This must be Anne. Come on right over here and sit down, sweetie," she said, patting the examination table.

Anne hopped up on the table, and Katie took her blood pressure, noting the results on the chart. "120 over 80. That's good." Then she took her temperature, also noting that on the chart. "Temperature is normal. Is she on any medications? Are there any issues that you are aware of?"

"No on both," Henry answered. "She seems fine."

"Are we doing a full exam today?"

"I guess so," Henry answered. "I want to make sure she is checked out head to toe."

"Okay," Katie pulled out the paper gown doctors provide that never seem to cover enough. "Anne, take off all your clothes and put the gown on open in the front." She laid out the necessary medical instruments for a full pelvic exam then left the room. Anne disrobed, donning the paper gown as instructed.

A few minutes later, Dr. Jackson entered with Katie. "Mornin', Henry. And this apple blossom must be Anne. Good mornin', little lady. Pleased to make your acquaintance," he said with a slight bow. "Let's have a look see at you then." He listened to her heart and lungs then examined her throat, ears, eyes, and neck for any lumps. Then he examined her arms and legs.

"Lie down now, honey," he instructed. Anne did. Dr. Jackson examined her abdomen and breasts. "So we are going to do a pelvic exam today?"

"Yes. I want to know if there is any indication that something happened to her, any signs of past abuse or injuries," Henry verified. He turned to Anne and said, "The doctor is going to examine your, uh"—he felt uncomfortable explaining this to her in front of the doctor—"female parts."

Dr. Jackson nodded, understanding Henry's concern then pulled out the stirrups and told Anne to put her feet on the cold steel. "This might smart a bit, honey," he warned, picking up the speculum then applied lubrication and inserted it inside Anne. "I am going to insert this instrument called a speculum. Can y'all feel where I am, sweet pea?" Anne winced a bit as the instrument stretched her, but she remained still during the procedure. Dr. Jackson removed the speculum and examined her with his hand. "I'm just gonna poke around a bit with my finger and see if everything's all right." He was particularly thorough in his examination of the entire area, looking for any indication of scars or physical abuse.

"Well," he said, taking off his gloves. "I checked her out from her bonnet to her bunions, and everything appears to be right as rain as near as I can tell. I don't see any indication of abuse or injury, either physical or sexual, although I do see indications of recent sexual activity." He looked up at Henry. "I reckon y'all had somethin' to do with that?"

"Yes," Henry confessed, his face turning red.

Dr. Jackson stood up and wrote on the chart on the shelf. "I would like to do a complete blood count and an electrolyte panel, a skeletal survey, and certainly, a CT scan of her brain to make sure there are no indications of internal injuries or abnormalities. We can take the blood here today, but y'all have to set up the X-rays and CT scan. I'll give you an order for it. I won't charge you for today, but can y'all handle the cost for the other tests?"

"Yes," Henry affirmed. "I can handle it." He had quite a bit of money saved up by staying in his parents' home.

"Okay. Anne, honey, it has been a pleasure. I will see you soon," he said, offering his hand to help her sit up. "Katie will be back to get the blood sample." He left the room, closing the door behind him.

Katie returned with a plastic bin with tubes and syringes wrapped in plastic. She put on her gloves then a tourniquet on Anne's arm and said, "This might hurt just a bit" when she inserted the needle into Anne's arm. Anne did not move but watched as the dark red liquid filled several small tubes. "Okay," she said when she took all the blood she needed. "Go ahead and get dressed. I'll be back with your orders."

When Katie left, Anne took off the gown and put her clothes back on, examining the Band-Aid and cotton ball taped to the inside of her arm. Katie returned in just a few minutes, knocked on the door, and came in with a clipboard and several sheets of paper.

"Okay, the doctor wants you to get a full set of X-rays and a CT scan. Here is a list of places you can go that will take her without insurance, but you will need to pay cash. Call us after you do to set up a return appointment."

"We will," Henry took the papers.

"Nice to meet you, Anne," Katie said, shaking Anne's hand. "We'll see you soon. Y'all are good to go."

They left the doctor's office and stopped at a burger place for lunch. "What is an X-ray? What is CT scan?" Anne asked when they were eating their hamburgers and fries.

"A CT scan is a test where they take a picture of what's inside you. Angela suggested that the memory loss may be due to a prior injury. The CT scan will tell us that. X-rays are where they take pictures of the bones inside of you. I just want to be sure we do everything we can to help you regain your memory and to make sure nothing happened to you."

"I would like to remember," she said. "All I see are the dreams."

"I know. We'll work on that too. Angela said maybe by writing the story, we can get the cause of the nightmares to come out. But we'll only go as fast as you feel you can handle."

Anne finished her lunch. "I am good," she replied.

"Okay," Henry said, already finished with his cheeseburger. "Are you up to working on it some more today?"

"Yes." They cleared their trays and headed home.

Once home, Anne retreated to her own art table to work on her latest painting of the dragons building the crystal mountains. The picture depicted three dragons in a circle with the pieces of the crystal floating over their heads, conducting what Anne now knew to be *telekinesis*. Fortunately, lately her dreams consisted of more and more of the happier day-to-day glimpses into the lives of the golden dragons before the nightmare took over. She slipped on her headphones to listen to a new audio book, *The Princess Bride*, then sprayed down her sheet to resume her painting.

Henry sat at his desk in the studio and turned on his laptop to do some research on memory loss. He flipped through countless Web pages pertaining to that subject and read all he could on the different types of amnesia: *retrograde, anterograde, posttraumatic, dissociative, lacunar, childhood transient global,* and on and on! He never guessed that there were so many types of amnesia! Anne had no difficulty remembering things since he met her. In fact, her memory was almost photographic. Her ability to see or hear something once then remember it was incredible! It was only her past that escaped her. About the only thing she struggled with was mastering the English language. So many words have double meanings, and most people speak in contractions or slang. All in all, she was holding her own when she spoke, even though she would get mixed up or confused once in a while. In a way, it was quite charming at times.

Until she had her medical test done and they got the results, no one could determine if this was physically or psychologically induced, or possibly both. He didn't think her amnesia was caused by a specific incident. He reasoned that a person who had amnesia due to a traumatic event would probably remember something prior to the event. Anne had no memories at all! Or perhaps she did, but somehow, her memories had been transformed into this fantasy world of mind-reading dragons and mountains made out of crystal. Nowhere could he find any example of anyone forgetting their past life and replacing it with an entirely new one, especially a fictitious one. Assuming he was right and her dreams were these distorted memories, it only served to make her situation more complex and unique.

He found the description of dissociative amnesia interesting because a person could forget his or her entire life. She not only forgot her life but she also forgot how to talk, walk, or even eat, regressing to the level of a newborn! Amnesia that would cause such a severe loss had to be from a significant event. He was anxious to get Anne tested.

His head hurt from researching amnesia. He took a break and played solitaire on the computer to get his mind off the enormity of the task ahead of him. Try as he might to clear his thoughts, that nagging question kept creeping back into his brain like a spider skittering across his synapses: What if? What if he did find out what happened? Could he truly handle it? What if the truth was something so horrific and unspeakable that it was unbearable? Could it destroy both of them if they found out? What if he stopped looking for answers and let her go on with no memories at all? Should he keep this new Anne all to himself, leaving the past behind and vowing to never to look back? Would that condemn the woman he loved to a lifetime of nightmares and unanswered questions? She was bright and intelligent and filled with curiosity. She already wondered what her real name was, when her birthday was, where she came from. He couldn't deny her that. His mind was spinning with the possibilities.

Finally, he'd had enough of the bright screen and closed the laptop, shutting it off. Anne was still engrossed in her paintings, her headphones on as she listened to her audio book. Henry smiled, got up from his chair, and touched her on the shoulder. She turned off the audio and took off her headphones.

"I can't work anymore. Do you want to come on a run with me?"

She nodded, putting her brush in the water and the headphones down on the table. They changed into running shorts and shoes, with a tank top for Anne. They left the house and started running down the street. Henry really didn't have a plan where to go; he just wanted to move. He would, however, keep to the neighborhood streets because it was dark. He knew these streets and neighborhood well and was running on autopilot.

It was on their way back that Henry noticed the black SUV following them. Something was seriously wrong here. He didn't want to alert Anne, so he decided to go somewhere public and get off the deserted streets. "Let's go to the gas station and get a drink," he told Anne, keeping an eye on the car. They sprinted out onto Tamiami Trail and ducked into the first building that was well lit, a small convenience store. The SUV followed, turning onto Tamiami. It slowed down as it passed their location before speeding up where it was swallowed by the night. Henry waited a few more minutes to make sure it didn't come back then guided Anne back through the small streets that would lead them home. Either he was going crazy seeing shadows and cars following them, or there really was something nefarious in Anne's past that had caught up with them. Whichever way he looked at it, he had a bad feeling about it.

32

After my wings are devoured, the Other orders the black dragons to hold down my beautiful tail. I thrash it back and forth in my pain and anger. Several of the dragons dig their long sharp claws into my tail, preventing the strong muscles within from hitting them. The Other pulls out the three fins from the end of my tail. Then he takes the crystal sword and begins to saw into my flesh where my tail joins my body. I fight with everything I have left to escape the agony, but I cannot move. I beg the Other to stop, but he continues to saw through my muscles. My vision fades, and my strength fails me as the pain overwhelms me. When my tail is severed, the Other throws it to the black dragons who fight over it to feast.

33

More Tests

June 30
Tuesday

Anne went for her X-rays and CT scans the next day. She was more nervous about the CT scan's narrow tube than the open but uncomfortable X-ray machine where the radiographer bent her body in ways it wasn't supposed to be bent. The technician and Henry assured her she would not get stuck in there. Henry had her bring along her audio book so that she could listen to her stories. She was enjoying the stories with rich characters, adventures, and romance. She did not understand a lot of what she was hearing, but of what she did understand she enjoyed.

She put on the hospital gown and lay on the table. As she was pushed in, she felt her heart racing and gripped the side of the table so tightly that her fingers turned white. But when the technician piped in her audio book, she soon settled in when the familiar voice of the audio book narrated the story where she had left off. The soothing voice of the reader had a calming effect that helped her relax while the machine hummed around her, probing deep into her body to reveal the secrets it held. Before the story was finished, the scan was over. The technician pulled her out and helped her sit up.

"Was it as bad as you thought?" he asked with a smile.

"I was scared at first, but then it was okay," she answered. Henry helped her off the table. She got dressed, and they left the CT scan room, stopping at the checkout desk on the way out. The woman behind the counter read the chart and said, "Are you paying cash or credit?"

"Credit," Henry replied, his wallet already open.

"That will be $1,500." Henry gave the woman his card, and she returned with something she called a receipt. "Your doctor will call you with the results," she said.

When they got in the car, Henry asked her if she was okay.

"Yes," she replied. "I was afraid at first, but my stories made it better."

"Good," Henry said. "Some people have a hard time in the enclosed space. What do you want to do with the rest of our day?"

"I would like to make more paintings. I want to get the pictures in my head on the paper."

"Home it is."

When they got home, Anne went to her art table to continue work on her paintings. They spent the remainder of their day together in the studio, Anne working on her drawings with her audiobooks and Henry working on his illustration while listening to that blaring music he called heavy metal. She did not like that music as much as the others. They took comfort in having the other near, as each retreated into his or her private space, occasionally interrupted by a nosey feline or attention-starved canine visitor, which happened frequently.

Anne noticed something odd. Out of all the surprise visits that came slobbering her way, Flack was not among them. Anne put her brushes down and went to find him. He was lying on his bed whimpering, his eyes sad. She picked him up and cuddled him, cooing softly to him.

"What's wrong?" Henry came to see why Anne left.

"Flack is dying," Anne whispered while rocking the little brown dog.

Henry stood still. "What do you mean? How do you know?"

"I know. I feel it."

Henry turned around and grabbed the car keys. "Let's go. We're going to the vet now!"

He helped Anne to her feet. She wrapped Flack in his blanket and followed Henry to the car. He held the door and helped them get in while Anne cradled Flack in one arm. Then when she was safely secured, she cuddled both arms around him tightly, petting his little head, love in her eyes.

Henry tried to hold back his tears as they pulled up to the vet's office, which was still open, this being one of their later nights. He jumped out, ran around, opened the door for Anne and Flack, and then opened the door to the vet's office.

"Can I help you?" the nice lady behind the counter asked. Her name tag said "Anne."

"He is dying," Anne informed her namesake.

"Let's get you right in to exam room number 3. I'll let Dr. Lewis know." She ushered them into a small exam room and shut the door.

Within two minutes, Dr. Lewis, the vet on call at the hospital, rushed into the room. "What's going on?" He had Flack's chart in his hand.

"Anne believes he's dying," Henry explained.

"Anne," Dr. Lewis said, examining the little dog who was having difficulty breathing, "why do you think he's dying?"

"I know. I feel it."

Dr. Lewis listened to Flack's heart, felt his abdomen, and nodded. "There is a chance you are correct, but I need to run a few tests to confirm. I can call you and let you know what I find out. Or do you want to wait?"

"We'll wait," Henry said, his arms around Anne. They both sat down on the bench in front of the island that served as an examination table while Dr. Lewis took Flack into the back of the hospital.

"How are you doing, sweetheart?" Henry rubbed Anne's back, knowing that if he was having such a difficult time dealing with another death, Anne must be too.

"I am fine," she said, and she indeed did not seem to be upset. "Flack is going to be happy in his new home."

Henry assumed this was Anne's way of dealing with the loss. Perhaps she was in denial and was seeing the dog going to a better place rather than facing the fact that the dog would be gone forever. But he wasn't going to break her bubble even if he didn't believe it. Maybe she couldn't face Flack's death because she would be reminded of the death she saw in her nightmares. He had to let her deal with this in her own way.

After what felt like an eternity, Dr. Lewis finally returned— without Flack. "You were right," he sighed. "Flack passed while we were doing the echocardiogram. His little heart gave out. He was ready to go. I am so sorry for your loss. He was one tough little pup."

Henry's efforts to keep the tears in failed, and they escaped from his eyes, making their way down his cheeks. He put his fingers up to brush them away, nodded, and extended his other hand to Dr. Lewis. "Thank you, sir, for trying."

Dr. Lewis gave him a box of Kleenex and offered it to Anne. She was not crying but had a peaceful look in her eyes, her mouth in a slight smile. "What do you want to do with him? I can offer cremation services, if you like."

"Thank you," Henry said, his voice cracking. "But I'll take him home and bury him in the backyard, where his brothers can still be near."

Dr. Lewis nodded and went to retrieve the body.

Henry put his hand on Anne's shoulder. "Are you sure you're okay?"

"I am okay." She put her hand on his. "I am happy for Flack. I see him running now with the other dogs in the bright place. Do not cry, Henry. This is a happy time for him. He no longer needs his cart. His legs are fine."

Henry had to use the Kleenex. Anne's statement made the tears come on stronger. He was glad she was doing okay because he didn't think he could be strong enough if she lost it too.

Dr. Lewis brought back a cardboard carrying box with Flack's body inside. Henry nodded, took the box and they left to take him home. The receptionist kindly offered her condolences, and told him they'd bill him instead of dealing with payment at that moment.

Once back home, Henry performed the sad task of digging the tiny grave with trembling hands and eyes blurred with tears. He buried his brave companion in the yard near the back fence, with all the other animals in attendance to say their own good-byes. He marked the grave with a large slab of granite he took from the front of the house. Flack's little wheelchair was buried with him.

34

While his sons gorge themselves on my tail, the Other covers me with his body, and I shriek when he enters me, the weight of his enormous form crushing me while his body tears me inside. He bites my back and shoulders, pulling out pieces of skin and muscle and swallowing them. Then he sears the wounds with his hot fiery breath. The agony is unbearable as he continues his attack, the other black dragons dancing around us in a circle and watching with glee in their red eyes. The more I try to get out from under him, the harder he bites while the other dragons laugh. I can only hope that if he kills me, the pain will stop.

35

Results Are In

July 1
Wednesday

Anne was sitting with Henry in the studio working on their book when the phone rang. It was Katie from Dr. Jackson's office. She moved closer to him so that she could hear. "Hi, Henry and Anne. We got all the test results back. Dr. Jackson wants to see you both to talk about them. Can you come in tomorrow around three o'clock?"

"Sure," Henry answered. "We'll be there. Thanks!" He ended the call and turned to Anne. "Dr. Jackson has the results of your tests back. Hopefully, we can find some answers."

"That is good," she replied. She too was anxious about what was going on inside her. She did not understand why she could not remember anything before Henry found her or why she had the same dreams night after night. She felt an uneasiness in her stomach after the call, hoping that Dr. Jackson would have some answers.

That night, Anne's nightmares were more intense than they had been in the last few days. "Anne," she heard Henry call her name, bringing her out of the darkness and quieting her screams in the dimly lit bedroom they shared. "Anne, wake up! It's okay," he whispered as he held her. "It's okay. You're with me. There are no dragons here. You're safe. It seems like the nightmares have been getting worse these last few nights. I wonder if you should talk to Angela."

"I will do what you think best," she said, snuggling deeper into his arms, her wet cheek dampening the hair on his chest. The bed grew crowded as several of their companions joined them in their concern for Anne.

"I'll call her tomorrow and set something up after we see Dr. Jackson." She continued to hold on to him until she finally fell back asleep.

Henry stayed awake for quite a while, staring into the dark room, his heart breaking for the woman in his arms. He could only imagine what she was going through each time the nightmares came. It wasn't just the nightmares though. How could anyone deal with losing an entire life? How would he react if it was him? He'd probably be a lot worse off than Anne. Despite the unknown horrors in her past, she always had a smile and a positive outlook on everything. She never let anything get her down. He snuggled closer to her, kissing her head and wishing her troubles away.

He thought he might have fallen back asleep and was also dreaming when he saw a dark shadow figure move quickly across the room then disappear. This seemed to be happening a lot lately. He wondered if maybe the house was haunted. As he drifted off to sleep, his last thought was "Who you gonna call?"

36

I lie in darkness, too weak to do anything else except wait for the black dragons to take me to the Other again. My back and neck are torn open from the Other's teeth. My beautiful wings are gone. My strong tail is gone. I will never again fly over the crystal mountains into the silver sky. I will never see my friends or the One. I will never play with the little dragons on the water while we chase the silver fish. I will never rest again at the bottom of the green oceans, the water cool against my skin. I will never see the white sun again. I will never know love.

37

Answers

July 2
Thursday

In the morning, Henry got out of bed, his head pounding while his body screamed at him for a few more hours of sleep. He would have been only too happy to comply, but there were animals that needed to be fed and a day of answers to be faced. So he ignored his body's protest and forced his weary bones to the bathroom. When finished, he was feeling refreshed, or at least as refreshed as one could feel before coffee. He headed to the kitchen and was happy to discover that Anne had already fed the animals. A wave of sadness rippled through his heart upon remembering that Flack was no longer among them.

"Thanks for feeding the hoard," he said, sitting at the table.

"You needed more sleep," Anne replied, placing a steaming cup of coffee in front of him.

"Oh, and thanks for this too! I thought I smelled dark roast but was afraid I was only dreaming." Henry grabbed her hand and kissed it before she could get away. One of the best things he taught her was how to make coffee in the morning. This was one of those moments where it paid off. He took a big slurp of the dark brew and felt life return as the hot liquid coursed through his system.

"I thought we might go to the beach today since we don't have to see Dr. Jackson until three o'clock. Would you like that?"

She smiled. "Yes!"

Henry knew that Anne loved the beach, and he was hoping that the outing would serve as a distraction, keeping both of their minds off the pending doctor appointment and the results.

Anne was really adventurous with her recently learned kitchen skills, and she treated Henry to a delicious breakfast of scrambled eggs, toast, coffee, and orange juice. Henry really didn't have to teach her too much; she picked up most of it just by watching him. She was a little nervous being around the flames of the gas stove at first. When a girl dreams of herself and everyone she loves being incinerated every night, being around fire was, understandably, upsetting and unsettling. But she handled it very well, and Henry was proud of how brave she was.

After breakfast, they divided up the tasks of preparing for a trip to the beach. Henry packed the blanket, beach towels, and suntan lotion before filling the cooler with ice and bottled water. Anne packed a bag of chips, grapes, and some whole wheat chicken wraps she made all by herself. The only thing left to do was to jump into their bathing suits—a hot pink bikini with matching floppy hat for Anne and swim trunks patterned after the American Flag for Henry. Once dressed, they slipped on their sandals and headed out to Venice Beach.

The beach was already crowded when they arrived. They cautiously tiptoed around the tourists, as if maneuvering a mine field, until they found a quiet spot at the bottom of a small hill. Henry spread out the blanket and placed their belongings along the edge facing the wind, anchoring it down so it wouldn't blow away. In moments, they were lathered up with sunscreen and racing each other to shore. Henry didn't hold back this time when they reached the water's edge. While still at a full gallop, he scooped up Anne in his arms and tossed her in. Anne squealed in shock and disappeared beneath the surface, only to emerge a moment later with her hands cupped, dowsing Henry in playful retaliation. The handsome couple laughed and giggled, chasing each other amongst the waves, splashing, grabbing, and tickling along the way. After a time, they decided to head in to enjoy the sun and relax.

Once back at their blanket, Anne joined Henry by his side as he put on his sunglasses and stretched out his lean muscular frame, tucking one arm under his head. Anne lay on her back, donning her beach hat, which she tilted forward, casting a speckled shadow across her face.

Listening to the heartbeat of the ocean waves upon the shore, Anne's thoughts were swept away with the current to the distant land in her dreams. She imagined herself lying on the top shelf of her home in the crystal mountains. The Florida sun was replaced by the white sun in the sky of the golden dragons, and it was Kenta, not Henry, by her side. Since her own memories abandoned her, maybe she could borrow someone else's for a while, even if they were only make-believe. Comforted by that thought, Anne slipped into a dreamless sleep.

After a while, Henry noticed Anne had nodded off, and he woke her up by stroking her cheek with the back of his hand. "Hey, Sleeping Beauty, if you don't turn over soon, you're going to go from medium well to extra crispy."

"Huh?" Anne replied, not comprehending.

"You'll get sunburned. Remember, we talked about this?"

"Yes, I remember. Why didn't you just say *that* instead of me getting more crispies?"

"You're right. I should have been more specific." Henry tried not to laugh. "Turn over. I'll put some suntan lotion on you." Anne did as instructed and rolled over onto her stomach, rearranged her hat, and rested her head on her arms. Henry squeezed a generous amount of coconut oil onto his hands then started to rub it on her back. Anne tensed up at first when the cool liquid touched her hot skin, and then he felt her muscles relax under his touch.

At one point, Henry unfastened the strap to her bikini, exposing her back and part of her breast to the warmth of the sun and his caress, causing Anne to gasp and bite her lower lip. He slowly worked his way down from her exposed breast to her sides and then down her back to the base of her spine, slipping his fingertips under the edge of her bikini bottom. When Henry applied oil to her upper thighs, Anne began to moan and tremble, her hips grinding ever so slightly into the hot sand.

"Is everything all right?" a clueless Henry inquired. One could almost hear the needle being scratched across the record as the music stopped. He just knelt there with his hands held up in front of him, like a surgeon preparing to operate. Anne turned and looked at him with wide eyes and a furrowed brow, making a low pleading groan in her throat, unable to speak. "What's the mat...Oh! Oh! I-I see," Henry said, looking down and feeling foolish. "Um, sorry about that. I didn't stop to think." He had a stupid smile on his face. Anne just rolled her eyes and took some deep breaths.

His mind had been preoccupied with the pending appointment with Dr. Jackson, but his body followed its own lead. "I'll make it up to you tonight. I promise." He sat back, wiping his hands on his suit. "Why don't we have something to eat?" Anxious to put this incident behind them, Henry was as clumsy as a boy with his prom date when he attempted to refasten Anne's bikini top. Partially because of his oily hands, but mostly because his own body had responded in kind. He had "Venice Beach Barbie" all oiled up and raring to go, and there wasn't a damn thing he could do about it at the moment. He now understood why sometimes mistakes were referred to as "boners." Only Henry could turn a simple outing to the beach into a trip down the erotic highway without trying or even being aware.

While Henry took their lunch out of the basket, he couldn't shake the feeling that he'd just been caught, like his parents had accidentally walked in on him and his girl. He felt like every eye on the beach was staring at him. It was all in his imagination of course, but for some reason, he couldn't bring himself to make eye contact with anyone. Halfway through eating her wrap, Anne reached over and gave Henry a reassuring kiss on the cheek. Then she hauled off and slugged him in the arm.

"I deserve that one. I admit that," Henry said humbly.

"Are things like this why Heidi calls you 'doofus'?"

"Yeah, pretty much."

"Okay, doofus."

As soon as they were finished eating, Henry told Anne it was time to go. They packed up the food, gathered their belongings, and headed to the car. They didn't bother washing the sand off their feet. Henry drove home barefoot.

Once home, they quickly put the food away and tossed their towels and swimsuits into the laundry basket. They showered together, but not before Anne made Henry make good on his promise. He was only too happy to comply.

Finally, they were satisfied, showered, and dressed, so they headed over to Dr. Jackson's office on Jacaranda Boulevard. Anne's trepidation of what they would hear began to creep back into her stomach, and she was breathing a little heavier. There had to be something wrong with her that caused her loss of memory. She hoped she would know something more today, anything.

Katie greeted them with a smile then led them to the examination room. "He'll be right with y'all," she said, depositing Anne's chart in the basket outside the room. A few minutes later, Dr. Jackson came in, chart in hand, and shook both of their hands.

"Howdy, nice to see you folks this fine day." He smiled. "I reckon y'all want to hear the results of Anne's tests." They both took a deep breath. "And"—he hesitated, scanning the charts—"everything is hunky-dory." Anne and Henry both looked at each other, their mouths slightly open.

"In fact," Dr. Jackson continued with incredulity in his voice, "I didn't find anything out of kilter. She is in perfect health. Her blood levels are exactly where they ought to be, her pap came back right as rain, the skeletal scan showed flawless bone structure, and the CT scan was a perfect brain scan. I've never seen anyone in such perfect health before. Readin' her results is like readin' a textbook. There's just nothing physically wrong with her that would explain the memory loss or the nightmares. She's fit as a fiddle."

"What do we do now?" Henry asked, amazed at the results.

"Well, I can't find a medical reason for her condition. Perhaps y'all should consider a psychological one. Might be good for Anne to have a chat with Dr. Rayback."

"I was going to call her this afternoon once we talked to you," Henry answered. "We'll try that and see what she has to say."

"I'm sorry I didn't find an easy solution," Dr. Jackson offered. "As long as we're talking here, did y'all want to talk about birth control?"

"I never thought about that," Henry admitted. "I probably should have a lot sooner."

"What is birth control?" Anne asked.

"Well," Dr. Jackson began, "you're a healthy young girl, and as near about as I can tell, y'all're engaged in sexual relations with Henry? Birth control is a way to make sure you don't get pregnant."

Henry let out a long breath then ran his hand over his short hair, shaking his head. "I haven't had to think about that for a long time because my prior partners always had that under control. I guess we should."

"Okay. How often do you two dance?"

"Just about every night," Henry admitted.

"All righty then. Since I know that Anne's system is healthy, and y'all're having sex quite frequently, I'm going to prescribe a birth control pill that needs to be taken daily. Let me know how she reacts to them."

"Thank you," Henry replied.

"As far as the memory loss, there isn't much I can do for her. I can give you something to help her sleep and maybe help with the nightmares. Do you want something for that?"

"No," Anne said. "I am scared, but I need to see what happens in my dreams. I do not want to lose them."

"Let me know what Dr. Rayback has to say." Dr. Jackson stood up from the stool. "If y'all change your mind, Anne, about the sleep aids, let me know about that as well. Hopefully we can get to the bottom of what's going on. Katie will be right back with a sample of a pill and a prescription if you tolerate it. If anything changes, call me immediately. Otherwise, I'll see you in six months to check her progress." He shook Henry's hand. "I have very much enjoyed meeting you Anne. You're a refreshing breath of air from my usual patients." He shook Anne's hand, smiling at her, and left.

Katie came back a few minutes later with several samples of the birth control pill that Dr. Jackson prescribed and a written prescription. "This should last for a while," she said. "Call us to make a return appointment." She took Anne's hand and smiled. "I look forward to seeing you again."

"I like meeting you too." Anne smiled.

On the way to the car, Henry called Angela's office and made an appointment with her for Monday. Anne hoped somewhere they would find the answer to her past.

38

I do not know how long I have endured the torment of the Other and his black dragons. They mock me, tossing the burned hides of my kind before me, to remind me that I am alone. I cannot even cry anymore. I do not have the strength. My creator, my guardian, even the little ones are consumed by the fires brought by the black dragons. I grieve each one as I endure the constant abuse from the Other. Each time he takes me, he gorges on my flesh, leaving my back raw. When he is finished with each attack, I am thrown into the darkness to cry alone. I wait until I can finally be released by death. I have nothing left but the memories and the anguish. It is so dark where I am, so lonely.

39

Tale of the Princess Dragon

July 3
Friday

Anne and Henry enjoyed writing their book together. Henry took out his laptop to continue the story where they left it, while Anne gathered her paintings.

Once upon a time, there was a kingdom of golden dragons who were called the Thraekenya. They lived on a crystal mountain in a land far, far away that was surrounded by a green ocean with a white sun in the sky. Although the dragons were all a beautiful golden color, they all had different colored wings: blue, green, orange, yellow, and white.

The Thraekenya were ruled over by two brothers, Aesmay and Saphan. Because Aesmay was the older brother, he was the king; and Saphan, his Captain. Aesmay and Saphan had iridescent wings that reflected all the colors of the other Thraekenya.

The Thraekenya lived in beautiful lairs that they made from the crystals of the mountains by using their minds to cut and move the large bricks. They were happy and flew high and wide over the mountains and swam in the green ocean where they dove to catch silver fish to eat. Then they lay out on the shelves of their lairs and soaked up the warmth of the white sun. At night, the sky was lit by the two bright moons circling in the sky overhead.

Aesmay had a daughter named Aeya, who fell in love with another dragon named Kenta. Aeya's wings were the prettiest of all the dragons and shimmered with traces of all the colors that moved over her iridescent wings like sunlight on the water. But Saphan secretly also loved Aeya and wanted her for himself. Every time he saw Aeya and Kenta together, he grew angier.

One day, Saphan told Aesmay that he wanted Aeya for himself. Aesmay told him that Aeya could not be with him because she had chosen another. Saphan decided that he did not want Aesmay to tell him what to do, so he came before him as Aesmay lay on the highest shelf and told the King that he would not obey his commands anymore.

Aesmay was sad that his brother was angry, but because he was king, he could not let Saphan disobey him. He told Saphan that if he did not obey the king's orders, he would have to leave the kingdom. Saphan refused to obey the king.

Then Aesmay banished Saphan and those of his army who were loyal to him and sent them to live on the other side of their world where black mountains spouting fire towered over dark waters. Aesmay put up a wall between the two sides of the world so that Saphan and his followers could not return to live with the Thraekenya.

After Saphan and his followers left, Aesmay was unhappy. He asked Aeya and Kenta to help him rule the Thraekenya. Aeya and Kenta helped Aesmay by judging the Thraekenya when they had disagreements between each other. Aesmay lay on his shelf and thought of his brother whom he had banished.

Saphan and his followers went to live on the other side of the world. When they thought about how angry they were, they began to change. They started to walk on their hind legs, and their feet grew long. Their beautiful wings grew gray, and their eyes turned red. Most of all, their beautiful golden skin turned black with hard scales. They called themselves Tannen. They ate the black rocks from the mountain and learned to create fire in their breath.

One day, the shield above the crystal mountain was suddenly torn, and Saphan and his followers came out of the sky with fire spewing from their mouths. Saphan went to where Aesmay lay and took a piece of the crystal mountain that he had hewn with his claws and killed Aesmay. The other Thraekenya were scattered as the Tannen attacked with the hot fire.

"Okay," Henry said after they agreed on the story to this point, "where do we go from here? We don't want to put that everyone was killed and you don't remember anything after this."

"We need to give them a happy ending," Anne said. "All princesses should have a happy ending."

"Okay, let's say that Kenta escapes the attack and comes back to rescue Aeya at some point. Like in your princess movies."

Anne smiled and nodded. "I'd like that."

Henry turned back to the laptop. "So Kenta escaped," he began to type.

> Kenta managed to escape by hiding deep in the ocean when Aeya was taken by Saphan and his army back to the black mountains.
>
> Aeya was sad about the death of her father and missed Kenta. Saphan told her that she would have to be his queen and rule over the Tannen. He treated her cruelly and kept her locked up in the center of the mountain where he had dug a deep tunnel with his claws.
>
> Kenta gathered up the Thraekenya who were scattered and brought them back to the top of the crystal mountain. They buried Aesmay deep in the sand under the water and mourned him for three days. Then when they had finished mourning their king, Kenta went to look for Aeya. He searched all the crystal mountains and everywhere in the green water. He knew he would have to go to the black mountains to look for Aeya because that was where Saphan would be holding her.
>
> Kenta created a long sword out of the crystal in the mountain and took down the barrier between the sides of the world. He flew off in search of Saphan and Aeya, his love.
>
> He flew for a long time and watched the world start to dim as he crossed over to the black mountains. The water grew darker, and the mountains lost the shine of the crystals. He knew he was getting closer to where Aeya was being held.

"Not bad so far," Henry observed. "I think this will be a good story."

"Is that an act of true love, what Kenta is doing?" Anne asked.

"Well," Henry said, "I guess that is love. He is willing to put his life on the line to go and save his princess. So what happens next?"

"He must find her."

> *Kenta flew until his wings ached. Finally, he reached the dark mountain where Saphan was hiding. He landed on the top of the mountain and called out for Saphan to face him.*
>
> *Saphan and the rest of the Tannen rose from the tunnels and surrounded him. They brought Aeya up with them, and Kenta's heart froze when he saw how sad she was.*
>
> *"Saphan," Kenta called, "let Aeya go. Let us settle this between ourselves."*
>
> *Saphan laughed. "Why would I let her go? She is so beautiful. She will be my queen. How can you stop me?"*
>
> *Kenta was afraid, but he knew that he could not leave his princess. He rose up on his hind legs so that he could look Saphan in the eyes and said, "I will never let her be your queen. I love her."*
>
> *All of the Tannen laughed and circled around Kenta. Aeya cried out to her love. Kenta prayed silently to the creator of all Thraekenya to give him the strength and held up his crystal sword. His mighty wings flapped hard to keep him balanced on his hind legs, but he was determined to meet his enemy on an equal level.*

"This is actually getting pretty exciting," Henry commented. "I'm really enjoying writing this story with you."

"Me too," Anne agreed. "Now what do we do?"

"They fight."

> *Kenta swung his sword at Saphan, only to be met with a flash of light when Saphan's black crystal sword connected with his. He swung again and again, only to meet Saphan's countermoves each time. They fought for a long time, growling at each other and slashing each other with their swords and their claws. Aeya wept as her love fought Saphan.*
>
> *Finally, when Saphan could fight no longer, he grabbed Aeya by her long neck and put his sword against it. "Stop or I will kill her!" he threatened.*

Kenta stopped his advance in midthrust. "No!" he cried. "I will not let any harm come to her." He threw down his sword and bowed before Saphan. He loved Aeya so much that he would offer his own life to save hers.

Suddenly, a bright light shot out from the dark clouds overhead. The rays of the white sun pierced through the darkness and burned the Tannen. "What magic is this!" cried Saphan as the smoke rose from his skin.

A loud voice was heard on the rays of white light. "Because Kenta was willing to give his life for Aeya, I will fight for him," the creator of all Thraekenya roared. Saphan and the rest of the Tannen crawled back into their tunnels and left Kenta and Aeya alone. They never bothered the Thraekenya again.

Kenta went to Aeya, and together, they flew home to the light and the crystal mountains. Because her father was dead, Aeya became the queen of the Thraekenya and Kenta became her king. The dragons could once more fly across the sky, swim in the water, and lie on their shelves. Queen Aeya and her Kenta lived happily ever after.

"The End," Henry said, typing the words. Okay, now all you have to do is give it a title and figure out which drawings go with the story. Do you want me to help you with that?"

"No, it is good for me to do the paintings," she replied. "It helps me making the dragons. What is 'title'?"

"What we call the book."

"I like the fairytales. Can we call it *Tale of the Princess Dragon?*"

"Then '*Tale of the Princess Dragon*' it is." Henry smiled and put the title on the story.

Henry printed out the text. "Okeydoke," he replied. "The illustrations are all yours. I will contact Elliott and see if he can shop for publishers who might be interested once we're done. I can send him the manuscript to get some feedback. Just tell me what text you want on each piece."

As she sorted through the finished pieces to determine which ones she could use and which ones she still needed to do, the meaning of an act of true love that they wrote about in their story latched on to her heart and did not let go. She wanted to know more about this kind of love. Was this what she felt for Henry? Did she ever feel this way before? She couldn't remember. Why was it so hard?

40

The black dragons come and drag me to the Other again. The Other hisses at me while he attacks that he hurts me because I did not choose him. He taunts me, reminding me that I am alone and that I am his. He has taken away all that I love. I am weak as much from despair as from the torture. When he does not taunt me, the other dragons take up his words, laughing at me while I cry. There is no one to help me. All I can do is hope that death will bring relief.

41

Fourth of July

July 4
Saturday

Henry and Anne arrived at James and Heidi's house at around ten o'clock in the morning on the Fourth of July. They joined the others, who were already poolside. Henry handed a copy of *Tale of the Princess Dragon* to Heidi and waited as she read it.

"This is wonderful!" Heidi exclaimed while they sat around the pool watching the kids swim. "I can't wait to see the illustrations!"

"Let me see! Let me see!" Nathan grabbed at the papers from Heidi's hands, dripping water because he just got out of the pool.

"Stop that, Nathan!" she yelled. "You're wet! You'll ruin the paper! Sit here next to mommy, and I'll read it to you. Nattie, wanna hear a story?" Nattie, who was already out of the pool following her brother, ran to her mother and climbed up into her lap, plugging her thumb in her mouth along the way. She used the beach towel her mom had wrapped around her as a surrogate blanket and laid her head on Heidi's chest. Meanwhile Nathan sat curled up against her on the side of the lounge chair. Heidi then read them the story, supplying different voices for each character. Even James was intrigued and stood behind her as she read, her voice transporting all of them into this strange and beautiful world created by Henry and Anne.

When Heidi finished, James stood up from where he was leaning on the back of the chair. "I have to say, that's pretty good! What is your next step? And please, Henry, let me negotiate any contract."

"Well," Henry replied, "first, of course I would want you in on any negotiations. I've asked Elliott to check out some publishers to see if anyone is interested. If we get an offer, then I'll need you to check it out please. In the meantime, Anne has a lot of work to do to complete the illustrations. She wants to do them all herself, and I'm okay with that."

Anne nodded. "I see the pictures in my head. It is easy to paint them."

James looked at her with concern. "Have you talked with Dr. Jackson yet about the test results?"

"Yes," Henry said. "There is nothing physically wrong with her that would explain either the memory loss or the nightmares. I've made another appointment to see Angela."

"I haven't found any more information on a fire in the area where someone has gone missing," James offered. "I've got a friend in Sarasota County looking into it. I also checked with someone in the Coast Guard for a fire on a boat, but nothing popped."

Heidi put Nattie down and handed the printed manuscript back to Henry, who returned it to the briefcase next to his chair. "We'll find out something, I'm sure, sweetie," she reassured Anne. "In the meantime, you are all ours!"

Nathan was bored. He hopped down off his mother's lap, got a running start, and jumped back in the pool, splashing all the adults. Little Nattie adjusted the small swimming floats around her tiny arms and followed Nathan in, dowsing the adults again.

"Well," Heidi said, water dripping off her head, "I guess it's swim time!"

"I couldn't agree more," Henry said, standing up. He offered one hand to his sister, the other to Anne. He tilted his chin towards James and said, "You comin'?"

"Wouldn't miss it for the world!" He grabbed his wife's free hand.

"Okay then, everyone, on three. One, two, three, GROUP CANNON BALL!" Henry screamed as the four of them charged the pool, leapt into the air, and came splashing down in a curled-up pile of arms and legs. Water sprayed out in every direction, followed by a huge wave. Nattie squealed and laughed and grabbed on to Nathan for dear life. The children were swept away in the ensuing tsunami and washed up on the steps leading into the pool.

"That was awesome, Uncle Henry. DO IT AGAIN!" Nathan pleaded.

"No, no," Heidi gasped, coughing. "Once is more than enough, thank you. I think I swallowed half of the pool."

"Aww, mom!" Nathan lamented.

"C'mon, Nate, let's show 'em how it's done. Do you think we can make an even bigger one?" Uncle Henry came to the rescue.

"Yeah!"

Cannon balls were continually launched into the pool until it was time for James to start the steaks and other assorted goodies, since the coals were ready and glowing red. They all got out, and Heidi and Anne went to the kitchen to retrieve the meat for the fire while Henry made sure the kids stayed out of the way.

In the kitchen, Anne noticed a pitcher of brightly colored liquid with cherries and pineapple floating on top. Thirsty and curious, she asked Heidi, "Can I taste please?" she asked.

"Sure," Heidi said. "Help yourself."

Anne took a hurricane glass sitting on the counter and filled it to the rim. She took a small sip at first, smacked her lips, smiled, and took a few more. "I like it," she said. Then she finished off the glass and poured another.

"Whoa, easy girl. Jim gets his rum from a client in Jamaica. That stuff'll knock you on your ass," Heidi warned.

Anne wasn't exactly sure what Heidi meant, and for some reason, she didn't care either. She was experiencing a tingly feeling all over her body and was in an inexplicably wonderful mood. She drank the second glass and refilled it again before following Heidi out with the plate of food for the barbeque with the pitcher in tow.

James stood at the ready with spatula and tongs, donning a 007 LICENSE TO GRILL novelty apron. A brush and a bowl of marinade lay waiting on the table by the outdoor kitchen. James took the first of the steaks off the plate and threw it on the fire.

"This stuff will knock your ass on," Anne proclaimed, taking another sip from her third glass of piña colada.

"Anne, honey," Henry sat up. "What the hell are you doing? You're not used to drinking."

"Did you know Jim gets this from a Jamaica? Whatever a Jamaica is? It tastes really good." She put the glass to her lips and guzzled it down, followed by a long, "BBRRRRRRRAAAAAAAAAPPPPP!" She held her hand to her lips with a look of surprise that turned into a giggle.

"Let her have as much as she wants," James called from the grill. "She's an adult."

"But she's not used to drinking," Heidi said. "She has no idea how this will affect her."

Anne steadied her glass then refilled it, spilling some on her hand. "I can choose," she said defiantly.

Henry shook his head in disbelief while he struggled with his next decision. "All right, but this is the last glass. I'm cutting you off." He took the nearly empty pitcher away from her. "I'll just keep an eye on you and make sure you don't hurt yourself."

Heidi shrugged. "Your problem if she pukes. I'm not cleaning it up," she said, going back into the house to bring out the plates and silverware. James had just plated the first of the meat that was ready and placed it on the patio table when Heidi returned.

"Dig in!"

Heidi prepared a couple of hot dogs off the platter, added some potato chips from the bag, and set Nathan and Nattie down to eat their dinner. Henry took a large steak and a sausage, a huge mound of potato salad, and a buttered corn-on-the-cob that had been roasted in the oven. Anne ate a chicken breast, an ear of corn, and a third as much potato salad as Henry, while Heidi finished the last steak. After dinner, Heidi brought out cupcakes with red, white, and blue frosting for dessert.

Anne tried to stand up to go to the bathroom and fell over onto Henry's chair.

"Whoa there, girl!" Henry caught her before she hurt herself. "You've had a bit too much to drink, young lady! I was afraid of this."

"I need...to peeeeeeeeeee!" She drew out the word, trying to hold on to Henry.

"She's wasted," James said, laughing.

Mercifully, the kids were too preoccupied to notice, sticking out their multicolored tongues at each other and laughing.

Henry stood up and put his arms around Anne's waist. "I'll help her go to the bathroom. Heidi, do you want to come along?"

"Oh no, thank you. I told you, if she blows chunks, it's your problem. I haven't held another girl's hair back while she called Ralph on the porcelain phone since...Well, never mind when. Just don't get any on my new rug."

Henry stood. "She's not going to hurl. She just has to take a leak." He hoped.

"First time for everything," James commented.

Henry wondered. Was this the first time she got drunk? Did she ever use drugs? Wouldn't that have shown in her test results? Would he ever know?

Thankfully, the trip to the bathroom was uneventful despite the fact that Henry had to guide Anne onto the seat. When they rejoined the group, it was time to pack everyone up to head out to see the fireworks. Henry debated taking Anne straight home to sleep it off, but she begged and pleaded because she was so looking forward to seeing fireworks for the first time. Not surprisingly, he gave into her; and they all climbed, or staggered, into James's SUV and headed out to the beach nearest the Venice jetty, which offered a spectacular view of the display. At the beach, Anne lost her balance getting out of the car and fell back onto the side of the vehicle.

"I feel thunny," she said, her speech slurring.

"You look thunny," Henry answered. "Come on." He put his arm around her waist, helping her to walk. "I've got you. James, can you get the chairs while I help Anne?"

"Sure, why not," James grumbled.

"Hey, you're the one who said, 'let her have all she wants,' remember?" Henry reminded him in a mocking tone.

"Yeah, yeah, I remember."

"Here, let me have the cooler. I can hold her up with one arm. She's just a little unsteady."

There was a little bit of beach left where they could all spread out. The sun lit up the sky with beautiful hues of blue and orange, flaming the clouds as it made its way down into the horizon. The crowded beach let creation know of its appreciation with an enthusiastic round of applause, a fitting opening act to the fireworks show.

"Where did the sun go?" Anne shouted. "Did it go swimming?"

"You've seen a sunset before," Henry said, smiling. "The sun doesn't really go into the water. It just looks like that. Sit down and enjoy the fireworks." He guided her to a beach chair and sat her down.

She did, just in time for the show to begin. The fireworks were set off on a boat several yards from the shore, so the blossoms of fiery beauty reflected over the surface of the water. Anne cried out when she saw the first one. "Flowers in the sky!" She stood unsteadily and pointed.

Henry made her sit back down. "There's going to be more," he said firmly. "Stay in your chair."

As the exploding blooms filled the sky and the "oohs" and "ahhs" came from the audience, Anne howled with delight at each display, clapping her hands together and calling out the colors of the blasts. The children joined her, and all three hollered at the display while the people nearest them responded with not-so-nice looks. Henry explained to them that it was her first time and that she had a bit too much to drink. It didn't help. And frankly, he really didn't care if they didn't like it. He was just trying to be nice.

The finale came when multiple fireworks filled the night sky with light, color, and thunder. Everyone on the beach made noise now, drowning out Anne and the kids. The complainers near them had moved to a different location, so Henry let her scream as loud as she wanted.

When the sky was dark except for the trailing lines of smoke and the smell of sulfur, the crowd headed to the parking lot and the mass of cars. Henry, Anne, Heidi, James, and the kids stayed behind for a few more minutes until the web of traffic was not as tangled. Then they headed back to the SUV, and James drove back to their house.

By the time they got back to the house, both Anne and the children had all passed out. James scooped up Nathan, and Heidi took Nattie. Henry tried to get Anne out of the car, but she couldn't stand up. The rum and the excitement of the show had finally taken their toll on her, forcing Henry to pick her up with an audible groan. With Anne slung over his shoulder like a sack of potatoes, Henry had an awkward time bending to kiss his tiny sister goodnight. "This has been a Fourth of July I won't soon forget. Thanks for everything." Henry took one of Anne's arms dangling in midair and helped her wave good-bye.

Back at his car, Henry propped Anne up against the passenger side while he opened the door. Anne's head hung down, and her hair covered her face as she rolled her head back and forth in a futile effort to stand up straight. Henry poured her into the seat, buckled her up, and lowered the seat so she could lie down. She sang a nonsensical tune to herself and kept her eyes closed.

When Henry got Anne home, he took her to the bedroom and put her right to bed. She was still humming her tune.

"Huuhhhh…Henry," Anne said, her eyes half-open. "I fly in the sky…You fly too?"

"Yes, I fly too, but not as high as you are at the moment." He pulled the blanket up to her neck. "Go to sleep." He kissed her on the forehead.

"I sleep," she slurred into a light snore.

Henry retreated to the bathroom, brushed his teeth, and splashed water on his face and head, letting it linger there to drip back into the sink. He watched the cares of the day disappear down the drain. When he joined Anne in bed, she was already in the throes of another nightmare. He held her as he did every night, but this time, Anne never woke up fully. He doubted very much if she would remember this dream or even how she got home and into bed.

When she finally settled down, Henry collapsed back down in the bed. Just before he shut his eyes, he saw that damn shadow dart across the room again. He sat up in his bed with a start, his head spinning. He became concerned about what he thought he'd been seeing lately. Was he getting paranoid, seeing shadows in his room and mysterious cars following him? Or were there legitimate reasons to be concerned? Maybe he needed to talk to Angela too so she could help him sort it all out. Finally, the beer and the late hour took their toll on him as well. He lay back down and fell into a deep sleep as soon as his head hit the pillow.

In the dark of the night, one corner of the room was swallowed in a deeper darkness. The mysterious black shadow oozed out of the corner and crept closer to the helpless couple, stopping at the foot of the bed. Slowly, it expanded and solidified into a huge grotesque, not-quite-humanlike form with glowing red eyes. Despite its mass, it moved silently as it made its way up along the side of the bed, stopping next to Anne's head. Anne's breath had turned to fog as the temperature in the room dropped dramatically. Leaning over her, its forked tongue whispered through jagged teeth into her shell-like ear, "Soooooon!"

42

After the Other has taken me one last time, he says that he is bored of hurting me. He orders the black dragons to take me away and throw me into the heart of the black mountain where the fire burns. He tells his sons that I am to be an offering to the Master in celebration of his victory. I wonder who this Master is as I am dragged away. I try to fight with what little strength I have and beg him not to throw me into the fire, but he does not hear me over the sound of his own laughter.

43

The Morning After

July 5
Sunday

Anne fought the demons in the night, screaming and dragging herself as well as the sheets and blankets off the bed and falling onto the floor. Henry jumped up and ran around the bed to see if she had hurt herself and to wake her from the nightmares as he did every night. Either the nightmare from earlier in the evening had returned or she was just now sober enough to fully react to it. They were soon joined by a never-ending parade of concerned pets streaming into the room and surrounding them, sniffing and licking Anne wherever they could once she was still.

Anne woke up on the floor, disoriented and tangled in the sheets. She put her hands on her head and moaned, obviously suffering from a pounding headache. Henry brought her a bottle of water along with a couple of aspirin. "Take these and drink some water." He handed her the aspirin first then opened the bottle for her.

She tried to drink the water and did manage to get most of it down, although some spilled on her breasts, one of which had popped out of her bikini top she still had on.

"Come on." Henry helped her to her feet, fixing her wardrobe malfunction along the way. She stood, still shaky, but she was able to stand on her own. "I'll make you some breakfast." He put one arm around her waist, and she put her arm around his neck and laid her head on his shoulder.

They started to walk a few feet when Anne stopped and promptly threw up all over Henry. Then she started to cry.

Henry just stood there for a long moment, blinking in surprise. It all happened so fast and unexpected that it took a few seconds for his brain to process. Then the odor of vomit wafted up his nose. *Well, that's disgusting!* He turned his attention back to Anne.

"Sweetheart, it's okay. Don't cry," Henry said, trying to reassure her while guiding her back to the bed to sit. He tried not to hug her and redistribute the mess. He squatted in front of her and grabbed a nearby wastebasket. He was in midsentence explaining to her what it was for when Anne blasted him with a second volley straight to the face. Anne's crying went off the chart, and Charlie and Sam jumped up and started licking him.

"GO...GET...DAMN IT!" Henry yelled.

"WWWWAAAAAHHHHHH!" Anne's crying went up an octave. *Perfect*, he thought as he grabbed a towel from the hamper and started to clean up the vomit on his face and bare chest. Then he wiped up the vomit on the floor, competing with the dogs. Finally, he had himself cleaned up enough so he could tend to Anne. She had fallen back onto the bed sobbing, tired, and weak.

"Anne? Honey? How are you doing?" Her only reply was a long somber groan. "Come on, we need to get you cleaned up." Henry grabbed both of her hands and helped her to her feet. He escorted her to the bathroom, where he helped her out of her swimsuit before he slipped off his shorts. He had her rinse her mouth and splash water on her face and wrist while he held a cold wet washcloth to the back of her neck.

"Do you remember if you've ever felt like this before?" he asked.

"No, and I never want to feel like this ever again." She winced at the sound of her own voice.

"Didn't think so. Brush your teeth and we'll jump into the shower together."

Anne did as instructed while Henry got the shower going. Soon the two of them were being bombarded by the steamy waters of the shower. Henry could feel his pores opening and the morning's mishap circling the drain. Anne was still among the walking dead, and she just leaned against him while he washed her as best he could from head to toe.

"That will make you feel better." Henry helped her out of the shower, wrapped a towel around her, and sat her back on the bed. He toweled himself dry and slipped into a pair of running shorts and a muscle shirt. Anne found the strength to drag a comb through her hair while Henry retrieved a pair of pink shorts and T-shirt for her to wear. He reasoned that would be enough to hold her until she felt better.

They made their way to the kitchen where Henry gave Charlie, Sam, and the rest of the menagerie a more suitable breakfast than blown chunks. For Anne, he prepared some herbal tea and dry toast. He needed to get her rehydrated and replace her electrolytes, but first he needed to settle her queasy stomach. He made himself a strong cup of coffee and ate a stale powdered doughnut which, up until now, had lain forgotten in a bag tucked in the back of the cupboard.

Anne started to feel a little better, the color coming back into her face as she sipped her tea and nibbled her toast.

"I think we'll just stay in today," he said. "You need a day of rest."

"What is rest?"

"Just doing nothing, I guess. A day where we don't have to go anywhere or do any work. We'll just hang out with the animals." They had been busy every day since he found her, and he also felt that a day to just relax might help them both.

They finished their breakfast, and Henry cleaned up the mess. Anne stayed in her seat for a while, petting each critter who came to say good morning. Henry opened the doggy door so that all the animals could go outside into the bright Florida morning sun.

After the morning chores were done, they went into the living room and sat on the sofa, turning on the television. The set came on to a morning church service where a pastor was in the middle of a sermon.

"Do you know," the pastor said, leaning on the pulpit on his forearm, the other hand pointed at the audience, "even if you were the only person on this earth that would ever believe in him, Jesus would still have gone to the cross for you? You mean that much to him. Jesus chose to suffer the pain he knew he would endure because we were all sinners. We didn't even know him yet, and still he chose to go to death on Calvary for us. He made the sacrifice.

"We need to be reminded why that sacrifice was made. You cannot earn your way into heaven. All your good deeds are as filthy rags to him. You cannot buy your way into heaven. God created gold, and man created greed and lusted after it. Jesus is the only way to be with the Father in heaven. Therefore, a sacrifice had to be made to make that way happen. Sacrifice would not be a sacrifice if someone could earn it."

Henry picked up the remote to change the channel, but Anne put her hand on it. "No, please, I want to hear."

Henry grimaced but put the remote down. He'd heard all this before and believed it all before God turned his back on him. But Anne sat on the edge of the sofa, concentrating on the words of the man in the impeccable black suit with perfect hair. *Didn't they all look like that?*

"When we look at Jesus's example, what we should learn from that is that we should be willing to make sacrifices in our lives for people we haven't even met yet. Maybe it's giving a little more of our money to support a charity." *It's always about the money.*

"Maybe it's giving more of our time to help the homeless at a shelter or a young mother who has been abused. The simple definition of sacrifice is giving up something that you want to keep, even if it hurts to do so. Parents know this better than anyone. How many evenings and weekends have you sacrificed to support your son or daughter's recital or soccer game? How many of you have worked a second job or put off buying a new car to pay for your child's college? Parents make these sacrifices out of love with no guarantee that their child will someday play at Carnegie Hall or sign some huge sports contract.

"God gave us his only son. Handed him over to the Pharisees and stood by and watched as they beat, mocked, and eventually killed him in one of the worst ways possible. God the Father gave up his only son's life with the hope that one day you would believe in him and become one of his children as well. He made us all with free will. He clings to the hope that you will one day use that gift of free will to willingly accept Jesus's sacrifice and be forgiven." He stood up and walked in front of the thin wooden pulpit with the raised cross on the stand.

"As God made a sacrifice, he calls us to follow him. Sacrifice is giving up something for someone else, even if they don't deserve it or even know about it. Even if no one knows about it! We certainly didn't know about God's sacrifice when it was made. And we certainly don't deserve it. Paul tells us in Ephesians, chapter 5, verses 1 and 2, to be 'imitators of God, as beloved children; and walk in love, just as Christ also loved you and gave Himself up for us, an offering and a sacrifice to God as a fragrant aroma.'"

The pastor walked back behind the pulpit and closed his Bible. "So the next time you see someone in need, don't worry about what the cost is or what glory you may obtain by it. Be willing to make the sacrifice just as Christ made the ultimate sacrifice just for you. Then you will truly know God's love, just for you." Music started to play in the background as the camera panned over the audience. Henry began to feel very uncomfortable; memories of a faith long-buried tried to rise to the surface of his heart.

Anne got off the sofa and sat on the floor in front of the television, focused on the words of the pastor.

"Everyone, please bow your heads. Have you accepted the sacrifice of Jesus?" he continued. "Have you acknowledged the sacrifice he made hanging on the cross, beaten and humiliated to the point of his death just so that you may have eternal life? The beauty of His sacrifice is that because He made it, you don't have to. All you have to do is accept that sacrifice and ask him to come into your heart as your Lord and Savior. As the choir sings 'Just as I Am,' I'll be waiting in front of the stage here with our trusted assistants alongside me, waiting for you to come forward and acknowledge that you accepted that sacrifice. Everyone, keep your heads down. Don't be afraid. Come on down."

One by one, several people got up from the audience and came to the stage where the people waiting there put their hands on the heads of those who came forward, their own heads bowed and their mouths moving. The music kept playing while more came down to the stage, hands held in front of them and heads bowed. Anne stood up and walked up to the television, her hand outstretched, then touched the screen.

Henry turned his head away, his mouth clenched and his breath forced. He'd made that walk before. It didn't mean anything! When he needed God or Jesus or whoever, no one was there! It took everything inside him not to change the channel and find a nice action movie or even see if the game had started yet, but he saw how Anne was responding and instead got up and left the room under the pretenses that he needed to go to the bathroom. He didn't want to say something in his anger that he would later regret.

Henry stayed in the bathroom for a few minutes, trying to keep the anger away. The specters of his losses haunted him like the demons in Anne's nightmares. He took several deep breaths, willing himself to let go until he finally felt his heart slow to a normal beat and his breathing become easier.

He went back to the living room and saw that the program had ended and the credits were rolling on the screen. Anne was still standing in front of the television, but she turned around when he came back in.

"Tell me about Jesus," she asked. Henry closed his eyes and sighed.

"I'll see if Pastor Jennings can meet with you. He's the pastor from my parents' church, South Bay Baptist. He can better explain things than I can."

"Okay," she said, nodding and coming back to sit on the sofa.

After that, Henry took control of the remote and found a good action movie where lots of things blew up, which made him feel much better. *There is real healing in big fiery explosions.* Then they watched the football game between Tampa Bay and Chicago, ate some popcorn, watched another movie starring that wonderful Austrian bodybuilder, where even more things blew up, then finally watched a comedy about knights in King Arthur's day presented by a British comedy troupe. They ordered Chinese food for dinner and did not leave the house at all. Henry put the morning out of his mind.

44

The black dragons drag me down to the tunnels, and I feel the heat of the fire as we near the center. I wonder if the pain of the fire will be better than the pain of my agony. All I can do is look forward to the release that death will bring. I must accept my fate. I am powerless to do anything to stop it. But I am afraid of what I will feel when the fire touches my skin. I have suffered so much pain. Can I endure much more? I can only hope it will be quick. The black dragons lift me up and throw me into the fire. I wait to feel the hot fire as it consumes what is left of me, wishing with everything inside me that I could be somewhere else, someone else.

45

Anne Meets Dr. Rayback

July 6
Monday

Anne sat on the sofa in Angela Rayback's office while Angela typed notes on her laptop. Henry sat beside her, his arm around her shoulders.

"Anne," Angela said, "let's start with what you remember before you met Henry."

"I do not remember anything." Anne shook her head. "There is nothing before Henry."

"Interesting." Angela typed on her laptop. "Henry thinks you may have been on a boat that caught fire, that maybe you fell into the ocean. How does that make you feel?"

Anne shrugged her shoulders. "It may be, but I do not remember a boat. I do not remember the fire, but I feel it."

"Henry says that the nightmares are getting worse? Can you tell me what is happening?"

Anne blinked her eyes rapidly against the tears that began to form, her hands trembling.

"It's okay, Anne. Take your time. You don't have to tell me if you don't want to."

They all sat quietly for several minutes while Anne took time to compose her thoughts. Finally, in a little voice, she spoke. "The black dragons come and kill all of the golden ones. I see my... father?...die at my feet. Then the dragons take me away to the black mountains where..." She stopped.

"Anne," Henry offered, "you don't have to talk about this if it's too difficult."

"Give her time, Henry," Angela suggested. "I'll only charge you for the hour, but we can take as long as we need. Anne, take a deep breath in through your nose and let it out through your mouth." Anne did. "Again." Anne took a few more deep breaths until the trembling stopped.

"Take your time," Angela encouraged her.

Anne nodded. "I am taken to the black mountains where Saphan...cuts off my wings...then my tail ..." She struggled to get the words out. "Then...he takes me."

"What do you mean 'takes you'," Henry asked, his brows furrowed. Anne could see that he was upset by what she was saying. She didn't want to make him angry, but they wanted her to talk about the dreams. She took his hand and held tightly.

"He...has sex with me...not like we do...he is hurting me...I do not want to."

"Anne, you don't have to say anything more," Henry said in a low voice. She felt his muscles tighten in the arm that was around her.

She closed her eyes and shook her head sharply. "No, I must."

Angela took her other hand. "It's okay, Anne. There's no one here that can harm you. You're safe here with me and Henry. No one is going to hurt you anymore."

Anne held on to both Henry's and Angela's hands as she continued. "He takes me and bites me, tearing out my skin...eating me...while the others laugh." She began weeping, letting go of the hands holding hers and burrowing herself in Henry's chest.

Angela sat back and took a deep breath. "I think that what she went through was more than a fire on a boat. It sounds like maybe she witnessed someone close to her being killed before she was viciously assaulted. You're sure that there were no reports of something like this from the police department?"

Henry shook his head. "Nothing that would match her description or that hasn't already been solved. If this happened, it was never reported to anyone so far as I've heard." He continued to hold on to Anne, stroking her back while she wept. "I never imagined it was as bad as this."

"One thing I don't understand is"—he hesitated a moment—"she is, or was, a virgin when I met her. And Dr. Jackson examined her completely and said she is in perfect health with no signs of prior abuse or injury. How could she have been sexually assaulted? Wouldn't there be physical evidence of that?"

"Well," Angela responded, "sexual assault is not always vaginal, but I would think Dr. Jackson would have found some scarring in any case." Angela noted this on her laptop. "Also, dreams of rape don't always mean a physical attack. It may be something totally unrelated to the actual act, such as when one feels betrayed or abused or humiliated. We have no way of knowing if the rape in her dreams is from an actual incident or something else."

"We may have an idea as to what caused her memory loss, but we still need to understand why these events manifest in dreams of dragons. It may be that the dragons attacking her in the dream world are the memories of her attack trying to get through. I am going to do some more research. In the meantime, Anne, are the drawings helping you?"

Anne had ceased weeping and now only sniffled, her eyes red and swollen. "Yes, I think I can talk about it now because I have drawn the dragons."

"Okay," Angela continued. "Keep up with your drawings. If you feel at any time though that the pictures are making you feel worse, try to focus on lighter subjects, like the animals."

"I can do that," Anne agreed.

"Henry, take pictures of her drawings and paintings and email them to me. They could be very helpful."

"I will."

"Also, I'd like to set up some sessions with you, maybe once a week while you are creating your paintings to see if we can uncover any of those lost memories. Your memory may even come back on its own." She took Anne's hand. "We will try to see what we can do to help you get back your life."

They stood up, and Angela reached out, taking Anne in her arms and hugging her. "It's going to be okay, Anne," she said, smiling. "We'll find out who you really are. I promise."

"Thank you," Henry said, hugging Angela next. "I can't tell you how much this means."

"Let's set up a time for next week? Wednesday at ten o'clock?"

Henry nodded, pulling out his checkbook to pay for the session. "We'll be here."

Angela put her hand on the checkbook. "No, Henry. It's okay. There's no charge."

"Thanks."

When they left Angela's office, they were both silent on the drive home. Henry pondered what the secrets revealed in the session meant—the answer to the dilemma that was Anne still unsolved. He knew that he was getting angry while she told them about her dreams. How could he not? It took everything inside him to keep it bottled up. But he was there for Anne, not for his own feelings. The rage that grew at the possibilities her story meant tied his stomach into knots. Yet there were no scars or evidence of a physical assault. What was done to this girl to leave her so deprived of memory but leave no visible scars? Was that kind of torture even possible? Henry was so lost in thought that he didn't notice the black sedan follow them home.

46

I wait to feel the heat of the inferno as it takes my life and ends my woe. I wish with all my heart to escape from the flames, to go to another place if only it were possible.

The fire surrounds me, but it does not touch me! I do not know what is happening. The fire fades away until I am surrounded by complete darkness. There is nothing but the darkness. I do not feel pain anymore, I do not feel anything. I am prisoner to the dark surrounding me, pulling me further in. Is this what it is to finally die? Am I finally free?

Where am I? What am I? Why cannot I feel anything? Am I alive? Am I breathing? Do I even exist? There is nothing before the blackness that swirls around me, and I do not know if it will ever end. How did I get here? What is happening to me!?

47

Pastor Jennings

July 7
Tuesday

Anne finally finished her paintings, and together, they put the text on each panel. Henry packaged up the drawings as carefully as he could and sent them to Elliott, who would shop around for a publisher or publish it through his company. It was a good feeling to finish the project, and they were both quite happy with the final result.

"Now that we've finished the book," Henry asked. "What are you going to work on now?"

Anne shrugged. "I do not know. I think I would like to learn more about what I heard on the television."

Henry said, "I'll give Pastor Jennings a call."

"I would like that," Anne said.

A few hours later, they sat in the office of Pastor Ron Jennings of South Bay Baptist Church. He was an older man with thinning blond hair that was gray at the temples. He had a remarkable smile that put you at ease the moment you met him. He was unusually fit for a man of the cloth and stood about six feet with Paul Newman blue eyes.

"Hello, Henry. And you must be Anne," he said, extending his hand. "How can I help you?"

"Anne saw a church service on TV where they had an altar call and has some questions."

"I think I might be able to help. Won't you sit down?"

When they were seated, Pastor Jennings smiled and looked at Anne. "What are your questions?"

"Tell me about Jesus," she began.

Pastor Jennings smiled and nodded. "Jesus is the Son of God. We believe that Jesus became the ultimate sacrifice to pay for all our sins. Another way to look at it is to realize that God is a perfect being. Because man is sinful, he cannot have communion with a perfect God. But God loved us so much that he sent his own son to be a sacrifice, to bridge the way for man to commune directly with God. That sacrifice was Jesus. Do you understand this so far?"

"What is love?" Anne asked. "And what is sacrifice?"

"Well"—Pastor Jennings steepled his fingers in front of him—"that is a very big question. There are many different kinds of love, and the term means different things to different people. For example, I can say 'I love chocolate cake' or 'I love to dance.' That is not really love, but we use that term to express how we feel about certain objects or foods or things we enjoy doing. Some people think that love is something you feel, like when someone says, 'I'm falling in love.'

"There is a love which is called *philia* love or 'brotherly love.' It's the bond between friends or soldiers who band together like brothers. It's not like the love a man has for a woman, for example.

"Then there is the love of family, which is called *storge* love. This is what you feel for your mother, father, or siblings. You love your mother differently than you would love a friend or a spouse.

"The love you would feel for your spouse can be described as *eros* love. It is the passionate love between a man and a woman that is expressed in a physical way. That's where people get confused when they say they are falling in love. *Eros* is more physical than the other types of love but is not by itself true love."

"Finally, there is unconditional love, or *agape*, which is the love that God has for all of us. Christ describes it best when he says in John 15:13: 'There is no greater love than this, that a man lay down his life for another.' *Agape* love means sacrifice or putting the needs of someone else above your own. This is the love that led Jesus to willingly die on the cross for our sins. John 3:16 expresses it well. 'God loved us so much that he sent his only son to die for our sins.' That is what true love, or the highest form of love, means. Do you understand?"

"I do not know," Anne said hesitantly. "I do not remember my family and do not have friends."

"How you feel toward Henry's family?" Pastor Jennings asked.

"Heidi and James make me feel like I am part of their family." She smiled. "I am happy inside here"—she pointed to her chest— "when I am with Nathan and Nattie."

Pastor Jennings leaned forward. "You can relate how you feel about them to how you would feel about your own family," he offered. "Does that make it any clearer? How do you feel when you are with Henry?"

She looked at Henry with longing in her eyes. "I do not want to be away from him. I hurt in here"—again she pointed to her chest— "when he is away from me." Henry took her hand to encourage her. "Everywhere inside me *needs* him.

"When we"—she glanced at Henry—"make love?" Henry blushed, a little embarrassed at discussing his sexual relationships in front of the pastor, but he nodded for her to continue. This was for her benefit, after all, not his. "When we make love," she continued, "I only know him. Nothing else is around me. I tickle inside, and I feel heat burning in me when I am with him. When he is inside me, we are like one body." She held out her hands with her palms facing up, shaking her head. "I do not know the words to tell you what I feel when we are together."

Pastor Jennings smiled and nodded. "You're doing just fine, Anne. That is a very good example of *eros* love." He looked at Henry over his glasses. "You and I will need to have a discussion about this another time, my friend." Henry fidgeted in his seat, the red color on his face getting brighter, knowing what the pastor wanted to talk about.

Pastor Jennings turned back to look at Anne. "I am glad that you have Henry and his family in your life. But it is the *agape* love that we all need. When you are willing to surrender everything you have and everything you want, even to the point of giving up your life for someone else, that is true love. That is sacrifice. It doesn't depend on what someone looks like, who he is, or even what he does, but it is truly from your own heart. This is the kind of love only God can give."

He took out his Bible and opened it. "Let me read something to you that might help explain love. Paul writes about love in his first letter to the Corinthians in chapter 13:

> Though I speak with the tongues of men and of angels, but have not love, I have become sounding brass or a clanging cymbal. And though I have the gift of prophecy, and understand all mysteries and all knowledge, and though I have all faith, so that I could remove mountains, but have not love, I am nothing. And though I bestow all my goods to feed the poor, and though I give my body to be burned, but have not love, it profits me nothing.
>
> Love suffers long and is kind; love does not envy; love does not parade itself, is not puffed up; does not behave rudely, does not seek its own, is not provoked, thinks no evil; does not rejoice in iniquity, but rejoices in the truth; bears all things, believes all things, hopes all things, endures all things. Love never fails.

"When we think about what Jesus did by going to the cross to die, that is the epitome of both love and sacrifice. God loves us so much he sacrificed his own son so that we could be with him. God loved his Son but knew that Jesus had to die for us to be able to come to the Father. And Jesus willingly submitted himself to become that sacrifice, knowing what it would cost him. That is the ultimate act of true love."

He closed the book and smiled at Anne. "I hope this has helped you."

"I will think about what you have told me," she said. "Thank you, Pastor."

Pastor Jennings took her hand in his. "I know it is a difficult concept to grasp, and I am here if you need to talk more about it."

Henry stood up and extended his hand to Anne to help her up. Pastor Jennings also stood and walked them to the door. "Please feel free to come see me any time you want to talk more about it." And to Henry, he said, "Take good care of her, my friend. I look forward to talking with you soon."

Henry gave the pastor an uneasy smile. He wasn't looking forward to that at all.

48

A bright flash of light replaces the black void I am in, and a voice softly speaks.

"Hello, my child. It is time for you to fulfill your destiny." The voice is soothing, making the fear go away.

"Who are you? Why can't I see you or touch you? How am I hearing you?"

"You are in-between. I am here to guide you to a new beginning."

"New beginning? I do not understand?"

"You will, in time. Do you remember who you are or where you came from?"

"No. I cannot remember."

"That is because your true destiny awaits. Hush, sleep now. When you awake, you will be renewed. It is time." The voice fades, and the nothingness returns.

I sense the body I now have but cannot see it. I cannot see anything. Cool liquid surrounds me. I am pushed by the cool liquid until I feel something firm under me. Then light begins to filter through the darkness, and shapes appear around me. Something approaches me.

"Heh…hello. Miss, are you okay?"

49

The Book Is Published

July 8
Wednesday

"We're going to be published!" Henry waved a letter over his head. "Elliot's company is going to publish the book. They'll be sending a contract."

Anne had been working on a still life of the shells she had collected. "I am very glad to hear that." She looked up and smiled.

"You did it, girl!" He hugged her then kissed the top of her head. "Guess I better call James and let him know we're going to need him after all." He punched in James's number on his phone.

While Henry talked to James, Anne dipped her brush into the cerulean blue glob of watercolor paint in her paint tray to use in the shadows of the shells. She listened to Henry explain the letter to James. She wasn't sure what it would mean to have her dreams printed in a book. The act of drawing out the dreams, although it didn't stop them, made them a little less intense. But now she would share them with many people.

Like Henry, she did not know why her dreams were about dragons. She wanted to find out what happened to her and, more importantly, who she really was. Did she have a family like Heidi and James? Why couldn't she remember anything about her childhood? The dreams were so real, so vivid, even to the point of knowing the names of the dragons in her nightmare world. She wondered if she would ever stop having nightmares. How could anyone forget so much in one world and remember so much in another? Did she really suffer such a trauma to take away her entire life? Why couldn't she remember?!

Henry got off the phone with James. "Let's go out and celebrate. I'm going to take you out to a movie and dinner at the pier. Come on, let's get cleaned up."

"I would like that," she said, putting her brush in the jar of water. They took a quick shower then she put on a white sundress with small flowers on it and white sandals. Henry chose to wear black slacks and a button-down black shirt with black loafers without socks.

Henry decided to go see a science fiction film recently released about an astronaut who crashes on another world where he meets a race of strange, glowing aliens. The story was about how the astronaut searches for a way back to his home world where he has a wife and two children, but while on the new world, he falls in love with one of the alien women who becomes pregnant with his child. When his shipmates finally find him years later, he has to choose to either return to his family on his home world or stay with his glowing bride and hybrid child. When he decides to stay, he and his new family are forced to fight his old comrades, who refuse to leave without him. In the midst of the struggle, he kills his best friend from the ship. He prevails over the crew of the starship and returns to his home, only to find that during the fight, his alien child was struck by falling debris when their home was hit by a laser cannon and died.

As the final scene of the movie played out, Anne wept for the astronaut and his family while Henry held her, whispering that it was only a movie and not real, although he too had a tear or two in his eyes. They sat together while the end credits rolled up the screen, and the rest of the audience filed out of the theatre. Henry picked up the empty tub of popcorn and their cup. "Let's go get something to eat, and after that, we'll go watch the sunset."

Henry parked by the beach, and they walked to the seafood restaurant. Several people lined the pier, fishing for sharks. Once seated, they enjoyed a garden salad, fresh crab legs, and a baked potato with a side of broccoli. Henry ordered hot chocolate chip cookies with ice cream for dessert. Anne rolled her eyes, relishing each decadent bite of the warm sweet chewy dough and the cold, melting ice cream on top.

After dinner, they walked back to the beach, took off their shoes, and sat on the sand along with the crowd of onlookers waiting to witness the beauty of a Florida sunset sink into the water. The sun slowly made its way to its watery grave, painting the clouds above the water with bright orange and yellow flames on a cerulean blue canvas. The sky gradually deepened in hue until the orange orb of the sun dipped into the dark blue ocean. Anne saw the scene as an artist wanting to capture it on canvas. Everyone clapped in appreciation at the spectacle of nature and eventually folded up their beach chairs and left. Henry and Anne stayed on the beach as the dark of night took its turn on the sky.

"Did you like the movie?" Henry asked Anne. They sat in the sand pushing up piles of it with their toes.

"It was beautiful," she replied. "I would love to go to that place."

"It's not real, Anne," he corrected her. "It's make-believe, like your princess movies."

The stars in the night sky started to reveal themselves, like a million lights being turned on one by one. Anne looked up at them. "Are there other places like that?"

Henry lay back on the sand. "I believe that there are other worlds. We can't be the only one. You have to think that in this whole universe, there must be other worlds where there is life. Our planet is like a piece of sand on the shore of the grand beach that is the universe. It's humbling to think of how small our world really is when you think about the billions of stars and planets up there."

Anne lay back with him, both ignoring the sand that crept into their clothes. "I know in here"—she pointed to her chest—"that there are other places too that we cannot see. Maybe a world like my dreams is out there somewhere."

"Maybe," Henry mused. "I have to think that there are so many possibilities of life, more than we can imagine. It's arrogant to think that we're the only life forms in the entire universe."

"Someday, I would like to see them all." Anne gazed at the sky, the stars sparkling in her wishful eyes.

"Me too. I have to think there is so much more we can experience and learn from other worlds. Can you imagine what they would look like?"

They remained lying on the sand watching more stars come out, the sound of the surf enchanting them to lose themselves in their imaginary journeys to exotic and alien lands. The beach became their solitary sanctuary.

Sometime later, Henry stretched his arms over his head and sighed. "Probably time we should head home." He turned to her, his head up while leaning on his elbow, and gazed upon her as she lay on the sand smiling at him. He wanted nothing more than to take her right there in the open on the sandy beach. He leaned down and kissed her passionately, and Anne responded by running her fingers through his hair before wrapping her arms around him and pulling him close. Together, their breathing deepened, and their hands began probing and caressing as if it were their first time.

There was something about the danger of being discovered on the public beach in the middle of the night that made the experience that much more exciting. Henry's kisses moved down her neck towards her breasts, and he nearly tore the strap of her sundress to expose them to his waiting mouth, while Anne worked to loosen his belt and undo his pants. The moon blushed as they gave into their passion, forgetting where they were or who might see. It was one of those special moments two lovers share when they are alone in the universe. Just the two of them; time and the earth held still so the moment was theirs and theirs alone. The moon rose a little higher behind them, carving out a path of light across the ocean and bathing them in the glow of true love.

Afterward, they relaxed on the moonlit beach, beyond which lay a black wall before them. It was around one o'clock in the morning. Henry said, "Now we really need to go." He stood up, adjusted his clothes, and brushed what sand he could from them. Then he reached out his hand to help her stand as she brushed sand from her dress, her sandals in her hand.

They kept their shoes off and made their way across the dark sands to try to find their way to the car in the moonlight. Henry thought he saw the gleam of the hood a few yards ahead and guided her to the wooden walkway over the wild grass to the sand-covered black asphalt of the parking lot.

50

The Attack

When they approached their car, Henry saw four men dressed in black standing near it, a black sedan parked next to it that looked disturbingly familiar. He slowly he held out his hand for Anne to stop and pushed her behind him. He whispered in the hope that only Anne would hear, "These are the guys who've been chasing us. We need to slip away." But it was too late; they had been spotted.

One of the men, a shorter man with blond hair sticking out of the black knit hat, walked around the car to where Henry and Anne stood. "Quite a show you two put on. Care to share some of that?" He sneered at Anne. "Hello, little lady. We've got someone who wants to meet you."

Henry dropped his shoes and assumed a fighting stance. "Run!" he shouted as the four men approached. Anne turned and took off, running away as fast as she could.

"Get her!" blondie shouted, pointing. Two of the men ran after Anne while blondie made his move on Henry. Henry brought his right fist forward, connecting with blondie's chin and knocking him into the car. The other man, a tall black man, ran around the vehicle with his fists raised, ready to strike at Henry. Henry spun around to his right and struck tall man's face with the back of his fist. When he turned to make sure Anne was running from the other two goons who chased after her, blondie recovered enough to land a blow on Henry's left cheek.

Henry staggered back but recovered his balance just in time to block tall guy's fist with his left forearm as it hammered toward him. He shot his right arm up, palm first and struck tall guy square in the nose, breaking the cartilage and sending him to the asphalt. Caught between the two, Henry took a punch to his lower back from blondie. With tall guy out of the fight, he turned around to face blondie, just in time to see the black SUV drive up with two more uninvited guests to the party.

Henry had to try and keep the odds against him to a minimum, so he punched blondie in the solar plexus, causing him to bend over. Then Henry grabbed the back of his head with both hands and pulled down while bringing his knee up into the brute's face. His Navy training was rusty, but not that rusty. As blondie hit the ground with an audible thud, one of the newcomers grabbed him from behind, wrapped his arm around Henry's neck, and squeezed. *Damn that guy was fast. Maybe I'm rustier than I thought.* The new guy's partner then started punching Henry in the gut. Henry held on to the arm squeezing his neck, used it as leverage, then brought his legs up, kicking the gut puncher in the chest and knocking him back.

Then he grabbed a hold of the new guy's thumb and snapped it back to loosen his hold, allowing Henry's elbow to connect to new guy's abdomen, breaking him free of the choke hold. But new guy's partner got back up and connected a left hook to Henry's jaw. New guy followed that with a punch to Henry's kidneys, causing him to fall. He got back up, turned around, braced himself, brought his fists up in front of him, and threw three quick right jabs at new guy then pivoted to his left with a side kick to new guy's partner. By that time, blondie had rejoined the fray, and all three came at Henry, surrounding him. *This is not where I want to be!* Tactically, this was the worst case scenario, not being able to keep all his opponents in his field of vision. The trio started punching and kicking him from all sides, and all he could do was to try and block as best he could. Until he felt the sting of the blade as it entered his side. He never saw it coming and had no idea who stabbed him.

Henry's first thought when he looked down at his shirt was that he was bleeding. The blade felt cold when it pierced his side, and he noted, almost as a detached observer, that it hurt, but not as much as he thought it should. The stabbing felt almost surreal, as if he were watching someone else grapple with the four attackers. Well, two really, because tall guy with the broken nose was too involved with his own pain to keep up his part of the attack, and one of the newcomers was rolling on the ground after a hard kick to his groin. When the first two who went after Anne came back without her, Henry felt a great sense of relief, despite his own predicament in now having to face six pissed-off attackers with a stab wound. It would all be worth it if Anne got away.

Henry felt one fist connect with his cheek and another to his stomach, sending him falling to the asphalt, his body starting to go into shock. He lay on the street cradled into a fetal position, his arms around his midsection, while the attackers kicked him over and over until the sudden and loud sound of a siren and the flashing lights of a Venice Police Department squad car interrupted the assault. By some miracle, someone must have witnessed the fray and called 911. The four who were still able to walk grabbed the two who were down, shoved them into the two vehicles, and sped off mere moments before the squad car arrived on the scene. Two patrolmen jumped out of the car and rushed over to Henry.

"Sir, are you all right?" a white male with a name tag that read "Harrison" said. He put his hand on Henry's shoulder.

"I've been stabbed," Henry grunted, turning onto his back, his arms still around his abdomen. The other officer, an African-American woman named "Wilson," was already on her portable radio calling for an ambulance.

"My girlfriend," Henry gasped. "Two of them ran off...after her. That way." He indicated north from the pier with his bloody hand. "They came back without her...I don't know where she is." He found it hard to breathe, let alone talk.

Officer Wilson quickly retrieved a first aid kit from the car while Officer Harrison was holding on to Henry's side, hands pressed against the wound in an effort to stop the bleeding.

"I'll go look for her," Wilson said, giving Harrison the first aid kit so that he could replace his hand with a padded bandage. "What is her name? What does she look like?"

"Anne. Her name is Anne. Blond hair, white dress." Henry stopped as a spasm of pain took his breath. "Tall, five feet ten inches, 130 pounds."

"Thanks," Wilson said, turning north to run down Harbor Drive. She had a flashlight in her hand and was calling Anne's name.

"We'll find her, sir," Harrison said, still holding the pad to the wound. "Can you tell me your name?"

"Henry Williford." Henry tried to get his wallet.

Officer Harrison reached into Henry's pocket and pulled out the black leather trifold wallet. "I got it, Mr. Williford." With one hand holding the bandages over Henry's wound, he flipped open the wallet with the other hand to get Henry's driver's license.

"Can you tell me what happened?" Harrison tried to keep Henry talking and awake.

"We...were on the beach late...came back to the car... black sedan."

"Take your time."

"Four guys waiting...I told Anne to run, and two of 'em...chased her. I held my own...against the other two...then second car came with...two more. During the fight...one stabbed me." Henry tried to laugh, but it hurt too much. "Should've seen the other guys!"

The ambulance arrived, and the paramedics got out, running over with their bag to help.

"Stab wound to the lower right quadrant of the abdomen," Harrison called out.

One of the paramedics, a woman with blonde hair tied back in a ponytail named "Henderson," knelt over Henry and quickly checked his vitals. Once she was satisfied that he was breathing on his own, she shined a light in his eyes. "Hello, sir. I'm a paramedic, and I'm going to take care of you. Can you tell me your name?"

"Henry Williford."

"Hi, Henry. I'm Jill. Henry, can you tell me where you are?"

"In a stupid parking lot...bleeding like a stuck pig...while my girlfriend is...all alone in the dark...where I should be...out there...looking for her," Henry gasped. "In Venice, Florida."

"Well, you're in no shape to help anyone at the moment. I'm sure the officers will find your girlfriend. What's her name?"

"Anne." Henry's replies were growing weaker by the moment.

"Okay, Henry, stay with me. Are you hurt anywhere else? Are there any other injuries I should know about?"

"No...I don't think so. Unless you think...numerous kicks and punches to my head, face, and vital organs count?"

"You're doing fine, Henry. My partner is here, and we're going to put you on a backboard then onto the gurney."

The other paramedic, a Hispanic male with a name tag that read "Garcia," pulled up the gurney and put a backboard on the ground. Officer Harrison stepped back. "Okay, Henry," Garcia said. "We're going to put you on the backboard and take you to the hospital. Ready on three?" They transferred him to the backboard and then to the gurney.

Henry waved his right hand, grimacing in pain. "Wait! Can't leave yet...Anne...need to find Anne...Is she okay?"

Henderson called it in as soon as Henry was secure. "Thirty two-year-old white male, with a single stab wound to lower right quadrant of the abdomen, also multiple contusions. He's breathing and alert, but he's in shock due to loss of blood. I'm going to start an IV and administer oxygen. Patient's name is Henry Williford." She added a few more pads over the wound and taped it down with medical tape.

Henderson looked at Officer Harrison. "Who is Anne?" She put a blanket over Henry.

"His girlfriend. He says she ran off north down Harbor Road. My partner is looking for her."

"We've got to go, Henry," Henderson said. "The officers will find Anne." She and Garcia lowered the gurney then lifted it up into the ambulance.

"No, please." Henry grabbed her arm. "Need to find her."

"Sir," she answered as kindly as she could but with a strong urgency, "you are in shock, and you're losing a lot of blood. How would Anne feel if we found her and lost you? They'll find her and bring her to the hospital as soon as they do."

Officer Harrison stepped up into the ambulance and took Henry's hand. "We'll stay here until we find her and bring her to you. You have my word."

Henry reluctantly nodded, closed his eyes, and lay back as Garcia got out of the back of the ambulance and into the driver's seat while Henderson took his vitals and communicated his status to the hospital. "Please let them find her," he prayed to a God he no longer believed in but now wanted with all of his heart to be there.

Anne did as Henry had instructed and turned around, running as fast as she could and catching her two would-be assailants flatfooted and off guard. She had a tremendous lead on them as she raced toward a bend in Harbor Drive that led to a thickly wooded area made up of palm trees and tall beach grass. She disappeared into the night, crossing the perimeter of the trees and darting left and right so she wouldn't leave a clear path for them to follow. At one point, she leapt over a small sand dune and curled up in a shallow section, hoping her white dress and blonde hair would blend in with the white sand of the beach. Her heart beat wildly in her chest, and the seconds ticked away like hours as she waited breathlessly to see if her ruse would work.

For the longest time, her pursuers were nowhere in sight. For a brief moment, she thought she may have eluded them until she heard the sound of their voices and heavy breathing.

"Where...the hell...did she...go?" the heavier of the two men gasped, sucking in air and holding his side.

"Man, we're going to be in deep trouble with the Master if we don't bring her back," his partner replied. "We better split up. You go left, and I'll go right. And be sure to keep each other in sight so she doesn't slip past us."

The two thugs split up, the mouth-breather headed right in Anne's direction. She couldn't see him, but she could hear him rustling through the tall grass, crunching dead twigs and sand as he trudged ever closer. Anne was on the verge of panic at the sound of his approach. *Crunch, crunch, crunch.* In moments he would be upon her. *Crunch, crunch, crunch.* If she bolted now, she would give away her position for sure. *Crunch, crunch, crunch.*

"Damn it, look!" the mouth-breather shouted, alerting his partner. "The cops are coming. See, there's a squad car heading our way." He pointed. "There, up the highway coming down the hill!"

"Crap! Yeah, I see it. Let's hustle back to the car and get the hell out of here. Better to come back empty-handed than get apprehended, I hope."

"The Master doesn't tolerate mistakes," Mouth-Breather replied.

They took off back to the parking lot and did not come by her hiding place again. She lay on the ground panting and shaking, frozen by fear. She felt sick to her stomach upon realizing Henry was alone against those evil men. But she was too afraid to go back. She lay there shivering until the light from the pending dawn was just starting to brighten up the dark, and she heard a voice calling her name.

"Anne," the voice called, "this is Officer Wilson of the Venice Police Department. I'm here to help you! Henry told me to find you!" Anne peeked over the edge of the sand and saw a woman, recognizing the police uniform. She slowly crawled out over the top of her hiding place.

"I'm here!" Anne proclaimed, waving her arms.

The officer pointed her flashlight in Anne's direction, blinding her as she rushed over to her position. "Are you Anne?"

"Yes, I am Anne?"

"Are you all right? Are you hurt?"

"I'm just very tired, cold, and thirsty. Where is Henry?"

"Henry is at the hospital, exactly where I suggest we take you and have you checked out. Besides, I don't think he'll rest for a moment until he knows you're all right," Officer Wilson said. "Officer Wilson to dispatch," she spoke into the walkie mic on her shoulder.

"Dispatch go for Wilson, over."

"I have the girl. Repeat, I have found the girl, Anne, missing at Venice Beach, over."

"Roger that. Do you need medical backup?"

"Negative, she is ambulatory and appears cognizant. I will transport her to the hospital in my unit and take her statement after she's been medically cleared. Wilson out."

"Copy that. Dispatch to Wilson, out."

"Why is Henry at the hospital?" Anne asked nervously.

"Same reason you're going, to get checked out. He did suffer a single stab wound during the fight, but the paramedics were on the scene right afterward, and he's in good hands."

"Henry," Anne sobbed, allowing herself to be led back to the squad car. Officer Wilson helped her into the backseat and sat with her to get more information. Harrison called dispatch to advise that they were en route to the hospital.

"First of all," Wilson said, "can you tell me what happened?"

"We went to the beach and stayed on the sand for a long time staring at the stars," Anne began. "We were almost back to our car when Henry saw another car that we had seen before with men waiting for us. They said someone wanted to meet me, and Henry told to run. I ran, and two of the men chased me into the trees where I hid until you found me. I heard them talking, and one of them saw your police car coming and they left. I was too afraid to go back."

"You're lucky. Someone from Public Works was nearby cleaning the visitor center and called it in. Did either of the men call the other by name?"

"No, but one did say something about 'the Master' not being pleased."

"Do you remember anything else? What did they look like?"

"One man was brown like you, and one man had hair like mine but short. I do not remember what the others looked like, but they had black pants and black shirts and black hats on their heads."

"Okay," Officer Wilson said, "you're doing great, Anne. We'll be at the hospital soon. I'll have you sign an official statement after you've been medically cleared. First, let's get you looked at and then reunite you with Henry." Anne sat silent while the tears flowed down her cheek. Why would anybody want to "meet" her? She desperately wanted answers about her past, but not if it would cause Henry harm, or worse.

51

At the Hospital

When the ambulance arrived at the hospital, Henry was in a stable but weak condition. The paramedics rolled the gurney in to the waiting arms of the emergency room staff. They rushed him to the trauma unit, and within seconds, they had cut off and removed all his clothes then covered him with a white sheet. One nurse inserted a catheter in Henry's arm, replacing the one the paramedics inserted in his hand. Then she started an IV that would administer the saline solution, medication, and, if necessary, a blood transfusion. Another nurse took his blood pressure, leaving the cuff attached to his arm so it could automatically recheck his pressure every fifteen minutes. The same nurse also attached a device to constantly monitor his pulse and hooked him up to the oxygen tank.

They were cleaning and irrigating his wound when Dr. John Turner came in. He introduced himself and began to examine the wound to determine the extent of the damage. Since the bleeding was under control, Dr. Turner ordered a CT scan to determine if there were any internal injuries prior to scheduling surgery. Henry was awake and able to answer questions from the nurse about his medical history and to sign the necessary forms. While they were itemizing and cataloging his personal effects, he persuaded the nurse to call his sister Heidi. The poor girl nearly dropped the phone from Heidi's high-pitched shriek reaction to the news. Henry would not be at all surprised if Heidi were to arrive at the hospital by the time the nurse hung up.

The nurse told him that the Venice Police cruiser pulled up to the ER entrance where an orderly was waiting with a wheelchair to transport Anne inside. They had radioed ahead to alert them to their arrival and to let Henry know Anne had been found and was safe. He teared up at the news and was finally able to calm down and relax after receiving it. A huge weight had been lifted off his shoulders, and he silently thanked God, just in case there was some small chance he really was there and had answered his prayer.

Before taking Anne to her own examination bay, they wheeled her in to see Henry to reunite the young couple. By now, the entire ER was buzzing with the story and was rooting for the two lovebirds to come out on top of this ordeal. Anne started crying when she saw Henry all hooked and wired up, with a bloodstained bandage on his abdomen. She jumped up out of the chair and ran to him, sobbing with joy and sadness. Henry did his best to hold her as he tore off his oxygen mask and kissed his girl. The nurse's station erupted with applause, and someone took a picture on their cell phone. The nurse assigned to Henry started to close the curtain, "Let's give them a moment."

Just then, someone else ripped the curtain out of her hand and in a loud voice said, "Moment my ass. What the hell happened, Henry?!" demanded Heidi.

There she stood with that look on her face that Henry had seen a million times. That look of concern mixed with love and tempered with anger that said "I can't wait until you get through this so I can kill you myself." She stood there wearing a mismatched pair of flip-flops, baggy shorts, and apparently had mistakenly put on one of James's T-shirts. Her hair was a mess, and Henry wasn't sure if she drove here or flew over on her broom.

In a weakened voice, Henry said, "It's a long story, and I'm really in no mood, nor do I have the strength to tell you at the moment. Right now, I need you to look after Anne for me while I'm in surgery."

Anne looked up at Heidi with tears in her eyes, dirt and sand in her hair and on her dress, and scratches on her face, hands, and legs. Heidi rushed to Anne's side and held her, and the two of them cried while Heidi slipped into her mother-slash-sister mode and tried to comfort her. Then she leaned over and kissed her brother. "I'm sorry. I'm here for you both. I just freaked out when the nurse called and said you had been attacked, stabbed, something about the police? You can imagine all the scenarios that played out in my head. You rest, Henry. I will not leave Anne's side."

Henry kissed her back and said, "Thanks, sis. I owe you one."

Heidi replied, "Shhh, you don't owe me anything. This isn't a favor. This is family pulling together in a crisis. You relax now. Rest and save your strength. And do what the doctors and nurses say or I'll have them give you an ice water enema." Henry winced from the pain as he laughed at her teasing. *She was teasing, right?*

"He'll be okay, Anne," Heidi encouraged the girl, holding her tightly. "They're going to take good care of him. It's time to take care of you now. You need to get back in the wheelchair and go with this nice nurse and let them have a look at you. I will be right here the whole time." Anne kissed Henry one last time and reluctantly obeyed. The nurse put the mask back on Henry's face, and they waved to each other as she was wheeled backwards to her own examination room. The technicians came to take Henry to get the CT scan while Heidi went with Anne.

"What happened?" Heidi finally had the opportunity to ask when they had Anne settled on a portable bed in her examination room.

"We were on our way home from the beach near the pier when men came out and tried to get me." Her eyes were red and puffy from crying, but she seemed to be steadier now that they were at the hospital. "Henry told me to run and I did, but two of them ran after me. I ran as fast as I could and hid." She looked up at Heidi. "I left Henry alone with the others!"

"It's what he wanted you to do, Anne. It's his job to protect you. He wouldn't have wanted it any other way. If you hadn't run, you would be a captive of those men, and Henry would probably still be right here with a stab wound worrying about you."

Anne shook her head. "I was too afraid to go back. I left him alone!"

"Anne," Heidi said in a voice that was both firm and gentle at the same time. "You couldn't have done anything to help. You did what you had to do to protect yourself. Don't feel bad about it."

"I will try."

"You have to be strong for Henry. He would feel terrible if he knew you were feeling guilty. How many were there?"

"There were four when I ran. I do not know what happened after that. I do know that one man said they wanted me for 'the Master.'"

"The Master?" Heidi asked. "Who the hell is that?"

"Probably some kind of drug lord or something," Officer Wilson answered. She was still there completing her report and jotting something in her notebook. "Mr. Williford was able to give us a description of the vehicles so we've put out a BOLO for them. If you can think of anything else, Anne, please let me know."

"I will. Thank you," Anne said as Officer Wilson left her examination room.

Moments later, a nurse walked in and had Anne put on a hospital gown. After taking her vitals, she got Anne a basin of hot water, a bar of soap, a towel, and a washcloth. Anne felt better as she freshened up while Heidi brushed the beach out of her hair. The ER doctor came in just as they were finishing up. He shined a light in Anne's eyes to check her pupils, had her follow his finger, squeeze his fingers with each hand, and answer a never-ending series of questions. He gave her a clean bill of health, ordered the nurse to treat the scratches, and prescribed an antibiotic to avoid infection. Heidi told him of her nursing background, so he left the girl in her charge. They returned to Henry's room and waited.

Just a few minutes later, the technicians brought Henry back. "All done!" the young man in the blue scrubs pushing the gurney said. "The doctor will see you once he gets the results."

Henry was propped up with pillows behind him and reached out to Anne. "Hi, honey," he said in a weak voice. "Are you okay?"

She took his hand. "I am okay. I am sorry I did not come back. I could not help you. I was too afraid!"

Henry shook his head. "It's my job to protect you, not yours to protect me. I will always be there to protect you. Besides, I had it all under control." He reached back to adjust the pillows behind him. Heidi stepped up and assisted.

"How do you feel?" Heidi asked as she straightened his bedding for him.

"Like a million bucks," he boasted. Heidi could tell he was trying not to let Anne know how much his side really hurt. But she knew her brother. She saw the pain on his face. He laid his head back and closed his eyes as if trying to will the pain away. The nurse came back to check Henry's vital signs. "We're still waiting for the results of the CT scan."

They all sat quietly for a while, each lost in thought and worry while the minutes ticked by. Henry had fallen asleep, worn out by the adrenaline rush he needed to fight the attackers and the loss of blood from the stab wound. Combined with a healthy dose of morphine, he was getting some badly needed rest. Heidi kept an eye on both Anne and Henry, watching the young girl struggle with her undeserved guilt about what happened.

Finally, Dr. Turner returned. "Well, Mr. Williford," Dr. Turner said, waking Henry up, a clipboard in his hands. "You are one lucky fellow. The knife seemed to have missed any major organs, although it did just nick your small intestine. We're going to take you to surgery to stop the internal bleeding and then close the wound up, but I don't think there will be any major repairs needed. After that, you'll be admitted for a couple of days, just to make sure the stitches hold and nothing else develops. In cases like this, one of the biggest risks is infection setting in afterward."

"Thank you," Henry groggily nodded. The doctor nodded in response then left.

Henry took Anne's hand. "Anne, when the surgery is over, you can't go back to the house. It's not safe. Heidi, can she stay with you for a few days?"

"Of course," Heidi replied.

"Just make sure you have Jim stop by the house and feed the animals."

"No, I need to be with them. I will be okay," Anne protested.

"You can't stay there alone and without protection," Henry insisted.

"James taught me how to use his shotgun, Henry," Heidi interjected. "You forget. I'm often alone with two kids when he's away on business. He made sure I was able to hold my own if the unthinkable were to happen. I will stay with Anne, and we'll keep Charlie close and the gun loaded and ready."

"We'll keep a patrol car near the house while you're in here," Officer Harrison, who was still in Henry's room added. "Probably our best chance of catching these guys is if they make another attempt anyway. With the description you gave us of the vehicles and your attackers, we plan on keeping an eye on your house anyway."

Henry nodded. Heidi knew he felt uneasy using Anne and her as bait, putting them in harm's way, but Heidi also knew that she would do anything for him, including putting herself in the line of fire. Despite her sometimes rough treatment of him, Heidi loved her brother fiercely.

Soon, a young female orderly with big brown eyes and long brown hair wearing green surgical scrubs came into the room pushing a gurney. "Okay, Mr. Williford. I'm going to take you to surgery now." She checked the name on his hospital ID bracelet and raised the bed to match the height of the gurney. She held it in place as he painfully scooted over and settled in. Anne and Heidi both kissed him one last time as the young orderly transferred his IV from the bed to the gurney.

"We'll be waiting when you get back," Heidi said, reassuring him as the orderly whisked him away. Heidi took Anne to the cafeteria to get her some breakfast then they went to the surgical waiting room and began their vigil.

About three hours later, the doctor came with the good news that the operation went smoothly and Henry would be out of recovery soon and checked into a regular room. A short while later, a nurse arrived and escorted them to the room where Henry was already resting. His mouth was dry, and he was still doped up from the anesthetic so he didn't say much, but the smile on his face said it all. Heidi was proud of how brave Anne was, holding back the tears she knew were bursting to get out. Anne kissed him gently on the cheek as if he were made of glass and might shatter at any moment. Henry had taken quite a beating in addition to being stabbed and was now very stiff, bruised, and swollen just about everywhere. Heidi kissed him too and whispered in his ear that she was going to take Anne home so she could rest as well. They both kissed him good-bye, and when she turned to look back before she left, he was already asleep.

On the ride home, Heidi called James and gave him an update on both Henry's and Anne's condition. Anne had been up all night, and her physical and emotional ordeal was taking its toll on her and it showed. She also instructed James to meet them at Henry's house and to bring the shotgun along with a box of ammo. He was waiting for them when they pulled up.

"I'm so glad you're here," James said with a relieved look on his face. "The police stopped by, and it was all I could do to explain why I was here with a loaded shotgun. Fortunately, they checked with the hospital, and both of us are on Henry's emergency call list." He turned his attention to Anne. "Oh, you poor thing. You look like you've been put through the ringer." Anne weakly returned his hug. "I already checked the perimeter of the house and the shed out back. There's no sign that anyone's been around or broken in. Just to be safe, once we're inside, you two stay put while I check out the house."

Once inside, Anne sat down on a chair nearest the front door and smiled when Charlie and his four-legged gang rushed up to greet her. A few moments later, James reappeared to announce the all clear. "I have serious reservations leaving you guys all alone with someone out after Anne. Both of you promise me that you won't open the door for anyone and to call 911 if anything suspicious at all happens."

"We promise," Heidi said. She needed James to be okay with leaving them. Heidi would stay with Anne as long as she needed to.

"I'm leaving now. I left the kids with grandma for a few days and will be working from home, so call if you need anything and I'll rush right over." James kissed them both good-bye.

Heidi immediately turned her attention to Anne.

"You need to get out of that dress and into a shower and wash out those scratches. Go!" Heidi pushed her to the bedroom. "I'll look after the animals."

Anne went into the bedroom and took off her dress, stepping into the hot water of the shower as it ran down her body and washed away the dirt, Henry's blood, and her tears. She replayed the scene over and over in her mind, the guilt of her escape at Henry's expense relentlessly pummeling her. She knew the reason she did not go back was because she was afraid, not because Henry told her to run. Right or wrong, in her heart, she had failed him.

When she got out of the shower, she put on panties and a T-shirt and climbed into bed, afraid and ashamed, doubting that she knew what true love really was. She wasn't willing to make the sacrifice to save Henry at her own expense. She began to doubt her feelings for Henry. How could she have left him like that? After all he had done for her, she didn't stay to help him, and he got hurt as a result. She cried, her tears telling her that she had failed the one she thought she loved. Anne wondered if she could really love if she couldn't make the right choices, to make the sacrifices love sometimes called for. She had failed. Maybe this was who she really was, and that thought scared her.

That night, Heidi, Charlie, and the shotgun were all curled up on an air mattress next to Anne's bed. She didn't dream of black dragons because she lay awake reliving the attack and the taunts of the Master wanting her. Is the past she so desperately wanted to uncover catching up to her? If so, why didn't she remember any of it, of them, of him? Maybe it would be better not to remember anything.

52

Thief in the Night

July 25
Saturday

It was ten days after the attack, and Henry was enjoying some time alone at home. After spending three days in the hospital and a week at home with Anne and Heidi taking care of his every need, he was all pampered out. They kept following him everywhere he went, treating him like an invalid, insisting on opening every door, fetching food from the fridge, retrieving the remote, and changing the channels when everyone knows you never get between a man and the TV remote. It could disrupt the balance of the space-time continuum or worse.

He was relishing his break from recuperation so he could actually have a few hours to recuperate. He sent Anne with Heidi to a home shopping party Heidi had been invited to long ago. Oh, she protested and refused at first, but he finally got her to agree. He ambled over to the refrigerator and grabbed a can of soda, because beer and pain meds don't mix, then he made his way to the sofa to watch a horror movie about a knife-wielding killer on the loose in a small town in Illinois, something he didn't think would help Anne's nightmares go away. Probably not the best movie to watch after what happened, but he really enjoyed horror movies.

The phone rang, showing the caller as Detective Ortega. Henry answered with a smile. "Good afternoon, detective! I hope this means you have good news!"

"I'm sorry, Henry. Our research didn't yield any results. But I did want to talk to you about what happened to you. Officer Wilson told me about the attack."

"Yeah, that's a real game changer for sure. The fact that they specifically targeted Anne lets me know they are somehow connected to her, and not in a good way."

"That brings me to the other possibility," Detective Ortega suggested. "I'm concerned with your report of the attackers talking about taking Anne to 'the Master.' Is that what they said?"

"Yeah," Henry frowned, remembering blondie's words. "I have no idea what they meant by that."

"Well, there is another possibility. Anne may have been involved in something a little darker than we thought."

"What do you mean?" Henry felt his stomach cramp with trepidation, making the wound hurt just a bit more.

"There is a small possibility that she may have been a victim of human trafficking. That would explain a lot of things, like why there are no records of a boat fire or missing person's report. These guys don't file reports with the Harbor Patrol or Coast Guard. They aggressively avoid them. It could also explain why she dreams of fires, attacks, and murder, and who this 'Master' may be. If your girl has already been bought and paid for, some rival cartel may have tried to abduct her, and something went horribly wrong. You better believe they will stop at nothing to fulfill their contract. I've tried to find any explanation for what could have happened, and when you add everything up, this seems like a very possible scenario."

Henry felt like he'd been kicked in the gut, the thought of Anne being sold on the black market tearing at his sanity. He was blinded by rage. "If any part of what you're saying is true, Ed, you better hope you find these assholes before I do." Henry was shaking, his pulse pounding in his ears.

"Just calm down, Henry. I'm sorry I brought this up," Detective Ortega apologized. "But I have to consider all possibilities. Please don't go off and do anything rash or impulsive, especially in your condition. It's just one of many possible scenarios. We have no other leads, and this recent event has me very concerned. I'm going to do some more digging and see if I can find any known traffickers who go by the name of 'master.' In the meantime, Henry, I suggest you be very careful from this point on. This is a very dangerous situation."

"Thanks, Ed," Henry said. "I will take all necessary precautions. Please let me know if you find out anything more."

Henry sat on the sofa for a few minutes, regretting that he let Anne out of his sight by sending her away. He felt guilty for being so selfish by putting his own needs before her safety. If anything happened to her now, he would never forgive himself. His mind absorbed what Detective Ortega told him, and even though he didn't want to face it, the explanation had to be considered. It would explain so much. The trauma she went through must have been so severe to wipe everything in her memory away. The nagging question that haunted him since he first met Anne rang out loud like a church bell in his ears. What could have possibly happened to this girl that caused her to regress almost to a newborn and yet leave no physical evidence of prior injuries or sexual assault? The answer that Detective Ortega suggested tore at his heart like a lion tears through its helpless prey. It just didn't make any sense.

He relived what Anne revealed about her dreams at Angela's office, the horror of being brutally raped multiple times, and then her body mutilated before being cast into the fire. He felt conflicting urges to cry for her or go out and kill someone, to run outside and scream at the universe for the pain inflicted on this girl who meant everything to him. He would face a thousand thugs with a thousand knives if he could take away what had been done to her!

He put in the DVD, picked up his drink, and put his bare feet on the coffee table, sliding it away from the sofa to accommodate his long legs. He was dressed only in his running shorts, going commando. He had to get his mind off the call or he would go insane. He hoped that the movie would do the trick.

Halfway through the movie, the dogs started barking at something outside. He paused the movie and went to the bedroom to get his gun then the lantern flashlight from under the kitchen sink. He slowly cracked open the back door to peek outside. He did not see anything, but he knew that didn't mean there was nothing dangerous lurking about. Henry opened the door wide enough to let the dogs out. He gave Charlie the command to heel, and he stayed glued to his hip as he led him around the house. Charlie was alert and sniffing the ground around them. After they made a complete circuit and found nothing, Henry took Charlie back inside. The dogs stayed near the back door, whining while they paced back and forth, reluctant to leave the kitchen. Even the cats were agitated and scattered to find a good hiding place. Henry headed back into the living room; and when he turned the corner from the kitchen, the black shadow crashed on top of him, taking him away into oblivion.

53

The Warehouse

When Henry awoke, the first thing he felt was the intense pain in his side. He looked down and saw that he was naked and bleeding from his stab wound; the bandages had been ripped off and the wound viciously reopened. His arms were stretched above him and to the sides, his wrists gripped by heavy metal shackles that cut into his skin. His legs were also spread wide with metal restraints right above his ankles. The blood from the gash in his side ran down his torso, along his hip, and then down his leg, pooling on top of the metal above his ankle. He looked to the side and saw that he was shackled between two poles in what appeared to be an old abandoned warehouse for boats. Other than a couple of hanging lights above him with hooded metal shades, the rest of the room was dark.

There were large shelves on one side of the building that still contained the remnants of old fishing boats. Several dock doors were on the side opposite the boat storage. An old metal desk stood in front of him on which two men sat. He felt a knot in the pit of his stomach when he realized that these men were the same ones who attacked them at the beach. They were both dressed as they were on that fateful night—in black jeans with black long sleeve shirts, leather gloves on their hands, and black knit caps on their heads. Henry imagined a white circle painted on the chest of their shirts that read THUG 1 and THUG 2. The tall guy was sitting on the edge of the desk while blondie sat in the metal chair behind the desk, and both had bandages over their noses. Henry smiled at his handiwork. *Let me down from here, jerkoffs, and I'll make a broken nose the least of your problems.*

"Where the hell am I?" Henry croaked, finding his throat dry and raw. He heard a reply, but it did not come from either of the two men.

Behind him, he heard a deep growling voice that didn't quite sound possible from a human throat say, "You are my guest, Mr. Williford."

"Wh-who the hell are you?" Henry tried to struggle against the chains but found that they were too taut to get any movement.

"Let's just say that we have a mutual…acquaintance," the voice rumbled.

Henry was finding it hard to breathe stretched out as he was. "Wh…What…do…you want…with Anne? You…leave…her… the hell…alone. I'll kill you…I swear!"

Blondie stood up and punched Henry's stab wound several times. Henry squeezed his eyes against the agonizing pain the punches caused.

The voice behind him oozed over the room like rancid honey. "Just be patient, my friend. You'll know soon enough. Stan"—the black man looked up—"make the call."

Stan took out Henry's cell phone and punched in a number. Henry's heart froze when he heard him say in a slimy voice, "Hello, Anne. We met the other night, but you were rude and ran off, remember?"

"Leave her…the hell…alone!" Henry struggled to pull his wrists out of the shackles. "Leave her alone!"

The voice in the dark chuckled. "Don't worry. She's an old friend. She'll be very surprised to see me again."

"I don't know why you…assholes are doing this…and I don't care. Do what you want…with me. Just leave her…out of it."

Stan and the other man both laughed as well. The voice continued. "She is the reason you are here. I could care less about you. Stan, you go ahead."

Stan held the phone up to his ear. Henry could hear Anne screaming into the phone. "Who is this? What do you want?"

"Calm down, sweetie," Stan said. "We've got your boy here. If you want to see him alive again, get into the black car waiting outside. We know where you are. Come alone. Don't even tell Heidi that you're leaving." There was a pause as Anne was speaking, but Henry could not make out what she was saying. Then Stan put the phone up to Henry. "Tell her you're fine, lover boy. She just wants to hear your voice."

Henry shouted, "Don't come here, Anne!...Call the police! Don't worry about m—" He stopped talking when blondie punched his stab wound again, causing it to gush fresh blood. Henry couldn't even double over in response; the chains cut into his flesh as his body tried. He rolled his eyes while the room turned red from the pain.

"Come alone and don't say anything to anybody if you want to find him alive when you get here. Be a good girl. Just get into the black car and everything will be just fine." Stan's voice smiled. He ended the call and spoke to the voice in the dark. "She's on her way." Stan then threw Henry's phone on the floor and stomped on it, crushing it.

"No," Henry whispered. "Anne, no."

The voice in the dark drew closer. Henry felt hot air brush against the skin on his back, and he tried to turn his head to see the face of the voice in the dark. "What do you...want with us?"

"All in good time, my friend," it said. "All will be revealed in good time. Stan, Ed, let's make our guest comfortable while we wait for my lady."

As Henry hung between the poles like a fly laced up in a spider's web, he tried to figure out who the mystery voice was. Was this the man from Anne's past who may have attacked her? Were these people the traffickers Detective Ortega warned him about? Was this asswipe the 'Master' Thug 1 and Thug 2 were yammering about the other night?

He only had a moment to contemplate the possibilities before Stan and Ed started beating him with wooden strips used to line the boats. They took turns hitting him in the back, legs, and side. He was grateful that they left the stab wound alone for the time being. He could take the beating on the rest of his body, letting his muscles absorb the blows, but the tender area in and around the wound was already burning. He closed his eyes, bit his lip, and tensed his body in anticipation of each blow. *Have your fun while you can, boys.* Henry tried to keep his courage up. *Payback's gonna be a bitch when I get loose.*

He didn't know how long it would take Anne to get to where they were. After about a half an hour of beating him with the wooden strips, Stan and Ed stopped, both breathing heavy from their labors. Henry felt his body relax just a little, bowing his head at the respite.

"Oh no!" The mysterious voice feigned distaste. "Our painting is uneven! As an artist, Mr. Williford, I'm sure you want your work to be balanced. Boys, you need to make sure that your 'brush strokes' are evenly distributed on our canvas. We must present a complete picture for my lady to help her understand the situation."

Stan and Ed sighed and took a drink of water from bottles on the desk. They turned their heads back and forth, cracking their necks and rolling their shoulders to loosen their muscles. Then they picked up the wooden "brushes" and began beating their human canvas again. This time, they hit Henry everywhere, including his stomach, chest, face, and groin. He tried not to cry out, but when they hit the wound on his side and more sensitive parts, he cursed them out. He was soon covered in horizontal red welts, some bleeding, with the flow of blood from his side intersecting the welts with dark red lines.

"Beautiful, isn't it?" the voice drawled. "I'm sure you couldn't do better yourself, Mr. Williford. My only regret is that we ruined that beautiful dragon tattoo, reminds me of my home. Oh well, couldn't be helped." The voice sounded closer now. "Maybe I should just call you Henry seeing as we are now friends. I hope you enjoyed our playtime," the voice continued. "The main event will be so much more fun! We have to show my lady only the best."

Henry's chin was on his chest as he struggled to breathe between being stretched out and the beating. He slowly lifted his head and tried to open his swollen eyes. "I...told...you...leave...her... alone...or...I swear" was all he managed to get out.

"Henry," the voice admonished, "you are in no position to make threats. So why don't you just sit back...well, hang back in your case, and enjoy the show!"

Henry heard the sound of a car pulling up and the doors closing. Anne was here!

Only an hour before, Anne was enjoying her outing with Heidi until she got a phone call that she thought was from Henry. Her legs gave out, and she fell into a chair when she realized it was one of her attackers from the other night. Panic overcame her as she struggled to remain calm and not alert anyone at the party to the seriousness of the situation. Henry was in trouble, and she wasn't going to run this time. She would follow the instructions to the letter and trust God to help them get through this.

After she hung up, she headed right to and then out the front door, where the car was waiting. She didn't answer any questions from Heidi or their host, briefly glancing at Heidi before she left, her fearful eyes trying to convey a message. When she approached the vehicle, the back door on the passenger side opened and a voice in the darkness instructed her to "Get in." Once inside, she could see that there were two men in black jeans, shirts, and knit caps, one with a gun pointed at her.

"Sit there and be quiet," he ordered her. "Give me your phone." When she did, he threw it out the window as the car sped away from the house. "Enjoy the ride. This is going to be a fun-filled evening for you."

On the way to her unknown destination, Anne's mind was trying to understand why someone would do this to her and Henry. She closed her eyes and remembered what she had learned about faith. She held her hands together and tried to form the right words for a prayer in her mind, asking the God she had come to trust to protect her and Henry and to give her strength to face whatever was waiting for her. She didn't even know if there really was a God or if he would hear her, but she found peace in believing he would.

Anne couldn't see where they were heading because the windows in the back were blackened along with a divider between the passenger compartment and the driver. The interior of the car and the seats were black. There was a small bar on the left side with a bottle of champagne. One of her companions poured some in a tall glass and offered it to her, but she refused. Other than that, they rode in silence, the men leering at her like she was a juicy steak about to be devoured.

When they finally reached their destination, the two men got out; and the shorter one held the door for her, holding out his hand to assist her as she exited the car. Her legs felt like jelly, and her heart was pounding in her chest. She had to force herself to take the next few steps as they escorted her into an old and very dark building. She was flanked by a man on either side of her, guns on their belts. They walked about fifty yards into the building to the only area that was lit by two hanging lamps.

There in the light she saw Henry. He was naked and strung between two poles with metal shackles around his wrists and above his ankles. Blood flowed from the wound in his side, and his body was covered with bloody welts that looked like red stripes surrounded by blue bruising. She cried out and tried to run to him, but she was held back by her abductors. A deep growling voice spoke in the darkness.

"Now, now, my dear," the voice oozed with glee. "Not so fast. I have been waiting for you for a long time."

"Who are you!" she cried, struggling against her captors.

"Don't you know?" the voice said. "Don't you remember?" And as he said that, a figure stepped out of the dark to reveal what could only be described as a dragon-man. He stood over seven feet high, with skin the color of India ink that was covered in scales on an anthropomorphic body. His nose and mouth appeared in human form, but with long sharp white teeth that extended over his lips. His ears were long and pointed, with ridges extending from the top of his ear down his cheek to the corners of his mouth and also extending into his hairless brow. The ridges outlined his chin with large spiked edges, ending in a horn-like appendage. His eyes were human in shape but red with no pupils. Large black wings were folded against his back, and his hands and feet had three-inch claws. He wore only a black cloth wrapped around his waist like a kilt. He walked up to Anne, grabbing her chin in his clawed hand while his forked tongue licked his lips, and said, "Hello, Aeya. How about a kiss for your beloved Saphan?"

Anne's head was spinning. Her legs folded under her, and she would have fallen if not for the two thugs who held her arms. She couldn't breathe, couldn't see, and couldn't move. There before her stood Saphan! How could he be real! He was only in her nightmares! A manifestation of her imagination! But there he was standing in front of her, changed some from the hellish figure in her nightmares, but it was him just the same. She knew it was him. He was real! This wasn't a nightmare! She felt the heat from his breath when he called her name. The room grew dark, and her vision blurred as she tried to comprehend what was happening.

"Get my lady a chair," Saphan hissed.

A metal chair slammed hard up against the back of her knees, forcing her to sit. She wanted to scream but couldn't muster any sound from her open mouth. A sharp intense pain filled her chest, brought on by each pulse of her rapidly beating heart, which magnified throughout her body. All the fear she had felt in her nightmares, combined with the shock at seeing Henry beaten and bleeding, converged on her like an avalanche of emotion, burying her in terror so intense that her body shut off and she passed out, slipping into the blackness.

54

Choices

"Wake up, my dear," she heard that evil voice command. "Come on. Don't spoil my game." She held her eyes shut tight, terrified to open them and find that the living nightmare was still there. "Open your eyes, Aeya. Open your eyes or I will slit your lover's throat."

She forced her tear-filled eyes to open to find that she too was naked like Henry but that she was lying on her back on the metal desk, her hands bound in front of her. She turned her head to see that Henry was still hanging between the poles, his head down. Saphan was kneeling on the floor and looking directly into Anne's eyes, his red eyes burning into her soul.

"Aeya." He smiled then stood up. "Imagine my surprise when I discovered you were still alive after I ordered you thrown into the fire." He walked around the table to stand near her head. "When my Tannen told me that there was no sign of your burnt body in the fire, I knew something wasn't right. I was so angry that I ate them all, one by one. It took me a long time to find you and to understand what happened."

"Let me tell you a story, my lady." Saphan walked around the desk. "When Aesmay defeated me and banished me to the black mountains, I wanted to die. I hated him, and I hated you! All I wanted was revenge on my dear brother and his offspring."

"But that is when my Master found me in the darkness. He promised me that he would give me the strength to defeat my enemy if I would serve him. I gladly accepted and gave all I had, and in exchange, my Master gave me the power of fire and the strength to defeat Aesmay."

Saphan looked up at the ceiling. His eyes closed, and he breathed heavily, his fists clenching and unclenching. "Aesmay was such a fool! He thought we were sent to guide the Thraekenya. He never understood we were meant to *rule* them! I can't tell you how delicious it felt when I plunged my crystal knife into your foolish father! To feel his pathetic life leave him at my hands and flow around my feet made my heart soar!"

Saphan leaned over Anne, his hot and foul breath burning her cheek. "Then taking you was the most stimulating and thrilling crown to my revenge! My only regret was he didn't last long enough to see it. To watch me take his precious and forbidden daughter would have been priceless! How tasty your flesh was, how… vulnerable…your body was under me!" He hesitated, stood up, and walked around the desk. "But the gift from my Master comes at a great price, and only you can give me back that which I paid."

Anne followed Saphan with her teary eyes. "What can I give you? I do not have anything!"

He kissed Anne's forehead. "You have Aesmay's powers, my dear! You have the power to change your appearance, which is what I want to get back." Saphan stood up and walked down along the side of the desk, dragging his claws down her body, leaving long, deep cuts on her skin. "And you chose our true appearance, which, as you can see, is something I can no longer do. This is the closest I can get to what I once was, caught between Thraekenya and Aeyohem. This was the cost I paid to gain my victory." He stood near her feet.

"I did not choose," Anne whispered. "I do not know what happened to me."

Saphan's laugh sounded like dogs snarling in a fight. "That's the fun part! You don't even *know* what you did!" He flapped his massive wings, lifted himself up, and hovered over her. He gripped her head and cupped her face in his clawed hands. "You have the ability to give me back my power, my lady."

Anne looked up at him, trembling. "I do not understand," she said, gagging from the stench of his fowl breath.

Saphan took one hand and extended his finger, the sharp claw pointed at Anne's chest. "You have Aesmay's heart." He dug his claw into her chest, ignoring her screams of pain. "Aesmay's heart *is* power, and when I have it, I will be restored to my former magnificence. There are so many new mates I can take on this world, and I do want to look my best."

"Leave her alone!" Henry yelled.

"Shut him up," Saphan ordered his servants. "I have no more use for his words." Stan reached up and shoved a dirty rag in Henry's mouth then sealed it with duct tape. Henry's words came out as muffled sounds.

"But," Saphan continued, "here is my dilemma. In order for me to gain your power, I cannot take it from you. You have to give it to me willingly. You see, you have Aesmay's authority because he gave it to you. You have to make a choice."

Anne shook her head. "I do not know what I have or how to give it to you."

"Lucky for you, I do. This is the choice you have to make. In order for me to have your power, you must surrender your heart to me, your physical heart. You will give yourself to me freely, unlike the last time, and I will take out your heart and consume it. But before I do, know that what you suffered before will be nothing compared to what you will suffer now.

"I know." He patted her cheek. "What kind of crappy choice is that? Only a fool would make it, unless that someone was properly motivated." He extended the longest claw on his left hand in front of Anne's face, and then soared over to Henry and stood next to him, extending his right hand behind Henry's back, almost as if in friendship. "The choice, my dear, is that if you do not give me what I need, you will watch while Henry dies a slow, painful death. I will rip him apart piece by delicious piece." At that moment, he plunged his claw deep into the knife wound on Henry's side and twisted it back and forth, expanding the wound, a fresh spurt of blood flowing heavily from the gash. Henry screamed into the gag, straining fervently at the restraints in his attempt to escape the pain. Saphan removed his claw, licking off Henry's blood. "The choice is yours, my lady. Give your heart to me or Henry will suffer everything you endured in your dragon form. You remember what that was like? EVERYTHING! And when I'm done with him, he will BURN. So, Aeya, what will it be, your life or your love?"

Anne wept bitterly. Somehow this was all real, but how could that be? How could Saphan force her to make such a choice? How could she endure the terrifying ordeal of Saphan's rape and torture? Could she live and watch Henry suffer them instead then to die such a horrible death? She fought to breathe, her lungs burning with fear as her heart pounded against her sternum. She couldn't move, her muscles losing all control as the terror worked its way through her body. Her nightmares were real! The realization of that made her sick, and she turned on her side and vomited over the desk until nothing was left inside. This just couldn't be real! She drew her knees up to her chest, sobbing into the ropes around her wrists as she held her hands up to her face. She had prayed and asked God to help! How could He let this happen? She felt abandoned like her nightmare in the cave, waiting for Saphan's minions to take her to him again. The despair was overwhelming, clouding her vision and her mind.

Saphan was losing his patience. He walked over to Henry and again dug his claw into the open wound. Then he slowly dragged his claw across Henry's abdomen, slicing through skin and muscle, like he was gutting a fish. Henry's intestines threatened to break through the wall of his abdomen at any moment. Henry screamed through his gag and wept, the tears running down his cheeks and onto the tape around his mouth.

"Take the gag out, Eddie. Let Mr. Williford convince her." Eddie ripped off the tape and pulled the oily rag out.

Henry gasped for breath. "Anne...please! Don't do this! Don't let him...take you! I can't...let you suffer...again. Please!"

"Okay, that's enough." Saphan waved his hand. "Put it back in." Ed stuffed the rag back into Henry's mouth and put fresh tape over it. Henry thrashed against his chains cutting his wrists and ankles deeper, the belly wound expanding as the dark puddle under him grew.

"Aeya," Saphan sighed, "how long do you think Henry will last if I take him now? I'd much rather have you, and I think deep down inside you would too. In his condition, he wouldn't last five minutes under one of…my size. Make the right choice! Right now, even if I try to kill you, you can transform and escape to live again in another realm like you did before. Henry can't. He will simply suffer then DIE! Then you will leave me no choice but to bring Heidi and the children over to play and start this all over again. NOW CHOOSE!" Saphan walked behind Henry, lifted his head up by his hair and started licking his face.

Anne's body seized, and her sight went black. But then she heard a voice saying, *"Do not be afraid, I am here. I will give you the strength to endure. I am here with you."* And she knew then what she had to do: an act of true love, a sacrifice. She knew now that she could and would make that choice. Her body relaxed as the finality of her fate was sealed.

She now understood what it meant to truly love someone because her love for Henry overcame the intense fear, even in the face of her own death. The greatest gift she could give Henry was to give her life so that he could live. She was now ready to make the sacrifice for love. Nothing else mattered anymore, but her love for Henry. Her cries quieted, and her heart stilled. Although she was still fearful of the pain and torment she would suffer, she felt peace in knowing that she had chosen love and that love would sustain her through the upcoming ordeal. She rolled back to face Saphan, who was now pressed up against Henry's back, his head down while he whispered in Henry's ear. Henry could only moan in reply behind the gag, his wet eyes shut tight against the anticipated assault.

Anne stared at him with defiance in her Sapphire eyes. "I will give you all of me, my heart and my body to do with as you will, in exchange for your promise that Henry will live."

"Bring him down," Saphan ordered, backing away from Henry. The four men took up the chains holding Henry up and loosened them, causing him to fall to the floor where his blood was pooling. "My lady has chosen. Bind up the wounds then throw him into the night."

"Bind it up with what?" Stan complained.

"I don't care. Use the duct tape. I promised my lady his life, and I don't want him bleeding to death out there."

Stan shrugged and retrieved Henry's shorts from a corner of the room, tore them up, and placed the torn pieces over the wounds while Ed wrapped duct tape around Henry's abdomen, bracing the wall against the breach. As soon as they pulled him to his feet, Henry tried to wrestle his way out of their grasp to reach Anne but was too weak to sustain the fight. "No, Anne! Please...don't do this! Please! I love you!"

"I have to do this," Anne whispered, tears streaming down her cheeks. She kept her eyes on him, wanting to remember his face while she endured what had to be. "I love you too, Henry, so very much! Go home to Heidi, James, and the kids. Live a good life and don't forget me. This is my gift of true love, my sacrifice for my love for you."

"Get him out of here," Saphan waved his hand, dismissing Henry.

"Please"—Henry fought to stay—"let me stay with her!"

"As much as I love an audience, I already have one—my six willing servants who are ready to play the game with me. You have your life, Mr. Williford. Aeya is mine. Take him far from here and leave him. If he can survive the night, he can find his own way home."

"No!" Henry shouted. "No!" But weakened by the loss of blood and the beating, he could not fight Saphan's men when they forced him out of the building and into the black sedan.

Anne watched them drag her love away. She could only lie on the desk, silently crying out to God to watch over Henry, and to give her the strength to endure what she knew was to come. She did not know what would happen if she died this time. She didn't really understand what Saphan had told her about her ability to transform her body and travel to another realm, but she knew that whatever was going to happen, when that time came it could not be changed. She closed her eyes and waited for the first strike, the tears that would never stop until her death washing into her hair and spilling onto the desk. Saphan removed his wrap and roared like one hundred lions as he stood over her, the sound hurting her ears and rattling the walls of the building.

55

Going Back

Henry tried to time how long the car had been traveling, but his head was pounding too badly. He could not see where they were going, but he tried to keep track of every direction they turned and any sounds he heard. He was on the floor of the back of the sedan, his hands bound behind him. They were not in a populated area. He did not hear any other traffic, and the road was bumpy; he knew that much. When the car stopped and the door opened, two of Saphan's sycophants dragged him out and dumped him on the side of the road.

They were in a heavily wooded area where there were no lights visible from any towns or cities. The men got back into the car and drove off, leaving Henry stranded and naked in the wild, weak from the torture he endured, with his hands still bound. He had a choice: either he could try to find his way to help or try to get back to where Anne was, wherever that was. It really was an easy choice after all. He could not leave her, and once he made it to his feet, he took off in the direction the sedan went.

Although the pain in his stomach was excruciating, the duct tape binding actually seemed to help. It was pitch-black in the middle of the night, but he could see the stars overhead and that gave him hope. He ran through a mental map of the area he thought he was in, based on the time it took for Anne to get there from the time they called her. He estimated they were maybe sixty miles from Venice, which could put them somewhere between Venice and Arcadia, Florida, possibly in the Myakka River State Park, but he didn't think there were any warehouses there. So it had to be beyond the park. He thought that the roads they travelled on were mostly rough, and the fact that there was no traffic around also made him believe that they were in an unincorporated area. As he ran, he tried not to despair, thinking of the hopelessness of trying to find her in time, but he had to try. He could not go back to his life without her, finally admitting that he was truly in love with her, the kind of love he knew would last even beyond the grave. If he could just stay alive until he got to her, he would tell her. A weaker man would have succumbed to the wound to his stomach, but his powerful physique was holding him together.

After he lost sight of the red taillights of the sedan, he decided to keep to the gravel road he was on until it intersected with a paved road. Henry stopped and reviewed the mental notes he took on his ride over here. The last turn they made before leaving the paved road for the bumpy unpaved road was left, so they had to go to the right to go back the way they came. So that was the direction he headed.

Henry's entire body ached from his ordeal, and his wounds were still bleeding. His throat was raw, and his left eye was partially swollen shut. Still, he ran on for what seemed like hours. He was not worried about the roads as much as he was on the alert for any signs of alligators that may be in the area. At one point, he passed a road sign that had been run over by someone long ago, leaving a jagged metal stump where the post used to be. He used the sharp edge to cut through the tape that was binding his hands. With his hands free, he could now use them to support his stomach and help hold himself together.

Once he thought he heard the sounds of cars on a highway somewhere to his left, but he kept off the main roads because that was consistent with the feel of the sedan on his way to the area where they forced him out of the car. He didn't think that a naked bleeding man running around would be allowed to roam free for very long. If he were seen, he would undoubtedly be picked up by the police who would take him to a hospital and away from Anne. He couldn't risk that, even if the police would act in his best interests. There was no time! He had to find her before Saphan took her heart. Besides, no one would believe him anyway.

While he was running, he implored the heavens above that he would find Anne still alive. He still struggled with his belief, but the farther he went with no sign of the place he believed they were keeping Anne, his fear led him to cry out. "God, if you're really...there," he managed between gulps of air as he ran. "Keep her alive...I...love...her ..." He hadn't knelt in prayer for a long time, but each time he fell to his knees when his strength gave out, he called out to his God for the strength to get up and keep going. One of those times, he noticed a puddle of rainwater and drank his fill, splashing water on his face. Maybe God was watching out for him after all. Maybe God really did love him, even when he couldn't see it. It was a miracle he was still alive and able to move at all, let alone run. With every step forward, he was finding his way back to his Heavenly Father.

His vision at times became blurry, and he pushed himself on only by sheer will, fighting off his body's threats to throw him into shock and shut down. The only thing keeping him going was the adrenaline rush caused by his intense desire to get to Anne. He hoped he was still traveling in the right direction. Henry tried to tap into the connection he felt with Anne the day he found her. Somehow, he sensed she was still alive, and her life force was pulling him toward her. *I'm coming, sweetheart. Just stay alive, and I will find you.* With newfound energy, he picked up the pace. The gravel crunched under his bare feet with each stride as the sky above started to lighten with the dawn.

Finally, he saw the top of a metal building several yards ahead. It was surrounded by a dense wild overgrowth of trees and bushes that obscured most of the sides of the building, but he could see that it was a rusted metal-sided building with several dock doors on one side of the building. The outside of the building matched what he saw inside the warehouse.

In the front, there was a parking lot with broken asphalt in several places where wild grass and weeds burst through. He noticed as he neared the structure that there were three black cars parked in front, the sedan in which he and Anne rode and two SUVs. A faded and peeling sign on the front of the building read "Miller's Boats."

In front of the building, two of Saphan's goons, Carl and Ed, were leaning on the sedan smoking, wearing only their black jeans. Henry ducked into the bushes and squatted.

"That was one fine piece!" Carl exclaimed.

"Tell me about it," Ed agreed. "Glad we got to have some of that. But tell me, Carl, wasn't that some weird stuff going on? I mean, I don't mind the rough stuff, but that was really intense."

"Yeah, I've bitten girls before, but not like that. But the Master insisted we bite hard. Did you drink her blood?"

"I did. Kinda found it added to the experience, if you know what I mean. Like we was vampires or something."

Carl shrugged. "I guess." He shuddered. "I still feel like I'm in a horror movie though. Be glad when this assignment is over. I'm still covered with blood."

"Do you think that stupid boyfriend of hers might have found his way to the main road and called for help?"

"No way, even if his guts didn't pop moments after we dumped him, the gators will get him before he finds any help. You saw all the blood on the floor and the beating we gave him. He's either already dead or passed out and soon will be."

Henry squatted behind the bushes that grew between the needle palms and high grass, feeling his blood boiling as he realized what they were discussing about Anne. But he had to be smart. He was naked, unarmed, and very weak. All it would take is one punch to his gut and he'd be done for sure. They both carried AR-15 high-powered rifles on their backs and what appeared to be a 9mm Glock on their belts. Henry looked around and picked up a chunk of the asphalt about the size of a football. He silently made his way through the trees and behind the vehicle where he waited for an opportunity. There was no way these guy would have dreamed he'd find his way back here, which would give him the much needed element of surprise.

Carl put out his cigarette, hefted his rifle to settle more comfortably on his back, and turned to head back into the warehouse. "Well, I guess we'd better go back. I wonder how far the Master has gone."

"Be right with you," Ed said. "I want to enjoy this smoke as much as I enjoyed her. I'm sure the Master isn't done playing yet."

When Carl entered the building, Henry saw his chance. He lifted the piece of pavement above his head with both hands, snuck up behind Ed, and brought it down with all his strength, connecting with Ed's surprised face as he turned around too late. Ed crumbled like a rag doll at his feet. Henry tried to take a deep breath, but it hurt when he did. He pulled the rifle off Ed's shoulder and took the handgun out of his belt. Then he slowly opened the door to enter the building, dreading what he might find.

The place was still dark except for the end of the building where the two hanging lamps barely illuminated the area where they were held. Henry saw Carl and the four other goons standing in front of the metal desk, laughing and cheering, two of whom were completely naked, and the other two were only partially dressed. Henry didn't have time to dwell on why they were in that state. He knew. But he had to get to Anne. He could not see beyond them to where she was. He stayed along the dock door side of the building and crept up to the scene.

What he saw when he was finally able to look took his breath away, freezing his heart and causing his stomach to seize up into a tight ball of pain extending down his legs. Saphan was naked and bent over the prone figure of Anne. His teeth were tearing out a large chunk of her shoulder as he continued his assault on her. His large black wings were spread above him, beating in time with his exertions. Henry watched in horror as Saphan threw back his head, Anne's flesh bloody in his mouth, gurgling with the blood while he howled before swallowing the piece. Then Saphan made one last violent thrust, gave a bloodcurdling yell, and stood up, satisfied. Henry could now see that he was covered in her blood.

Anne had several bite wounds all over her body, and it appeared three of her fingers were gone. Her long golden hair had been ripped from her scalp and laid in heaps around her head. Her beautiful breasts were mutilated from the bite wounds, and the blood in the area between her still spread legs evidenced the savagery of her violation. Blood flowed over the desk, spilling onto the floor in a wide puddle around it. She was still alive though, her head to the side staring into the dark with eyes open, red with tears while Saphan consumed her piece by piece.

"Nooo!" Henry screamed as he ran to where Anne was. Carl was the only one who had a weapon on; the others had left their guns on the floor with the rest of their clothes, not expecting anyone to find the warehouse. Carl reached for his gun and fired, but Henry shot him in the chest first before he had time to aim. The other cowards dove to the floor to retrieve their guns in a feeble attempt to return fire but were not fast enough. Henry peppered the area where they laid with fire, not sure if the bullets found their mark. He turned the automatic rifle on Saphan and held the trigger down.

Saphan laughed as the bullets bounced off his hard scaly skin. "That won't work on me, Mr. Williford." He thumped his chest with his fist. "Skin as hard as dragon scales you see. Wait a minute. I'm almost done here. I'll play with you after." And with that, he took his clawed hand, thrust it deep into Anne's chest, and pulled out her still beating heart. She gasped as her body lifted with her heart; and once the heart was severed, she fell back to the desk with a wet slap, sending splatters of blood in a macabre fountain around her.

Henry screamed with everything inside him, tearing his throat and his vocal cords, and ran to Anne, only to meet head on the hardened fist of Saphan. Henry collapsed in defeat, crushed by the knowledge that he was too late. Anne, the love of his life, was dead. Saphan held Anne's heart up, his roar thundering in Henry's ears, then feasted on his prize.

56

Heaven

Light…I am surrounded by a bright light that shines warm around me, brighter even than the white sun of my home. I am lying on a soft bed with satin pillows under my head. The light comes from a man standing by me dressed in a white robe that blinds me in its brilliance. I cannot see his face clearly but hear his voice when he says, "Welcome, Anne."

"Where am I?"

"You are in my home." The man touches my cheek with his hand.

"Saphan took my heart!" I am afraid to know the answer but ask the question anyway. "Am I dead?"

"No." He smiles with such a soft smile. "You are merely in transition."

"What is happening to me?"

He holds my hand. "Saphan was wrong. He cannot take your power by taking your heart because, even though you gave it to him willingly, it was done with love for Henry."

"I do not understand." I try to sit up, and he helps me.

"Anne, when Aesmay and Saphan were created, they were not as you remember them. They were the Aeyohem, the Firstborn, but they chose to take the form of the Thraekenya when they inherited the world of the golden dragons. You are not from the dragon realm but came directly from Aesmay's heart out of his love. You were not hatched from an egg but created in the form you are now. Who you are now is your true self.

"Only by love can this gift be given. It cannot be transferred or taken by any other means. As you know, Aesmay and Saphan were forbidden to mate, but Aesmay never told you why. The Aeyohem are pure and without sin. If they mate or sin in any way, they break their vow to me and become one of the Fallen, stripped of their transformative power

and condemned to eternal fire. Saphan chose to disobey his vow and has become one of the Fallen.

"But as for Aesmay, after many years of faithful service to me and to the golden dragons of the Thraekenya, Aesmay came to me and pleaded for a child. He offered his Aeyohem heart in exchange for a dragon heart and a mortal life. I agreed and used his heart to create you. When Aesmay gave his heart to create you, he willingly gave you all his authority and power to control the appearance of your body and to travel between the many realms of Aeyoronis. You too are one of the Aeyohem. This is the power Saphan lost in his fall and the power he wanted restored to him but can never have.

"It was I who transformed you from Aeyohem to Thraekenya and sent you back to the Thraekenya. Aesmay would tell you the truth about who you really are and where you came from someday, but he wanted to wait until the twilight of his years before revealing your ability to transform and visit other realms. He could not bear the thought of losing you. He loved you that much. He died before he had the opportunity. Because you did not know you were Aeyohem and the vow on your heart came from Aesmay who never broke it, you alone of the Aeyohem are forgiven.

"That is why when you were cast into the fire and wished you could be somewhere else, someone else, you were transported to the in-between place where I transformed you. That is why you did not know what it meant to be human when you were found. I have always had a plan for you, Aeya, for your future and your hope. And it has been that you be with Henry in your human form. Henry's finding you was no accident. It was by design. You were meant to be together."

I look at my body, which looks so much like my human body, but glowing with a translucent light under my skin. And I realize I have large white wings behind me that unfold into a beautiful display of iridescent feathers. My body feels strong and powerful, as if I can lift up the sky.

The man places his hand on my cheek. "Besides, Saphan cannot take what has already been surrendered. You gave your heart to Henry when you gave your life for his."

Suddenly, I am flooded with memories of my life as the Thraekenya called Aeya, daughter of Aesmay, and I know that it is all real. My heart leaps in my chest as the revelation of my entire existence unfolds. But when I remember the destruction of my world, my heart hurts when I feel the death of each of the Thraekenya. "Why did they have to die?" *I look up with tears in my eyes.*

"Do not cry, little one." *The man wipes away my tears.* "When Aesmay surrendered his authority to you, dominion over the Thraekenya was given to Saphan to do as he willed. Aesmay knew that by giving his heart to you, he surrendered his own life to Saphan. But your suffering was the pain of birth that brought you into a new life with Henry and with me."

"What happens to me now?"

"I will give you the power to defeat your enemy. Return and avenge my children, your family. But then, because you are unique among your kind, having lived as a human without knowing your true form, you must choose your destiny. If you want to remain in this form, you will live forever with me in my home here, where you may be sent to other worlds to bring the good news to those realms, retaining the power you now have. There is much work to be done and many worlds that need to hear about me. However, you will never be with Henry again."

"If you choose to stay with Henry, you must do so in a consecrated union. You will become fully human, subject to all the frailties of man, including your allotment to die. You will no longer be able to change your form or travel to the realms of Aeyoronis. Someday, you will die and return here to be with me forever. But there are also greater works that I have planned for you and Henry."

"Also, my child, I have a gift for you. Because I know what you have suffered and what you have lost, I will give you back all the memories of your kind regardless of your choice, but I will take away all the pain you have endured."

"Why would you do this for me?"

"Because I have been waiting for you since the time you were first created, child of the Firstborn. I have always loved you, Aeya." *He kisses my forehead.*

With His kiss, all the pain and sorrow of my torture, exile, and death washes away like the sand under the waves of the beach. My spirit soars, and I weep with infinite joy as the fear carried so long in my heart evaporates. I feel a peace deeper than the oceans cover me, and I know in my heart that everything will be all right now; there will be no more nightmares. And I finally know what true love really is.

The man takes my hand. "Do not worry about Henry. Give him the gift you have received with a kiss. Tell him who you are. It will all be as it should be. And know that even when you may face difficult times ahead, I will always be with you here." He points to my heart.

I cry and hug him. "Thank you, but I do not even know your name."

"Yes, you do." He smiles as the light begins to fade away.

57

Final Battle

Henry crouched on the floor of the warehouse, his head in his hands as the tears flowed from his broken heart. He was too late to save Anne who lay lifeless on the old metal desk, her heart consumed by Saphan. He knew he was also going to die here in this old broken-down warehouse. It didn't matter anymore anyway. Anne was gone. His reason for living was gone. He didn't want to face life without her. He just prayed that it would be quick.

Saphan swallowed the last of the organ and turned toward Henry. "I gave you the chance to live, you pathetic fool. With my princess gone, I am free from my promise. I am going to enjoy your agony and humiliation when I take you. You will be my desert!"

Henry held up the guns and stood, shaking his head, weapons raised before him. He realized his hope for a quick death wasn't going to happen. "Try and do what you want, Saphan, I don't care anymore. Without Anne, I'm ready to die. But know that I won't go easy. I'm going to take you down with me, you son of a bitch!" He felt like a child kicking the toes of a giant, bracing his legs for a fight he knew he could not win but also could not walk away from. Saphan approached, smiling, Anne's blood dripping off his teeth, his massive body poised for another round. Henry swallowed hard and waited, fingers hovering over the triggers of the guns in his hands. Saphan reached out his claws to grab his prey.

Suddenly, a bright light blazed from where Anne's devastated body laid. Henry gazed astonished, realizing the light was coming from her remains, increasing in intensity and closing the wounds on her body. Her form began to grow larger and transformed into an enormous golden dragon, like the ones in her drawings. Her torso lengthened into a serpentine shape and her hands and feet grew long and sprouted sharp claws. Her head stretched out into the long head of a dragon, and her eyes became pure white. She grew until her massive form touched the ceiling. When the transformation was complete, she spoke. "*I am Aeya of the Aeyohem and last of the Thraekenya, and I will avenge my father and my kind.*"

Saphan spun around and cried out in surprise at the sight of Aeya's transformation. "How is this possible? I took your heart! You...you gave me your heart!" Terrified, he backed away from the glowing dragon that filled the room, real fear on his face. Panic consumed him when he attempted to morph into his own dragon form and could not.

The large golden dragon queen faced her enemy. "*My heart is not my power. You ate my flesh. The power of the Aeyohem heart is the love that it holds. I have no love for you!*" The glowing dragon descended on the black dragon-man, tearing his black-scaled body to pieces with her sharp teeth and long claws. Saphan struggled to fight her; but locked into his current form, he no longer had the power or the fire that he once did. The powerful black dragon that once destroyed the Thraekenya was gone, and only the twisted caricature of a half man, half dragon survived, no match for the power of the massive golden dragon who filled the warehouse.

Saphan shrieked in agony and horror as she ripped him to pieces, each severed scrap bursting into flames before disintegrating into black dust, until he was decimated and reduced to a pile of putrid black ash lying on the floor. Without a body, a black wisp of shadow fled across the warehouse and out into the night sky, perhaps doomed to remain in a noncorporeal existence.

Henry stared in open mouth bewilderment while the woman he loved transformed into a mystical dragon creature capable of destroying the powerful demon enemy. He could not wrap his mind around what he was seeing! He must have already died and was in Heaven, or if he was still alive, he must be so in shock that he was hallucinating. What he was witnessing was impossible!

When Saphan was no more, Anne's dragon-shape shrank back into a figure that looked like Anne but with glowing skin, and large iridescent feathered wings on her back. She started to walk toward him. "Henry," she called, "it's me, Anne."

"I don't understand." Henry shook his head, his voice when he found it coming out almost as a squeak. "I watched you die! Then I saw you turn into a dragon! Now you're an…an *angel*? What *are* you?" He backed away from her until he hit the wall. His head was spinning, and his knees were ready to buckle.

"I am Aeya, and I am Anne," she said, holding out her hands in supplication to him for understanding. "Aesmay was my father, but he wasn't always a dragon. He and Saphan were the Aeyohem, the Firstborn, with the power to change their appearance and travel to different realms. They chose the form of the dragons to guide the Thraekenya.

"My father surrendered his own heart to the Great Creator to bring me into existence, giving me his power to change my form and travel to other realms. I was unaware I had this power for my father had not yet revealed it to me. When Saphan cursed me and threw me into the fires of the black mountain, God intervened, transforming me into the human form you know as Anne, and then He sent me to be with you. That is why you found me like you did, why I had no memories. But now I know who I really am. I am Aeya one of the Aeyohem, the Firstborn. What you see before you is who I truly am. But, Henry, my love, I am also Anne, the human woman who loves you with all my heart. Please, Henry! Believe me!"

Henry stood staring at her. "You're a dragon!" he cried. "How is that even possible?!" He looked at her, shaking his head, his mouth open and his eyes pleading. He sank down onto the floor, his mind and body both in shock. "You're a dragon!" he repeated over and over.

Anne's face softened, her arms out to him. "I don't know how it happened, but I know that it is true. When I died, I went to a place where I met a man, and He showed me who I really was. He healed me and sent me back to be with you." She began to cry. "I love you! God sent me here to this world so that I could be with *you*! That is why the dragon in your dreams when your mom died gave you peace, the dragon you made into the tattoo. Henry, we *are* meant to be together!" The light from her body dimmed as she assumed her human form again, her wings disappearing and the golden gleam of her skin returning to its normal color. "I love you, Henry."

Henry didn't say anything for a while, remaining on the floor rocking back and forth, his lips pressed together in a tight frown, his arms in front of his face, clenched fists on his head. His heart was warring with his intellect as the incredulity over what he just witnessed struggled with the love he felt for Anne in his heart. What does anyone feel when faced with the truth, however fantastic it may be, of one's true love? What wins out, love or truth? Is love based on what one is on the outside or what one is inside? Henry knew that Anne was his true love, and that they were connected, they were meant to be together. Of that he was certain. But was it even possible for him love such an incredible being?! It, she, was Anne, but it was something *more*!

Henry felt like the entire weight of the world was crashing down on him. But the possibility of life without Anne was far more painful than a thousand deaths. To be loved by this miraculous creature was a journey he could not imagine living without. And like Anne before him, suddenly he was filled with peace, the realization that he did love Anne with all his heart, broke through the shock, giving him clarity and resolve.

Finally, he took a painful breath and pushed himself up from the floor and stood before her. The battle was over. In the end, true love won out.

"It all makes sense now," he nodded coming toward her. "I know it's crazy, but I believe you!" He took her hand, tears flowing down his face. "Anne or Aeya, whomever you are, I love you! I want you with me forever. I don't care what you are. I can't lose you again. I love you more than life itself!"

With his whole being focused on the woman he now knew just how much he loved, he didn't see Ed creep back into the warehouse and crawl behind the metal desk, picking up one of the loose guns lying on the floor by Carl's body. Henry heard the pop of the gun as it fired a heartbeat before the bullet slammed into his left side between his fourth and fifth ribs, puncturing his lung. The shot caused Henry's body to bend sideways and threw him five feet, where he collapsed in a heap on the floor.

Henry felt intense pain in his chest, as if something had exploded inside him. His lung collapsed, and it was as if all the air had been sucked out of the room. The pain was unlike anything he had suffered to this point, making even his abdomen laceration pale in comparison. He couldn't talk, couldn't move; every breath was a painful struggle, as if his lungs were being cut by a thousand knives.

He saw Anne begin to change again, the large white wings on her back extending, her skin glowing with a bright light. It was like watching a scene from a movie in slow motion. In her hand, she held a fiery sword that created circles of fire in the air when she swung it down to slay the remaining servant of Saphan as he emptied what was left in the gun at her. He screamed a bloodcurdling sound when the fire of her wrath wrapped itself around him, scorching him, then extending to the bodies of the others who were dead, feeding on them until all that remained were just the charred outlines of where they lay. Their souls were given long ago to the Master and they were sent to reap their rewards. Nothing was left of the attackers but ashes, their clothes, and guns.

Henry tried to call out to her but could not make any sound. His vision began to fade, the aggregate of the injuries his body sustained finally claiming him, the blood from the chest wound flowing out to join the puddle under the chains, draining him of any remaining strength he had. He knew he was bleeding to death. He could feel his heart beat slowing down inside his chest. *Thump, thump...thump......thump.* Then the pain faded, and all feeling in his body was gone. Henry felt only a great sense of peace and euphoria. This was it. He was dying. He whispered a prayer, "Forgive me."

His last thought as he slipped into oblivion was would he see Anne in Heaven.

With the enemy gone, Anne transformed back into her human form. She ran over to Henry, who was lying still in a puddle on the floor, white as her wings, at the point of death. She held him in her arms, his body limp and lifeless. But she was not afraid. She had the assurance in her heart from the Man that everything was going to be all right. Anne knew what to do. She leaned over Henry's battered form and kissed his open lips.

Henry's body burned with an intense heat from the inside, searing his side, his lung, and across his abdomen. The burning coursed through his body, touching every wound he sustained, knitting together flesh, muscle, and tissue, shoring up the wall to hold in the breach, erasing the red and blue welts, the healing paintbrush filling them in with a healthy flesh tone. Henry writhed on the floor as the unseen flames coursed through every part of him.

Finally, the burning stopped and was replaced by absolute joy. Henry woke and looked at his naked form, seeing that his wounds were healed, even the gunshot. Anne smiled with that wonderful, open, face-splitting smile. He sat up and pulled the duct tape off his abdomen to find that the wound had sealed, a thin pink scar where the slash that opened his belly had been. He felt strong, the shock from the wounds, the beating, and the blood loss replaced by renewed energy, giving him back his life. Henry and Anne were in awe at the power that saved them both, unbounded joy filling their hearts.

At that moment, the child inside Henry stood triumphant on the hill, the flag of victory waving over his head. Henry found his faith again, and he knew that God was real and that He had always been there, through his mom's death, through his dad's passing, and even through Heather's death. God was real, and Henry knew he would never doubt again. Henry and Anne were both weeping with copious tears, holding each other in a tight embrace.

Finally, Henry stood, helping Anne up.

"Where do we go from here?" he asked after several minutes of just enjoying each other's company. "Do you..." He hesitated. "Do you go back to Heaven now? Will I ever see you again?"

She smiled as she held his hand. "No. I am staying here with you. I have made my choice, and I choose you."

"Can you be with me and still be an..." He still couldn't get used to the idea of what she really was. "An angel?"

"Aeyohem," she corrected.

"Aeyohem. Isn't that against some kind of code or something?"

She looked down and slowly nodded her head. "It is true that I cannot live among the Aeyohem and yet be with you as we have been. But I am unique among my kind because I have lived as a human in ignorance of my true nature. For me to stay with you though, I must give up my life as an Aeyohem and remain in human form, with all the limits and vulnerabilities, including my allotment to die."

"Would you want to give up that kind of power? To be able to travel to different realms changing how you look? To live forever? For me?" Henry couldn't fathom such a choice.

She looked up at him and smiled that wonderful smile. "Yes!"

58

Going Home

Henry searched near where the remains of the attackers still smoldered, checking the clothes left on the floor until he found some car keys. He also picked up a pair of pants and put them on. They must have been Stan's because they were too long, but at least he wasn't naked anymore. Even though he was healed, the blood from the injuries covered them both. He tried to wipe off as much as he could with the remaining clothes. Anne's clothes were in a corner near the desk where she retrieved them. Once dressed, they went outside, trying all the cars until they found one that the key started. It was the black sedan that had taken them both. "Let's go home," Henry said.

"You need to let me be the one to talk to the police," Henry advised her while they were driving down Route 72 on their way back to Venice. "I don't think they'd believe us if we told them the truth that you're an angel."

"Why would they not believe us? It is the truth," Anne protested.

"I know, honey. But some people have a hard time believing in angels, demons, and especially dragons. I know. I was one of them until I saw it with my own eyes. They will call you delusional or fanatical or worse, insane, which may earn you a trip to the mental hospital. Some people just can't deal with the impossible."

"I do not understand." She frowned. "Nothing is impossible. But I will do as you say."

"Just let me do all the talking. My healing will be difficult enough for them to swallow. You coming back from the dead as a shape-shifting angel who ripped apart a dragon demon with your bare teeth, heck, I feel crazy just saying it and I was there. Besides, we now have the makings of a sequel to our book."

When they pulled up to the house, the police were already there with several squad cars topped with flashing lights. Officers were going into and out of the house. Henry pulled into the driveway, and the car was immediately surrounded by officers with guns drawn, shouting commands that they get out of the car with their hands up. Henry and Anne slowly got out, hands in the air.

"Get down on the ground!" one officer commanded. Henry and Anne both lay down on the grass where officers converged on them, pulling their hands behind their backs and handcuffing them until Officer Harrison, who was also on the scene, noticed it was them.

"Wait," he yelled. "Those are the victims! Oh my god! Mr. Williford, miss, are you all right? We've been looking all over for you since your sister called to report the abduction!" He ran over and unlocked the handcuffs then helped Henry to his feet. Henry was still covered in his own blood despite his efforts to clean it up. Another officer released Anne and helped her to stand up. Henry heard one of the officers calling for an ambulance.

"Thank you. I'm okay," Henry said. "We were held at a warehouse, Miller's Boats, down off Route 72 near to Arcadia. We were both tortured by someone called 'the Master' who wanted to get back at Anne and used me as bait. I was shot in the side and my stomach cut open, but somehow I'm fine now. The blood you see is from those injuries."

"That's impossible," an officer named Vaquero said. "If you were shot in the lungs, you'd be in much worse shape that you are now. You should be dead."

Henry turned and showed him the scar. "I know. I can't really explain it. I thought I was dead after the bullet hit me. Believe me, I have never felt such intense pain in my entire life. But something happened that can only be described as a miracle because I'm okay now." He also showed him the scar on his abdomen, a pink line almost the entire width of his waistline. "This is where they cut me. Officer Harrison can vouch that I didn't have this scar a few days ago."

"He's right," Harrison confirmed. "I was on the scene when he was stabbed ten days ago. I was the first responder and administered first aid. There was no cut like that on him then."

Vaquero shook his head in disbelief.

Harrison turned to Anne. "And you, Anne, are you okay? Did this Master hurt you in any way?"

"Yes," she answered. "I was...taken...by the Master and the others. They bit me and cut me. But God has healed me also."

"Are you saying you were raped?" Officer Wilson who was also on the scene came up when she heard that.

"Yes," Anne replied. Officer Wilson put her hand on Anne's back in a show of support.

"How did you get away?" Harrison asked. "What happened to this Master guy and the others?"

"I'm not really sure," Henry replied. "But it was some kind of explosion that took them all out. There were six guys, but there isn't much left to identify them though."

"Sit down," Harrison directed, making Henry sit back on the grass. "The ambulance is on its way. We're going to take you both to the hospital."

"How did you get this car?" Vaquero asked. "It's the car that your sister reported was involved in the abduction."

"We were able to escape the warehouse and found the keys in the ignition so we took the car."

"We'll send a tow truck to take it to impound. Do you know what caused the explosion?"

"No," Henry lied. "We were restrained at the time but were far enough away from the blast to avoid getting hit by it. It's strange though because nothing else burned."

Officer Vaquero didn't look very convinced. "Just the same, best if you don't leave the state and be available if we have any other questions once we have a chance to investigate the scene." Henry nodded.

Just then the ambulance pulled up, siren blaring and lights flashing. The paramedics ran to Henry and made him lie on the grass while they checked him for any wound that would have caused the immense amount of blood still there. Henry assured them he was fine and stood up, getting on the gurney under his own power. For the second time in as many weeks, Henry would take an ambulance ride to the hospital, even though he asserted he was okay.

"You are going too, ma'am," Vaquero said to Anne. "You both need to be checked out."

The paramedics secured Henry in the ambulance then helped Anne step in, putting a blanket around her shoulders as she sat by Henry. Once she was seated, they sped off, the police still at the house, documenting the scene and scratching their heads.

Henry did not get a chance to see the condition of the house since he was taken, which was probably a good thing for him. When Harrison told him about the damage, he cringed. Chairs from the dining room set were broken, apparently thrown across the room, the books on the shelf all knocked to the floor, the sofa ripped to shreds, and his beautiful eighty-four-inch plasma television smashed. Henry's blood left a trail leading from the living room where he was attacked to the back door and into the backyard.

He was relieved when he found out that the animals were gone, having been retrieved by James and Heidi, safe at their house. All except Charlie. The brave canine suffered a broken leg. He must have tried to defend his master against the creature that took him. He was at the vet where he was getting extra special care for his heroic efforts. Henry felt his chest tighten at the news of his faithful companion's injury. He closed his eyes against the tears, so soon after losing Flack.

In the emergency room, they checked Henry and Anne out from head to toe. The doctors and nurses were amazed at the freshly healed scars from injuries on Henry that were not there when he was in the same emergency room a few days ago, other than the one-inch stab wound on his right side. Several doctors came and checked out Henry, subjecting him to CT scans, X-rays, and MRIs. They compared the results to the ones from ten days ago but were unable to believe that what they saw were obviously new injuries but appeared as if they had been healed for three months. No one could believe it, hence the several different tests they subjected Henry to in their search for a reason.

Anne was also examined thoroughly and subjected to a sexual assault test. All the results showed no sign of injury or assault, which caused some to question her account of the rape.

Henry heard later that the police found the warehouse and photographed the scene, taking samples of the large pools of blood under the hanging chains that had held Henry and on the desk where Anne had died, confirming that it was indeed blood from Henry and Anne. With the amount of blood found, the experts couldn't believe that either were still alive. No one could have survived such a massive loss, but nonetheless, the evidence was clear and they were obviously alive. The forensic evidence on the desk indicated semen from seven distinct individuals in addition to Anne's blood, which confirmed her account of the gang rape and her torture. It was evident that something horrible had happened there, and that both Henry and Anne were gravely injured at some point.

The charred remains of the six human assailants was also collected and tested. The identities of the six human assailants were confirmed as the contributors to the semen; however, they could not identify one sample that contained some human DNA but something else that could not be identified. The conclusion of the forensic team was that the bodies had been consumed in a manner consistent with spontaneous human combustion, but they could not declare a definitive cause of the fire. Other than the human remains, no other material was burned. However, it was clear that whatever consumed the bodies was not caused by anything Henry or Anne had done. There were no traces of an accelerant on any of the bodies or at the crime scene. Henry and Anne were eventually cleared of any culpability in their deaths.

Finally, after several hours and tests, one doctor, an older man, Dr. John Geller, one of the chief doctors in the hospital, said with a smile, "I believe you, Mr. Williford. There is no other explanation other than to believe that this was truly a miracle. We can't do more than God can, so I think you can go home now."

Henry smiled, extending his hand. "Thank you, Dr. Geller."

Heidi and James arrived, having been informed by the police that Henry and Anne were found. They brought fresh clothes for the couple. Heidi hugged Henry as tight as she could once he was dressed. It was evident Heidi had been crying, but when she saw them, the joy on their faces shining though like freshly scrubbed skin, she smiled.

"Something changed," she said when she stepped back. "Someday you will need to tell me what happened."

He kissed her forehead and promised, "I will. But I need to do something first. Did you pick up that item I asked you to retrieve from the house?"

"I did," Heidi replied with a wink, slipping something into Henry's hand.

Henry got down on his knees in front of Anne, in the middle of the emergency room, and with all the attending doctors, nurses, police, and paramedics watching, he uttered the words that he knew made Anne's heart soar. "Anne, I know I am not Prince Charming, but will you marry me?" he asked, holding up the ring he intended for Heather. It was meant to be worn by his true love, and now, it finally would be. It was Henry's way of casting off the last bitter memory of his past.

"Well, you may not be a prince, but you are charming." Anne paused. "Yes!" she barely got the word out. "Of course I will." The entire emergency room burst out in applause as the couple kissed. Heidi lost it. She was crying so uncontrollably that Jim had to guide her to a chair.

Henry and Anne looked at each other and laughed, saying in unison, "And they lived happily ever after?"

Epilogue

Anne and Henry remained apart until they were married in a small ceremony in Heidi and James' backyard, with Pastor Jennings conducting the service and some of their new friends from South Bay in attendance. Nattie and Nathan even behaved themselves as they walked down the aisle as flower girl and ring bearer.

Tale of the Princess Dragon was published and became a huge success, selling over a million copies. After their honeymoon in Hawaii, they travelled around the country for various events and book signings.

One day, they were at a bookstore in downtown Chicago for a book signing. The lines of readers at the store reached to the door and into the street with parents and their children holding on to their copies of the large picture book. Anne and Henry sat at the table, pens in hand, signing the many copies of the book placed in front of them and taking the time to greet and thank each fan.

One young mother had her two children with her, who appeared to be five and ten years of age. She put her open book in front of Anne, smiling with excitement as Anne signed the book, asking her to sign "With love to Crystal." Anne smiled and wrote the words. Her reading and writing abilities were now up to par with where she should be, and like Henry, she had a great love for books.

Crystal thanked her and when she turned to leave the table asked, "Will there be a sequel?"

Anne smiled as she looked at Henry, then winked at the children as she handed Crystal the book. "You never know! There are so many possibilities out there!"